ALTHEA
DESTINY'S GLITCHES BOOK TWO

Z.K. COLE

Althea – Destiny's Glitches Book 2

Copyright © 2024 by Z.K. Cole.

All rights reserved.

This is a work of fiction. Names, characters, places and incidents are either the products of the author's imagination or are used fictitiously. Any resemblance to actual persons, living or dead, businesses, establishments, events or locales is entirely coincidental.

No part of this book may be reproduced in any form or by electronic or mechanical means, including information storage and retrieval systems, without written permission from the author, except for the use of brief quotations in a book review. This book may not be redistributed to others for commercial or non-commercial purposes.

Cover design by Sarah at AngelicSeraphan Designs

ALTHEA

DESTINY'S GLITCHES
BOOK 2

Z.K. Cole

CONTENT WARNING

This book contains explicit sexual content. It also includes references to emotional abuse. Practising self-care is important, so please don't read this book if this subject upsets you. If you have any questions about this, please don't hesitate to contact me at zkcoleauthor@gmail.com or on my Facebook page.

This book is written by a British author, and as such, the following story will contain a mixture of English slang, dialect, regional colloquialisms and other quirky spellings. Having said that, you may notice some American spellings for certain words. This is because, as an avid reader, these words sound more pleasing when reading. It has been done intentionally and is not a mistake. This book has been edited, but if you spot any typos, please reach out to the author via social media channels. Please do not report it to Amazon, as this feature can lead to a book being taken down.

This book is enrolled in Kindle Unlimited, which means it is not legally available on any platform other than Amazon. If you have downloaded this book from somewhere else, this is book piracy and can lead to the book being removed.

To my Bestie.
You are my sister from another mister.
My ride or die.
*For over fifteen years, you've supported me
through so much, including this crazy
journey I'm on now.*
Everyone needs a friend like you.
Love you always.

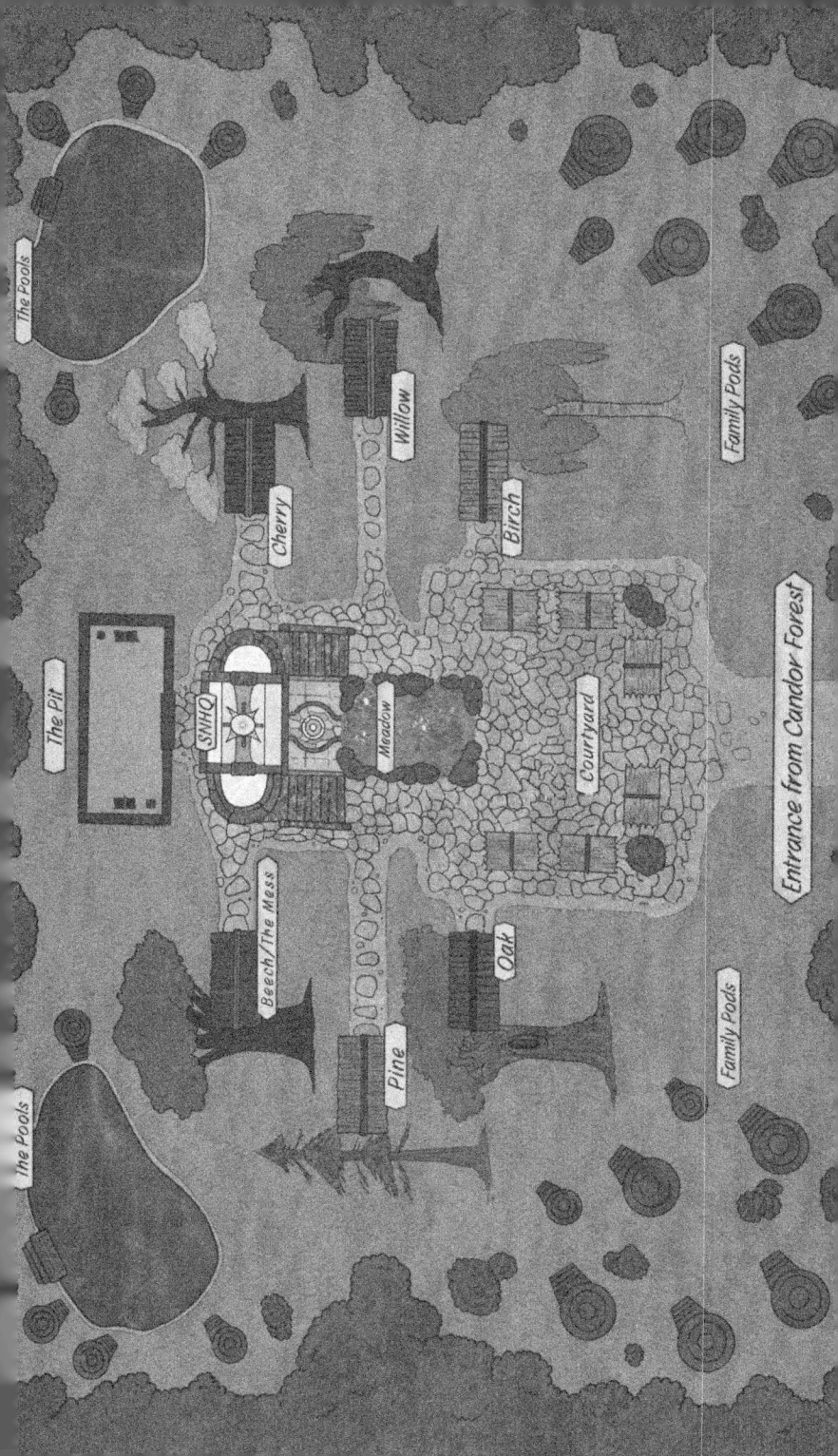

CHAPTER ONE

My fists pound relentlessly against the makeshift dummy, sawdust floating on the wind as my father's words echo in my mind.

Defect, Useless, Pathetic.

A small sample of the names he's called me over the years, and they replay in my mind on a torturous loop. I hear them with every punch I throw, even as my knuckles bleed and the sawdust-filled sack ruptures. I've been maiming the dummy for too long, yet I can't bring myself to stop.

Tomorrow, I'll depart from my home, leave behind my pack, and say goodbye to my best friend. Only one of these losses will truly hurt. My father finally achieved his goal, auctioning his daughter off to the highest bidder. I should be thankful. At least I've met the man I'm being forced into a union with. All the other times, I was kept in the dark about who I was being offered to.

The outcome, however, is always the same. When they discover I'm a defective shifter, they back out of the agreement, unwilling to accept me and my imperfections. I can't blame them, and there's a twisted satisfaction in seeing the deals fall apart. Even with the fury I face from my father afterwards, it's worth it.

I should have known the time would come when he eventually succeeded. At twenty-one, I've endured his attempts to force a mating since I was sixteen, the age when my true defective nature first became apparent. The memory of that moment is as vivid as if it was yesterday, the same anger and frustration still sweeping through me as I continue to destroy my dummy.

Though I was born with an animal spirit inside me, I soon recognised I was different from the rest of my pack. Unlike others my age, I couldn't shift forms. Most pups shift for the first time at the age of three, some earlier under the guidance of their alpha. Since my alpha loathes me, the opportunity didn't present itself until I turned nine.

Before my father even commanded it, I knew nothing would happen. My animal is there, and I'm able to sense some of her emotions, but the connection between us is wrong, broken. When I couldn't shift, my father's anger burned brighter, his hatred of me vindicated as he spewed his nasty insults at me. I was a defect, a stain on the shifter community. I should mention my father's hatred of me started from birth, blaming me for my mother's death, so when I sought answers about my differences, I was only ever met with aggression and resentment.

After my failed shift, his attitude towards me was either disdain or anger. This got so much worse the day I turned sixteen. When a shifter comes into maturity, there is a celebration, after which you run with the pack for the first time. I was upset not to be joining the others, but by this point, that feeling was a constant state for me. Ignoring the stares and whispered comments from the other pack members, when the time came for everyone to shift, I watched on in envy.

Being the pack's defect and outcast, I was left to clean up the mess while they went off and revelled. Stewing in my anger and frustration, my animal mirrored my emotions, the two of us raging against the injustice of it all. It was in this heightened state that I experienced my first, albeit partial, shift.

My ears started to twitch, then my fingers, jerky energy moving through me as my frustration mounted. When the sensation subsided, my hearing was impeccable, and my nails had shifted into claws. I waited for the rest of me to change, my excitement quickly diminishing when I realised that was as far as the shift would go. As I examined these new changes to my body, I soon discovered I was not alone. The pack had returned from their run to witness my partial shift.

Shock and confusion were widespread throughout the pack. My eyes sought out my father's, looking to my alpha for answers. All I got was fury and disappointment. With tears brimming in my eyes and my face burning with humiliation, my father delivered the words that still plague me to this day.

"You have been nothing but a disappointment since the day you were born. Now, when you should be training for your birthright, you present me with this. What must I have done wrong to deserve such a failure as a daughter? You disgust me."

His words struck me with the force of a physical hit to the chest, the pack watching on, snickering and murmuring as my heart broke in two. Only my best friend Angie stood separately from them, the eyes of her tiger shining with sympathy and anger. As a younger pack member, she could do nothing as my father continued his irate rant.

"You are lucky I don't exile you from the pack and leave you to fend for yourself. Leave my sight as I cannot stand to look upon the disaster you turned out to be."

So I ran, with tears streaming down my face and my animal's sorrow thrumming through me.

After that day, his efforts to get rid of me increased.

Just the memory causes me to hammer against the dummy so hard that I'm forced to stop, my skin hanging from my knuckles and the ground painted with my blood. My lungs expel harshly, the pain from my hands a mere echo compared to the pain inflicted on me over the years by the man who sired me.

Since that day, I've been treated worse than dirt. I am the pack's punching bag, maid and overall skivvy. My only joys in life are the small amounts of time I spend with Angie and the rigorous training I put myself through. I've watched countless hours of YouTube videos for years, learning how to fight and defend myself, all useless in the scheme of things. I'll never be an alpha. Yet the routine and the knowledge I've gained help settle the piece of my soul I'm unable to connect with.

The only time my animal is at peace is when I'm training, the constant strain on my muscles like a balm to her worries. I should state that I've no idea what type of animal I have. My father is a Lion, and my mother was a Leopard, so I can only assume I'm a cat of some sort. Not that it matters. I might as well be human in the eyes of my pack.

Grabbing my bottle of water, I take a long pull to quench my thirst while looking around what is essentially a training ground. It's my back garden, one I've spent years renovating to become a home gym.

Everything is made of wood, the only material I have free access to, thanks to the forest surrounding our land.

I suppose I'll miss this too, the tranquillity of the land, the freedom to use this space as my own. Our territory lies in the secluded region of Applecross, a peninsula located in highland Scotland. The mountains and expansive sea with the golden sandy beaches make the place majestic, and the forest provides plenty of wildlife to hunt. I'd enjoy living here if it wasn't for my pack and my father.

My father used to be the alpha of the pack I was born into, but when my mother died, he became unstable. Reasonable, considering he'd lost his true mate. It wasn't long before the pack saw him as a weakness, and the challenges started to come. From the stories I've heard, he didn't even try to defend himself, too lost in his grief to care what was going on around him.

Sadly, that also meant he had no care for his daughter, his only child and the last piece of his mate he had left.

All I have is hearsay as I don't remember much from my earlier years other than anxiety, but we travelled to different packs where my father would enter more alpha challenges. He lost more than he won, but his animal would not allow him to give up on being an alpha. Apparently, we come from a long line of alpha Lions, so he could never settle for anything less. With every new pack came a new nanny to provide the basic care for me that he never could.

We travelled all over the country, picking up followers on the way who supported him. I never understood what they supported about him. To me, he's a complete jackass, yet when he had enough followers, we eventually remained in Applecross.

I was eleven when we settled here, and as the pack grew, more children came with it. I remained the outcast, never fitting in with others and watching from the sidelines because I was different. By thirteen, my father had enough of the nannies and deemed me old enough to look after myself. What he actually meant was that I was old enough to look after him, and I have been doing so ever since.

Making my way back to the house, my mind wonders what my new life will entail. Will my new mate let me continue with my training?

Will he expect me to be in the kitchen all the time? Will I be bound to the house the way I am now, the defect hidden away inside?

I could scream at the unfairness of it all, giving up one sheltered life for another.

Entering through the back door, I head straight to the kitchen, swiping the first aid kit along the way. My hands are a mess, and though I heal faster than a human, I heal slower than other shifters. One more weird kink in my DNA that irritates my father.

As I wash my hands, I peer out of the kitchen window, realisation and sadness washing over me. I'll no longer see this incredible view when I'm washing the dishes or get to enjoy the bay and its beautiful blue waters. What will unfold in this next chapter of my life?

Tomorrow, I'll leave for the Supernatural Headquarters, or SNHQ, to mate with a man I met once two years ago and join a pack I know nothing about. I doubt my father has told them I'm defective—if he had, they wouldn't want me—plus he'll get some sort of sick satisfaction leaving it to me to tell them.

Will they kick me out when they discover my secret? Will the alpha shun me immediately? The numerous questions and not knowing may drive me insane before I even get there. If my memory serves me well, the man I'm forced to mate is a handsome man, one I felt not a single thing for. I was introduced to him briefly when he arrived with his father, and after the initial introduction, they swiftly headed to my father's office to broker the deal.

I remember being surprised I wasn't whisked away that day. My father quickly assured me I would leave, but their alpha thought waiting until I was twenty-one was appropriate. I knew this annoyed him, but he had to agree, or he would not come off well in the eyes of another pack.

I understand most matings are chosen, supernaturals that pledge to be together for as long as they live. I just always hoped for more. If I'm honest, I wanted a true mate.

That thought belongs to the little girl who used to dream about her true mate coming to rescue her from this horrid life. For him to arrive and take all her problems away while declaring his undying love.

Believe me, I'm laughing at myself. It was a fairy tale, one I'm far too jaded and old to believe in. The only person who can make my life better is me. I just have no idea how to do it. I've thought about running several times, leaving the pack and going rogue. It's the campfire stories that have stopped me. According to a few older members of the pack that I'd heard discussing me one evening—when a shifter tries to go it alone, it drives the animal to madness, the bonds between pack keeping our animals grounded.

With my situation, I can't be sure if the same would apply. I've been too afraid to find out. If things don't work out at SNHQ, I may discover the truth sooner than I'd hoped. I've already decided if they reject me, I will not be coming back here. The reality of my life is crushing me—this place is too toxic for me to stay in any longer. It is crippling me with anxiety, constantly on guard for when the next verbal attack will come and how deep it will cut. My animal grows more restless every day too, my partial shifts occurring more often, which I'm certain is down to my mood.

No, if I'm rejected from SNHQ, I'd rather live as a human than return to this place. If only I had the courage to tell my father this.

Caught up in my sombre thoughts as I'm cleaning my hands, I fail to notice the time.

"Damnit," I snap, heading to the fridge and pulling out the ingredients for dinner.

If I don't have a meal ready for him when he walks through the door, my evening will turn into a soundtrack of his greatest hits. One of his favourites is that all I'm good for is cooking and cleaning.

This kitchen is my domain. Everything is set out how I like, allowing me to move around the ageing room on autopilot. The whole house is huge yet terribly outdated. We have all the modern kitchen appliances you could want, but the blue wallpaper is yellowing and peeling. The dark brown cupboards are tattered and falling apart. I've tried to spruce the place over the years and fix things up, but there's only so much you can do with limited supplies. When I asked my father to buy some paint, he barked at me for an hour about how he wouldn't waste his money on things like that.

He's happy to gamble with the pack's money, though, isn't he.

I discovered his dirty secret about six months ago, the bills piling up even though the pack contributes a fair amount of money to my father. I couldn't care less if he runs the pack into the ground. They all deserve each other, as far as I'm concerned.

As I'm chopping the vegetables, the sound of an engine causes me to blanch. He's not supposed to be home for at least another two hours.

My shoulders tense along with my animal when his boots pound against the front steps. I busy myself, pulling out pans and furiously chopping vegetables when he enters the kitchen. I don't look up, don't make eye contact with him as I wait for the reason he's home so early.

"You need to prepare a feast for tonight," he barks, his deep voice grating on my nerves.

My heart skips a few beats. When a shifter leaves to join another pack, it's tradition for the current pack to have a celebration, a way to wish the shifter luck and good fortune. I believed with my history, they'd be likely to celebrate once I was gone. Could I have been wrong?

I'm about to engage with him for the first time in weeks when he opens his spiteful mouth.

"Don't get any ideas. It's for the Wick's, they're expecting."

Of course it is. Why do I never learn? Why do I cling to the hope he has some feelings other than disgust and resentment for me. I had hoped to spend at least a little time with Angie today before I left, but with a feast to prepare, I'll have no time.

My fury quickly rises, my ears and fingers trembling as I struggle to hold back my emotions. My animal's rage is palpable, the dismissal of shifter tradition cutting through her like a blade. My fingers change, nails growing into claws with brown fur surrounding the nail bed. My sensitive hearing picks up on my father's heavy breathing, the water dripping from the tap and the soft waves outside the window. All those things pale in comparison to the red mist at the edges of my vision.

"Put that shit away," he snarls. "You're already an embarrassment. Why must you make it worse? It's not surprising you can't shift; your animal is probably as defective as you are. Useless the both of you."

Oh, look, it's number two of his greatest hits.

I hate it when he talks about my animal. Whatever is wrong with us is not her fault. She tries to make me stronger, to show me her strength, but he will never see that. All his insults do is rile me up further, which makes it impossible to stop the partial shift. I've tried to tell him this before, but he never listens.

"Get the feast made, and don't you dare show yourself to the pack looking like that," he sneers, his tone dripping with venom before storming out of the house.

My hands continue to shake long after he's gone. Cooking anything is out of the question until I can get these claws to go away.

The funny thing is, sometimes I understand his hatred towards me. I'm the reason his true mate is no longer here. Many times, I've wished it was me that died and not her, that she could have lived, and they would have been happy. If I had been the one to die, they could have tried again. They would have been together.

I recognise no one is to blame. I was a baby, and labour can be complicated. I just wish my father could see he has a piece of my mother right here, a piece he treats worse than dirt. What would she make of his behaviour? Would she be disappointed with him? Would she hate him for it?

A knock at the back door startles me from my thoughts. Only one person comes to the back, and a smile spreads across my face as I walk over to answer it.

"That fucker, what has he said to you now!" Angie yells, taking in my ears and claws.

"Nothing I haven't heard before. What are you doing here?"

I open the door to let her through, and she waltzes into the kitchen, "I heard about the feast and knew that shifter shit would be making you do all the work, cutting into our time together."

"So you came to rescue me?"

"Next best thing. I came to help, so put me to work," she claps her hands, looking around the kitchen.

Overcome with sadness at leaving this incredible woman behind, I hug her. My action surprises her, but she's soon returning my hug, her arms banding around me tightly.

"Can't breathe," I choke teasingly when her shifter strength becomes too much.

When she pulls away from me, her blue eyes shine with tears.

"Oh no, don't start. We have all afternoon and will get nothing done if you start."

"Fine," she pouts, "but be warned, I'm an emotional shit today."

That makes two of us.

CHAPTER TWO

Angie's distracting presence is precisely what I needed to get through the rest of today. After a few minutes in her company, my claws and ears recede, my animal calming enough for my own emotions to settle. We catch up over coffee before the gruelling work of cooking for thirty-odd shifters begins.

"You're better at baking, so you can make a start on the cake, and I'll make the stew," I tell Angie, gathering all the ingredients we'll need.

"Seriously," she moans. "I can't help eating all the mixture, and I need to watch my figure in case Jake ever asks me to mate him."

"You know you could ask him, right? It's the 21st century, and women can do stuff like that now," I point out, my voice dripping with sarcasm.

"Haha, very funny. Forgive me for being a romantic and wanting him to ask me. Plus, at this stage, he should be begging me to be his mate."

She's not wrong. Angie is a catch and way too good for this pack.

"So, where do your parents think you are this afternoon?" I ask wryly, knowing she always gives them a location that doesn't involve me. The poor woman would get hours of hassle if they knew how much time we spent together. It's not as much time as I would like, but it's more than her parents would find acceptable.

"Are you kidding? This is your last day. I told them I was coming here, and if they didn't like it, I could always move to SNHQ with you."

"You did not!"

"I did. I'm sick of their disapproving bullshit. You haven't even done anything to them, to anyone for that matter!"

"You're going to get grief for that later."

"Yeah, well, maybe I'll be the one to give them grief. Judgemental bitches."

Angie loves her parents, and I'm confident they will forgive her for ever associating with me once I'm out of the picture. She has tried to reason with them over the years and defend me to them, but if the alpha doesn't like me, nobody else will. I'm surprised Angie has stuck around me as long as she has. Then again, she's not a sheep like the rest of the pack.

We met when she joined my father's pack nine years ago. They had moved up from the south, her parents looking for a more remote pack after they'd experienced some trouble in their last one. While my father was getting acquainted with her parents, I was out in the garden playing when an energetic bundle of blonde curly hair came bounding my way, asking if I wanted to be her best friend. It was the first time any child had taken notice of me, and we instantly connected.

The first few years of our friendship were easy. Her parents didn't hate me and allowed us to spend time together, but that all changed the night of the pack gathering. My father's public shaming made me the pariah of the pack—everyone turned against me overnight. Don't get me wrong, I wasn't exactly flush with friends before that point, but most people stopped talking to me altogether after that night. Angie was the only one who didn't change. If anything, it made her more determined to stick by me.

I'll miss her more than I can express, and the thought of not having her close by has tears springing to my eyes.

"What's been going on with you and Jake then?" I ask to distract myself, mainly so I don't end up crying into the stew.

She regales me with the details of her date with Jake the previous night, her face animated and her smile wide when she talks about him. It's surprising they're not true mates based on their strong feelings towards each other. I have a suspicion the only reason he hasn't asked her to mate him is because of me. We've met briefly a few times, but he hasn't said more than four words to me, his disapproval of mine and Angie's friendship written all over his face. I personally don't like the arrogant prick, but he makes Angie happy, and that's all I care about.

"Do you remember anything about the man you're being forced to mate?" Angie's softly spoken question causes my shoulders to tense. For a second, I'd forgotten all about tomorrow.

I screw my nose up, my mind trying to recall the day we met, "Just that he was tall and had lovely grey eyes, but that's about it. We barely said more than two words to each other."

"At least he's not old and fat then."

"I guess there is that. I just..." my words trail off. It's pointless to keep wishing for a different outcome.

"Just what?" Angie coxes.

"It doesn't matter. He could be the nicest guy in the world, but the second he finds out I'm a defect, everything will change."

"You are not a defect. I hate when you call yourself that."

"But I am broken, Angie," I state dejectedly, "Call it whatever you want. There is something fundamentally wrong with me and my animal. Staying here is not good for us, but I don't think going there will be either."

"You don't know that." Angie strides across from the other side of the kitchen, her hands on my shoulders forcing me to turn towards her.

"I need you to promise something for me, actually two things. The first is that you won't ever forget about me. That you'll call me whenever you can."

"That's the easiest promise I'll ever make. If it's within my power to contact you, I'll do it daily. What's the second promise?"

"Regardless of what this mate of yours is like, find yourself some friends and get the answers you need. I've been doing some research on SNHQ, and the place is a hive of activity for supernaturals. Someone there must know what's happening with you. They'll have books, elders, hell, they could even have sears. You need to be like a cat with yarn. Never stop searching for your answers. Never stop annoying people with your questions. I can't bear the thought of you being there and disappearing inside yourself even more."

When her blue eyes fill with tears, there is no stopping them from trailing down her cheeks. My ears and fingers thrum with energy as my own sadness pushes to the surface.

"What if they reject me?" I whisper, my worst fear coming to the forefront of my mind. "What if they find out what I am, and I'm forced to leave. I can't come back here, Angie, I can't."

"Then you travel all over the shifter damn country, and you find your answers some other way. What you fail to realise, my beautiful best friend is that even if they reject you, you'll finally be free."

Will I? Yes, I'll be free of my father, but what if the madness sets in from being without a pack? Immersing myself in the human world could work for a short time, but what if I partially shift in front of them? How will they react?

There are too many unknowns. Too many unanswered questions. It would be better for everyone if I—

"Stop it," Angie shakes me by the shoulders. "I see where your head is going, and this is exactly what I'm talking about. You have to fight, Thea. You have to stop seeing yourself as a defect, a problem to be solved or removed. You have so much to offer, but no one will see that if you don't show them. Promise me, promise me you will fight, and you will live."

Her eyes burn with fire, her hands tightening as if she's forcing me to accept her message. In my misery over being forced to mate someone, I'd forgotten what SNHQ is supposed to represent. A safe haven for all supernaturals. Perhaps Angie's right. There could be someone there who knows what's wrong with me. I've been sheltered for a long time, never having the opportunity to seek answers from someone other than my alpha.

"I promise," I tell her fiercely, a small dash of confidence igniting at the possibilities my new home could present.

"Good. Now let's stop with the tears, and we can scoff some of these tasty treats before anyone notices."

She plasters a smile on her face, but her eyes can't lie. She's worried for me. She knows as well as I do my life will turn out one of two ways. Either I'll find the help I need and become someone new, or I'll wither away under the constant negative reactions and become a shell of myself. Either way, it's too soon to tell.

Angie has made some additional cupcakes for us both, and as we eat and laugh, I thank my friend for her constant support, for keeping me sane, and never letting me give up. It turns out to be the perfect day and when the sun begins to set, I reluctantly pull away from our happy bubble, readying the food to be transported to our meeting area.

Between our house and the Beta's house is a large area of land we use for our social gatherings, picnic tables are set up and the start of the evening is always signified with a bonfire. When I start to gather the platters to take over, Angie surprises me by collecting some and following me.

"What are you doing?"

"I'm helping you with the food."

"Angie," I sigh. "If my father sees you, it will get us both into trouble."

"I don't give a shit, Thea. The fact you even have to do this when you're leaving tomorrow disgusts me. I am a grown woman and will help my best friend in whatever way I can before she leaves." Her tone becomes loud and irate, her eyes swirling with the brown of her tiger when her anger takes over.

"Okay, Angie, okay." I placate, knowing I won't be able to stop her from doing this. "Thank you."

Outside, a few shifters wait at the meeting area, the bonfire now built and ready to be lit. With the arrival of food, more make their way over. All of them ignore me, and none of them thank me for the feast they are about to consume. It doesn't surprise me, and I don't have the energy to be bothered by it. They may be a shitty pack, but one last night with them all, and I can put this part of my life to bed.

It takes Angie and me two trips to get the food set up, and as we're walking back to the house, my father's hulking figure approaches.

"Angie, leave," he demands, an extra kick of alpha power lacing his command.

She wants to disobey him, it's written all over her face, but she can't. An alpha's order is final. She meets my gaze, defiance and sorrow warring within her. When she turns to leave, I stare at my feet, waiting for my own orders.

"House, now," he barks, storming away and expecting me to follow.

The force of his command washes over me, but at the same time, my animal rises, and the compulsion to follow lessens. My brows furrow. I've never dared defy my alpha's orders, yet something's different. The need to obey diminished and could easily be ignored. However, years of doing as I'm told are still well ingrained within me, and I shuffle back to the house.

When I enter, my whole body is on high alert, my ears and fingers itching with the need to shift. My father stands in the kitchen, his demanding presence an eyesore in my space. A quick glance at his face tells me that whatever words spill from his lips are meant to hurt me.

I stand with my back ramrod straight and wait, always waiting on this spiteful man.

"You are not to attend tonight."

My eyes flick to his in surprise, loathing shining back at me from blue eyes so much like my own. Looking away, I stare at the floor, questions filtering through my mind. Why can't I attend? What could I have done wrong to warrant such an action? Is it because Angie helped me with the feast? I might not like my pack, and I'm angry he would avoid tradition because of me, but he has never banned me from a pack gathering. I would love nothing more than to scream all my questions at him. Instead, my voice comes out as a soft whisper.

"Is there a reason I cannot attend?"

"The gathering is for the pack, and you are no longer pack."

He means to hurt me, and I hate him, but it bothers me his actions still impact me deeply. I'm momentarily distracted by a snarl echoing in my head, my animal making her displeasure known.

"I... I am a pack member," I state, my ire slowly rising at his blatant enjoyment of cutting me down.

"No, you are not. You are a defective shifter I have allowed to live on my land for far too long. Come tomorrow, that will no longer be the case."

"Why do you hate me so much?" I seethe, my calm control slipping. "What could I have possibly done to deserve such cruel treatment from my own father."

Regrettably, with my anger comes a shift. When the changes come over me, my father hisses, taking a step back away from me.

"Defective," he snarls. "This is why I don't want you anywhere near my pack. Deliver the rest of the food and return here. The next time I see your face will be when you are leaving."

He storms across the kitchen, stopping beside me, "Your mother would be ashamed of you."

And there it is, his greatest number-one hit. A shot to the heart with the power to break me. He hardly ever mentions her, yet when he does, it's to tell me how disappointed in me she would have been. My tears burn the back of my eyes, and I fight hard against them, refusing to let them fall. I will not give this bastard the satisfaction of knowing how much he hurts me.

He waits, watching my reactions, looking to see how his words affect me.

When he doesn't get the response he wants, he storms out of the house, and my shoulders drop, a howl of pain echoing in my head. I'm not stupid. My father has never loved me, and most days, he ignores me altogether, and we live in silence. But his hatred towards me, the pleasure he gets from torturing me, is something I've never been able to comprehend. I have been an exceptional daughter, doing everything that has been asked of me and never once shying away from my responsibilities. This last blow is too far.

My already fractured heart has been brutalised enough. After today, I will never see him as my father or my alpha ever again. I am done trying to please him, to stick to the shadows and not draw attention to myself, to bend over backwards for his every whim in the hopes he'll throw some scraps of affection my way. When he walked out of that door, he might as well have been dead to me.

Admiration pours through me from my animal, and it affects me greatly. Despite being an innocent bystander to his harsh and unjust treatment, she admires me for not breaking. Even when I believe I'm alone and flawed, she sees beyond that. She loves and relies on me. Though we may never meet, her presence is a comforting reminder that I am never truly alone.

I spend a few minutes basking in her support, and by the time my heart stops racing, and my anger fades, my ears and fingers are normal again. I have one more drop-off with the food. I'm tempted to leave it and hide in the woods for a few hours, but I want my father to see his actions have done nothing to me. It might not be the truth, but it's the truth I'll show him.

Collecting the last two platters, I hold my head up high and head back over to the meeting area. Nearly the whole pack is in attendance now, and I sense their stares as if they're crawling across my skin. I bite my tongue the entire way, the pain a distraction from focusing on their negativity. When I drop off the last platter, I look around, raise my chin and look down my nose at them, disgust evident on my face. I register a few looks of surprise. After all, I've never been so brazen at a gathering.

I don't say anything. I simply let my disappointment and resentment shine through. When I'm satisfied everyone has gotten the message, I walk away, whistling a tune all the way back to the house, not a care in the world.

The second I'm behind the closed door, I pant, my heart pounding over what I just did. Apart from Angie, every member of this pack should be ashamed of themselves. They have never once stepped in. Never once thought of the struggles I go through daily not having access to my animal. They're all aware of how my father treats me, and not one person has ever bothered to check-in. If I had been attending the gathering tonight, I wouldn't have behaved that way. My father did me a favour by banning me. Now they know exactly how I feel about them and their so-called pack.

News of my behaviour will undoubtedly reach my father, but his opinion no longer concerns me. Angie is right. I should fight and stand up for myself because that felt empowering. I can't be sure what awaits me at SNHQ, but it has to be better than this. I'll exploit every inch of the place, just like I've been exploited my whole life. I'll gather as much information as possible, and if it doesn't suit me, I'll move on. If the madness takes me, so be it. I'd rather have the madness than live this way any longer.

For the first time since finding out about my departure, something other than fear and nausea twists inside me. The first spark of hope, or perhaps acceptance, fills me with a new purpose.

Within that spark is also defiance. For all the years I've been good, taken everything my twisted father has done or said to me, I want to be bad.

My lips curl, ideas floating around my mind. The noise from the gathering tells me things are getting started, so I will have a few hours to enact my plans.

I run upstairs so quick that I end up falling up most of them, laughter blossoming out of me, both from my crazy idea and my excitement. Pausing at the threshold of my father's room, I contemplate if this is the right thing to do when a jolt from my animal pushes me the last few steps. I'm only ever allowed in my father's room to put his clothes away. Even then, I'm in and out as fast as possible, the smell of his space making my nose itch.

Reaching into his drawers, I take out all his white T-shirts and shirts and a pair of red socks. You can see where I'm going with this.

It's childish, I admit, but the thought of him stumbling across the pink clothes when I'm gone has maniacal laughter ringing in my head. Taking the clothes back to the kitchen, I put them in the wash, smiling the whole time. After that, I switch out the sugar for salt and remove every scrap of toilet paper except the one we'll need for the morning. Then I move on to his favourite chair, the monstrosity in our living room.

When he's home, he either stays in his room or sits in this brown leather recliner, barking orders out for me to follow. He treats it like a throne, and I hate it. Carefully taking the half-opened can of sardines, I place it under the chair, my arm scraping against the metal bars underneath. It will take a few days for him to notice, but when he does, he won't be able to get his arm through the gap, and he'll be forced to either take it apart or throw it out.

The best part about all these little transgressions is my father will know it was me. I'll be long gone by the time he notices, but when he discovers what I've done, it'll be like giving him the middle finger. I'm almost disappointed I won't get to see his face.

By the time I've fixed myself something to eat and had a shower, the load of washing has finished, and my father's shirts are a hideous pastel pink. I chuckle to myself the whole time I'm folding and putting them away, making sure they're under enough clothes so he doesn't immediately notice them. Before leaving his room, the frame on his bedside table draws my attention, the only picture of my mother in our whole house.

I'm sure he hides it away in here because he doesn't want me to look at her or study our similarities. I pick up the frame reverently, stroking my finger down the face of the mystery woman who is my mother. She looks young and happy in the picture, the sun shining against her dark red hair, the exact same shade as mine. Our features are so similar this could be a picture of me. The only differences are our eyes. Where I have my father's crystal blue eyes, hers are dark brown and pretty.

Is this why my father hates me so much, because I look like her? Do I remind him of her so much it hurts him to look at me? If he wasn't such a bastard, I'd love nothing more than to talk about her, find out all her likes and dislikes, and how they met and fell in love.

Placing a kiss against the photo, I say goodbye, knowing this will be the last time I see her.

I leave the room, closing the door to his bedroom, and on a chapter of my life I want nothing more to do with.

CHAPTER THREE

I'm running, no, not running, sprinting with vigour.

My feet thud against verdant grass, propelling me forward with an unnatural speed. I struggle to grasp my surroundings, searching for anything familiar. All I notice is an endless sea of grass under a sky that shimmers with an unusual hue.

Hurtling forward at this breakneck speed, I glance down, and a wave of confusion clouds my mind as my heart races. Instead of two legs, I find myself driven by light brown paws with long claws.

What is going on? Is this my animal?

I decelerate, letting the realisation dawn on me. I'm dreaming. I've never dreamt of her before, and I don't usually sense her when I'm sleeping. Is my animal making her presence known, and if so, what's changed?

Attempting to get a better look at myself, I try to glimpse my tail or some identifiable features, but my efforts only cause a hazy and obscured image. Whenever I focus on a different part of me, a veil masks my vision, keeping my true form hidden.

The push to see through my blurred vision is nauseating, so I shift my focus to the scenery. Initially, it appeared desolate. However, I can now make out a structure in the distance. Drawn to it, I move forward, and after a few strides of my paws, I find myself sprinting once more.

As I approach, I marvel at my fluid movements in this form. Going from sixty to suddenly two miles per hour is disconcerting, yet my happiness far outweighs any discomfort. I need to know what this all means and why I am now dreaming in shifter form. Have we fixed what was broken? Am I no longer a defect? I should enjoy this moment, but I'm distracted by the many questions and this strange structure.

Six towering wooden posts stand embedded in the ground, evenly spaced and arranged in a pattern I'm unable to decipher from my viewpoint. Circling the structure, I note a concrete altar in the centre.

Why would I dream of myself in my shifter form, in a location I've never seen before?

I circle the structure three times and, on the third pass, change back to two feet. I don't feel the shift from animal to human, the transformation so swift I have to question if I imagined it all. I can't have. If that were possible, I would have been doing it for years. The loss of my animal form brings sadness surging to the surface. I may not have been able to see what I was, but for those brief moments, I've never felt more alive.

Resting my head against one of the wooden posts, I sigh, hoping to conjure her again. Instantly, a barrage of images engulfs me. The first is of myself looking happy, but when I strain to make out more details, another image swiftly emerges. It's a blonde woman, her eyes an intense shade of green and unfamiliar. When the next image flashes, it's a new woman, her features obscured with only black hair detectable.

Three more women materialise, and with each vision, the clarity diminishes. Following the last figure, the scene turns ominous. Flames consume buildings, streets lie abandoned, and blood saturates everything. Recoiling, I pull away from the posts and survey my surroundings. I remain in the strange meadow with only these wooden pillars for company.

Chills cascade down my arms and neck, and an oppressive silence hangs heavily. I sense a presence, as if someone is watching me from the shadows.

"Six will connect, six to save all," a whisper reverberates around me.

I see no one, yet it doesn't stop me from moving away from the structure and running in the opposite direction.

With a few yards separating me from the wooden posts, a chant starts that stops me dead in my tracks.

"Find the six, find the six, find the six."

I cover my ears, desperate to mute the relentless drone. As suddenly as it began, the chanting stops, that uncomfortable silence wrapping itself around me. I don't have time to be relieved or confused before something shoves me from behind, sending me tumbling forward.

"Get up now," my father's voice yanks me out of the dream, the pounding of his fist against my door reverberating through my skull.

The small clock on my bedside reads 3am. Why the hell is my father waking me so early? And while I'm asking questions, I'll never get the answers to what the hell was that dream about? Was that my animal or a manifestation of my hopes? Who are the six, why should I find them, and who the hell shoved me?

The connection between my animal and me is still weak. Could the dream have been trying to tell me something? I'm a big believer that our dreams mean more to us than we realise, that they are sub-context to what is unfolding in our lives.

The sounds of my father moving around the house pause my speculating mind, confusion causing my head to tilt as I listen more closely. It's then I see my packed bag. Of course, I'm leaving today.

The journey to SNHQ will take hours from here by car, hence the early wake-up call. I gathered he'd want me gone early so he could get on with life without me. I just didn't think we would be setting off in the early morning hours. I was hoping to say a proper goodbye to Angie. I wouldn't put it past him to do this purposefully, one final metaphorical kick to the gut before he doesn't have any control over me.

It's disappointing, but I'm determined yesterday will not be the last day I see her. Whatever I need to do at SNHQ to see or speak to her, I'll do it.

Pulling back the covers, I cringe at the sweat stains on my nightshirt. Clearly, I'm going to need a quick shower before going anywhere. Silently rising from the bed, I collect the essentials and tip-toe to the bathroom. Several times, my father has interrupted me mid-shower, demanding I leave the bathroom so he can use it. If I'm quiet, I can usually get through the whole thing, and his vengeful ass doesn't have a chance to kick me out.

I make it to the bathroom without running into him and have the quickest shower possible, grimacing as always at the smell of the shampoo and soap. His male products are the only thing I have access to. My father refused to spend money on me, including feminine products. Thankfully, I've had Angie to help me out in that regard over the years.

Will my new mate allow me to choose products to my liking, or will I be forced to use his things in the same way? This new life is going to take some getting used to. Even if he doesn't turn out to be as bad as my father, the smells, location, and surroundings will all be new. Everything I've known over the last ten years will be completely different, and though I won't miss this place, it will be a hard adjustment to make.

Shuffling back to my room, I dress quickly in tattered blue jeans and a black T-shirt, the nicest clothes I own. Collecting all the belongings I'll be taking with me and glancing one last time around my bedroom, I make my way downstairs, desperate for a coffee to shake my morning fog.

My father is nowhere to be seen, so I take the opportunity to make myself some toast as I wait for the kettle to boil. It's strange. I hate this kitchen and what it represents, but I will miss it. The time I've spent here alone has been some of my most peaceful. Living with a mate, I don't imagine I will have any space of my own.

I've been ignoring the fear that rears its ugly head when it comes to intimacy, shoving it to the back of my mind and pretending it doesn't exist. I've never had a boyfriend or kissed anyone before. I only discovered porn about a year ago, and I'm not sure what to make of it. Will my mate expect me to be intimate immediately, or will there be some form of courtship first? These are all questions that could have been asked when this arrangement was made. I doubt my father cared enough to ask.

Lost in thought, the sound of my father's footsteps on the stairs only registers when he's close. Instinctively, the breakfast preparation begins, my meal forgotten and cooling on the table. The ingrained response to his presence is infuriating. It's my last day. I ought to tell him to make his own damn food. Maybe in some alternate universe, I'd have the courage, but here, the old routine of catering to him persists.

Tension courses through every fibre as he settles at the table. He typically lounges in front of the TV until his meal is served. Is this a deliberate attempt to rattle me? As I prepare his meal, my eyes strain with the need to look at him, fearing what will happen if I do. I try my best to ignore him, but with his gaze on me, my actions turn jerky, and my nerves are taut. My animal brushes against my mind, trying to temper my anxiety, but it barely registers in the presence of my father.

Once his breakfast is ready, I set it before him without waiting for an acknowledgement, which he wouldn't offer anyway. Drifting towards the sink, I begin washing the dishes, anything to distract myself from his existence.

"Do you think you will have it easy there?" he asks casually, the deceptive normalcy of his tone making my defences immediately go up.

"I don't know," I respond indifferently.

The silence hangs between us. There is so much unsaid, so many years of hurt. Is he having regrets? Does he wish he'd done things differently? My body is coiled so tightly, like a mouse trap readying to snap, waiting for his next words, the next blow.

"I haven't told them you're a defect. I won't either, or they might not take you. You'll likely be an outcast once they find out."

"That should make you happy then." The flippant response flies out of my mouth before I can stop it.

He slams his fist on the table, the impact making me jump, "You will speak to me with respect," he yells. "You may not be of my pack, but I am still an alpha, and you will address me as such. I will not have a defect disrespecting me in my home or in front of another alpha. Do I make myself clear?"

"Yes, alpha," I mumble, my eyes cast down, my shoulders so tense they sit by my ears.

He shoves his plate across the table and stands, about to leave the room, until my voice stops him.

"I would change it if I could. I would give my life for hers." My confession is barely above a whisper, but he hears it, his shoulders stiffening at the mention of my mother.

He stands with his back to me. The tension is unbearable as I wait to see if he'll react. I know he misses her and wishes every day she was here. I can't blame him. I wish she was here, and I've never even met her.

"I would give your life for hers a thousand times over," he says softly, leaving the room and breaking my heart into pieces.

You'd think I'd learn. I never do. Maybe, on some level, I put myself in this position on purpose, saying things he will only answer with a nasty response so he can reaffirm what I already think about myself. I am a nobody, pathetic, useless and defective.

I'll stick by my promise to Angie. I'll fight for my answers and find myself. What good it will do remains to be seen. Perhaps this is all I'm meant to be in this life, an anomaly in the universe who isn't meant to exist. Maybe that will be my truth.

There is nothing left for me to do here, so picking up my things, I put my coat on and wait outside until my father is ready. The morning air's chill seeps through my shabby jacket and into my skin, a refreshing cleanse washing through me, removing the stain of my old life and starting with a clean slate for my new one. At least, that's how I like to view it.

I linger for thirty minutes in the dark before he eventually emerges from the house. He doesn't say anything as he makes his way over to one of the two cars he owns. Hefting my bags, I approach the vehicle with a final glance around. As I'm about to throw my bags into the car and climb in, the sound of my name being called stops me.

Spotting a familiar blonde figure sprinting at full speed, a laugh explodes out of me. My best friend, still clad in her pyjamas, is racing towards me as if the world is about to end. Not even casting a look at my father, I race to meet her. We collide midway, both of us tumbling to the ground. With laughter still spilling from me, I stand and extend my hand to help her up.

"I was so worried I might miss you!" she says in a rush. "If I'd have known I wasn't going to see you last night—"

"I know, me too," I hold her hands and look at her sweet face. "Listen, before he tells you to leave, I need to tell you something. Thank you. Thank you for being my friend when nobody else would, for always looking out for me and for just being you. I'll miss you so much, but I promise I will see you again."

Her eyes shimmer and fill with tears, as do mine, "While you're making promises, you better keep the ones you made yesterday, right?

You give them hell, Thea, you hear me! Don't take any shit from them, and don't let them treat you any differently, you are special, not different, and you need to make them see that like I do."

My father blares the car horn, the engine running, and our time up, "I love you, Angie. I'll call soon, okay."

She pulls me into a bone-crushing hug, and with another blast of the horn, we pull apart, and I head over to the waiting car. Opening the rear door, I climb in and turn to see her still standing there, tears trailing down her face. I roll down the window, smiling as best I can, even as I leave a piece of my heart behind.

As we pass by, she screams at the top of her lungs, "I love you, Thea. You're the best shifter I've ever met!"

A silent chuckle escapes me, knowing she said that more for my father's benefit than mine. I blow her a kiss and watch her a second more as we pull away. When she's no longer in sight, I settle in for the journey, a small part of me left behind and the rest of me moving forward into the unknown.

CHAPTER FOUR

I'VE LOST THE WILL to live.

Five hours trapped in this car with my megalomaniac father, nothing but silence and my own thoughts to keep me company. I've over analysed every aspect of my life, every interaction between me and my father and everything that's still to come.

Even my animal's frustration has reached me, and I can't blame her. I'm annoying myself. I've tried to fall asleep, but with my father's presence, I can't manage it. I sense him growing restless, too. Shifters, by nature, dislike confinement, and after being trapped in a car for five hours, the silence is suffocating. I'm surprised he hasn't left me by the roadside and headed back home.

The closer we get to our destination, the landscape begins to change, giving way to an expansive forest. Trees stretch endlessly in every direction, densely packed, making the area seem even more remote than I had envisioned. After another twenty minutes, we arrive at a seemingly random rest stop on the forest's edge. The surroundings offer no clue, leaving me puzzled about why my father would choose this location to stop. The engine goes silent, and he exits the car as I scan the area, looking for any sign of SNHQ. Trees dominate the view, with no buildings, pathways, or even hints of an entrance in sight.

A fleeting pang of fear courses through me as I briefly entertain the idea my father might simply be abandoning me here without any intention of taking me to SNHQ. Would he drive all this way to do that? Would it make things easier for me if he did?

Still looking around, trying to figure out where we are, he bangs on the car, "Get out," he barks.

I swing the car door open and step out, taking a moment to relish a satisfying stretch. Grasping my bags, I shut the car door with a thud. My father shoots me a glare, mouth opening as if to reprimand me, but he's interrupted. A figure suddenly emerges from the trees. And I don't mean from a break in the foliage or a hidden pathway. He quite literally materialises from the very heart of the trees!

My father steps forward, exchanging a handshake and pleasantries with the man. After their brief exchange, they both shift their attention to me.

"Althea, it's nice to meet you. My name is Damiean. I trust your journey here was comfortable?" the man remarks, his face familiar but not one I can place.

"It was, thank you," I reply with a courteous tone, choosing to keep the awful experience to myself.

"As the leader of SNHQ, I wanted to be the one to greet you and introduce you to your new home. We've prepared everything for your arrival, so if you'll please follow me to my office," he says, gesturing towards the dense trees. It's then recognition dawns on me. I've seen this man before on TV. He represents the supernatural community.

As we follow, I'm left wondering if the forest is his office or if he believes I can simply pass through the trees. Nonetheless, I trail after him and my father as they lead the way.

Pausing briefly, I take a tentative step into the forest. A slithering sensation skims across my skin as I step through, presumably some sort of magical barrier. I'll need to adapt to the use of magic in this place. I've only ever been around shifters, so interacting with other supernaturals will take some getting used to.

Emerging on the other side of the trees, an enchanting village unfurls before my eyes. A surreal but vibrant community tucked inside a forest, bustling life nestled within the embrace of trees and earth.

Walking behind my father and Damiean, my head whips from side to side, my eyes consuming as many details as possible. The smells, the sights, even the air has a magical quality, and I instantly fall in love with the place.

The wooden buildings, characterised by large windows, are arranged around a bustling courtyard. Generous spaces lie between each modern-looking building, and people buzz around the market stalls in the courtyard. Glimpses between the buildings reveal endless trees, evoking a burst of joy from my animal. If we ever resolve our predicament, I sense she would enjoy it here.

As we pass through the centre of the courtyard, a gentle pulsing sensation tugs at my chest, the feeling causing me to pause. Is this my animal's way of saying she likes it here? Before I can understand the cause, I find myself needing to catch up with my father and Damiean, who have moved on.

Walking up the ornate and beautiful steps at the edge of the courtyard, we head towards the most imposing building. Its stark modern appearance contrasts with the rest of SNHQ's structures, making it stand out against the forest backdrop. Some curious looks follow us, as others remain indifferent to our presence. Still, my anxiety intensifies with the sheer number of people around. This bustling environment is a far cry from the smaller pack life I'm accustomed to, and with more people comes more judgment.

Damiean faces me, and for a fleeting moment, I detect the hint of a frown. It vanishes so swiftly I may have imagined it.

"So, Althea, as I'm sure your father has explained, while the circumstances of you being here have changed, I'm positive we can still help you adjust to your new life."

My head cocks to the side, and I frown, trying to decipher his meaning. He seems to notice my bewilderment, but my father interjects before we can address it. "Actually, I haven't had the opportunity to discuss it with her," he remarks nonchalantly, continuing his stride.

"Discuss what, exactly?" I query, my tone edged with caution.

"Perhaps it's best we discuss this in my office," Damiean proposes, his arm held out to indicate the waiting elevator.

As we ride the elevator up several floors, my mind whirls with possible outcomes. What did he mean by the circumstances have changed? Has my father brokered another deal for me besides finding a mate? What new life is Damiean alluding to?

By the time we reach his office, doubt plagues me. Damiean seems like a nice enough man, but I'll be wary until I know exactly what 'new life' they have planned for me.

"Please, take a seat," Damiean says. "Could I get either of you a drink?"

Agreeing to the offered drink, I settle into a chair opposite the expansive desk as my father remains standing. Anxious energy causes my foot to tap rhythmically, my thoughts gravitating towards whatever additional chaos he might have introduced to my life.

My gaze drifts to Damiean as he prepares the drinks. His appearance is strikingly more handsome than I recall from seeing him on the news. His manner of speaking hints at his seasoned supernatural age, yet he looks no older than thirty. The allure of his dark hair and eyes briefly captivates me.

He smiles kindly as he hands me the drink, and I remind myself of his influential position as the leader of SNHQ. This man could hold considerable sway over my fate, and I may be trading one tyrant for another. Another flicker of a frown crosses his face as if he's experiencing something unpleasant, but again, it's brief. Once he has distributed the drinks and takes his seat, the look is gone and I steel myself for the conversation ahead, ensuring my father remains within my view.

"Initially, the plan was for you to be paired with the next prospective Alpha, Anubis. But since that agreement was made, Anubis has discovered his true mate," Damiean clarifies. The information is surprising and not what I was expecting.

"That's wonderful news for him. It's truly a blessing they found each other," I respond, genuinely happy with the outcome and not just because of what it could mean for me.

"Indeed, they are fortunate," Damiean states, his voice filled with fondness. "However, their union raised concerns regarding your prior arrangement."

I look fleetingly to my father. Why would he not tell me this? Surely, the point of bringing me here was to get rid of me.

"These things are beyond our control. I hope they'll both find happiness together," I say cautiously, waiting for my father to intervene.

As if on cue, he emits a disgruntled growl. "You will be mated to someone," he asserts with resolve.

"If they are both in agreement," Damiean quickly clarifies. "All we are proposing, for the time being, is a meeting between the two of you."

"No, the agreement was she would be mated," my father states, about to argue further until Damiean interrupts.

"Sir, I'm not sure how you are used to dealing with things in your pack, but I can assure you, we do not force matings here," Damiean says more forcefully, a hint of disapproval in his voice.

Whilst my father continues to push his own agenda, I'm distracted from the conversation when the strange tugging sensation returns. It was dull and faint in the courtyard, but now it's insistent enough that I can't ignore it. My animal notices it, too, sending a flurry of emotions my way. The most dominant among them is elation. Does she know something I don't? Is this our connection I'm suddenly experiencing?

I'm left bewildered as the sensation intensifies. The voices of my father and Damiean are background noise, the conversation a quiet buzz as I contemplate if I should make them aware of my situation. As if something is trying to pull me towards it, I open my mouth to speak when a knock sounds at the door.

Damiean cocks his head to the side, alarm registering on his face, though it's not clear what could have caused the expression. "Excuse me, I need to get this."

When Damiean approaches the door, the sensation deepens, some unseen power on the verge of jerking me out of my seat. I hear snippets of Damiean's conversation with a male and female on the other side of the door but find it hard to concentrate on anything other than the feeling in my chest.

Moments later, he broadens the doorway, allowing the couple to enter. I instantly recognise the man as Anubis, which adds to my confusion. It's as if the force pulling at me emanates from him, but that's impossible, given he already has a true mate.

The woman first glances at my father. Then her gaze shifts to me, and I'm taken aback, drawing in a sharp breath.

"It's you!" she shouts.

The force within my chest builds up until it snaps into a solid connection, linking me to the blonde woman from my dreams. We lock eyes, mutual shock mirrored in our expressions. Suddenly, flames erupt from her hands as tears shine in her eyes. Anubis swiftly envelops her in a comforting embrace, murmuring soothing words so gently that I'm unable to catch them. As he lays his hands over hers, the flames subside.

I watch the scene with an odd sense of detachment, my mind grappling with the confusing events. Emotions that aren't solely my own swirl within me—confusion and awe. Dizziness threatens to overtake me, and my mind becomes jumbled as the blonde woman's gaze meets mine once more. She hurries to my side, and when her hand touches my arm, a profound sense of peace washes over me. My animal responds with a surge of affection towards her, increasing my confusion.

"It's okay, just breathe. I'm not sure what's happening, but we'll figure it out," she whispers reassuringly.

"What is the meaning of this?" my father intervenes from his position near the window.

For some reason, I don't want to make him aware of what's occurred. I couldn't explain it for a start, and I think it's best if he doesn't know. A wave of apprehension washes over me as I search for the words to offer him without revealing the truth. The woman, her back turned to my father, seems to sense my predicament, offering me a wink before pivoting to face my father.

"Sorry, she looks like the spitting image of an old friend of mine, but I see I'm mistaken now," she turns back to face me. "Sorry for shouting at you like that. The resemblance was just a bit shocking."

"No... no problem," I stutter, unsure why she's covering for me yet grateful.

Damiean is looking at the woman with complete bafflement, but she seems to convey something he recognises because he clears his throat and makes introductions, "Althea, I believe you've met Anubis previously, and the woman before you is Kali, Anubis's true mate."

The woman from my dream is Anubis's true mate. What does this mean? Why on earth would I dream of her? And what the hell formed between us? I have so many questions that even my questions have questions.

My father, not appreciating being left out of the introductions, ignores Anubis and Kali and continues his conversation with Damiean, "Is the shifter mating her also attending this meeting?"

It doesn't escape my notice he can't even call me his daughter.

"Who said Bran was mating your daughter?" Anubis asks, emphasising the word daughter with a level of hostility my father doesn't appreciate. Seems I'm not the only one to notice his lack of respect for me.

"I said," my father snaps, turning his attention to Anubis. "The agreement was for you to mate her, and if you no longer can, then you need to provide an alternative."

Isn't it nice that he makes me sound like some kind of goods to be traded?

"Honestly, what is it with you alphas trying to marry off your kids! I thought you were a progressive species?" Kali grumbles, throwing her hands in the air with exasperation. I almost laugh out loud, stopping myself in time when I remember who's in the room. I must say, I like this woman already.

My father ignores Kali's comment and turns to Damiean instead, "Can we please get this over and done with? I have places I need to be. Call the shifter who will mate with her, and I will be on my way."

"Well, aren't you just the loving father figure?" Kali snarls with narrowed eyes. My father growls at her, forcing Anubis to react immediately and growling much more aggressively.

Hearing my father growl at Kali and seeing the disrespect in his eyes when he looks at her makes my blood boil. I've known this woman for under five minutes, but the urge to protect and shield her from him is so strong that it not only forces a partial shift, it forces me out of my chair.

"If I don't mate with someone, am I welcome here? To join this pack?" I ask, addressing Damiean as the leader here.

"Yes, absolutely. As I was saying, if you are interested, we can arrange a meeting with a suitable shifter."

"Okay, thank you. I'm not interested in being mated, but I would like to stay."

"You only leave my pack if I allow it, and I will allow it on the condition you will be mated. That way, you can never come back," Father says through gritted teeth.

I have no idea what comes over me, but I lock eyes with him. Instead of the usual coerced respect, I defiantly meet his gaze, disgust and loathing flowing within me from my animal. He's no longer my alpha, no longer my father or someone who can demand respect. Even if I couldn't stay here, I would never leave with him.

Kali moves to stand beside me, her presence an unexpected source of comfort, bolstering me with an intangible strength. As a lesser shifter, I should be compelled to break eye contact first in a show of submission. Today is different. Something about this peculiar bond with Kali gives me a newfound sense of freedom from him, my tormentor.

As our eyes continue to clash, a bead of sweat forms on his brow. My heart races, realising the significance of that minor detail. Challenging an alpha's dominance begins with a stare. The lesser shifter usually grows uncomfortable, the discomfort intensifying the longer the gaze holds.

Never did I imagine, after enduring years of his abuse, there would come a day when I, his defective daughter, might appear more dominant than him. I'm not sure of the implications or how I'm even doing it, and there's no time to fully grasp it, but one realisation stands out.

"It seems, father," I say with a touch of scorn, "you're not alpha enough to keep me in your pack."

His façade is cracking, revealing the strain underneath and the touch of fear in his eyes.

"Leave," I command, my voice carrying a new assertiveness. "I will never endure your degrading remarks or follow your every demand again. You've lost your grip on me. You. Are. Nothing."

I tremble, but it's not from fear. A whirlwind of emotions—liberation, excitement, and astonishment, among others—swirl within me. Simultaneously, the connection with Kali pulses with joy and pride.

The erratic surge I recognise from a partial shift vibrates, though my ears and fingers are already transformed. With all the emotions cascading through me, there's an unfamiliar tingling sensation just above my upper lip as another shift completes. Still maintaining eye contact with my father, my hand rises to my face, finding a lone whisker jutting out from the left side.

That's new.

My father's eyes widen in surprise before narrowing, sweat now pouring down his head. "I'm sure everyone will be thrilled to learn there's a defective shifter among them."

With his scathing statement, he breaks our gaze and surprise nearly knocks me off balance.

I am more alpha than my father.

Kali's steadying presence is there, keeping me upright and grounded. Despite being a stranger, I've never felt more gratitude toward anyone in such a moment. My father's gaze sweeps the room, settling back on me with less confidence than before.

A malicious grin suddenly pulls at his lips, a sign he's about to spew more hate. "I'm sure the actual alpha will be less than pleased with this latest development. A defect in the pack will ruin everything, just like you have done for me all these years."

If he aims to hurt me, he fails. I'll face that challenge when it comes, as I've faced this challenge against him and won.

"Althea will have no problem with the pack here, and as future alpha, I'll make sure she is well looked after and thrives under our protection." The insinuation is clear in Anubis's tone. The few sentences my father has uttered since Anubis entered the room have told him everything he needs to know about what kind of man and shifter my father is.

"I haven't released her from my pack yet," my father snarls. His face contorted with rage at the blatant disrespect Anubis is showing him.

"I think we both realise that's not required," Anubis huffs with laughter. "She won the dominance challenge, and under shifter hierarchy, she is no longer bound to you or your pack."

Have I fallen asleep in the car, and this is a dream? I won a dominance challenge against my father, Anubis is defending me, Kali is supporting me, and even Damiean has moved to stand by me in a show of solidarity. How is this all happening when I've known these people for less than ten minutes?

If it wasn't completely inappropriate, I'd be cheering and clapping right now.

My father sensing his audience has shifted to my side, growls in my direction before moving purposefully towards the exit. Before he departs, I deliver one last message.

"Mother would be so disappointed in you," I state, my voice brimming with quiet confidence.

He pauses, his shoulders rigid—my words have struck a chord. He chooses not to reply, storming out and letting the door slam in his wake.

CHAPTER FIVE

In the fleeting silence, I'm overcome with... relief. Kali is once more by my side, gently guiding me to a chair as my thoughts race, replaying the surreal events. Today has taken turns I never could have anticipated. My animal's presence is soothing, offering comfort and reassurance while reminding me of the whisker on my face.

Is this another sign of our growing connection? Has getting away from my old pack somehow allowed our connection to be repaired? If I find out my father and his pack are the reason for my problems, I will freak out.

"You doing okay?" Kali asks gently, studying me from her crouched position. "It seems something big went down for you, and speaking from experience, I get how it can take some time to process."

"I..." Am I okay? Did all that happen? Seeing the woman before me, I could be mistaking this for another dream. I pinch my arm, the pain real enough to prove I'm not dreaming.

"I'm great," I chuckle, my tone tinged with hysteria.

"Let me make everyone a drink, and we can talk," Damiean suggests, moving over to the drink station in his office.

While he's busy, I stare into the beautiful green eyes of the woman I dreamt about, "This is all so bizarre. I dreamt of you last night."

"Me too, that's kind of why I went all leaky when I first saw you. I recognised you from my dream. We were on our way over here to discuss it with Damiean when I felt the bond," she touches her chest, resting her hand over the position of our connection.

"Bond? What do you mean by bond? Isn't that normally a true mate kind of thing?"

"I'm new to all this supernatural stuff, but yeah, I think so."

"I don't mean to interrupt," Anubis says, looking at me and Kali, "I can see you've had a lot to deal with, but could someone please explain what the hell is going on?"

"Yes, I would second that comment, Anubis," Damiean adds, handing out our drinks before taking a seat on his desk.

"I'm sorry you all had to witness that," I start. "My father and I have a complicated relationship. Well, we don't have a relationship at all. I may have sounded harsh, but it's no worse than what he's done to me over the years."

These people are strangers to me, so I'm compelled to defend myself and my actions before they form any judgments about me. I'm still partially shifted, revealing my defective nature, and the anticipation of someone pointing it out has me on edge.

"Sounds like you weren't harsh enough," Anubis mumbles from behind his cup.

"Right?" Kali yells, hearing Anubis's comment. "I mean, what a complete asshole. Who the fuck does he think he is to treat you that way. Dick!"

A startled laugh escapes me at her general use of vulgar names for my father, all of them true, but it's only something I've ever thought about in my head. To hear her casually calling him out is shocking but hilarious.

"I agree with Kali's assessment, but could you share your perspective? Given your father's actions, it's evident that your previous pack wasn't a supportive environment. We might need to investigate this," Damiean comments, exchanging a concerned glance with Anubis.

"Oh no, he treats everyone in the pack fine, if that's what you mean," I have no idea why I'm defending him. "It was only ever me that was the issue."

"I thought there was something amiss with him the day we came to visit," Anubis says. "He was very insistent you leave with us immediately, stating it would be good for the alliance. It was my insistence you were too young that stopped it from happening. Seeing how he's treated you, I wish I had done things differently."

"You weren't to know," I respond, shocked by Anubis's genuine annoyance at the situation. "I was the outsider, or defect as he liked to call me—"

"Fucking stupid bastard," Kali interrupts quietly, her anger filtering down the bond we now share as a gentle breeze suddenly blows through the room.

Kali's eyes get comically wide, and she stands from her crouched position, taking a chair next to Anubis and sitting on her hands, "I'm sorry, you were saying."

Her strange behaviour is confusing, but I offer her a small smile before continuing, "My father has hated me since the day I was born. There were complications with my delivery, and after my birth, my mother died. He's blamed me for it since my first breath."

The glass Kali has just picked up cracks in her hand, the liquid leaking through before twirling around in front of her and becoming a small cyclone right before my eyes.

"Shit," she snaps. Placing the glass down, she carefully seizes the cyclone in her hands, her eyes scanning the office frantically. Striding over to the window, she swings it open and forces the liquid out. As a sound from the window wafts our way, Kali winces.

"Sorry," she yells to someone outside, quickly slamming the window shut and shuffling back to her seat.

Anubis and Damiean do nothing to hide their amusement. If anything, it all appears to be a normal occurrence.

"I'm sorry, I'm not normally this leaky. I think hearing your story and feeling the emotions that accompany it will take some adjustment. Expect more bizarre crap while you're talking, and just ignore it. You'll be fine, please, continue."

This woman is utterly chaotic, and I find her completely endearing. As someone who's struggled to control her own magic, I also have a lot of sympathy for her.

"Okay," I smile at her. Taking a deep breath, I prepare myself to share my story with these people. "From an early age, I knew something was wrong with me because I've never been able to shift into my animal. I can sense her, and she's always there, but even with an alpha command, I cannot bring her out. Around my sixteenth birthday, there was a pack gathering, I was angry at not being involved, and my emotions triggered a partial shift. I can shift my ears and fingers, but that's all. Oh, and this," I point to the one lone whisker. "This has never emerged before until today."

My sentences tumble out quickly, nerves making me ramble and worry about potential rejection. Damiean might have already offered me a place here, and Anubis confronted my father on my behalf, but they did so before I made them aware of my challenges. Now they are informed, I steel myself for their response.

"That can't be a coincidence, can it?" Kali queries, her head whipping back and forth between me and Damiean.

What coincidence is she referring to, and how could it be connected to me? There is so much going on here that I need help keeping track of what I should be processing first.

"I feel your confusion, and I'm right there with you," Kali says, her hand once again going to where the bond resides between us. "Long story short, I'm an orphan and never knew I was supernatural. On my sixteenth birthday, I got these powers and didn't know what the hell was happening. Four weeks ago, I came here looking for help and found out I was an elemental, only my powers don't work as they should. I have some kind of restriction around them, which means I only have a small amount of control. When I'm emotional, they tend to leak out of me, which you've seen for yourself."

Her experience closely mirrors my own, and a surge of hope rises within me. "I can only shift partially when I'm overwhelmed with emotions. Any strong feelings will act as a trigger for the shift." Turning to Damiean, I ask, "Could we be facing the same problem?"

Damiean pauses his intense note-taking to answer my question. "Given this revelation, I'll need to conduct further research. However, it is peculiar for both of you to experience the same issues with your magical abilities."

This is incredible. In under an hour of being here, I've made more progress and have more insight into my situation than I ever have before.

"So, you're aware of your animal but can't connect with her?" Anubis's expression shows concern, and I fear he might say I'm not fit to join their pack.

"No, I only occasionally sense her emotions, usually when I'm overwhelmed with my own feelings."

"I'm so sorry," he expresses sincerely, "I can't imagine what that must be like." The genuine compassion in his tone is encouraging. It doesn't hint at rejection, and I take it as a positive sign.

Kali's worry for me resonates down our bond, amplifying the pressing questions building within me. "Now you've heard my story. Care to enlighten me on this bond between us?"

She regards me with a furrowed brow, "I got nothing."

"Very reassuring," I deadpan, my lips pulling at the corners.

Subtly prodding at the bond, I watch Kali for any response. She grins, and moments later, a gentle pull registers, suggesting she's doing the same. "This is so strange. What could it mean?" I pose, seeking an answer from anyone.

"The only thing I can compare it to is my mate bond with Anubis, but this is different. It's more like family," she offers with a shrug.

Anubis gazes at Kali with a puzzled expression, "Alright, both of you need to elaborate. What exactly went down when we came in here?"

"The pull I felt in my chest on our way to Damiean's office is a bond but with Althea. It has a sort of family essence to it." When she reiterates the term, the description resonates deeply with me. It truly feels that way—like I'm familiar with her, even without knowing her. Admittedly, that might sound confusing, but I'm navigating this mystery in real time and coming up with the best conclusion I can.

"Family? That's highly unusual." Damiean comments, looking lost in deep contemplation.

"Does that mean she could be a sister to me?" Kali asks, hope and excitement gleaming in her eyes.

"I wouldn't classify it as 'sisters' per se, perhaps more akin to distant relatives," Damiean suggests. Rising from his chair, he paces the room and, after a moment, gravitates to his bookshelf. Perusing its vast collection, he searches the shelves, retrieving an ancient-looking book.

Returning to his desk, he carefully opens the book and scans the yellowing pages. "Kali, as we're aware, your restrictions stem from an incredibly powerful source. Despite our extensive research, I haven't identified anyone with such immense power. If we assume Althea shares similar limitations, then there's likely a broader significance at play."

"What could that be?" Kali and I say at the same time.

Damiean smiles softly, still scanning the contents of the book. "My initial theory was your parents cast the spell, perhaps to ensure your safety while you lived among humans. But with Althea echoing a similar sentiment, that can't be it. Plus, there's the matter of your unique bond."

With her chin propped in her hand, Kali frowns. "We need Oberon," she huffs. Anubis responds with a soft chuckle, placing a reassuring hand on her back.

Damiean gives a distracted nod before continuing, "Setting aside the restriction for now, the intriguing part is that two entirely different species share a bond reminiscent of family ties. That introduces a fresh perspective for our investigation."

"In what way?" Anubis inquires.

"There are a plethora of tales about the origins of the first supernaturals," Damiean starts.

"Shifter spirit," Anubis and I blurt out in unison.

Kali looks between us, her brows furrowed once more in confusion.

Pausing to glance at each of us, Damiean chuckles, "The two of you are off the mark, and you know it." He shakes his head, still smiling. Turning to Kali, he adds, "Let me enlighten you with the accurate narrative before these two fill your thoughts with their whimsical tales."

"We all have our beliefs," I retort, defending our shifter spirit.

"Indeed, Althea. Every species cherishes its beliefs, but all origins trace back to a starting point. The most ancient documentation we possess points to supernaturals being an amalgamation of all species. While their exact origins remain unclear, this record stands as the earliest evidence we have."

Damiean picks up the book from his desk, carefully displaying the page towards us. The language is not anything I recognise, so it's the roughly drawn picture that gains my attention. Six beings are depicted, their forms tall but otherwise, none descript.

"Our oldest manuscripts suggest these primordial supernaturals encompassed attributes from all identified species. They possessed magic, consumed blood, had the ability to shape-shift, and could command the elements, to name a few. It's theorised that a few of these 'originals,' to use a makeshift term, descended to Earth and intermingled with early humans. Instead of passing on their entire spectrum of abilities, when their DNA combined with human genes, only one specific power got transmitted. From these unions, our distinct supernatural lineages emerged."

The concept of the originals is new to me, but my life has been sheltered. The idea that our lineage might be traced back to one of these primordial beings is staggering. I can see Kali is equally captivated, absorbing the details of Damiean's theory.

Pointing back and forth between Kali and myself, I ask the pivotal question, "How does this relate to the bond we share?"

"If you follow your family lineage far enough, it's conceivable that both of you could trace back to the original supernaturals. Historically, there's been no documented bond between species outside the realm of a true mate connection. Given that the originals are as close as one can get to different species sharing familial ties, it raises questions about your ancestry."

"Even if we are descendants of the originals, we're fundamentally different species now. How would the bond come into it?" I interject, still unsure how this links to our situation.

Damiean's exhalation is audible as he carefully shuts the book. "That's precisely the part that eludes me. If you're indeed descendants of the originals, then this could drastically alter the direction of my research."

"I have a headache," Kali remarks, echoing my sentiments.

Damiean rises to replace the book back on its shelf, "Given our current uncertainties and Althea's recent arrival, it might be best to continue this discussion after I've had an opportunity for further research."

His comment brings a pang of disappointment, but considering the physical and emotional journey I've been on today, a meal and a break from the confusing events sound appealing.

As Kali rises, Anubis does the same. Unexpectedly, the weight of my situation hits me. I have no mate, haven't met the pack's alpha, and I'm unfamiliar with my surroundings. What does my life hold for me now? I'd prepared myself for a life of servitude and possible isolation. This sudden freedom is unsettling.

Kali peers down at me, concern etched on her features. "What's wrong?"

I'm surprised by her question. I didn't say or do anything to indicate something was wrong, "What do you mean?"

She seems confused and looks to Anubis for a second before turning back to me, "I can sense something from you, I think. It's not as strong as the mate bond, but a second ago, it seemed as if you were almost panicking."

"I... I wasn't..." Sighing, I recognise there is no point in keeping my feelings from her. This bond will reveal my true worries anyway.

"I'm not sure what to do now." God, I sound so pathetic. "What I mean is, I'm not used to having my own freedom. I await the next demand and carry out the action. Where do I go now? What do I do with myself? I have no idea what is expected of me."

Their collective sympathetic gazes settle on me with an intensity that makes me shift uncomfortably. Damiean is the first to break the silence. "I apologise, Althea. Given your father's behaviour, I appear to have overlooked my usual courtesies. Welcome to SNHQ. I am Damiean Thorax and the leader of the British division," he finishes, a mischievous smirk highlighting his handsome features.

"I got that much," I chuckle, some of the tension easing in me.

Getting up from his desk, he smiles and takes a seat beside me. "From what I've observed, life hasn't always been kind to you. Firstly, I want to assure you that you won't be pressured into any relationships here, and you're welcome to stay for as long as you wish. We've prepared a place for you to stay. Tomorrow, we can discuss your role and future here with us. Everyone here contributes in their own way, and if you wish to stay, we'll find the right fit for you. For now, take some time to relax and familiarise yourself with the place."

It's all so surreal. I kind of want to pinch myself again. To think I was apprehensive about coming here. His kind response brings about a sense of peace, and for the first time since arriving, I begin to relax enough for my ears, fingers and one whisker to withdraw.

"Which apartment block will she be in?" Kali queries on my behalf.

"I've chosen Oak," Damiean replies, standing to open a drawer and handing a key over to me. "Given that you're new here as well, I thought it'd be helpful for Althea to have someone nearby who has been in a similar situation."

A surge of joy travels across the bond, and I cast a puzzled glance at Kali. While the bond gives an impression of familiarity between us, I wonder why she would be excited living close to the defective shifter.

"Come on, Althea, I'll show you where we keep all the food, and then you can see your place."

At the mention of food, my stomach rumbles loudly. Partial shifting often leaves me with an appetite, and skipping breakfast today, courtesy of my father didn't help. I grab my bags and stand, ready to accompany Kali and Anubis out of the office. Before I leave, I pause to face Damiean, "Thank you, truly. Being here means a lot to me, and I promise to do my part."

He acknowledges my statement with a nod and a warm smile. I seem to be making a lot of promises lately, but I intend to keep them all.

Exiting the office, I sidle up to Kali, whispering, "Tell me more about this food."

CHAPTER SIX

As we exit the SNHQ head building, Kali gestures towards a large building, advising of the canteen and the wonderful food on offer. As we make our way there, my mind is singularly focused on food, all other noise from this morning drowned out by my hunger. It's not quite lunchtime, but as I haven't eaten anything other than a few bites of toast, my stomach and animal are making their displeasure clear.

Having lived with my father, I've grown accustomed to eating less than most shifters. Judging from Kali's enthusiasm about the food here, that might soon change. Walking through the beautiful courtyard, Kali animatedly talks about all the food she's experienced since being here and my mouth waters at the possibilities.

When we arrive at the canteen, I'm relieved to see it's nearly empty when we walk in. After the day's events, the last thing I want is to be the centre of any attention. Kali and Anubis find an unoccupied table, and I'm momentarily puzzled when Kali settles into a chair. Given her earlier excitement about the food, I'd expected her to be at the front of any queue.

"I know what you're thinking. Apparently, it's a shifter thing to get their mate food. I'm not complaining, as he always brings me the best stuff," she explains, looking adoringly at Anubis.

Ah of course, a shifter custom I have witnessed many times. "It's true. I've seen it in my former pack. The males would be insulted if the females attempted to serve themselves."

Kali gives an eye-roll at this, while Anubis appears uneasy. "Would you like me to grab something for you too, Althea?"

"It's kind of you to offer, Anubis, but I'd rather join you," I reply, noting how his shoulders relax at my response. I've heard a shifter mate is inherently aware of their partner's preferences. So, his gesture to fetch my food, while thoughtful, would be a challenging task considering we've only just met.

Following Anubis to the buffet spread, my eyes widen in amazement at the sight of burgers, pasta, pastries, salads, and more. The variety seems endless, and my stomach twists painfully, the need for food intense.

"Is there a limit on what I can have?" I whisper to Anubis.

He laughs loudly, "No, Althea, have as much as you like."

Without further preamble, I excitedly grab two plates, one for wholesome choices and another for indulgent treats. Anubis laughs lightly at my eagerness as I stack my plates. "I appreciate things didn't pan out as you expected, but I hope we can still be friends?"

As I reach for a burger, I halt and meet his gaze. "Absolutely, I'd like that. I'm happy you found your true mate. It's a blessing. And honestly, we both knew there was no romantic spark between us," I say, motioning between the two of us.

He nods in agreement as he fills plates for both Kali and himself. "From one shifter to another, if you ever need assistance or support, don't hesitate to ask."

"I'll remember that, Anubis, thank you." A sudden urge strikes me, an unexpected thought I'm compelled to voice. "I might have only known Kali an hour, but I have to say, if you hurt her, I'm going to make you suffer."

He smiles broadly, "There's no need for concern on that front. Kali means everything to me." He pauses his filling of the plates, something occurring to him. "It seems this bond is influencing your protective instincts. It makes me happy, knowing she has someone else who genuinely cares about her like I do."

I nod absentmindedly as I ponder his words. Could it be instinct that prompted me to voice such protective thoughts? It's unusual for me to be so brazen, and despite only having met Kali, I felt an uncontrollable urge to warn him. I'll need to explore this, but for now, the tantalising array of food distracts me. Heaping our plates with generous amounts, we head back to Kali, who's practically vibrating in her seat, her eyes eagerly tracking our laden plates.

The moment Anubis sets her plate down, Kali almost skewers his fingers in her eagerness, and I chuckle at her ravenous appetite. Savouring her first bite, she pauses briefly to plant a kiss on Anubis's cheek, then dives back into her meal. With a suppressed giggle, I begin on my own food.

The initial taste of my burger has me groaning in delight. It is undoubtedly the most delicious thing I've ever had.

"Didn't I tell you it was amazing?" Kali says, her hand over her mouth as she continues to eat. I'm enjoying my burger far too much to respond verbally, instead nodding enthusiastically and rolling my eyes. We all eat in contented silence for the next few moments, revelling in the simple pleasure of satisfying our hunger.

When I finish my first plate, I suddenly remember something Kali mentioned earlier. "Can you tell me more about your dream? Did you also have your first one last night?"

Kali's eyes grow large, and she carefully places her fork down, swallowing her food. "Oh my days, it slipped my mind," she admits, dragging a hand down her face. "The whole reason we were at Damiean's office was to discuss my dream and see what he would make of it. Last night was the first time your face came into sharp focus. That's why I was so taken aback. Until then, all the women in the dreams had blurred faces."

"That's the same for me, but last night was the first time dreaming of you and that strange place."

"I've had them a few times now, in each one, wooden posts, whispering voices, the images of six women, yourself included, and then the images start to get weird. Blood and death, that sort of thing. This last dream was different."

She hesitates, her expression distant and an edge of fear pulsing along our bond. Anubis clasps her hand firmly, silently providing his support. She meets my gaze and offers a sad smile. "Someone was attacking me in this last one. I didn't see their face, but they were trying to kill me. It all felt so real and took place here in the forest of SNHQ. It freaked the shit out of me. I woke up screaming, and Anubis suggested speaking with Damiean about it."

"I'm sorry, Kali, that sounds terrible."

She nods, shaking away her sombre expression. "What did you see in yours?"

"Six wooden posts with an altar in the middle. When I leaned my head against the post, the images started." I forego mentioning my animal, as it seems irrelevant to the whole dream and could just be wishful thinking on my part. "All the images were blurred until they became sinister."

"Be warned, in my dream, the altar also causes the images to start. Learned my lesson with that one. Have you heard the voice?"

"Yes, but it was more like chanting. Find the six repeatedly until something shoved me, and I woke up."

"I'm really not happy that it sounds like you are part of this six Feisty," Anubis grumbles, listening intently to our conversation.

"You and me both, Wolf Man," Kali nods in agreement. "What are the odds of us having the same dream? Both have restricted access to our magic and are now connected by this bond. It's all got to mean something, right?"

"I would think so, and I'm guessing it's nothing good."

"And that is exactly what worries me," Anubis frowns. "Before you arrived, Althea, I could have put it down to any number of things, but now it's sounding more ominous by the second. We need to fill Damiean in on the details."

"Right. I should also tell Oberon," Kali says, turning her attention to me. "Oberon is the brains behind our rag-tag group. You'll likely meet him and the rest of the guys later. I'm sure they'll take an instant liking to you."

Hearing about their group, anxiety courses through me. The realisation I'd need to meet not only the pack but also the other residents of SNHQ slipped my mind. I'm not ready to deal with that type of pressure yet. Anubis seems empathetic to my situation, but I wonder if it's because his mate shares a similar problem to me. The non-judgmental time spent with them has been refreshing, and I'm not looking forward to that changing.

"She's freaking out," Kali whispers to Anubis. "Why are you freaking out?"

The bond we share is truly special, but I predict moments of frustration in my future with Kali's ability to sense every intense emotion or reaction I have.

"I struggle in group settings," I admit ashamedly. "I know I was part of a pack, but I was often isolated, pushed to the sidelines in shame. I'm anxious about being scrutinised by others and facing their judgments."

Water suddenly trickles from Kali's fingers, and Anubis emits a low growl, "Althea, trust me when I say that will not happen, and you're safe here. Oberon might be a tad direct in his quest for knowledge, but rest assured, you won't face any judgment. What's happening to you and Kali isn't something you can control. It's something that's been done to you. We'll do everything in our power to set things right."

I am relieved he would view the situation that way. I never considered the possibility of this being done to me, someone being responsible for the broken connection with my animal. "Could you explain more about these restrictions and their impact?"

"Honestly, we don't know much," Kali sighs, clearly bothered by the lack of information. "As we currently understand it, the 'restrictions,' as we call them, is a powerful spell. Designed to prevent us from fully accessing or controlling our magic. In my case, that means when I experience strong emotions, my elements react. Since mating with Anubis, it has weakened the restrictions somewhat, which is why I now leak everywhere. The elements can escape the cage easier, so to speak, but the core of my magic is still locked down, limiting my control."

"And the same could be said for me?" I ask hopefully. "I could have some type of magical cage trapping my animal?"

"I wish I knew," she shrugs. "Based on my experiences and what you've been through, it seems likely it could be the same thing."

I nod, thinking of my own situation and how I've been forced to live my life. "What confuses me is the motive. Why would anyone take such measures to restrict us like this?"

"Well, that's the bloody million-pound question, isn't it. What is so unique or threatening about us that someone felt compelled to devise such a powerful spell to control us? We need to uncover that mystery, and I suspect the answers might lie in these strange dreams."

We speculate for some time as we finish our meals. We've both lived such different lives that it's hard to find a common factor that could link us together in a way that would explain all this. With a belly full of food and all the revelations from today, exhaustion pulls at me. Whether from the early start, hearty meal or the weight of the day's information, I can't suppress the yawn from escaping.

Seeing this, Kali smiles softly, suggesting I get some rest and show me where I'll be staying.

"Girl, just wait until you see it. I was so excited I almost pissed myself," she snorts as we leave the canteen and head over to the Oak building. As we walk, I share snippets about Applecross and my life there, glossing over how miserable I was and that I mainly stayed confined to the house.

Arriving at the Oak building, I'm surprised by its contemporary design, especially compared to its exterior. Given the buildings' wooden construction, I envisioned a more rustic interior, not the sleek luxury I'm currently seeing. The entrance has an open yet cosy vibe, with a relaxed lounge area offering a clear view of the courtyard. We ascend to the third floor via an elevator, and when I show Kali my key, her face lights up.

"Looks like we're neighbours! Anubis and I are right over there," she says happily, pointing to the door across from mine.

"Do you mind if I come in with you? You can say no, but I kind of want to see your reaction."

Her eagerness is infectious, and it feels right to share this moment.

"I'll leave you two to explore," Anubis chimes in. "Remember, Althea, if you need anything, we're just across the hall."

"Thanks, Anubis. And please, you can both call me Thea." He acknowledges with a nod, after which he swiftly kisses Kali and heads to his apartment. Kali's face takes on a dreamy expression as she watches him leave. Grinning at her, I tease, "Let's get this tour started so you can hurry back to him."

"Is it that obvious?"

"Yep," I reply, putting the key in the door.

When the door opens, I'm left in sheer awe. My initial thought is how expansive the place is for one person. The combination of the living room and kitchen is nothing short of amazing, and the endless stretch of trees visible from the window elevates the view to breathtaking.

The pristine cream walls are adorned with green accents, lending a vibrant touch of colour to the space. State-of-the-art appliances dot the area, and a large TV is prominently displayed on the wall. I venture deeper into the room, spinning around to absorb every detail. The entire apartment projects a modern aesthetic and is a far cry from where I've come from.

Kali stands by the kitchen, observing me with a broad grin. "Incredible, isn't it?"

"Just to clarify," I begin, still in disbelief. "This entire space is mine. I don't have to share it with anyone?"

"Yep, every inch," she affirms. "It's all yours."

I set my bags down, continually discovering new details, pictures and flowers, and even dishcloths have been provided. It's all so... astonishing.

"Judging by that look, you're as stunned as I was when I first saw my place," she remarks. "I think you'll grow to love it here, Thea."

Her eyes drop to the floor, revealing a hint of unease. "You might not know me well, and I've never truly had any close friends, so I'm not sure I'll be any good at it, but if you need a friend..." she gestures vaguely, appearing surprisingly fragile. My heart twinges in sympathy. How could someone as delightful as her not have friends?

"I'd be honoured to be your friend, Kali," I tell her sincerely. "I only have one close friend and I never got to spend much time with her. Having one I could spend time with freely would mean a lot to me."

Her face lights up with a heartfelt smile. Drawn by an impulse, I embrace her briefly. Whether it's the bond we share or the recognition of mutual struggles, I sense a deep connection blooming between us.

"I'll let you get settled in your new place. If you need anything, use the iPad over there. And trust me, it covers pretty much everything. Just unlock it and browse the catalogue. You'll get the idea. Remember, we're across the hall if you need anything," she says, heading towards the door, with me trailing behind.

Pausing, she spins around, a thought striking her. "We'll be in the canteen at around six. Feel free to join us for dinner."

"Thank you. And I truly appreciate your support today, especially with my father. It was nice to have another person in my corner for a change."

"Always here for you. Catch you later." With that, she exits, and I secure the door after her.

Despite all my preconceived notions about coming here, nothing could have prepared me for the surprise that is Kali. I'm not being forced to mate with anyone. I have an apartment solely for me, with no mate to share it with, and I beat my father in an alpha challenge. And yet all those things pale compared to the friend, or rather family, I've gained. Even gone, if I concentrate hard enough, I sense her happiness, her excitement. Obviously, some mysterious force ties us together, but I find myself dismissing it, grateful I'm not on this journey alone.

Moving over to the plush green couch, my legs give out, and I sink into the soft material, internalising everything that's happened over the last few hours. I woke up this morning to my father's demands, and now here I sit, a free woman. Able to make my own decisions and decide how I want my life to be from now on. So why is the overriding emotion fear?

Is it because I have no clue who I am, how I should behave and what I want from life. Sure, I've fantasised over the years, but now the opportunity presents itself, I'm lost.

Who am I if not the pack's defect? What do I do with myself all day if not waiting on commands? As much as I've prayed for this moment, now it's here, its daunting. I may have a reason for the problems with my animal, but there's still no resolution in sight. How do I contribute to the pack if I can't access my animal?

In response to the worries clouding my mind, my animal sends a surge of comfort, her presence brushing against my mind. It calms some of my racing thoughts, allowing me to fill my lungs and exhale loudly.

"Are you the reason I was able to challenge my father today?" I ask aloud, still looking for answers on how it was even possible.

I get nothing from my animal, which I expect, but it's one more thing I have no answer for.

Driving myself insane with worry will get me nowhere, and as I don't have any more information to add to the mysteries surrounding me, I get up to explore the rest of the apartment.

The bedroom and bathroom match the elegance of the other rooms, and when I catch sight of the shower, my limbs automatically burst into a happy dance. At last, I can shower without the fear of being interrupted or pulled out halfway through a shave.

Picking up my bags from the living room, I move everything to the bedroom and start unpacking. Having little in the way of possessions means the task only takes me a few minutes, after which I decide to indulge in an extra-long shower. To my delight, feminine shampoo and conditioner are available, both of which I use liberally, savouring the scent of strawberries. When I finally step out, my fingers have pruned, but I'm surrounded by a delightful aroma, and my hair has never felt better.

The extended shower didn't revive me as I'd hoped. Glancing at the large bed, the allure is too much—I need some shut-eye. After the emotional whirlwind and the early start to the day, a brief nap is beckoning. Sliding into the bed, I release a sigh of sheer contentment. It's unbelievably comfortable, and I might have to stay here a little longer than planned. Nestling in, I quickly drift off to sleep.

CHAPTER SEVEN

I FIND MYSELF SPRINTING again. The sensation of four legs pushing me forward and the touch of grass on my paws is unmistakable. Still, I see no further details of what I am.

The agony of being in a dream as a shifter but unable to perceive any specifics feels almost wicked. Why would my subconscious torment me this way!

Despite my frustration, I recognise the peculiar dreamscape, the wooden posts visible in the distance. Given my previous dream and conversation with Kali, I'm wary as I make my way towards the structure, my hackles raising against the strange nature of this place. Knowing touching one of the posts or the altar will set off the run of images, I slow my pace as I get closer, not all that eager for a repeat of last time.

I believe Kali was correct in that this dream may be the only thing to provide the answers we're looking for. It's also what worries me most. Neither of us has been lucky in this life so far. With the menacing warnings for the six and the images we've been shown, I fear our run of bad luck is set to continue.

A few feet away from the posts, my form morphs, transitioning back to my human self. I almost backtrack, wanting to remain in my shifter form a little longer. The urge for answers must surpass that desire for now. I'm not seeking them for just myself anymore. Whatever information is revealed could also impact Kali. Approaching the posts, I examine them more closely than before. They seem ordinary—merely tall, dark-brown pillars rooted in the earth.

I acknowledge the need to touch them, but I'm hesitating. I can handle the images of the women, it's the following ones I dread. My attention shifts to the altar at the centre, thinking it's worth an exploration—after all, I'm not sure when I might return to this place.

Navigating between two of the posts, I head towards the altar. Etched into the stone is an unusual mark. A hexagon with a pentagram inside is segmented into six parts, each section holding a different and unique symbol. I've never seen it before, yet I can't deny the strong pull towards it. The symbol that catches my eye the most features a circle at the top, leading down to a swirl, flanked by arrows on both sides. It's new to me, but there's a hint of familiarity to it, a sense of recognition in the corners of my mind.

Kali warned me what would happen if I touched the altar, but my fingers itch to trace the design, to feel the circle's grooves and follow the swirl pattern. In an almost trance-like state, my fingers connect with the symbol, and the images begin.

Again, the first image is of me looking happy, only this time, before it moves on to the next one, my smile fades. My eyes widen in fear before my mouth opens on a scream. The following image shows Kali, tears running down her face as her mouth morphs from smiling to screaming, back to smiling again. The disturbing sight sends a shiver of fear down my spine, and I'm relieved when the next woman appears. The rest of the women fly by too fast for me to see any details about them other than their hair colour.

When the blood and death images start, I want to close my eyes against the grisly specifics. Instead, I force myself to watch, scanning every detail to see if there are any hidden clues. It's hard to detect if there is any due to the amount of blood that seems to flow from one to the next.

Studying one particularly disturbing image of a field of bodies, all torn apart in the most savage way, a whisper on the wind catches my attention. "Six to connect, six will determine the fate of all."

An evil and menacing smile flashes in my mind before something grips me around my throat. I'm forced to remove my hand from the altar and take a step back, my windpipe being crushed under the weight of a force I can't see.

Panic sets in, and I scratch at my throat frantically, but there's nothing there. I manage to turn my head enough to look behind me. Again, I see nothing. As black dots dance on the edge of my vision, the voice reverberates, "Find the six. Six will save all."

I jolt awake, gasping for air as if trying to fill every corner of my lungs. Instinctively, I touch my neck, confirming there's no harm done. While there's no pain, it's as if the phantom force is still there, clutching at me. I lie still for a moment, waiting for my breaths to find their rhythm, clutching the sheets to steady my trembling hands.

I won't pretend otherwise. That was downright terrifying.

Lying here, I realise my claws have extended, tearing through the sheets. I sit up to inspect the damage when something else grabs my attention. I feel my face and discover whiskers—two on each side. Another sign of my growing connection to my animal? Touching them, I find they're quite receptive, reacting to the slightest contact.

I'm not sensing much in the way of emotions from my animal other than her initial excitement at meeting Kali. The connection doesn't appear to be any stronger. Which begs the question, are we getting closer, or is this new development a response to the dream?

Setting that aside, for now, I refocus my attention back on the dream. All the odd references to the number six, those symbols, and the images, but the pressing question is, why was someone trying to kill me? Who could it be? Given that the whispering person was trying to take my life, I don't think I will find the six. They can do their own damn dirty work. Lunatics.

Once my heart settles from its frantic pace, I glance at the nightstand and register the time: 6:55am. What in the shifter gods—I've been out for over fifteen hours! What on earth is going on with me? I typically struggle to get a full eight hours of sleep.

Perhaps I was more drained than I realised, or maybe the bed has some magical hold on me. Either way, after that frankly horrifying dream, I'm eager to get up. Stretching out of bed, I head straight for the bathroom. Catching my reflection, I release a bark of laughter when seeing my wild hair. It seems to be defying gravity, making me resemble a hybrid of Edward Scissorhands and a lion, my shifted ears invisible under the mountain of hair.

The soothing effects of a shower allow my partial shift to reverse, meaning I can clean without stabbing myself. I've not had much opportunity to practise using my claws. By the time my emotions have settled enough to think clearly, they've usually disappeared. Perhaps I could practise getting angry, see if I can control a partial shift and use the results in a more active way. My musings continue as I head to the wardrobe and select my clothes for the day, a miserable task considering my lack of options. In the end, I opt for the same pair of jeans I wore yesterday, a black vest top and a blue sweater with only two holes in the sleeve. I desperately need to sort out my clothing situation.

Moving on to my hair, I decide to let its natural beauty shine today. With the unruly tresses now under control thanks to a thorough conditioning, I leave it to air dry, taking a moment to appreciate its newfound silkiness. A loud growl erupts from my stomach as I check out my reflection. After such a long nap, it demands attention. I make a beeline for the kitchen, hoping to whip up a quick meal. A glance around the fridge's contents reveals only the essentials, not nearly enough for the substantial meal I had in mind.

Standing in the kitchen, the cold surface of the refrigerator becomes the resting place for my fingers, which idly drum a rhythm. Mentally, I sort through my options. Given the fantastic food I enjoyed at the canteen yesterday, it seems the most logical place for a meal. Yet the thought of walking there solo wracks me with anxiety. I remember how to get there, but I'd rather not do it alone until I get a sense of the locals. Perhaps I could knock on Kali's door and see if she's up? Then again, if she's not, I don't want to disturb her.

Why am I being so indecisive? I won't know how good or bad this place is until I give it a chance. I can't spend every waking moment anticipating my father's shadow at every turn or waiting for the degrading comments. Even if people choose to glance my way or murmur behind hushed tones, that behaviour isn't new to me. My skin is thicker than that.

My racing thoughts are jolted, and I nearly jump out of my skin when a knock sounds against the door. Reacting to my sudden surge of emotions, my claws emerge, puncturing the fridge door with four deep gashes. Shifter gods, if I carry on this way, I'll be facing a hefty repair bill.

Stepping forward tentatively, I realise halfway to the door that there is likely only one person it can be and considering the bond feels stronger now, the person on the other side of the door must be Kali.

The moment I open the door, she dives right in, "Who do I need to kill?"

Taken aback, I reply, "I'm sorry?"

"You've got all kinds of negative energy coming from you, and you're partially shifted. So again, who's upset you, and who do I need to kill."

Trying to read her expression, I note the seriousness in her eyes as they dart around my apartment. The combination of her words and demeanour strikes me as comical, and a squark of laughter bursts from me.

"That's more like it. Loving the new whiskers, by the way," she comments, pointing to my face. "I'm serious. If someone has upset you, point me in their direction. With both of our emotions running through me, I'll just go leak all over them."

I shake my head in amusement. This woman is delightfully mad in all the best ways.

Seeing her genuine concern, I'm quick to reassure her, "I'm fine. It's more of an internal crisis."

"Oh. I'm good at those. My first two weeks here were filled with them. Do you want to talk it out?"

We gravitate towards the couch. As I settle in, she sits beside me, her expression and the bond between us radiating curiosity. I hesitate momentarily before saying softly, "It's nothing, really."

Seeing her arched brow, I remember it's pointless to withhold anything from her.

"It all started with another one of those dreams, which I'll get to in a minute, but what set me off was breakfast. I woke up hungry, found almost nothing in the fridge, and realised I'd need to go to the canteen. That's when the crisis started."

"Because you don't like the canteen?" Kali frowns. "Because you're mad when you're hungry?"

"No, nothing like that. It was the idea of walking to the canteen alone," I confess, my head shaking with frustration. "It sounds weak, but... I'm afraid. When I believed I was destined to mate with someone, I guess there was an underlying sense of protection. Regardless of his feelings towards me, he would've been obligated to stand by me, and I would've essentially belonged to the pack. With that no longer being the case, and with my newfound freedom, I'm lost."

Exhaling with exasperation, I continue, "I've been through enough critique and mockery for things beyond my control. The moment I step outside, and rumours about me spread, the cycle will start all over again. And this time, I'm in a strange place, with new people and new judgements. I've longed for this freedom for as long as I can remember, but now that it's within reach, I'm afraid to take it."

"Oh, Thea," Kali mutters sadly, "It sickens me what your father and that pack have done to you. But do you know something great about this place?"

"What?"

"You can start over, become whoever you want to be, and that might be scary at first, but you're not alone. If you don't mind a dud for a friend, I'll be with you every step of the way. I can't promise people won't talk about you because they do about me. I can promise that if you ever feel uncomfortable, we deal with it together. Finding out who you are will take time and if I've learnt anything from being afraid of my own shadow, it's the baby steps you take that matter the most."

"But what if I'm always going to be a shifter with no access to her animal. How do I fit into the pack like that because I didn't back home."

"Look, I can't say I understand all the inner workings of why a pack is important to shifters, but so what if you can't shift. I'm sure once you find out who the real Thea is, there'll be other ways for you to become an important member of this community."

I want to trust her words, but if the pack rejects me, facing a life shunned by my own kind is a frightening prospect. And what will happen if I succumb to the madness?

"You're still freaking out," Kali observes, pivoting to face me as she grasps my hands reassuringly. "Take a deep breath, Thea. At this moment, there are no expectations on your shoulders. Relish that freedom and let yourself live. Trust me, the reality won't be as bad as what's going on in your head."

She has a point, the only person putting pressure on me is myself. I should try to relax, take each day as it comes and see how this plays out. If the madness does become a problem, I can always ask Anubis for help and with Kali's backing, I'm sure he would.

"Okay, you're right," I exhale loudly. "Thank you. After twenty-one years of being told I'm worthless and a defect, I'm finding it hard to get out of that mindset and see this for the opportunity that it is."

"No problem, gal pal," Kali replies, then winces and smacks her forehead. "Let's pretend I didn't just say that. It sounded way cooler in my mind."

"Agreed," I giggle.

"Casually side-stepping around my weird awkwardness. Tell me about your dream."

I recount every aspect of what I saw, from Kali's unsettling display of happiness and pain to the sinister blood and death field I'd found myself in. Lastly, I mention the attack, or rather what felt like a near-death experience.

"Why are these dreams suddenly attacking us? Do you think whoever the voice is wants us dead?"

"I don't think so. Why tell us to find the six and then try to kill part of the six. If that's what we are, it doesn't make sense. Maybe whoever is trying to kill us is separate from the voice? What worries me is how far the dream would've gone had I not woken up. You can die in your dreams, right?"

"Jesus' fuck, we need a clue," Kali moans, rubbing at her head. "I wonder what triggered the dreams?"

"What do you mean?"

"Well, I've had three of them now, the last one being where I nearly died. And you've only just started having yours, so what's the trigger? Why now after twenty-one years?"

"Something tells me we'll only find that out once we find those other women in the images."

"That's what I'm afraid of. How do we find them when we can't see what they look like? Is it a coincidence you turned up here a month after I did, or is someone planning this? There are too many variables and too many mysteries. We need to mention these dreams to the guys and Damiean. I don't know enough about the supernatural world, and I don't think you do either. We need their help in figuring all this out."

"Okay, sure, if you think it will help."

"Great," she slaps her thighs, standing up. "I'm going to get my fine ass man of a mate, and then we'll all walk over to the canteen, yeah?"

"I think I'll meet you there. Take some of those baby steps."

"Baby steps," she smiles. "See you in about twenty?"

"Sure. And thank you again. Even without this bond, I'd be glad I met you. It boggles my mind why you didn't have friends before, but you're shaping up to be an amazing one for me."

"Aww fuck, thanks," she says, her cheeks reddening slightly. "I'm a hoot, right? Maybe it's all the swearing that puts people off. I should try and get a handle on that."

"Nope, don't you dare. I love your candour. I almost died of happiness when you called my father an asshole. If people don't like you for who you are, then they are not worth bothering with."

She gives me a sharp, scrutinising look, "Alright, I get it. I'll heed my own advice as well. Now, shoo. If you've only got twenty minutes, you'll have to make it a quicky."

"Oh, Thea, what could you possibly be insinuating. Hmmm, now I think about it. Catch you soon," she grins, skipping excitedly from my apartment over to hers.

I let out a soft laugh as I shut my apartment door behind me and head outside. With both Kali's wisdom and my own thoughts echoing in my mind, I stride towards the canteen, praying for confidence.

CHAPTER EIGHT

Exiting the Oak building, I'm greeted by the wonderful early morning atmosphere. The sun's rays bathe everything in light, complemented by a gentle breeze carrying the scent of oak and timber—a soothing reminder of my surroundings. At this early hour, the courtyard has yet to spring to life the way I witnessed yesterday.

Enjoying my stroll, I spot a man ahead, laboriously ascending the stairs with an oversized box blocking his view. I contemplate rushing to help him, but given my hesitation about mingling with the locals, I opt to continue my lazy walk.

As I follow him up the stairs, I discreetly observe him from behind. His toned build and blonde hair are the only features visible to me. Despite his obscured vision, his confident steps indicate he's familiar with the area. However, just a few steps shy of the top, he takes a spectacular tumble. He and the box part ways, its contents scattering in all directions.

"Oh Fuck!" he yells, remaining in his sprawled position at the top of the steps.

It takes me only a second to make up my mind before I jog up to him and offer some help.

"Um, hi, are you okay?" I ask, holding out my hand to help him up.

"Yeah, but please don't tell anyone you saw that." He clasps my extended hand and, with my assistance, regains his footing. Once he's standing, I get a clear view of his face, and... Wow.

The man is gorgeous, no, not gorgeous, stunning. Strong features with slightly shaggy blonde hair and bright ice-blue eyes. Without being overly dramatic, he looks like an angel.

"I'm Castiel," he says, a smirk pulling at his lips and his hand still in mine.

"Castiel," I murmur "I'm... I'm Thea," I utter nervously.

"Ah yes, the new shifter from Scotland. It's nice to meet you, Thea. Kali and Anubis said you were here, though neither mentioned how beautiful you are."

I find myself caught off guard by his compliment. Never have I encountered a man such as him, and to hear him call me beautiful causes my thoughts to momentarily scatter. His piercing blue eyes hold mine with an intensity that feels almost physical. The warmth of a blush spreads across my cheeks, and I get the distinct impression he notices.

"Do you need help with your box?" I offer, hoping to mask my nervousness.

His gaze shifts from me as if suddenly recalling his task, and he surveys the items from his box now strewn across the path.

"That would be great, thanks."

I step forward, helping to gather what appears to be a uniform—T-shirts and trousers, all in the same dark blue. Once everything is returned to the box, he stands holding it, seemingly lost in thought.

"Think you could walk with me, keep me from making a tit of myself?"

"Sure," I snicker. "Where are you going?"

"I need to get these uniforms over to The Pit."

"The Pit?"

"Yeah, it's what we call our training centre."

"Training centre? I didn't realise you had something like that here."

"We run a programme for training supernaturals, more than ever it seems now. It's how we keep things in order, both in here and out in the world."

"Okay, you're good to go," I tell him as we set off walking, watching the direction he's headed in.

The idea of a training centre causes excitement to rush through me. I did wonder if I would be allowed to continue with my own training. Now that I have no mate holding me back, I think getting into this training program could be good for me. Maybe that's where I'll find a place to fit in.

"So, how are you settling in?"

"Good."

"Do you want to tell your face that," he quips, his eyes alight with humour.

"Well, it is taking some getting used to," I tell him, lightly touching his arm and directing him around a dip in the path. "This place is much bigger than I'm used to, and I've slept for fifteen hours, so I've not had much chance to get to grips with things."

"Got ya. It's a good place, we look after our own, and all pull together. It's nice to be part of a community like that."

"Yeah, I can imagine." Watching from the sidelines of my old pack, I always wanted to be part of the community, to be more involved in the pack gatherings and not just the cleaner. If things work out here the way I hope, this could be my community, something I'm finding more appealing by the second.

We quickly arrive at the training centre, and as the gates swing open to reveal its expanse, my steps falter. For someone who has trained relentlessly, this venue feels sacred. The walls are adorned with more weapons than I can identify, complemented by training mats and, most impressively, authentic training dummies.

I'm so engrossed in every detail of the training centre that I don't realise Castiel has slipped away with the box. When he returns, he has an amused expression on his face. "I don't think I've ever seen someone as enthralled by this place as you. Do you train?"

"Only my whole life," I gush, too overcome with this place to care if I'm acting like a complete goon.

"Oh yeah? What are you training for?" Castiel asks causally.

A pang of regret hits me as I deliberate how to answer his question. I'm not exactly training for a specific reason, more so to be prepared. Something in my expression must give away my feelings, as he clearly picks up on it.

"Sorry, you looked like you went somewhere difficult."

He's perceptive, and I find I like that, "No, it's fine, I'm not training for anything. I should have been the next alpha of my pack, but... I'm not." I don't feel like telling him the whole story.

"Want to show me what you've got?" he asks, a playful challenge in his gaze.

A wave of eager anticipation courses through me, pulling at the corner of my lips. The rare occasions I've sparred with Angie come to mind, and the prospect of testing my skills against someone new thrills me. My animal responds keenly too, her excitement filtering through to me in anticipation of the potential challenge Castiel sets before us.

"Absolutely!"

I head to the benches, shedding my sweater and easing into a few preliminary stretches to warm up. I sense Castiel's lingering gaze on me, but when I turn to meet his eyes, he swiftly looks away. Being admired by a gorgeous guy isn't the worst way to start my day.

"So, what kind of training have you done?"

"I've dabbled in a bit of everything by watching videos on YouTube. I find I'm more comfortable with kickboxing, but I've done karate, jujitsu, judo and freestyle."

"I remember Kali saying something similar when she first got here. Not a problem, we can harness what you've got and work from there." Based on his comment, it sounds like he is underestimating me. I can't wait to prove him wrong.

He throws me a set of gloves, and after putting them on, I walk over to the training mats. Shaking out my shoulders, I move towards him to touch gloves, keeping the contact light. We circle around each other, and I watch how he moves, how he holds himself, keeping myself light on my feet as he watches me.

I throw a reaching jab, which he blocks and then another, which he pushes away. I continue to throw them so I can get a feel for how he blocks and moves. From his expression, I gather he thinks this is all too easy. His guard comes down slightly, and when I throw another, he bats it away easily.

"Come on, Thea, is that all you got? You've not even laid a glove on me."

Bringing my guard up, a secretive smile pulls at my lips. I raise my leg to make it seem like I'm about to swing a kick at him, and when he lowers his guard to protect himself, I see my opening. I deliver a swift jab, cross to his face and then hit him with an almighty lead hook to the temple. While he's dazed and disorientated, I grab him by his shoulder and waist and throw him over my hip.

He lands with a thud, and I stand above him, grinning.

"You okay down there, Castiel? You've not even laid a glove on me," I taunt.

His smile is tight as he jumps up and shakes off the impact of the throw. "Yep, totally fine, you got lucky. Well done," he says quickly.

"Lucky? Is that what you call it? Looks like I kicked your ass."

"Nah, I must have slipped. Not bad, now let's test your defensive skills."

He's a little too eager, and I get my guard up in time for him to throw a jab and cross. I block both easily and wait for the next set. He's predictable and throws the same punches.

"Come on, Castiel, are you even trying? I get better training than this when I fight against my homemade dummy."

He steps towards me and tries to hit me with a combination. When he throws a lead hook, my arm immediately comes up to protect my ears. His speed is impressive, and he moves quicker now to throw a lead uppercut, a rear uppercut and a cross. I dance away from each move, leaning left and right to avoid the delivery. Sensing he's not getting anywhere with his punches, he swings his leg out and attempts to hit me with a rear roundhouse.

I bring my knee up to block him, and when he leans back to swing a rear sidekick to my stomach, I block it by bringing my arm down hard and pushing his leg away.

Back in my stance, with my guard up, I grin behind my gloves. He's yet to get a hit on me, and I detect a hint of frustration from him.

"Good defensive work," he says a little breathlessly. "Now I see you know your stuff. Let's really go for it."

To be honest, it looked like he was. Me, I'm just getting warmed up.

I wait to see what he has in mind, and when he paces towards me and throws a lead hook, I dodge back as it swings past my face. His move forces me to take a step back, and at the same time, he steps forward with a rear hook. I anticipate the move, so my guard is already up, protecting the side of my face.

With his hand still up by my face, his arm is outstretched, and I quickly swing my arm under his to lock his forearm in place. With no way to guard himself now that I have his arm, I deliver a hammer fist to his chest. I try not to put too much power behind it, just enough to knock him off balance, and as he's recovering, I grab his neck and push his head down to meet my knee.

I stop a few centimetres away from making the impact and let go of him.

"Fuck! I give, I give. Please don't impale me on those things."

Confused, I release him, only to notice I've shifted again, my claws piercing through the boxing gloves. Mortified, I turn away, urgently searching for a way out of this situation.

Castiel collapses to the floor, breathing heavily. I'm sure he mumbles something that sounds an awful lot like savage bitch, causing a bark of laughter to burst out of me. He wanted to see what I could do, and I showed him.

"I didn't hurt you, did I?" I ask, my back still to him as I will the shift to go away. Damn it, things were going so well.

"Nah, I'm good," he wheezes. "You definitely have skills. We could use someone like you to help train the new recruits."

"Really?" I turn around surprised, heart pounding with excitement at the prospect until I catch another glimpse of myself. Like anyone would want me near a bunch of new recruits.

"Absolutely. I'm ashamed to say that we don't have any female trainers, so it would be good to get your perspective on things.

"But..." He can clearly see for himself that I'm not like other shifters. Why hasn't he mentioned it?

"But what?" He cocks his head to the side, confusion marring his features.

"Well," I gesture to my hands, not able to articulate what a mess I am. "I have a control issue."

"You mean your badass claws and cute ears?"

"Well, yes, but it's a little more complex than that. I'm a defective shifter."

His face darkens over the term defective, "I don't see a defective shifter," he asserts firmly. "I see a brave woman who has been subjected to something terrible. I don't know your full story, Thea, but

Kali shared you may have the same restrictions as her, which means whatever is going on now in no way makes you defective."

I'm shocked by his sincere and unwavering perspective. He might not be completely aware of my story, but his firm stand against the term "defective" is refreshing. This is not at all what I expected after half an hour of knowing him, and I find his support restores some of my confidence.

"Thank you. I appreciate you saying that. Are you sure I would be a good fit for that kind of position? My… limitations may cause issues."

"Are you kidding? Just teaching the recruits the basics of combat is half the challenge. With skills like you have, you won't even need access to your shifter side. Are you sure you're self-taught?"

I beam at his praise, "Yep. There wasn't much to do in my old pack, so I had a lot of time on my hands."

"Well, if Damiean hasn't assigned you a job yet and it's okay with you, I would like to recommend you join the training team."

"What! You're sure?"

"Absolutely. The number we have to train is going up every day, and the extra skills will take some pressure off the rest of us."

"Then I accept. Thank you." My smile feels impossibly wide. This job seems like a perfect fit for me. I have the skills to fight and feel I would do a good job teaching others. What more could I want?

"Don't thank me yet. These last lot of recruits are hard work. You might be cursing me in a few days," he grins as we start our warm-down stretches.

Once we finish, we return to the benches. I hand him the gloves, and as I slip my sweater back on, I catch him stealing another glance. Far from being bothered, I'm amused by his evident interest. I've never been in the spotlight of attention with a guy before. Being isolated from the pack, there wasn't much in the way of men my age and any that were wouldn't come near the defect.

I find myself standing uncertainly, at a loss for words around him. My stomach suddenly grumbles loudly, reminding me of my earlier hunger. Castiel raises his brows, "Guess we worked up an appetite. You want to get some breakfast?" His grin carries a hint of overconfidence, and though I shouldn't, I'm quite drawn to it.

"Sure, sounds good."

Leaving The Pit, his proposal that I train the recruits reverberates in my mind. My initial elation is slowly overshadowed by a growing apprehension. As enticing as the position sounds, doubts about my suitability for it creep in. How would recruits react to a shifter like me, one who's defective? If I'm tasked with guiding other shifters, would they respect and follow my lead? Given the role, I assume I'd hold some authority, but how could I effectively lead, feeling as fractured as I do?

The dream, fresh and barely minutes old, feels like it's already slipping through my fingers.

"So, what was your old home like?" Castiel asks, interrupting my wavering thoughts.

I share some details with him, skimming over specifics and focusing on the picturesque beauty of the land. I'm not sure what Kali and Anubis might have told him, but I prefer not to delve deep into my shifter complexities and my life before here.

I quickly begin asking him questions, turning his attention away from me. He tells me of his experiences at SNHQ and his responsibilities here. I discover he's a witch and has spent his entire life here alongside his mother. He never mentions his father, so I refrain from prying.

Talking with him feels effortless, and as we approach the canteen, a part of me wishes we could continue our easy conversation. The bustling noise of the canteen hits my ears even before Castiel courteously holds the door for me. Once the room unfolds before my eyes, I'm stunned.

As a supernatural, I've seen and heard plenty of stories about other races, but seeing them all gathered in one place is a sight to behold. Vampires, Fae, Elves, Pixies, they're all here. I even glimpse a Kitsune, which, until this moment, I wasn't even sure existed.

"Don't worry, you get used to it. I hardly even notice it anymore." Castiel tells me as he cocks his head over to the line waiting for food.

"Is there someone from every race living here?" I ask him quietly.

"Mostly, yeah. The only supernaturals we've never had, and for obvious reasons, are Mermaids."

"This is incredible," I comment, my mouth slightly agape as I rudely stare at the occupants of the canteen. Thankfully, no one seems to notice my gawking as we walk through the congregation of beings. The presence of so many is slightly overwhelming but fascinating.

The queue begins to shift, and despite my hunger, I opt for a single plate today, unlike yesterday's two. I stack it generously with bacon, sausage, pancakes, and bread. As I attempt to precariously place another sausage on top of the mound, Castiel's laughter causes me to jump, and I drop it.

"You can come back for more," he continues to chuckle, picking up the sausage from the ground and passing me another.

Instead of continuing my balancing act with the sausage, I pop it into my mouth. His eyes momentarily widen before settling into a confident smirk. Rolling my eyes yet smiling with my mouthful, I step aside to let him serve himself.

With our plates full, he directs us to the same table where I sat with Kali and Anubis the day before. A sizable, imposing man is already seated there, engrossed in his meal. I'm on the verge of proposing a different table due to the man's daunting presence when Castiel offers him a friendly greeting.

"Yo, Balbur, how's it going?"

"You're late this morning. Thought I was going to have to come and drag you out of bed," the big guy responds, his tone deep and rough.

"Nope, just had my ass handed to me by a pretty girl," Castiel says, winking at me as he sits down. A slight smirk pulls at the corner of my lips, and I try my best to ignore the heat rising in my cheeks. Castiel is very free with his compliments, and I see heated cheeks as a regular thing in my future.

The large man, Balbur, pauses, his fork suspended mid-air, looking intently at Castiel to see if he's serious. Castiel gestures towards me, prompting Balbur to direct his gaze my way. The first detail that strikes me is the depth of his eyes. I've never encountered such pitch-black irises, which appear eerie until I absorb his complete appearance. His raven-black hair contrasts against his pale skin, and I instantly recognise him as a vampire.

"Is it true what he says?" he asks me, his tone intense.

As he zeroes in on me, his formidable stature makes me hesitant to confirm the truth, fearing he might be offended. I shoot a brief, searching glance at Castiel, who reassures me with a subtle smile and a slight nod. Turning my attention back to Balbur, I nod in acknowledgement, not quite mustering the courage to verbalise it.

His laughter booms, causing me to startle and almost drop my plate. I stand still, a shocked expression on my face, watching this imposing figure dissolve into hearty chuckles. Once he regains his composure, he gestures to the chair beside him, inviting me to sit.

"Please sit down and tell me in vivid detail how you beat him."

CHAPTER NINE

As I settle into the seat beside Balbur, I recount my training session with Castiel. Between bites of his food, he questions me about specific techniques, and chuckles at the ease with which I managed to take Castiel down. I feel a tinge of guilt for possibly embarrassing Castiel, but when I glance his way and spot his good-natured smile, I sense he's taking it all in his stride.

"I wish I was there to see it. Will you show me again sometime?" Balbur asks, his delighted eagerness making his request hard to refuse.

"I don't think that will be necessary," Castiel quickly jumps in. "She can go up against you next time."

My eyes go wide at his suggestion. While I enjoy pushing my limits, tackling this towering figure would be an enormous task.

Balbur notices my apprehension and chuckles softly, his deep tenor resonating around the room. "Don't look so worried," he teases, his large eyes crinkling with amusement. "I promise I'd hold back a bit."

His words give me pause, and I consider his proposal. "Well, I've never sparred with a vampire before. It might be a useful experience."

He gently claps me on the back, his strength evident even in that small gesture. "That's the spirit," he says with an approving grin.

We delve deeper into our meal, and Balbur formally introduces himself. The three of us talk among ourselves and I learn Balbur is a key member of the training team. Given his imposing stature, this information hardly comes as a shock. He asks me a few questions but maintains a balance of genuine interest without being overly intrusive.

Both Castiel and Balbur share details about their roles in training new recruits and their daily routines. It's an extensive programme run by these two, along with Anubis, who is the leader, and Bran and Oberon, whom I've yet to meet. Their training focuses on recognising each supernatural being's strengths and weaknesses while promoting unity. They regularly update the program based on new threats and knowledge from the human and supernatural worlds.

It's evident as the conversation unfolds that the aim of the Supernatural Defence and Training Programme, or SDTP for short, is deeply anchored in magical integration. Hearing about the recruit's daily routine, I once again question my ability to be involved. While I can fight with the best of them, assisting the recruits in areas such as physical and magical fitness is an impossible task. How can I help shifters practice their transitioning speed when I can't shift myself.

The idea of joining them excites me, but given my situation, I doubt I'm suitable for the job, no matter how much I want it.

Pushing aside my sombre thoughts, I re-engage in the conversation with Castiel and Balbur, enjoying the ease I feel in their company. Their friendship is infectious, and I find it amusing when they complete each other's thoughts and share playful banter. They keep me engaged throughout, asking questions about my life without prying. By the time Kali and Anubis join us, I'm laughing heartily at Castiel as he describes a training session gone wrong between Kali and Balbur.

Anubis pauses briefly to say good morning but doesn't stop, heading straight for the food to make a plate up for himself and Kali. Before I can get a word out to Kali, Balbur jumps in like an excited kid with a secret.

"Thea kicked Castiel's ass this morning!"

Kali looks between us both, "I'm sorry, what? How? And I bloody missed it!"

Laughing, I start to tell her what happened, but then Anubis sits down with their food, and Kali turns to him, "Thea kicked Castiel's ass this morning."

Anubis's eyes widen, and he also looks between us both for confirmation.

"Okay, can we stop saying she kicked my ass? It was more like getting in a few good hits, and I was being a gentleman."

"Um... Yeah, that's not how it happened at all."

Retelling the actual version of events to Kali and Anubis, everyone laughs at Castiel's expense. I would feel bad for him, but he has that cocky smirk in place, which I'm guessing can't be good for me.

"She's training with Balbur next," Castiel tells them.

"Oh, girl, I'm so sorry. Any skill you thought you had goes out of the window when you train with Balbur. Plus, he likes to make you exercise a lot."

Hearing Balbur's snort of amusement, I can't help wondering what I've let myself in for. Is he as formidable as the others suggest, or is this an initiation of sorts? Given his size, I'd imagine him a difficult opponent, but it doesn't matter if I'm not up to par now. I'll simply work harder until I am. Even if I'm not suitable for the job Castiel has in mind, I'm hopeful I'll still be able to use the facilities.

"Where have Bran and Oberon got to this morning?" Castiel asks, looking pointedly at the two vacant chairs.

Anubis briefly glances at me before diverting his eyes, "Bran is helping my father with something, and Oberon is helping Damiean with the missing people case."

"How's that going?" Kali asks, her expression turning grave.

"Not good by all accounts. The number is now up to five hundred and forty-two, and the human government is in full panic mode."

"Erm, you have me a little lost here," I interject. "What's going on with the humans?"

Kali responds, her voice conveying her worry as she explains the situation. "You haven't heard? Around four weeks ago, people began disappearing, initially in the London area. Now, it's expanding to nearby areas. It's not just the odd person, either. They're being taken in large quantities."

"Well, then, someone must have seen something?"

"That's the thing, no one's seen anything. It's like they disappeared into thin air."

"Damiean and Oberon are no closer to finding a link between the people or the areas?" Balbur asks, his food forgotten as he directs his question to Anubis.

"No. They're looking into some rebel groups that have recently popped back up on our radar. It's unlikely they'd have the power to do something like this, but Damiean thinks it's worth exploring. They might not be responsible, but they could have information. There's also talk about us going down to London to see if we can assist. Damiean is placating the government by sending down as many teams as we can spare, but sooner or later, we will have to show our faces and answer their questions in person."

Kali casts an anxious glance at Anubis, who in turn offers her a reassuring hand squeeze. "It will probably be resolved soon," Anubis implies, though the lack of certainty in his tone suggests otherwise. Clearly, the situation weighs on him.

Before I get a chance to probe further, Damiean enters the canteen. Spotting us, he greets us with a nod and approaches our table.

"Good morning, everyone. Althea, I'm glad I found you. Are you happy for us to have our discussion here? It seems Oberon has taken over my office and is proving quite difficult to remove."

The group's collective laughter indicates this is a regular behaviour of his. Before I can answer Damiean's question, Castiel jumps in, "Damiean, have you settled on a role for Thea?"

"Not yet," Damiean responds. "I wanted to consult with Althea first."

Castiel directs a cheeky grin at me, "Well, you can skip the consultation. She'd be a fantastic fit for the training team."

Damiean, a bit taken aback, arches an eyebrow and turns his gaze to me, weighing Castiel's suggestion. After a moment, he asks, "Althea, is this a path you'd be keen on exploring?"

Bless Castiel for his input. I appreciate he's trying to help, but how do I tell Damiean that despite it being my dream job, I'm not the right fit. They need someone who is in control of their magic, not someone who could sprout ears from being easily startled.

"I—"

"Perhaps don't answer just yet, Althea. How about a trial period? If Castiel thinks you would be right for the job and if you're willing, I think it could be worth exploring."

"Honestly, Thea, if you can kick Castiel's ass, you'd make a great addition. It's a full-on sausage fest as it is now, and they could use a woman's energy," Kali adds, sharing a coy glance with Damiean.

Do they know what I'm thinking, or are they trying to ease my concerns about my situation? Their tremendous support is amazing, but it's in my nature to question where all this is coming from. I am deeply grateful for their generosity and appreciate their efforts, but I find myself asking why? What could they be gaining from helping me this way?

"Forgive the intrusion, Althea, but I can indeed hear your thoughts. I usually try to avoid doing so, but when someone is as concerned as you are, the thoughts can become quite loud," Damiean explains, a slightly contrite look on his face.

"Have you been able to hear them since I got here?"

"Generally, yes," he concedes. "But as I mentioned, I make an effort to block them out. I felt it necessary to address it now to alleviate your concerns. We take care of everyone here, but you and Kali are unique cases and deserve a chance at a good life. In fact, by joining the training team, you'd be helping me. We might gain insights into how the restrictions manifest differently for both of you, thus getting closer to realising how this all came about."

"And you're not just saying that to make me feel better?"

"Not at all. As I said, try it out for a short term. If the role doesn't suit you due to your situation, we can explore other options. And if you ever want to revisit this path, we can reconsider it later."

Presented that way, it's difficult to decline. Strangely, his ability to read my thoughts doesn't unsettle me much. In the end, it might save me the trouble of voicing my hesitations.

"Yes, I'll accept the trial period. Thank you. I'll try to keep my partial shifts to a minimum, though that may not be possible."

"Hell no," Castiel pipes up. "I thought it was awesome. Made you look super badass."

I smile at his earnest and enthusiastic response, "You might think so, but what about the others, the recruits. Plus, I've never trained anyone be—"

I'm cut off mid-sentence by a strange pulsing in my chest. I cock my head questionably to Kali, wondering what she's trying to communicate with me.

"What is it?" she asks. "You're feeling something, but I can't sense what it is."

"That's not coming from you?" My hand reaches for my chest as the pulsing becomes intense. "It's like when we first met, but..."

"Stronger?" She finishes.

"Yes. Much. Do you know what it is?" I ask, and the smile spreading across her face suggests she might.

"I have an inkling," she says, looking around the now nearly empty canteen.

When the doors suddenly open and two men walk in, my eyes are immediately drawn to them, the feeling in my chest magnifying by a thousand. My eyes scan over the very handsome, dark-skinned man, but he's not the one to hold my attention. It's the male next to him, that is. My animal's excitement hits me at the same time the world around me disappears, all except for the male walking this way.

Somewhere in the back of my mind, I register the similarities between him and his brother, yet to me, he is the most attractive man I have ever seen. His hair is dark brown and longer than his brothers, and he wears it in a tousled manner. He possesses those stunning grey stormy eyes, and the slight bump on his nose gives a distinct masculinity to his features. With sun-kissed skin and a cleanly shaven face, he lacks any trace of a beard—a look I find particularly appealing.

When he reaches the table, the other man with green eyes says something to make him laugh, and I'm utterly captivated by the sound and sight of his carefree nature. Kali says something to me quietly, but I don't hear, too enthralled by the male, the urges and the emotions my animal is shoving towards me. She has never shown interest in a male before, which can only mean one thing.

"Hey guys," Kali says, drawing my attention to her. "Thea, I'd like you to meet Oberon and Bran."

Two very different sets of eyes swing my way, my own meeting the grey ones of the male, who now looks at me with surprise.

"Oberon, Bran, this is—"

"My mate," Bran whispers in awe.

When he speaks those words, two things happen. First, it feels as if my entire world tilts, shifting on its axis and forever changing. The second is an unexpected partial shift. The shift is embarrassing, especially in front of someone who might be my destined mate, but it's the new change that truly startles me. There's a slight flare of pain in my coccyx before something pushes against my trousers. It suddenly feels like they are too tight for me, and as something twitches near my backside, I jump up in alarm.

"Thea, are you okay?" Kali asks, jumping up from the table now, too.

"Fine. I'm fine. I have to go." I rush out, turning and running from the table as fast as my feet will carry me, which surprisingly is very fast.

I'm out the door and at the bottom of the courtyard steps before I register the voice behind me calling my name. I slow down, allowing time for Kali to catch up with me. By the time she does, I notice the leaves falling from her hair as if she's shedding.

"What happened back there. You just met your true mate, right?"

"I... I can't talk about it here. Come back to my apartment with me?"

"Sure, let's go."

CHAPTER TEN

It takes considerable effort not to run so Kali can keep up with me. I feel truly out of control, and until I can get behind closed doors, I don't think I'll be able to settle. My animal bombards me with confusing emotions—one minute longing and the next anger. I've just run away from my true mate, and I have something growing from my ass.

My rational bandwidth is tapped out for today.

When we reach my apartment I quickly usher Kali inside, shutting and locking the door behind us.

"Come on, girl, spill it. What has you so freaked out? Is it because you partially shifted when you saw Bran? Because I have to say, the whiskers just make you look freaking adorable."

"Oh, shifter gods, I wish it was the whiskers," I moan, mortified but unable to keep it to myself any longer. "It's this," I say, turning around and pointing to my backside.

The few moments of silence are agony as I wait for her response.

"Um, well, Thea, you appear to have a fucking snake in your ass."

"I know," I groan loudly. "Of all the times for a new partial shift, it had to be when meeting my mate."

"I don't want to look at it or anything. That's a lie, I kind of do, but what is it?"

"It's my tail or rather my animals' tail."

"Oh shit."

"Exactly, Kali, exactly."

A few more moments of silence go by before Kali bursts into fits of laughter. I turn to scowl at her, not at all appreciating the fact that she finds this funny. Unfortunately, I can feel her amusement through our bond, so it's hard to ignore, and a smile pulls at my lips without conscious thought.

"Fucking hell, Thea," she screeches loudly. "You literally got a boner when you saw your mate."

She falls to her knees, her laughter consuming her to the point of gasping for air in between each bout. Each chuckle and breath releases a mist from her lips, which swiftly evaporates before the next appears. As she grabs onto the couch for support, the green fabric begins to crystallise into ice.

"Laugh it up, leaky," I grumble, still trying to hide my amusement. "Do not turn my new apartment into an igloo."

Following my gaze, Kali turns her attention to the now-frozen couch, which only triggers another bout of giggles and snorts from her. As I contemplate examining my tail to discern its origin or type, a sudden twinge at the base of my spine signals I'm too late.

In my amusement, I've calmed enough that the partial shift has receded, and I'm back to my proper freaked-out human form. I'm thrilled I seem to be connecting deeper to my animal, but I could have done without the tail at the exact moment I met my mate.

"Okay, okay, I'm composed. I'm good," Kali tells herself, pushing up from the floor.

"You sure? I just humiliated myself in front of my mate, but as long as you're good," I state dryly.

"Oh, please. You could have sprouted horns and he would still find you the sexiest woman alive. True mates, remember, it's like, ingrained into us or some shit."

Gods, do I hope she's right. Maybe I can pretend it never emerged. There was just some other emergency. I don't think he saw anything, and I could fabricate some reason why I ran out of there.

"Trust me, you're overthinking it," Kali assures me. "He wanted to come after you, but I could sense your distress. I told him to hang tight so I could talk to you."

"Really?"

"Absolutely. The guys had to all but hold him back. You're golden, don't worry."

"Okay. Thank you."

Her words ease my mind somewhat, and I relax a little more, heading over to the couch and sinking into the soft material.

"You finished leaking everywhere?" I ask with a raised brow.

"For now, but if your emotions start spiralling, I'm promising nothing."

I lean my head back against the couch, filling my lungs with air before expelling loudly, "What the hell is wrong with us, Kali? Do you think we'll always be this way?"

"Honestly, I have no clue about either question. I'd like to think we'll figure it out, but I've learnt not to get my hopes up."

"So we'll be a couple of defec—"

"Ah, we do not use that word anymore. I am banning it from your vocabulary."

"What would you call us then?"

"Awesome?" she grins. "Nah, I'd say we're glitches. We are exactly who we are meant to be. We just glitch out every now and then."

"Glitches? I like that, but I'd hardly say it's every now and then. I've only been here two days and shifted more in that time than I have in five years."

"That's a good thing, right?" she asks, getting more comfortable on the couch and facing me. "Means you're getting closer to your animal?"

As if in response to Kali's question, my animal stirs, sending a wave of happiness that causes me some concern.

"I think so, I just... I worry. I have no control over it. What will people's reactions be? What if I hurt someone? She would never hurt anyone intentionally but say I'm training a recruit, and my claws pop out like they did this morning. I could end up gouging someone's eyes out."

"Is that why you were hesitating over taking the training job?"

"Wouldn't you, given your leaking problem?"

"Maybe, but if we don't put ourselves in these situations, challenge ourselves, then what kind of life will we have?"

I see where she's coming from, but it doesn't help my situation. I want to help others, and I'd love to be a trainer, but am I being selfish at the cost of someone's safety?

"Look, when I first got here, I was a wreck. I'd just been attacked and blew up the café where I worked. When I finally found this place, I nearly got myself killed by stumbling across their shield. This whole world was completely new to me. Then I found out I might never be normal and discovered I had a true mate without fully understanding what that meant. I spent most of that time freaked out, in denial, or on the edge of losing my sanity. Throughout all that, do you know what pulled me back and kept me grounded?"

"What?"

"This place. The people here, the friends and family I've made. They helped me realise while I might not be considered normal, I can still have a normal life, so long as I don't shut myself off from it."

"But what about your leaking? Aren't you scared you might hurt someone?"

"I was, and I nearly have. My first attempt in class to create a tree did not go well," she huffs before smiling fondly at the memory. "It's only by practising that I'll learn more about how to use my powers. If one day the control comes, great. If not, then I'll get better at reacting on the spot. My point is, don't *not* do something because you're worried about how things might turn out. Go for it with everything you've got, and then worry about the glitches later."

"I'm not sure I'll make a good leader," I admit. "I've been trampled on most of my life by my father, and yesterday was the first time I've ever told him. I think I only did that because you were there. How am I supposed to lead a group of fighters if I couldn't even stand up to my father?"

"You'll learn, Thea. Nobody is expecting you to pick it up straight away. You need time to grow into the role and find out what works best for you. If it will help, you can practise with me. I'm still training with the guys, but we could do a few sessions a week, give you a chance to go all out without worrying.

"You wouldn't mind?"

"No, not at all. That's what friends do for each other. You're not alone, remember."

"Thank you, Kali, truly. You're an incredibly wonderful person, and I'm lucky to call you a friend."

"Incredibly wonderful, that's a first," she snorts. "I also answer to fucking awesome."

"As you should," I giggle.

Spending time with Kali and sharing my innermost thoughts has been therapeutic. Her non-judgmental nature and insightful feedback make conversations flow easily, and I feel completely at ease in her company. She reminds me of Angie, though Kali is much more straightforward. It's hard to believe this is only my second day here. I'm still coming to grips with the whirlwind of events and the sheer luck of how things have unfolded.

"So Bran is your true mate. How's your head processing that one?" Kali asks with a gleam in her eyes.

"I don't think it has yet. If I tell you something, do you promise not to laugh?"

"I will do my very best. That's as much as I can give you," she shrugs.

"Good enough. When I was little, I always dreamed of having a true mate, someone who would turn up to the pack lands, see how I was being treated and rain down hell on my behalf before whisking me away. That dream faded as I got older, and my father tried to sell me off to different packs. I became resigned to the fact I would never have a true mate or pick my own, for that matter. I came here knowing I could be trading one bad situation for another, and I did nothing to stop it. Finding my true mate here, I feel like that little girl again."

"Son of a bitch, Thea," Kali sniffles. "That's so goddamn cute. It couldn't happen to a better person."

Experiencing Kali's profound shift from sadness to joy through our connection and seeing a tear roll down her face, I instinctively reach out to comfort her. When I touch her hand, it's damp. Glancing down, I notice a change in my own hand. My claws aren't extended, but my skin has taken on a light beige hue, with hair emerging from my knuckles and fingers.

"Did you cause that, or did I?"

"I'm not sure," I say, inspecting my hand closer and taking note of every aspect of the fur.

"Do you have an idea what your animal could be?" Kali asks, looking over at my hand as she wipes her own on her jeans.

"My father is a lion, and my mother was a leopard, so I'd presume one of them."

"Hmm, going off the colour there, I'm guessing lion."

I agree, and there's a twinge of disappointment. I had hoped after all the years my father spent tormenting me, I would take after my mother.

"No matter what you are, you will be nothing like your father," Kali says, reading the situation for what it is.

"I've only ever seen a picture of my mother, and I look exactly like her. I guess I was hoping my animal would be the same."

"Even if she's not, you're still a complete badass. Anubis explained a little about what developed in the office yesterday when you stood up to your father. He said it's unheard of for a non-alpha to be able to challenge an alpha that way, and yet you did. That's got to mean something."

"Honestly, I still can't wrap my head around it. When he growled at you, something in me snapped. I've never disobeyed my father, was afraid to even look him in the eye but when my animal pushed to the surface, I embraced her. For the first time in my life, I think he could see that she was there and she was not backing down. I have no idea what it all means or how I did it, but it was the most liberating feeling."

"It also sounds like it was long overdue," Kali grumbles. "Now you've had that liberating moment, you need to embrace your shifter side. Don't shy away from your partial shifts. Encourage and enjoy them. It will be hard, but it will help you learn. Speaking from experience, it took me time to trust my elements, and I'm still not there completely, but every day gets easier. I look at my leaking as a good sign, a way to connect with my elements and grow stronger."

"But you still fear them?"

"Of course. It's only natural to fear something you can't control. I just try not to let it bother me as much these days. This place and the guys help with that. They act as if my leaking is completely normal, and that takes away some of the worry."

"They do seem like a great group. Castiel and Balbur made me feel very welcome this morning."

"What is it, Damiean said to me?" Kali thinks for a moment before her eyes light up. "Surround yourself with a good support group. That's what we are for you. Our very own glitches support group."

Chuckling at Kali's take on our situation, I realise she's right. After meeting some of the others today, having a support group could work in my favour and help me adjust quicker to this new life.

When the pulsing in my chest suddenly kicks up again, my hand immediately goes to the spot, rubbing the sensation and now recognising what it means. I have a true mate. All these years of dreaming and resigning myself to the inevitable forced mating, and now here I sit, a bond pulsing in my chest.

How my life has changed so much.

"Looks like the guys could only keep him contained for so long," Kali grins excitedly. "Are you ready to spend some time with your mate?"

I grin shyly, the thought a crazy notion, yet one I'm insanely excited for, "I guess we'll find out."

CHAPTER ELEVEN

KALI RISES FROM THE couch, and I stand, following her to the door. That intense sensation surges in my chest, compelling me towards the entrance even without Kali's urging. As she eagerly swings the door open, Anubis and Bran are revealed on the other side. Anubis swiftly grabs Kali by the waist, whisking her away from my apartment.

"Feisty, I believe these two need some time alone. Want to go home?" he growls softly against her ear.

"Hell yes," she breathes huskily before looking back at me. "Enjoy," she grins and waltzes off with Anubis, patting Bran on the arm before leaving the two of us alone.

Our eyes meet the second we're alone, and the bond pounds fiercely in my chest. My animal surges to the surface, practically begging to be near her mate. The overload of emotions and the intense gaze of my mate can only lead to one thing. A single blink is all it takes for the shift to emerge, the unfortunate tail reappearing and making me jump.

"Very cute," Bran mutters, eyeing my ears and whiskers.

Would he still think I was cute if he could see my tail?

"It's a pleasure to meet you, mate. Is everything okay?" he asks, leaning against the wall as I block the doorway.

"I..." my voice fails me, too many conflicting emotions overloading my senses, causing me to stumble over what I should say.

Appearing concerned, he stands straight, stepping towards me, "Thea, are you well? Do you need anything? Would you like me to go?"

"No!" I blurt, the word ripping from my lips at the thought of him leaving. "Would... would you like to come in?" I manage.

His answering smile devastates my already fractured brain, but I somehow control myself and move out of the doorway, keeping my back to the door. His presence in my new apartment makes my animal purr inside me, another first. Whilst I am thankful for any sign my animal is reaching out, does it all have to manifest for the first time in front of my new mate.

"Would you like a drink?" I ask, shutting the door and praying he says no.

"Sure," he smirks, a playfulness in his gaze.

I internally curse myself for even offering, knowing that means I will have to turn my back on him. Instead, I sidestep once, then twice, keeping him in my line of sight. He appears to find the whole thing amusing, but my embarrassment is mounting with every second.

"So, you're Anubis's brother, younger or older?" I ask as I reach the kitchen island and use it as a shield.

"Younger, is that a problem?" His tone makes me pause, the defensive note in his question confusing me.

"No," I say, reaching for two glasses and wishing for a less awkward introduction between us.

I only have juice in the fridge and as I pour us both a glass, he leans against the back of my couch.

"I should imagine this is all a bit of a disappointment for you. Going from the alpha to second best."

I stop with my hand midway to pouring the second glass, the bite in his tone making me spin on the spot and meet his gaze.

"Excuse me?"

His eyes narrow slightly, "I just mean, to find out the alpha is no longer available, you didn't want to meet his replacement, and now it turns out I'm your mate anyway. I had hoped we could have discussed getting to know each other before you made up your mind, but I see that may be a waste of time."

I frown, my confusion increasing the more he talks, "I'm sorry, I have no idea what you're talking about."

"It's fine, I should have expected this. I was hoping you would at least give me a chance, but clearly, that's not something that's going to happen."

"Okay, stop," I demand, raising my hand so that he stops speaking. "You have completely lost me here, but I'm not sure I like what you're insinuating."

"Oh, come on," he snorts. "First, you're not interested in meeting with me. Then, in the canteen, we meet and find out we're true mates, and you run off. Now you're behaving like you can't stand to be near me. I'm sorry I can't be the alpha you so clearly want."

How in all the heavens has he misread the situation so wrongly? Is this the impression I've given him?

"Bran, listen, I'm—"

"Forget it, Thea. Thank you for not wasting my time. Have a nice life," he says, storming towards the door.

So many things unfold at once. I knock over one of the glasses, fur materialises on my hands, and my animal surges forward, anger radiating through our bond, which in turn flames my own anger. The bond between me and Bran forces me from behind the kitchen island.

"Who the hell do you think you are," I snarl at his back before he can leave. "You don't know the first thing about me, yet you come into my apartment and judge me."

"It—"

"No, you're done talking," I snap at him. "I have been judged my whole life, and the one person I thought I would never receive that from was my true mate. You don't have the first clue about me, why I ran off earlier or any of the things I am going through now. It's so easy for you to stand there and throw blame at me for your own insecurities."

I can only assume this fire is coming from so many places. My animal, my bond with Kali, my bond with Bran. I'm not sure if the old Thea would have spoken to her mate this way, but the new Thea, she is done being people's door mat.

"After your assumptions, it's me that should be thanking you. I won't waste my time on a mate that doesn't deserve me."

"You're hot when you're mad," he says suddenly, confusing me again.

"I don't care. How dare you judge me and—"

"And make completely wrong assumptions? Given how you've behaved so far, what am I supposed to think?" he questions, striding across the room and closing the gap between us.

"How about you don't make any assumption at all and ask me rationally why I'm behaving like an idiot."

The corner of his lip twitches, distracting me from my tirade.

"Alright then. Why did you avoid our meeting yesterday, why did you take off earlier, and why are you constantly keeping space between us?"

I attempt to speak, trying to convey the emotions I've been grappling with.

"You know what, I don't care." He grips me around the waist, his lips crashing down onto mine.

My synapses go haywire, and my eyes widen in surprise. His soft lips knead against mine as his hand trails into my hair and angles my head slightly. Deepening the kiss, he groans low in the back of his throat. I melt into him as the bond between us pulses with a strength so fierce it takes my breath away.

When I gasp, Bran takes full advantage, his tongue sliding against mine in a sensual dance. He pulls me closer, his hands now firm against my back as he wrecks me from just one kiss. Utterly desperate for more of his touch, more of his lips, I groan in frustration when he pulls back, a smirk playing at the edge of those perfect lips.

"I don't want to be rude or misread the situation again, but is that a tail in your pants or are you just happy to see me?"

Mortification lasts a split second before laughter bubbles out of me, and I lean my head against his chest. I can feel his amusement through the rumbling of his chest, and after taking a minute to compose myself, I look up into his captivating grey eyes.

"I'm sorry," he says, pushing my hair to the side so he can use his thumb to push my chin higher. "I shouldn't have jumped to conclusions, and you're absolutely right that it had more to do with my own insecurities."

I search his eyes, surprised to see a vulnerability that resonates with me. Our insecurities can make us do stupid things, so I decide to give him the benefit of the doubt.

"Would you like that drink so we can sit and talk now?" Talking is the last thing I want to do when the bond and my animal are pushing for something more, but we need to clear the air before this goes any further.

"Let me get it so I can redeem myself slightly. You take a seat."

I follow his suggestion, letting him finish the drinks. As I try to settle on the couch, I jolt back up after landing on my tail. If this keeps happening, it's going to be an issue. Opting to stand, I lean against the dining table, observing Bran as he busies himself in the kitchen.

He's strikingly handsome, with a tall stature and a robust build, moving with the fluidity of a panther. The sunlight streaming in from the windows illuminates the coppery hues in his hair that had previously escaped my notice. As he pivots in my direction with the drinks, his tantalising lips curve into a playful grin, lending him a more youthful and carefree look.

Handing me the glass of juice, my body vibrates with the need to be near him, the bond begging for me to touch him, kiss him, make him mine.

"Do you want to sit?" he asks, his eyes directing me to the couch.

"I'll stand for now. I'm having some difficulties that I'm still trying to navigate."

"And would that be the reason you ran out of the canteen?"

"Yes, I... I don't even know where to start." I place my glass on the table and pace back and forth, the movement helping me concentrate on what I want to say.

"I'm not like other shifters, I'm a def... I have some control issues, glitches as Kali calls them. The tail is a new one for me. It materialised for the first time when I saw you. I was embarrassed, so I ran."

"Shit, I'm sorry, Thea. Kali has had a hard time with her restrictions, and as a shifter myself, I can't even begin to grasp what it must be like for you."

I nod along, but I'm sick of thinking and over-analysing my own problems. "What would make you think I wasn't happy to have you as a mate? I realise my behaviour hasn't been normal, but we haven't even spoken until today."

"Bruised ego?" he offers, his expression contrite. "It sounds pathetic admitting it out loud."

"Anymore pathetic than trying to hide your tail from your mate?"

"Fair point," he guffaws. "In all honesty, I wasn't happy when I found out I would be stepping in as Anubis's replacement. I wanted to pick my own mate, not have one arranged for me. The day you arrived, I came up with so many reasons it would never work, but when I found out you didn't even want to meet me, it stung."

"I love my brother, I do. It's just that being the only male in my family not to be an alpha, I've always felt like second best. When you refused the meeting, those feelings came back. Then, when you ran, I needed to know why, if it was so bad to be mated to someone who wasn't an alpha."

I'd guess it would be tough having an alpha for both a father and a brother. Add in my odd behaviour, and I can see his point of view.

"I'm sorry you felt that way, Bran, but it was never about you. It was about me needing control over my own life, wanting the freedom to make my own choices rather than being told what to do. When Damiean offered me a chance to stay without a mate, I eagerly took it. Had I known you were my true mate, my actions would've been different. I was simply searching for my freedom."

"And do you still want that freedom? To not be tied down to a mate?"

"A true mate is different," I murmur shyly. "I'm not being forced into anything. You're destined to be mine."

"And don't you ever forget it, baby," he says, his tone deep as a sinful smile plays at the edges of his lips.

The bond chooses that moment to surge again between us, along with a flurry of emotions from my animal, causing me to reach for my chest. Bran watches the movement, a touch of concern in his gaze, "Does it hurt you?"

"No. It's just taking some getting used to. Does yours feel intense, like it could pull you across the room?"

"It does. It's taking everything in me not to shift, and I hear it doesn't get any easier the more time we spend together."

"Your animal is driving you crazy, too? What is your other half?"

"A bear," he states proudly. "And right now, all he wants is to meet his mate."

A twinge of sorrow courses through me. Naturally, he'd want to meet his mate, but the reality is that it might remain an unfulfilled desire. My animal is just as eager. Will this longing always be there between us, something we'll learn to live with? The years I fantasised about a true mate, it never occurred to me how our animals might react. The bond with a true mate is anchored deep in our soul. They complete you. But what becomes of that bond if your soul is fragmented or damaged? How can Bran ever have happiness if his animal remains unsatisfied?

"Thea, are you okay?" Bran questions softly.

"For once, I would love to say yes and mean it," I mumble. My pacing begins again, something I've always done to help get my thoughts in order.

"How will this work, Bran? How can you be satisfied with me when our animals may never get to meet? I come with so much baggage and damage. I'm conflicted with every decision I try to make, a mess of emotions and half of the time, I don't know who they belong to."

Bran walks over to me, placing his hands on my arms to stop my pacing. "First of all, you're my mate, my true mate. No matter how our animals feel, I will always be satisfied with who the fates chose for me. We don't know each other yet, and that will come with time, but your baggage doesn't scare me. If anything, I like it. Someone as stunningly beautiful as you must have a flaw," he says, his eyes flashing mischievously.

The bond throbs powerfully within my chest, and his touch sends a pleasant shiver across my skin, yet I feel calm. His presence seems to settle some of the chaos inside me, and my lips twitch with amusement.

"You think I'm beautiful?"

He looks at me incredulously, as if I've said something highly offensive, before throwing his head back and murmuring. "Gods, how does my mate not see how beautiful she is?"

"Well, except for Castiel, I've never had a compliment before."

"What do you mean except for Castiel? What has he been saying to you?" he growls low, his expression swiftly changing to one of annoyance.

"Nothing," I'm quick to defend. "He just said that Kali and Anubis hadn't said I was beautiful. I'm sure he was just being kind."

"Hmm, we'll see about that."

"It doesn't matter either way. I only care what you think about me," I respond coyly.

My remark dispels his irritation, replacing it with a joyful expression. While I acknowledge Castiel's allure and undeniable good looks, now, gazing up at Bran, I recognise the pull I felt towards Castiel pales compared to the magnetism Bran exerts on me. His closeness intensifies the bond, sending waves of longing through my body, a connection so potent I can physically feel the pull.

"I'm glad to hear that, Thea," he says, stepping closer and invading my senses. Placing his finger under my chin, he tilts my head back, his eyes clashing with mine. "Do you want this bond?"

"I do," I reply with no hesitation. "But I would like us to get to know each other a little first if that's okay?"

"Of course. I would never rush you. I just needed to be sure this is something you want. If you're fine with it, I'd like to spend the day with you. Get to know my mate more intimately."

"Sounds perfect."

CHAPTER TWELVE

THE NEXT FEW HOURS are enlightening as we stay in my apartment, swapping tales about our lives. He delves into his past, recounting his childhood at SNHQ and his journey into the training programme. Bran has a way with words that's mesmerising. He's lively and comical, making it seem as if I was right there with him in those moments. Hearing about the mischief he and Anubis caused, I can't help but sympathise with his parents for the handful they must have been.

Entering the training programme appeared to stabilise them both. It's clear Bran was initially a challenge, but with Anubis's guidance, he's evolved into one of the top trainers. He might not admit it outright, but I can read between the lines of his modesty.

When he begins questioning me about my life, I feel it's only fair to bare it all, hoping he grasps the depth of my struggles and what I aim to overcome.

"The earliest years of my life are mostly a blur. What I do recall is my father wasn't around much. And when he was, there was this undercurrent of tension. I'm not sure if it was a deep intuition about his emotions or my animal sensing his hostility, but I always felt this need to steer clear of him," I explain, starting at the beginning to paint a true picture of my life to this point.

"When we relocated to a pack in Cumbria, my father brought in a nanny for me. I was only five then, and she quickly became a cherished figure in my life. More than just caring for me, she educated me. She taught me to read, write, and even cook. For a moment, it felt as if I had a mother. One day, when she fell ill and couldn't be with me, my world crumbled. Tears streamed down my face, and in my anguish, I stupidly expressed my concern to my father. I just wanted to make sure she was alright, but a part of me thinks I should have known he would use it against me. Admitting my attachment to Lydia was a mistake. When he realised our bond, she disappeared from my life, and I was alone again."

My eyes mist at the memory, the image of Lydia and her kind face coming to mind. Bran's hand brushes across mine, "It's okay if you'd rather not talk about this stuff. It's hard to hear, and I imagine it was even harder to live through."

"No, it's fine. I want to share it with you. All the good and the bad, perhaps then you can see where I am now and where I want to be in the future. If you're going to be my mate, I'll need your support."

"Forever and always," he responds, not missing a beat.

"Really? After only knowing me for a short amount of time," I snort, the start of this relationship surprising me at every turn.

"Hey, when you know, you know," he says, his eyes shining with sincerity. "So, what happened after your father got rid of Lydia?"

"Not long after, we moved again," I continue. "To be honest, I lost track of the packs and the location. I withdrew, barely speaking to anyone unless I had to. By the time we made it to Applecross, I was ten. I'd had four other nannies, but none looked after me like Lydia did. They never had the same warmth. I suspect that was because they knew something wasn't right with me, and it made them wary."

"As the alpha's daughter, I was always with him at gatherings or meetings when required, but as I got older and the other kids my age were shifting and playing, it became more noticeable to everyone that I wasn't doing the same. When the other adults started questioning it, my father dragged me home and commanded me to shift. Obviously, it didn't work, which enraged my father even more. We left that pack the next day and travelled until we settled in Applecross."

"I'm finding it hard to get my head around him treating you like that. How could he blame you for something you had no control over?" he growls angrily.

I shrug my shoulders, "I'll never know his reasons, only that losing his true mate affected him deeply and messed with his head."

He seems to consider this briefly before responding, "As hard as I'm sure that was, you were a baby, his daughter. He should have been able to see past his grief to be there for you."

"Perhaps, but who knows what it must be like to go through something like that. It could have changed him so fundamentally he could never be anything different. In my head, I've made excuses for him so many times and tried to justify his behaviour. In the end, it didn't matter. He would never speak about my mother or even mention her unless it was to tell me she would be disappointed in how I turned out."

A menacing growl rips from his throat, "Too far. He had no right to blame you and certainly no right to insinuate her feelings on the matter. I'm sorry, Thea, but I hope I never have to meet your father."

"Oh, don't worry about that. After the way things ended yesterday, it's very unlikely I will ever see him again."

"Please tell me you got some closure, some type of revenge."

"In a sense," I say, grinning, the thrill from yesterday's challenge still fresh in my mind. I share with Bran the events that unfolded when I turned sixteen, followed by the treatment I endured after. He looks as if he's on the verge of storming out to confront my father, but his demeanour changes once I mention the challenge.

"It was incredible, Bran," I tell him, becoming animated myself. "For years, I was shackled by my father's commands, following his every order without complaint. I never talked back and always presented a submissive front when around him because that's all I ever knew. He intimated me so much that I often went out of my way to avoid his path or make sure he had no grounds to criticise me. The day before I left to come here, he banned me from the pack gathering, declaring I was no longer pack."

Bran growls again, and I wave him off, "That's not the point. Right before he said it, he tried to use an alpha command to make me return to the house. My animal was perpetually restless or irate whenever I was around him, yet something changed that day. When he issued the command, it clashed with a surge from my animal, and to my surprise, it barely influenced me. I was taken aback sure, but it wasn't until the episode in Damiean's office I truly understood. With how things were going in my old pack, I may have been pushed too far and reached that point on my own, but the moment my father disrespected Kali, my animal and I had enough. I instinctively entered the challenge, not even pausing to consider it," I laugh with a shake of my head.

"Do you want to know the astounding part? There was no resistance, no urge to look away. Despite my father being a powerful alpha for years, there I was, standing up to him with the confidence of an old-timer. It was surreal."

"Then what happened?" Bran asks eagerly, hooked to every word spilling from my lips.

I describe it all in detail. How I felt, what I said, every emotion my animal was experiencing. By the end of my tale, Bran is smiling ear to ear, a proud gleam in his eyes. "I'm glad you had your moment, babe."

Our bond pulses hearing him call me babe. Such a simple word, and yet it holds so much meaning for me, a sign of acceptance.

"Do you mind if I ask about your animal?" he asks a moment later.

"Sure, though I'm not sure there's much I can tell you."

"Do you know what your animal is?"

"No. My father is a lion, and my mother was a leopard."

"And when you say you feel her, what do you mean? You talk as if your emotions are separate from each other."

"They are," I frown confused. "When I'm feeling down, she picks me up. She was always angry whenever my father was around, whereas I was more intimidated. We feel and react differently depending on the situation. Is that not the same for you and your bear?"

"Not exactly. We can react differently, but our feelings are the same. If I was down, my bear would be too. Where I might go a few rounds with Anubis to alleviate that feeling, my bear would want to go hunting. If we were angry, I would think logically about what I needed to do next. My bear would be ruled by instinct, looking to remove whatever has made us angry. It can result in a power struggle over who controls the situation, but ultimately, we both feel the same way; we just want to deal with it differently."

I pause to reflect on what he's saying, could this be another way I'm different to everybody else? Is this why I'm broken because my animal and I are separate? Angie and I have discussed our animals countless times in the past, but thinking back, I can't ever remember her referring to her tiger separately.

"Are you okay?" Bran asks after I've been silent for too long.

"Confused," I admit. "I've only ever had one friend and I guess I never picked up on how she spoke about her animal differently than me."

"I'm sure it's nothing. Could even be a by-product of the way this damn restriction spell works on shifters."

Given his connection with Kali, he's well-informed about my magical challenges and sympathetic to the issues with my animal. He's unwaveringly optimistic as we discuss more theories, convinced we will find a solution. As we continue to talk, what I enjoy most about spending time with him is his light-hearted manner. It goes a long way in helping me relax, and it's nice to be around someone who doesn't take things too seriously. When our conversation shifts to my potential future role here, I share my reservations about assuming a position as a trainer.

"I'm grateful for the opportunity. It's a dream job for me, just not sure how I'm supposed to navigate the role."

"What worries you the most about it?" he asks, lifting a piece of my hair and twirling it around his fingers.

"The leadership side of things. As well as teaching others when I don't have a handle on my magic."

"I'm sure we can make some accommodations. You can work on the physical side of things at first."

"What do you mean?"

"Our programme has changed slightly because we have so many new recruits. Normally, we would have physical and magical fitness to begin with, and then in the early afternoon, we'd focus on tactics, strategy, lore and weaponry. Later in the afternoon we would cover combat drills and specialised skills development. With things the way they are with the humans, more supernaturals are arriving by the minute. We now have to focus less on the collaborative and specialised working and more on the basic combat skills to get everyone battle ready should the need arise."

"Do you think that's going to be a possibility? The humans and supernaturals at war?"

"At this moment, no. Whatever is going on out there is big and is only getting worse. We need to be prepared for anything and everything. We'll do that by making sure everybody is prepared and combat-ready. I will not have anyone fighting that either doesn't want to be there or is not ready."

"I have to say, your light-hearted nature is calming and comforting for me, but seeing this commanding side of you, I find it very appealing," I comment, my cheeks blushing slightly at my honesty.

"Oh mate, you haven't seen anything yet," his tone deepens, and I feel the vibration of his words through my chest.

The bond pulsates, hammering at me as if to remind me of the goal with Bran and its eagerness for me to move things along. A part of me loves the idea, but I do need a little time.

"Sorry, you were saying something about me working on the more physical side of the training. What did you mean by that? I'm having a hard time staying focused, but the type of programme you've just described sounds very magically based."

"Tell me about it," he mumbles, trying to adjust himself without being obvious.

After shuffling in his seat, he clears his throat and continues, "As I said, we need to be battle-ready just in case, but we also need to send more teams across the country to help eliminate some of the risks. Most of the people turning up now have been isolated to their own clans, packs or covens. To send them on assignment, we need to ensure they can fight alongside other supernaturals who are not of the same species. I think that's where you could help.

"For you, it won't matter what species they are or what magic they have. We only need to focus on whether they can fight and work as a team. If you can teach them that, hone in on their skills and pull the best out of them, they'll be ready to go on assignment. And if it makes you more comfortable as you're getting to grips with things, you could take on a smaller group and work on their physical training, leaving the magical training to one of us."

"I guess that could work," I say, considering his proposal. "There's also the issue that I'm not very assertive. Will they even listen to me?"

"If they know what's good for them," he jokes. At least, I think it's a joke.

Taking hold of my hand and pulling me closer so I'm pressed against his side, his arm snakes around my shoulder. "What about if you shadow me for a period until you're secure with how things are run. I could show you the ropes, so to speak, and I'd be more than happy to stay back after work and go over everything in fine detail. In fact, I insist on it."

"But would we get much work done?" I flirt, already seeing where his mind is wandering.

"Doubt it, but it'll be fun."

I interlace our fingers together, wondering if this would be my most sensible option. I expected some sort of training, so maybe shadowing Bran wouldn't be such a bad idea. Plus, the idea of watching him work is very tempting.

When his fingers trace over mine and slowly make their way up my arm, I shiver, the sensation surprisingly erotic. All thoughts of work and training flee as my mind becomes focused on the pattern his fingers are trailing across my body. He's only touching my arm, yet I feel it everywhere, and my breathing turns laboured, my pulse and bond pounding in time with each other. When he reaches the collar of my shirt and traces the line across my neck, a sigh leaves my lips.

Working his hand across my collarbone, his fingers tangle in my hair as he firmly massages the back of my head, the slight pull on my roots making my head fall back.

He continues his sweet torture, alternating between massaging and pulling lightly at my hair. More breathy moans escape me, lost in a state of extreme arousal and relaxation. I feel a slight puff of air against my face before his firm lips are placed against my cheek. The softest kisses are dropped lightly all along my jawline, and I pant in time with his lips.

I need him with a desperation so intense that my legs clench, my body wound so tight and begging for more.

"Bran," I breathe huskily.

He nibbles on my lobe, goosebumps rising along my neck and shoulder, "What do you need, baby?" he asks, his tone low and his voice rough.

I don't know what the hell I need. For him to stop this torture? Continue? When the bond pulls maddingly at me, my animal joins in, pushing me forward with an enthusiasm rivalling my own. The sensation of losing control washes over me. I appreciate and crave Bran's advances, but the flood of emotions and stimuli makes it hard for me to fully surrender. In a fleeting instant, I recognise my need for a bit more time.

"Bran, I'm sorry," I mumble, sitting up straight but not moving away. "I'm—"

"Please, babe, you don't have to say anything. We've only known each other a few hours and I think the bond is trying to push the connection. How about we get out of here and get some food?"

"Thank you. That sounds great."

He pulls me up from the couch, planting a firm yet chaste kiss against my lips, "Don't worry, mate, I will have my way with you, but only when we're both ready."

Shifter gods, the deep tenor of his promise travels directly between my legs, and I'm tempted to take him up on the offer now. Before I can voice this, he's leading me out of the apartment and into the fresh, cool air, calming some of my rampant urges.

Let's hope I can make it through dinner without embarrassing myself.

CHAPTER THIRTEEN

"What the fuck. Why are the Throne brothers snatching up all the pretty girls," Castiel complains when Bran and I walk into the canteen hand in hand.

I'd had my reservations about his display of affection when he grabbed my hand on the way over here, and despite it sending the bond haywire, it settles the agitated emotions of my animal.

"Because we're hot and have true mates," Bran smiles proudly.

"Whatever," Castiel moans. "Good luck to you, Thea."

"Thanks. I think."

Bran doesn't comment further, turning to me with an excited look, "Can I fix you up a plate of food?"

Ah, shifter tradition, one I'm looking forward to seeing how it plays out, "That would be lovely, thank you."

He pulls out my chair for me, and as I sit with Castiel and Balbur, he wanders over to the other side of the canteen. My eyes track him all the way across, drawn to him with an intensity that feels natural.

"Another one fallen to a true mate. There must be something in the air," Castiel grumbles.

"You'd want the same in a heartbeat if it were possible," Balbur comments. "I know I would."

"I'm sure you two gentlemen have no problem with women," I point out, noting their sombre expressions.

"It's not the same," Castiel utters. "Ever since Kali came along and now you, seeing two of my best friends fall so hard, it kind of gives you a new perspective."

I'm surprised by Castiel's comment and the open honesty he's displaying. He seemed like a man very sure of himself when we first met, yet the man that sits before me is yearning for something more, and I want to help. To help both of them.

"If it can happen for me, it can for both of you. Don't stop searching or give up on that perfect mate. I'm sure they're out there somewhere, and when fate decides the time is right, you'll meet them."

Some gut feeling prompts me to tell them that, and I'm confident it's true.

"Thank you, Thea. That's very kind of you to say," Balbur smiles, a hint of his usual cheerfulness returning. Castiel also appears to have improved with my remark, that cocky smirk coming out to play.

"Hey guys," Kali says, making her way over to the table with Anubis. She takes the chair next to me, and when Anubis goes to get her food, she leans in close.

"Everything go okay with you and Bran? I was feeling some anger from you at one point and nearly came over to make sure he was treating you right."

I grin at Kali, grateful for her concern, "Everything is great. A little misunderstanding initially, but that's all cleared up now."

"Good. I would hate to have to kick my brother's ass," she chuckles, looking over in his direction.

With our men occupied, I use the opportunity to quietly ask Kali some questions about the bond. "When you and Anubis first discovered your bond, did you... did you want to..." Damn it, how do I say this without embarrassing myself.

"Screw like rabbits every time we were near each other?"

"Yes!" I exclaim. "It's so intense, and I'm trying to keep a level head, but every time we're near, it's like I'm going to crawl out of my skin."

"Preaching to the choir, sister. At one point, it got so bad with Anubis that I nearly went all the way with him in Damiean's office."

"You didn't?"

"Yep, only stopped because Damiean and Ann walked in."

"What did you do? How did you stop it from driving you crazy?"

"We accepted the bond," she shrugs. "It was the only way to tamper down the need, the desire."

Castiel makes a muffled noise at the end of the table. Kali and I turn to see him with that signature smirk of his in place.

"Apologies, ladies, but you're not being as quiet as you think you are, and I'm finding this conversation absolutely fascinating."

"Pervert," Kali laughs as my face flames with embarrassment. Perhaps I should have waited until we were alone before asking her these questions.

I clam up after that, deciding I should talk to Kali about this later. When Bran and Anubis come back to the table with our plates, the selection of food takes my mind off my mortification. My grin is broad as I observe the array of food Bran has provided for me. I'm not a picky eater and will eat most things, but my favourite is pasta. Any type of pasta, too, it doesn't matter. As is shifter custom, Bran has absolutely nailed it.

Three different pastas fill my plate, along with a side salad and a selection of breads. I wouldn't have picked anything better myself, and when I smile up at him in gratitude, his eyes shine triumphantly. Anubis chuckles quietly, observing our interaction before handing Kali her meal, and both men take a seat with their own meals.

"Thank you, Bran, this is perfect," I say, picking up my fork and happily eating.

"It's still crazy to me how they just know," Kali adds. "Is it like some sort of voice in your mind that tells you what we'll like?"

"No, Feisty, it's more instinctual than that. If the food I'm preparing is for you, I just go with what feels right."

"Makes no sense to me, but I'm not complaining."

As we settle in to enjoy our meal, Oberon arrives, sitting at the table, a plate in one hand and a laptop in the other.

"Hi, I'm Oberon. I don't believe we have formally met."

"Yes. Hi, Oberon. Sorry about before, I was having some shifter difficulties." I explain, not wanting to appear rude for running out before.

"No problem. I've heard that you may have the same issue as Kali?"

His eyes assess me with keen interest, and for a split second, I want to hide away, to not talk to anyone about my issues and just be normal.

"Don't mind him, Thea," Kali says. "I have him working on the restrictions, and that's all he can seem to focus on now. Isn't that right, O?"

Hearing about the restrictions, I suddenly find myself wanting to talk with him, eager to grasp what insights he might have gathered.

"Ah yes, Damiean said something about you not leaving his office. Have you made much progress?"

"Not as much as I would have liked," Oberon shakes his head disappointedly. "I'm narrowing down some different options at the moment, trying to eliminate the most unlikely scenarios. Collecting some data from you about how the restriction works for a shifter might help my research further."

"Okay, sure, what do you need to know?"

"Can you tell me about your connection with your animal?"

"Since I was born, I've been aware of her presence, but the connection seems fractured. It's only during intense emotional moments that she resonates with me. As if in my heightened state, the barrier between us falters, and she's able to channel a fragment of herself into me."

"And it's always been this way?" Oberon asks, taking notes as I try to explain my situation.

"Mostly yes. Our connection changed again when I was sixteen and had my first partial shift."

"Were you able to sense her more after that?"

"No, not necessarily. Only in the past year have I felt her presence more keenly. I can't pinpoint what changed, but my emotional responses seem to surface faster than usual, and when they do, I feel her."

When I finish speaking, Oberon continues his notes, and I realise you can hear a pin drop at the table, everyone quiet as they listen intently to what I'm saying. This is the first time I've ever discussed this side of myself without fear or ramifications, and as liberating as it is, I don't like being the centre of everyone's attention.

"What do you think, O?" Kali jumps in. "Crazy coincidence or strategically planned?"

"Based on Thea's experiences, I'm ruling out coincidence. There are too many parallels between your situation," he states confidently.

"What about a curse?" Castiel offers. "It's not unheard of for curses to restrict people in some way or another. Granted, it would still have to be immensely powerful, but curses can be broken."

"I considered that possibility when examining Kali's situation. But given that Thea is experiencing the same, the odds of a curse being placed on both simultaneously, leading to identical limitations, seems unlikely."

A few more theories are thrown around, and as the discussion continues, Bran places his hand on my knee. Presumably the gesture is meant to offer comfort while myself and Kali's situation is discussed. The only thing it does is divert my attention from the conversation, all my focus now on the hand that traces small circles above my knee.

Even through my jeans, my skin breaks out in goosebumps, his touch creating a chain reaction everywhere. The bond pulses heavily in my chest, and when his hand slides slightly higher on my leg, it takes considerable strength not to moan.

How can a simple touch create so much heat within me? His fingers trace swirls along my thigh, making my heart beat faster and my animal surge to the surface.

"Bran," Anubis warns, looking over at me.

Through my frenzy of emotions, I don't immediately notice the partial shift until I feel something drip down my chin. Wiping my hand against my face, it comes away red with blood, and I blink several times in confusion.

There's some commotion around me, yet all my attention is on the canines that have poked through my bottom lip. They're long, longer than my father's and incredibly sharp.

"Thea!" Kali shouts, her face coming into my field of vision. "Are you okay? What happened?"

"Yeath, I'mh fineth. Justh anothher..." I stop talking, struggling with my words around the huge canines. Looking past her to see our table empty, chairs strewn about and food all over the table. "Whath going onth?" I ask with a lisp, looking around for Bran.

"He..." Kali bites her lip, trying to hide her smile. "Well, let's just say he had a negative reaction to seeing you bleeding." She nods her head towards the rest of the room.

When I turn to see what has her interest, I gasp, taking in the carnage. It looks as if a bull has charged right through the centre, with tables and chairs upturned and food everywhere.

"He shifted into his bear and went a tad crazy," Kali explains. "The guys had to drag him out of here before he did any more damage."

"Where isth he?" I ask, jumping to my feet.

"They took him outside, but before you see him, you might want to clean the blood off your chin." She offers me a napkin and guides me until its clear.

"Very cool teeth, by the way. Also, your eyes look awesome, swirling with gold. Any idea what triggered the partial shift? Was it your arousal?" She asks, whispering the last part.

"Oh godth, I thinth soth. You felt thatht?"

Her laughter breaks free, and I roll my eyes. "I'm sorry, it's hard to take you seriously when you sound like that," she giggles. "In answer to your question, yes, but I tried to block it as soon as I recognised what it was. I'm not one to pry."

I don't know if I can carry on like this. The bond is... too much.

"Are you ready to accept it?"

"Honesthly, I'm noth sthure. Ugh, thith isth a nighthmare," I try to say. Based on Kali's squinted eyes and restrained smile, she's struggling to understand me.

For the next few minutes, I pace around the room, keeping myself calm so my emotions settle enough that the canines recede.

"That was interesting."

"And hilarious, don't forget hilarious," Kali adds with a snort.

"Not helping! What am I going to do?"

"Right, let's try this again. Are you ready to accept the bond?" she asks, repeating her earlier question.

"I'm not sure. I like Bran a lot, but I haven't even known him a day yet. I was hoping to have a bit more time to get my head around all the changes that have occurred over the last twenty-four hours."

"I know, right! These supernaturals love to move fast," she huffs, walking through the canteen with me. "My only advice is to keep contact to a minimum if you're not ready to accept the bond. It will be hard because it can make you a tad mindless, but it can be done. I think I lasted a day after our first kiss before I caved."

"We've already kissed," I admit.

"Oh jeez, well then, good luck to you, girl."

"Thanks," I laugh humourlessly.

By the time we've picked our way through the tables, I'm no closer to figuring out what I should do. When we exit the canteen to see the guys waiting for us, the sight of Bran looking frazzled causes my pace to increase.

"Are you alright?" We both ask at the same time.

"Come on, guys, let's leave these lovebirds to it. Wolf Man, I need chocolate." Kali saddles up to Anubis and after saying goodbye, the group disperses, leaving Bran and I alone.

"I'm sorry about that," Bran says, nodding his head towards the canteen. "My bear went a little wild when he thought you were hurt."

"This isn't going to be easy, is it, taking our time and getting to know each other?"

"It doesn't seem that way, no. We just need to be a little more mindful, and... I'll try not to touch you too much. From what Anubis has told me, it can make things worse."

I'm disappointed, and my animal isn't thrilled with the idea either, but it's for the best, at least until we've spent more time together.

"Can I walk you home?"

"Sure, I'd like that."

CHAPTER FOURTEEN

When I wake the next day and see the clock flashing 6am, a groan escapes me. I've hardly slept, constantly restless throughout the night. After Bran escorted me home, I was drained, yet when my head touched the pillow, my mind began to race. I attempted to shut it out, even resorted to pacing, but nothing worked. Ultimately, I managed to snatch a mere three hours of undisturbed sleep.

Now faced with the prospect of my first day at work, I can barely focus as I step out of the shower. The unexpected sound of a knock at the door gives me pause, water still dripping from my body and hair. Securing the towel firmly around me, I cautiously make my way to the living room. As a familiar pull tugs at my chest, I instantly recognise who's waiting outside.

Opening the door a crack, I peer out to see my mate standing there looking as gorgeous as ever with two coffees in one hand and a large bag in the other.

"Good morning, my beautiful mate," he says cheerfully with a dazzling smile. "I have your uniform for you and some strong coffee."

Smiling at the thoughtful gesture and the smell of coffee, I open the door wider and invite him in.

"Shifter gods, you are seriously testing my restraint," he mumbles up to the ceiling before his heat-filled eyes slowly peruse my towel-clad body.

"Here," he says, holding out the bag. "For the sake of my sanity, would you please get dressed?"

I chuckle softly, accepting the bag from him before swiftly retreating to the bedroom. Opening the bag, I take out several pieces, my anticipation heightening with each one. It's my first time owning new clothes, let alone a uniform, and this is far from ordinary. The deep black trousers mould to my legs as if tailor-made for me, the fabric incredibly lightweight and flexible. Next is a black button-down shirt that fits me perfectly. Who picked these clothes, and how did they get my measurements? The ensemble is completed with a dark brown leather vest and sleek black boots.

Inspecting myself in the mirror, my reflection looks foreign. I look strong and confident. The deep colours of my outfit contrast sharply with my fiery red hair, making it pop vividly. Not to boast, but I look like a warrior, and these clothes are a shield, my armour against the world. Grabbing a hair tie, I pull my mass of hair into a high ponytail, and my look is complete.

The anxiety that accompanies wearing this uniform is undeniable, but the strong pulsing in my chest and the presence of my mate in the next room eclipse those feelings for the moment. I only have so much capacity to deal with the range of emotions that could potentially drown me. I'm relieved my animal is quiet this morning, allowing me to adjust without bombarding me with feelings for our mate.

I find Bran relaxing on my couch, his coffee in hand, and when I enter the room, he pauses, his cup halfway to his mouth.

"Gods, babe, you look like you fell straight from my dreams," he growls, his eyes taking in every inch of me.

I blush under his gaze but straighten my back to seem more confident, enjoying his reaction to seeing me this way.

"We may notice a decline in concentration once you start training the recruits. Either that or everyone is going to want you as a trainer."

"Oh, please. You're only saying that because you're my mate."

"Nope. I'm saying that to prepare you for the reality." He stands from the couch, taking a step closer to me. "Please forgive me in advance, but until the bond is complete, I may act a little possessive."

I gulp at the heat banked in his eyes, his pupils flaring before a dark orange colour swirls within his eyes and replaces the usual grey.

"Are you okay?" I ask, knowing the colour change signifies his bear is close to the surface.

The bond between us tugs hard, causing me to gasp as desire rushes through me. He continues to gaze at me, and I want nothing more than for him to rip this uniform from me and make me his.

A knock at the door breaks our intense connection, and a different bond demands my focus. The timing of Kali's arrival is both disappointing and a relief, the conflicting emotions giving me a metaphorical whiplash. I distance myself from Bran and approach the door, revealing Kali and Anubis waiting on the other side.

"Woah, Thea, you look hot!" Kali states, her eyes searching behind me until she spots Bran. "Did we arrive just in time?" She asks quietly, a knowing smile on her face.

I smirk at her less than subtle interruption and send a wave of gratitude down our connection. I want this bond with Bran, but I need to get to know him, and without her presence this morning, the bond may have robbed that from me.

It's frustratingly confusing to go from acceptance to resistance in a matter of seconds.

"You alright, brother?" Anubis asks, his voice full of amusement.

"I'm sorry," Bran rushes out. "For all the times I teased you, I'm sorry. I get it now."

We all share a laugh as Bran joins us, dragging a hand over his face. As we leave the apartment and head for the elevator, Kali strategically positions herself between Bran and me, a welcome barrier that helps keep our intense connection at bay.

"Any more dreams last night?" Kali checks as we exist the Oak building and head to the canteen.

"No, I didn't sleep long enough to dream," I grumble and then notice Bran holding out a coffee cup he brought with him this morning. I take it gratefully, inhaling the rich aromas.

"You ever had trouble sleeping before?" Kali questions.

"No, but I'm guessing it's due to the new surroundings."

"I wouldn't be so sure. I thought the same thing until I realised it was the bond keeping me awake. Something to do with missing a piece of ourselves. Only once Anubis confirmed he wasn't sleeping either did it all fall into place."

I look over to Bran, raising my eyebrow in question.

"Afraid so, babe, hence the strong coffee. I managed about three hours."

This is ridiculous. How can the bond change us so fundamentally until it's forged? Our actions are determined by it, and now our sleep patterns. Am I being selfish by wanting a little more time?

"Hey, don't stress about it," Kali whispers softly. "When the time is right, you'll know."

I want to trust Kali's certainty, but just walking near him, it feels like he's a homing beacon, calling and pulling me towards him. I'm aware he has no control over the situation either, and he says I can take all the time I need, but at what cost to us both.

When we arrive at the canteen, Kali and I find a spot to sit at our usual table as our mates go to fetch breakfast for us. My thoughts continue to swing back and forth as the others talk, and I'm so preoccupied that I don't hear Castiel's question until he gestures to catch my attention.

"I'm sorry, I was miles away. What did you say?"

"I was just asking if you're looking forward to your first day. Bran mentioned you would shadow him, but if you need any support or pointers, the rest of us are here for you, too."

"Thanks, I appreciate that. I'm excited, if a little nervous. I think I'll be okay once I've had a day to get my bearings."

"It took me more than a day," Balbur chuckles. "The older recruits are manageable, but it's the teenagers you've got to keep an eye on. They're brimming with confidence and believe they're invincible. It took me weeks to figure out how to connect with them and get them to listen."

"Dude, you're supposed to be encouraging, not putting her off," Castiel comments, shaking his head in exasperation.

"It's fine," I say. "I'd rather hear your difficulties so I can be prepared for it."

"I think you'll do just fine, Thea. You have a commanding presence about you that I'm sure will make the recruits sit up and take notice," Kali assures.

"You think so? I've never seen myself that way before. I've been a doormat most of my life, so I'm surprised to hear you say that."

"Things are different now. You'll be different. Just wait and see."

"Have you started seeing the future, Blondie?" Castiel teases.

"I see an ass kicking in your future," she retorts with a grin.

Anubis and Bran approach, setting our plates down with a generous helping of food. "Are you threatening my men again, Feisty?" Anubis asks with amusement.

"Me? Never." She replies sweetly.

When Bran places my plate in front of me, the sight of bacon, eggs and toast elicits a warm smile.

"Thank you," I say gratefully.

Instead of sitting next to me, Bran opts for the chair across, presumably to maintain some space between us and make things easier. As we enjoy our breakfast, the group discusses today's arrangements and the aspects I'll observe. Bran will primarily focus on physical combat while I shadow him, but we've collectively decided it would benefit me to witness a magical session as well. Midway through our meal, Oberon joins us. He refrains from eating, choosing to sit with his laptop and swivelling the screen towards us to reveal the results of his investigations.

"Have either of you ever seen this before?" He asks, a hint of eagerness in his tone.

The image on his screen displays an ancient scroll, its text indecipherable, but it's the symbols that send a chill down my spine, causing me to abruptly abandon my meal. At the heart of the page are the very symbols from our dream, the ones engraved on the altar.

"Where did you find that?" Kali whispers, her eyes glued to the screen.

"It was inside the crate we received from the European division. It's the strangest thing. It appeared as a single piece of paper resting at the bottom. I've checked it against all our available sources, but I can't decipher these," he says, motioning to the text.

"Are you familiar with these symbols?" Bran checks, a frown marring his face as he studies me.

"Yes. It's from our dreams. In the centre of the wooden posts is an altar of sorts, and these symbols are engraved on the top."

It's surreal to see these symbols outside the dream realm and displayed so casually on Oberon's laptop. As in the dream, my gaze fixates on the same symbol, the lines appearing more faded than what I've seen previously, yet the intricate swirls still beckon me to trace my fingers over them.

"Have you ever seen this symbol before?" Kali asks Oberon, pointing to one that looks like smoke.

"No, never," he answers. "I haven't seen any of them before. Why do you ask specifically about that one?"

"It's the one I always feel drawn to in the dream."

"Strange, for me, it's this one," I tell her, pointing to the right.

"So, you've both encountered all six symbols but are drawn to a different one?" Oberon notes, jotting down observations and circling the symbols we've identified.

"Do you think that's significant?" Anubis asks, now studying the symbols.

"I'm not sure. I'm waiting to hear back from Damiean's contact in Europe to see where this scroll came from and if they can help with the translation."

"Good. If anything else comes back, let us know immediately," Anubis demands.

Castiel leans over the table to view the laptop more closely, "If you've both seen these symbols before and you're drawn to different ones, I guess it stands to reason that the other four could relate to women in your dreams?"

"But what's the connection?" Bran questions. "Do they relate specifically to each woman, or do they represent something else about them?"

"Six women, six symbols and lots of whispering and chanting about finding the six. It seems more prophecy related to me," Balbur comments. "I hate to say it, but until you find the others, you may not get any answers."

I rub at my head, tension pulsing around my temples as different theories run through my mind. "Until the dreams reveal more information, there's no way to find the other woman. Both Kali and I only saw each other the day before we met. Something tells me when the next woman is revealed, we will meet her shortly after."

Oberon nods, listening intently, "I agree, Thea. The dreams appear to be the key for any information relating to this, and until more is revealed, we're sitting ducks, so to speak."

My gaze lingers, fixated on the image for a few seconds more until Oberon retrieves the laptop to resume his research.

"Do you think those symbols could have something to do with our restrictions?" I ask Kali, wondering if the only consistent thing we've seen in the dreams could be leading us somewhere we've not thought of.

"Your guess would be as good as mine. I think the only positive here is at least we didn't make this shit up. We're not suffering from shared delusion."

"I guess that's true," I say distractedly.

"If anyone can figure it out, Oberon will," Bran says, trying to reassure me. "Are you ready to leave, or would you like something else to eat?"

"No, I'm good," I respond, my stomach churning with nerves as my first day at work is about to begin.

I rise from the table alongside the rest of the group, and as we make our way towards The Pit, Kali says goodbye, heading into SNHQ for her lessons.

"Give them hell, Thea!" she shouts before leaving.

Chuckling at Kali's infectious enthusiasm, I follow the guys, feeling only moderately prepared for the journey ahead.

CHAPTER FIFTEEN

THE PIT IS QUIET when we first arrive, the recruits not in attendance for another half an hour. Bran takes the time to show me around, pointing out various areas of interest I will need to be aware of as part of the staff. His demeanour is professional and commanding, doing nothing to tramp down my arousal for him.

Heading to a building at the rear of the training centre, he holds the door open for me as I step into a decently sized office. Inside are a couple of red couches, a refrigerator, a desk, and a set of tables and chairs tucked into a distant corner.

"This is our downtime spot between mentoring the recruits—think of it as our unofficial office. Feel free to grab any refreshments, and the restroom is just over there. It's a single restroom but does have a lock," he explains, guiding me through the room.

He gestures to another door behind the desk, "This leads to our equipment storage." As we approach and he swings the door open, the room reveals an array of training essentials: dummies, mats, gloves, pads, and even a small boxing ring. Every piece of equipment appears state of the art, making my gym back home look pathetic.

"This is amazing. I feel like I'm part of a waking dream," I comment, running my hands over the equipment.

"I understand that completely," he utters, and when I turn to question him, his eyes are trained only on me. "I never thought I'd have a true mate, let alone one as beautiful as you. Now here you stand, surrounded by the other love in my life, and I feel I've died and gone to heaven."

"That's very sweet of you to say, Bran," I mummer with a hint of shyness.

"Not sweet, babe, just the truth," he smirks. "Speaking of dreams coming true, could I take you on a date tonight?"

I grin coyly at his dream-coming-true comment, feeling butterflies and my animal's excitement, clearly happy at the thought of us being closer.

"I would love that," I reply, trying to keep any nervousness out of my voice.

He gestures towards the door leading out to The Pit, and I follow beside him, keenly aware of the bond yearning to connect with him. Outside, the recruits have started to arrive, and Bran turns to me with a mischievous smile.

"Ready to see me in action, babe?"

"Impress me," I smirk, and he raises his eyebrows at my challenge.

His smile broadens as I follow him to where the recruits have gathered. Among them are a mix of youngsters, some appearing almost too young to have completed school. When the other guys come over to join us, the recruits take notice of their trainers' presence and organise themselves into orderly lines, awaiting their instructions. I position myself to the side behind the guys, uncertain of how to occupy myself and already feeling out of my depth.

"Okay, everyone, you might have noticed we have a new addition with us today," Anubis begins, motioning towards me and stepping aside so I stand alongside them. "This is trainer Althea. She's new to our team and brings exceptional combat training skills. She'll observe over the next day or two to acquaint herself with our program. I expect each of you to treat Althea with the same respect you show the rest of us."

My heart beats rapidly throughout Anubis's speech. He portrays me as if I possess years of experience, and as the recruits regard me with a mix of curiosity and admiration, I feel a tingling sensation in my ears and fingers.

Please, gods, not now. Let me at least make it through the introductions.

Fortunately, Anubis doesn't prompt me to say anything, and when he starts outlining the day's sessions, I take a few discreet deep breaths, hoping to stave off the impending shift. The subtle brush of fingers across my hand takes all of my attention as Bran rhythmically traces circles across my palm. My hands are behind my back so no one can see, but I'm tempted to pull away, already trying to control too many emotions, so I don't shift.

He changes the pattern slightly, and I'm so focused on what he is doing that I miss most of what Anubis says. By the time Anubis has finished with his instructions, the tingling in my ears and fingers is gone and my breathing has evened out. Could Bran tell I was close to shifting? Did he sense something, and this was his way of helping me?

When the group disperses and I turn to Bran, he gives me a knowing wink, and a smile stretches wide over my face. He did know. He was distracting me so I could keep calm and not embarrass myself.

Damn, the fates chose well with this one.

The thirty recruits divide into four groups, with Balbur and Castiel each guiding their respective groups out of The Pit toward the lakes. The recruits follow the guys with palpable excitement, and I overhear a few of them murmuring about practising their water skills. It doesn't seem like the groups have been divided by species, as even vampires are making their way to the lakes. I am eager to learn more about the training taking place there and mentally make a note to ask Bran about it later.

Anubis takes five of the remaining fifteen recruits, leading them to the mats to commence their combat training. This leaves Bran with a group of ten, and I'm genuinely curious to see what he has in store for them.

"Alright, everyone, first things first, I want all of you warmed up. You know the routine, so let's get to it."

I hear a few groans as the recruits go to the far side of the arena and begin their warm-up exercises. Bran observes the recruits undergo a rigorous regimen, far more intense than anything I've witnessed before. Push-ups, squats, lunges, burpees—it's all there, but with the added challenge of the floor shifting slightly beneath them.

It takes me a while to notice, as I'm so focused on the exercises themselves, but when I see a few of them stumbling, that's when I realise the floor is moving beneath their feet. The sand beneath them shifts every few minutes, changing direction each time. I sympathise with the recruits, yet I'm curious about how I would fare working out on a constantly shifting floor. It would undoubtedly be a unique challenge, unlike anything I've experienced before.

Bran closely monitors the recruits throughout, offering suggestions and encouragement as we near the half-hour mark. When he signals the end of the warm-up and the recruits reach for their water bottles, the questions burst from me about the moving floor.

"Something Castiel takes great pride in," Bran tells me. "He's spelled the floor to move to keep the recruits on their toes. They need to be prepared for anything, even with simple warm-up exercises."

"They seemed to do well."

"I should hope so. They've been doing it for about three weeks now."

My gaze remains fixed on the floor as I try to detect any signs of where it changes or any magical properties it might possess.

"You want to try it, don't you?" he laughs.

"I do. I've always tried to push myself, and working out on that floor would be the ultimate challenge."

"Maybe after we've finished today's session, you could give it a go. I wouldn't mind watching over you while you do."

"Hmm, I imagine you'd take great pleasure from it," I respond quietly, my lips pulling at the corner.

"You have no idea, babe, watching you bounce around, getting all sweaty," he growls low before shaking his head. "Damn it, I need to stop. I've seen Anubis struggle with training when he was, shall we say, excited. I teased him mercilessly for it, so I can't have him doing the same to me."

I giggle when Bran retreats away from me, the heat still in his eyes but his professional demeanour slipping back into place. Something about being around Bran makes me throw caution to the wind and say whatever is on my mind. I need to get a handle on that when we're working together.

Throughout the morning, Bran challenges the recruits, evaluating their strength and endurance by subjecting them to various scenarios they could encounter on assignment. They take a break for the afternoon, during which I have lunch with Anubis and Bran. I excitedly pepper them with questions about the recruits' training regimens, combat training and the techniques they employ.

Neither of them appears to mind my enthusiasm. In fact, if anything, they seem to enjoy going into the specifics and explaining how they've adapted the programme over the years. It's evidenced by how they talk about it this programme means a lot to them.

By the time we've wrapped up our meal and leave the canteen, my bond with Kali pulsates in my chest, revealing my friend is close by.

When her smiling face comes into view, my animal surges with happiness. It's strange to me how she responds to Kali, and if it wasn't for my mate bond with Bran, I would think my animal had an attraction to her. However, through my mate bond, I can sense the difference between her attraction to Bran and her happiness at seeing her family.

"So, how was your morning? Did you enjoy it?" Kali asks cheerily.

"I did. It's incredible the structure they have with the recruits and how they adjust the regimes depending on the supernatural. Did you know they had a moving floor?"

"Urgh, don't even get me started on that thing. I'm still trying to get through a full session. Castiel thinks it's hilarious."

"I can't wait to try it."

"Oh gods, you're one of them, aren't you? Someone who enjoys exercise."

I laugh at her playful disgust and go on to share what I've noticed and some of my thoughts regarding the combat training. She listens intently, offering words of encouragement or praise, and I'm struck by how lucky I am to have her in my life.

By the time Bran has assembled his group again, I'm genuinely eager to see what challenges they'll face in the afternoon.

"Feisty, you're working with Balbur today," Anubis smirks unapologetically.

"Oh shit on a stick, really?" She whines. "Can't I just train with Thea?"

"You're going to give me a complex if you keep reacting this way," Balbur chuckles, his arms crossed over his broad chest.

"It's good for you, Feisty. Balbur keeps you honest and grounded, and when you can beat him, you can beat anyone," Anubis adds.

"You just want my frustration afterwards," she grumbles as she heads over to Balbur.

Returning my focus to Bran, he briefs the recruits on their afternoon's agenda, emphasising hand-to-hand combat, weapons training, and defensive tactics. Organising them into pairs, Bran provides clear directives regarding their areas of concentration, and the afternoon of combat training kicks off.

I observe him closely as he moves among the groups, pushing them to their limits and making necessary corrections. His authoritative demeanour is undeniably attractive, and I'm more engrossed in watching him than the recruits.

When one group grapples with the challenges of weapons training, Bran steps in to demonstrate, showcasing his mastery of the sword. He effortlessly overcomes his opponent while instructing the recruits, and my animal surges into overdrive. Witnessing him handle the sword with such natural ease, defeating his adversary and imparting knowledge, proves overwhelming for my female hormones.

Despite my best efforts to ignore the shift, it's impossible. Everything changes quickly, and even my canines lengthen, extending beyond my lower lip. I slam my hand over my mouth, concealing the elongated teeth and silently chastising my animal for her reactions. To make matters worse, I cannot divert my gaze from Bran, despite it not being in my best interest.

Taking deep, calming breaths proves ineffective, and my customary pacing is out of the question, as it would only draw attention to my condition. My focus becomes intensely fixated on Bran, and I can't help but track the path of a solitary bead of sweat trickling down his temple, a part of me wishing I were that droplet.

Subtly shifting my stance to the left, I try to divert my attention and inadvertently catch his scent—a blend of cinnamon and leather—which hits me square in the face. The effect is a cascade of reactions. First, my thighs clench involuntarily, then our bond pulses, and most unsettling of all, a purr inexplicably rumbles in my chest.

I sense the faint vibration, but the more I'm enveloped in Bran's scent, the louder it grows. It resonates within my chest with an unmistakable intensity, a noisy and undeniable purring I am powerless to suppress. Observing Bran throughout the morning and witnessing his swordplay, the surge of emotions becomes overwhelming, and my animal purrs in recognition of her mate.

With my ears, fingers, teeth, tail, whiskers and this new development, there's no point in denying or concealing the fact that I've shifted. The recruits were bound to discover the truth sooner or later, so the timing shouldn't matter. If only the purring wasn't so loud.

Bran locks eyes with me, his expression shifting as he realises the noise emanates from me. A broad smile spreads across his face, and while he's momentarily distracted, the sparring partner he is facing seizes the opportunity and strikes at him.

A fierce and resounding growl rips from my throat, echoing loudly and causing the sparring partner to instinctively recoil. As if Bran anticipated the entire sequence of events, he gracefully swings his sword and strikes, halting the blade just inches before it can cleanly sever the man's head.

"If I've told you once, I've told you a thousand times. Never get distracted."

I'm genuinely impressed by how expertly Bran managed to flip the situation. If I didn't know better, I'd believe it was all premeditated, but given I've never growled or purred this way before, he couldn't have predicted how it would unfold. He directs the other recruits to resume their training and heads over to me, jogging in my direction.

"That was so damn hot," he announces without preamble.

"I'thm sorry. I don'th knothw whath came over me," I cringe when my speech doesn't come out right. "I've never purrethed before."

This revelation only appears to bring more joy to Bran, and my animal, once again, makes her appreciation for his reactions apparent, resuming her low purring. I've always wanted a deeper connection with her, but why does she have to assert herself during these inopportune moments? I'm sure to the recruits, I must appear unhinged.

Bran smiles softly at me and places a gentle kiss on my cheek. "You can purr for me anytime, babe," he utters, walking away and resuming his training.

For the rest of the afternoon, I have no choice but to observe the session in my half-shifted state, teeth and all. If nothing else, at least the recruits will be used to seeing me this way now.

CHAPTER SIXTEEN

Instead of loitering with the guys or heading to the canteen for dinner, I drag Kali to my apartment to help me prepare for my date. The partial shift, which in the presence of Bran has lasted most of the afternoon, shows no signs of fading. Now, coupled with my nervousness about the first date, it's even more persistent.

"Whoa, where's the fire?" Kali asks as I all but run back to the apartment block, not wanting the whole village to see me this way.

"I neeth ttho geth ttho my aprathment, quickly," I try to say around my large teeth.

"If your teeth are going to be a regular thing, you need to get used to talking with them. I can hardly understand a word you're saying."

I don't try to respond as we head into Oak and take the elevator to our floor. Before we can make it to my apartment, Kali stops me outside of hers.

"Wait, I have an idea." She disappears inside her apartment and returns a few minutes later with a bottle of wine.

"This might help with the teeth," she grins, shaking the bottle enticingly.

"Andth howth am I suthposed to drinth it."

"No idea what you just said, but I also brought a straw," she laughs, pulling the straw from behind her back.

Instead of attempting to speak, I convey my gratitude through our bond, opening the door to my apartment and inviting her in. She quickly secures two glasses, pouring us both a generous measure. I've drank a few times before in the past. Angie would sneak bottles of her mum's wine, and we would drink it all down on the bay. The downside of shifter metabolism was we were never intoxicated for long.

"Here, get this down you. Hopefully, it will settle you enough so that your teeth retract, and I can understand you. Either that or you'll find the whole situation more amusing," she snorts, handing me the wine glass and straw.

I take a sip, enjoying the fruity taste as it explodes across my tongue. Moving over to the couch, Kali and I sit in silence until half my glass is gone, and I start to relax. Within the next few sips, my canines rescind.

"See, now isn't that better. You just needed to de-stress a bit. You've had a lot thrown at you in the last two days."

"Thank you for this," I say, holding up my glass, my words normal. "If this keeps up, you'll have to learn a new language, part human and part shifter."

"I could do that. Towards the end there, I was getting some of it. Do you want to talk about what brought on the shift?"

"I thought it was obvious," I sigh. "I can't control myself around Bran. Just watching him today sent my animal into a meltdown. She's pushing closer to the surface and there's a part of me insanely happy about it, but the timing of her reactions is always when I need it the least."

"And is the bond causing it?"

"Presumably, I've never felt this close to her. Perhaps the bond is helping, encouraging her to come out more. Other than when she's lusting after Bran or you're near, I don't feel her all that much."

"Me?" she asks in surprise.

"Yes. When you're close and I feel our bond, she's happy, content."

"Aww, that's so fucking sweet." She grins wide, her hand going to her chest where the bond resides.

"It is, and I wouldn't trade our bond for anything, but I'm struggling with all the emotions. Between our bond, my connection with Bran and the influx of feelings from my animal, I'm having a hard time finding myself in it all. I'm worried it will all accumulate, and I won't be able to contain it. I'll break."

"Oh girl, you are preaching to the choir," she says, holding her glass up in a toast. "Before I accepted the bond with Anubis, I was all over the place and didn't recognise my own feelings from what the bond wanted. It drove me insane, and I was questioning everything."

"What did you do?" I ask, turning towards her and getting more comfortable. If anyone understands what I'm going through, it's Kali.

"Honestly, I questioned everything until I drove myself insane, then waited until my head and heart got on the same page, which didn't take too long. When I accepted the bond, things became easier. Well, that's a lie. My emotions are still all over the place, and I leak elements like a tap, but I think that's more to do with the restrictions."

"So you're saying everything will settle down if I accept the bond?"

"It did for me, but you need to decide if that's what you want. The bond can drive you to distraction when your mate is around, so you need to be sure if it's something you want."

"I do want it. There's just something holding me back."

"Can you tell me what that is?"

I think about her question, trying to discern my feelings from my animal and my bonds. I felt I needed time for us to get to know each other, but now I'm not too sure. Is that the only thing holding me back, or is it something more? For the first time ever, I'm free. Will being mated with Bran take some of that freedom away? When I explain all this to Kali, she nods in understanding.

"The only advice I have there is that the bond hasn't felt that way for me. Knowing Bran the way I do, I think he would openly encourage any freedom you want. He's aware of your past, so I'm confident he would be mindful about that."

"I also have the issue that I still need to meet the alpha and join the pack. What if they don't accept me?"

"Ha, after meeting the alpha, you might be dodging a bullet there. He's an asshole."

In the most unladylike manner, I splutter some of my wine out, shocked at hearing Kali speak of the alpha that way.

"Why? Is he controlling like my father? What has he done?" I'm desperate to hear the gossip on this pack's alpha. For me, this is akin to a soap opera.

"I wouldn't say he was as bad as your father, but he isn't impressed with having an elemental as a daughter-in-law."

"What!" I screech too loudly. "Why?"

Kali tells me the story of when she first met Anubis's father and how he treated her and has barely spoken to her since.

"What an idiot! How dare he judge you like that. Who does he think he is? I have a good mind to go speak to him myself."

The fire in my belly is unusual, and on closer inspection, I realise it's coming from my animal. She is not happy with the alpha's treatment of my friend.

"Don't worry, I have him handled. He doesn't intimidate me, much to his disgust," she snickers. "Anyway, back to you and Bran."

Talking to Kali for the next thirty minutes, I go back and forth. In my heart, I want to dive into the bond with both feet, and in my head, I'm thinking I still need a bit more time. We end up having another glass of wine as we talk, and I'm a little tipsy by the time I reach the bottom of the glass.

"Enough of all this talk!" I shout louder than necessary. "You have to help me get ready for my first-ever date!"

She giggles as I pull her from the couch and into my bedroom, "Now that I can help with. As a first-timer myself, I was a nervous wreck on my first date with Anubis."

Opening the wardrobe doors, I peer inside and instantly recoil at my outfit choices.

"Oh dear," Kali says, looking over my selection of clothes. "Please tell me you've ordered some new stuff because this is depressing, and that's coming from someone who barely had anything when I got here."

"I haven't got around to it yet. What am I going to do, everything I own has holes in or stains."

"Your father is a knobhead."

"Right!" I laugh. "These clothes are the only items I could get my hands on over the years or what my friend Angie could get for me."

"Okay, wait here and let me see what I have. You're a little taller than me, but we might be able to work something together."

She leaves my apartment quickly, and as I wait, I sit on the bed, staring at my abysmal collection. It occurs to me I haven't called Angie since I got here, and I instantly feel guilty. She'll no doubt be worrying, and here I am, enjoying my life and about to go on a date. I resolve that I will ring her tonight to give her all the details.

When Kali returns, she has a wide grin on her face, "Unless you want to wear hoody or workout clothes, I haven't got anything date-worthy, but I do have an idea."

She holds out a large dark green shirt that I know must be one of Anubis's.

"First of all, how is that date-worthy? And second, won't he mind me using his shirt for a date with his brother?"

"No, he won't mind, and this is what we're going to do."

Kali and I spend the following hour preparing, which mainly involves her lounging on my bed as I shower, and then assisting me in assembling my outfit. Thanks to the conditioner I now have at my disposal, my hair looks incredible, the various shades of red more pronounced. I've always had naturally straight hair, so leaving it to air dry gives it a healthy sheen it's never possessed before.

Following Kali's guidance, I slip into the only pair of black jeans I have. They have a faint pen stain, but it's not particularly noticeable. I top it off with a black cami, then don the green shirt over it, leaving the buttons undone and tying the shirt's ends in a knot just above my waist. My old trainers, barely holding together, are replaced with my new work boots, completing my outfit perfectly. Retrieving a hairpin from the bathroom, I pull back one side of my hair and am ready to go.

"Girl, you make Anubis's shirt look hot. I do believe you are date-ready."

It's funny because the outfit isn't overly girly or what I envisioned wearing on a date, yet I love it. I feel sexy and confident, which is foreign to me.

"Are you ready to date your mate?" Kali laughs from the bed.

"As I'll ever be," I respond, the butterflies in my stomach taking flight now the time has come.

Kali jumps up from the bed, linking her arm through mine and leading me out of the bedroom.

"Thank you for this," I tell her, pointing at my outfit. "I don't think I'd be able to do half the stuff I have since I got here if it weren't for you."

"Nah, you would. You just wouldn't have an awesome sidekick," she snorts. "You never have to thank me. I'm happy to do it. I love having a female friend."

"Me too," I smile.

We continue chatting for a little longer until the sensation of my mate's proximity causes my chest to pulse with anticipation. A few seconds later, when he knocks on the door, my nerves escalate so abruptly that it triggers a partial shift. Fortunately, it's limited to my ears and fingers. This wasn't the appearance I had in mind.

"Bless ya, you just can't catch a break, can you?" Kali comments, following me to the door.

"Exactly! Worst timing ever."

Opening the door to see my gorgeous mate smiling back at me, the nerves are tapered by excitement. My first date, and it's with my true mate, the man I will spend forever with. No pressure.

CHAPTER SEVENTEEN

"Shifter gods, babe! You look smoking," Bran remarks enthusiastically, his eyes trailing down to my feet and back up again. "I hit the true mate jackpot with you."

A blush naturally rises to my cheeks in response to his comment and the intense heat that swirls within his eyes, the colour shifting slightly between grey and orange.

Kali comes up behind me, and I feel her amusement trickling through the bond. "Bro, pick your jaw up off the floor. You have a date to get to."

When she passes by me to exit the apartment, her grin is wide, "You two kids have fun now, and behave yourselves."

"Later, Sis," Bran shouts over his shoulder, his eyes never leaving mine.

The Bran who stands before me is notably more refined than I'm used to seeing, with his tousled brown hair pushed back, revealing more of his striking face. He's impeccably dressed in dark blue trousers and a white t-shirt beneath a blue shirt. As my gaze travels downward, I suddenly spot the bouquet of flowers in his hand.

"Are those for me?" I ask, nodding towards the flowers.

"They are," he replies, holding them out for me to take. "Next to you, their beauty pales in comparison."

Oh gods, why does he have to be so sweet. With the bond and my animal, I can already sense my self-control starting to waver. I accept his flowers, offering a coy smile in response to his compliment.

"Come in while I find a vase for these." Bringing the flowers to my nose, I inhale the beautiful floral scent. Having never received flowers before, I get a strong sense that Bran will provide many firsts for me over the coming weeks.

"So, where are you taking me for our date?" I inquire, my hands trembling with nerves as I carefully trim the flowers and place them in a vase.

"I figured we'd do something a little different. I've been busy preparing a surprise for you," he answers, his voice carrying a touch of excitement.

"Well, you've certainly piqued my curiosity. Shall we get going?" When tingling suddenly starts in my face, I groan. Not now, not now.

"What's wrong?" he asks, placing his hand on my shoulder and causing arousal to surge through me. When I turn to face him, I don't know if I'm embarrassed or disappointed in myself.

"Maybe we should stay in. It doesn't look like I'm going to have much control over myself tonight," I say, pointing to the whiskers that have now sprouted on my face.

"If it bothers you or makes you uncomfortable, I don't mind staying in. Personally, the whole package is really doing it for me."

My eyes widen in disbelief, "You don't mind my partially shifted state?"

"What! Are you kidding me? Not at all. I think you look sexy as hell. Why, what do you see when you shift like this?"

His question takes me by surprise. I've always thought of myself as a defect and that my partial shifts were embarrassing, something I should hide. When I tell him this, he scoffs.

"Babe, I don't want to push or make you uncomfortable, but if it was left to me, I would show you off to the world. Your shifts are just as beautiful as every other part of you."

He runs a finger across one of my whiskers, and the sensation travels straight to between my thighs. I jolt, taking a step back and gasping.

"Sorry, they're quite sensitive," I explain when he looks worried.

A mischievous grin spreads across his face, and he steps towards me before he seems to think better of it. Taking a deep breath, his eyes swirl again before settling on his usual grey.

"As long as I'm with you, I don't care where we are. So, we can stay here and eat or head to the surprise, and you can show the village what a badass you are."

It's hard to say no to going out when he puts it like that. Plus, I can see he's also having difficulty with this, and I don't want to ruin his surprise.

Squaring my shoulders, my emotional defences spring into action, shielding me from any potential judgments. "Let's go out," I inform him, my demeanour taking on a detached quality as I adopt my 'nothing can hurt me' facade.

He looks at me questioningly, but I stride to the door, ready to leave and hoping he follows.

"Are you sure you want to do this?" He checks, leaving the apartment with me.

"I do. I'm just preparing myself."

"Preparing for what?"

"The stares, the whispers, the judgement."

"If any of those things were to happen, which is unlikely, they would only happen once," he growls softly.

We exit the Oak building, and the courtyard is quiet, with only a few people milling around. I walk with my back straight and my head high, trying to present an image of confidence.

"Babe, you look like you're about to march into battle," Bran chuckles. Taking steps to close the gap between us, he drapes his arm over my shoulders. His height allows him to hold me this way comfortably, and my body vibrates with the connection between us. It does something else I don't expect. It relaxes me.

My shoulders drop, and I lean into his touch, savouring the warmth and presence of my mate beside me.

"Much better," he murmurs close to my ear.

As we amble along, I notice a few passersby stealing curious glances in our direction. Surprisingly, I find myself unfazed by their attention. Perhaps having my mate close contributes to my new sense of calm? Or it could be I'm distracted by my constant state of arousal.

Regardless of the reason, I don't overthink it. Instead, I savour the experience of walking and talking with Bran. Everything is effortless with him. Our conversation flows easily, discussing our day at work and my evening with Kali.

"Please tell me you didn't plan our date at the canteen?" I scoff when I see we're heading that way.

"Babe," he gasps. "I'm shocked you would even think that. I do have some game."

"Hmmm, we'll see about that."

We sweep across the area, passing by the canteen, SNHQ, and The Pit, gradually ascending toward the top of the village.

Beyond The Pit lies an expansive meadow adorned with lush greenery, seamlessly transitioning into the village's surrounding forest. Flanking this picturesque clearing on both sides are two immense bodies of water, affectionately referred to as The Pools. The moon casts its luminous reflection off the waters, and with the fragrance of the pine trees, I can't imagine a more romantic setting for our first date.

Under Bran's guidance, we make our way to the right pool, and as we approach a small dock, I catch sight of the small cottage-like dwellings scattered along the water's edge.

"I figured you wouldn't have had the chance to make it up here yet, and it's one of my favourite spots," Bran says as he leads me towards a trail of twinkling fairy lights that beckon us towards a dock.

At the far end of the dock lies a beautifully laid-out picnic blanket adorned with cushions, enough food for a family, and two bottles of wine.

"I can't believe you did all this for me," I whisper, my eyes watering when I spot the array of pasta dishes he's brought.

"You like it then?"

If my eyes don't deceive me, he appears a little nervous.

"I love it. Thank you." Standing on my tiptoes, I place a kiss on his cheek to show my gratitude.

When I pull away, his chest rumbles with the sound of his bear, his eyes almost entirely orange. He squeezes my hand affectionately before putting some distance between us.

"I'm sorry. I thought I would have better control, but the bond is—"

"It's alright, you don't have to explain. If anyone can understand what you're going through, it's me."

He nods, smiling tightly. "Shall we sit?"

I knew it would be a challenge to spend time together with our bond continually fuelling our desires. Still, it's a hurdle we need to overcome if we ever hope to know each other better. My hesitance lies in making the right decision, even when I want nothing more than to throw away my caution and take what is mine.

Maybe we should have made things easier for us both and had our first date over the phone.

Taking a seat on the blankets, Bran settles opposite me and begins to portion out the food, generously piling pasta onto my plate and pouring me a glass of wine.

"So, besides being an incredibly beautiful shifter, who is Thea?" He asks, handing me a glass of wine as some tension leaves his shoulders. "I find myself wanting to know every detail about you."

I take a sip of my wine while mulling over his question. "Honestly, Bran, I'm not sure there's much to tell," I admit, gazing into the water. "I don't know what I like or dislike because I've never had the chance to figure it out."

There's a brief silence, and when I turn to him, his eyes are once more swirling with the orange of his bear. He shakes his head, dispelling whatever thoughts had his bear surfacing before gently pressing for more, "There must be something you can tell me about yourself. Any hopes or dreams?"

"I guess there's my training. The countless hours watching videos to become strong, hoping that if I ever became an alpha, I'd be ready."

"And is that something you want? To be an alpha?"

I shake my head, "Not particularly. I was born into a line of alpha's and thought it should be my destiny, but considering my... condition, that's unlikely to ever happen."

"You never know what the future holds, babe," he adds boldly. "What else? Did you have any dreams when you were little? I used to dream of being an astronaut."

I giggle, imagining a little Bran running around in a space suit. "Only one thing comes to mind, but I can't tell you. It's too embarrassing."

"Now I must know," he demands playfully. "Go on, spill the beans on little Thea."

"Fine." I sigh in defeat. "I used to dream about meeting my true mate. He would come to rescue me, avenge me and whisk me away to somewhere safe."

His smile falters at my confession. "I wish there was some way to find out if you had a true mate. If I'd known you existed, I would have been your saviour."

And I believe him. Judging by how he's responded to every detail I've shared about my life, he would have arrived at my side at the earliest opportunity, confronting my father and firmly putting him in his place. The thought brings a smile to my face.

"Enough about me. Tell me everything about you?"

It's his turn to ponder my question as I start on my food and pour us more wine.

"I enjoy action movies, food and sleep—"

"I don't think that's necessarily specific to you," I chuckle. "Everyone enjoys those things."

"Not everyone does it as well as me," he grins. "I've dabbled playing a few instruments and handle the drums fairly well, but it's not something I do often. My job means a lot to me, and I take the responsibility seriously, but I'm also lucky I work with some of the finest men you'd ever meet. Oh, and I am the king at poker and monopoly."

"Really? I didn't have you pegged as the board game sort."

"I enjoy anything that involves a bit of competition."

Based on his previous admission about being second place, I can guess who he thinks his main competition is. You wouldn't know watching him and his brother together, they have a deep respect for one another, even if they do tease each other mercilessly. "And besides astronaut, do you have any dreams?"

"You mean other than mating the women of my dreams and maybe having a family at some point?"

"Family?" I choke out, shocked. "You've thought about having kids?"

"Haven't you?"

"Erm, not really. Given my situation, it's not something I've ever considered. I'm not averse to the idea, but it's not something I want in the immediate future. Do you?"

"No, not immediately. I just love being around kids. Something about their innocence resonates with me. It's why I always dress up as Santa at Christmas time. The kids love it, and so do I."

It shouldn't surprise me. He has a childlike enthusiasm when he speaks about things he enjoys. On the other hand, after watching him this morning, the domineering side of him is all man.

We talk for the next few hours about nothing and everything. We cover childhood, teenage years and early adulthood. I don't have much to contribute without bringing down the tone of the conversation, but I relish listening to Bran recount stories about his life. When he shares his favourite films and books, he paints such a vivid picture with his words. I feel like I've seen the film and read the books. Throughout our conversation, he mentally compiles a list of all the movies he thinks I'll enjoy, already envisioning the hours we'll spend together, cuddled on the couch.

We maintain a respectable distance during the entire night, but being in his proximity does little to quell the turbulence of my emotions, thanks to the persistent influence of my animal. Despite my efforts, my partial shift remains, allowing me to closely scrutinise the transformations. The fur encircling my nails resembles a lion, and when I ask Bran about my other shifts, he seems to agree with the lion-like association.

"Would it bother you, being the same as your father?"

"In a way, yes, but she's still my animal. Just because my father is an asshole doesn't mean she is. I had hoped to be more like my mother so it would be as if I had a piece of her with me."

He nods sadly, quiet for a moment. "I can't comprehend what it must be like to only feel your animal occasionally and to never have met her. I wish there was some way I could help you connect with her."

"You already are," I tell him, hoping I'm not pushing things too far by admitting that.

"I am?" He questions, a hint of optimism in his tone.

"I've never shifted for this long before. Being around you and having the bond constantly pulling at me brings her to the surface in a way she's never done before."

"And that's good, right?"

"Yeah, it's good," I laugh. "Her timing is just terrible sometimes."

Talking to Bran, I don't think I've ever felt this connected with someone, physically or mentally. Though we both have work the next day, we talk into the small hours of the morning, and when Bran suggests calling it a night, I'm disappointed.

For the walk back, he holds my hand the whole way, and the butterflies in my stomach refuse to settle. By the time we reach my apartment, my skin feels alive, and the bond is consuming, pushing against me harder.

"I don't want this to end, but thank you for the most amazing night and for making me feel special."

"It was truly my pleasure," he utters softly, his gaze smouldering. His hand snakes around my waist, and he gently pulls me towards him until my chest brushes against his. Now firmly pressed to him, his hand grazes up my side, leaving a trail of burning desire as he slowly works his way higher to entwine his finger through my hair.

With a firm grip at the base of my roots, my eyes clash with his. A combination of orange and grey ignites as he gazes at me with so much passion, I can barely contain the moan that wants to escape.

The first touch of his lips is soft and sensual, a worship against my mouth before he loses his control.

With an almost inaudible growl, he seizes my lips, dominating and controlling the kiss, sending the bond into overdrive. I moan against him, my desire so strong that when he lightly grazes his tongue against my lip, I grant him the access to destroy me.

And Gods, does he destroy me.

Pushing me up against the wall, I feel every hard edge of his body against mine. He reveres me with his tongue, his hands tightly clutching me as if I was his anchor. My need for him overwhelms me. My animal, the bond, and even myself are ready to throw all reservations aside and ask him inside. When he suddenly pulls back, his eyes are blazing and completely orange, his breathing heavy as he leans his forehead against mine.

"Dreams do come true," he whispers reverently. "You are too perfect, babe. If I don't go now, things will develop beyond our control."

I nod, not trusting myself to speak. I want to beg him to come inside, to extinguish the flames he's ignited within me, to ease the ache he's created. Instead, when he releases me, I take a deep, steadying breath and grab the door handle, heading inside before the bond takes my choices away from me. His voice stops me before I close the door.

"Thank you for the most incredible date," he smiles softly, and I watch him walk down the hallway, our bond pulling incessantly.

As I close the door, my animal snarls in my head, and I roll my eyes. I'm not going to last another twenty-four hours.

CHAPTER EIGHTEEN

Being so late when I finally got into bed, it would have been nice to have slept peacefully before the sun rose but of course, that doesn't turn out to be the case. I can only assume Kali is correct that the bond is keeping me awake, and given that my mind was consumed by Bran, it's not an unreasonable theory. By 5am, I abandon any attempt to sleep and get out of bed.

Work doesn't start for another four hours, but I get ready anyway to give myself something to do. It occupies me for a mere forty minutes before restlessness sets in. I find myself pacing around the living room, dissecting every detail of our date from the previous night. Given our time together, I wonder how much more I can discover about Bran before acknowledging and embracing the bond. In truth, I should be ready to solidify the connection and progress with my mate, but there remains a lingering hesitation.

After a night of contemplation, deciphering my feelings from my animal and the bond proves to be challenging. If I approach the situation analytically, my hesitation boils down to two things. The first revolves around my animal and the challenges we face. Despite Bran's assurance these issues don't concern him, I'm still determining whether he can genuinely dismiss its significance until more time has passed. How can he be sure that the strained bond with my animal won't hinder our connection in the future? Can we be confident that it won't negatively impact our relationship down the line?

The second aspect is my newfound freedom. It ranks lower on the list of concerns, but it still contributes to my insecurities. For the first time, I'm free to discover who I am and where I belong in this world. I don't believe Bran would hold me back from my journey of self-discovery, but in any decision I make, I would need to consider his feelings when all I want to do is what makes me happy.

For instance, what if I can't find the answers I need here and decide to travel in search of someone who can help me. Will Bran come too, leaving his pack and family behind? He would probably agree readily if it meant my happiness, but is it fair of me to ask that?

Another fleeting concern, though perhaps it should weigh more heavily, is the pack life. I have yet to encounter the alpha, and the absence of any initiative from his side is concerning. Is he already aware of my issues and choosing to ignore my presence? Should I take the initiative and seek him out? If I do, what role am I expected to play? The prospect of not liking the pack, opting not to join, and risking the potential consequences is another dilemma. Is it fair for me to make such a decision, especially when considering Bran? Would the risk of madness even be a concern if I were bonded to Bran?

The constant turmoil and questions are like an itch in my brain I cannot scratch.

Checking the time and seeing its 6.30am, I decide there is only one person who can help me with this, who truly knows the extent of what I've been through and what I should do now. I just hope she's not angry with me for ringing so early. Making a fresh mug of coffee, I take the iPad to the couch and get comfortable for this conversation.

It takes two rings before she answers, her voice sounding groggy with sleep, "Who the hell has a death wish ringing me this early?"

"Your one and only true best friend," I smile, comforted by hearing her voice.

"Thea! Oh my gods, Thea, is that really you?"

"It is, are you okay? Do you need a minute?"

"Yep, give me two seconds." I hear her shuffling around over the other end of the phone, her door opening before the sound of the kettle reaches me. I can envisage precisely what she's doing now.

She'll want to go into every detail of my time here so far, and to do that, she needs a drink and someplace comfortable and quiet.

"You know we could still talk while you do all that?"

"Shhhh, I'm composing all the questions in my head. I'm almost done."

A soft chuckle escapes me as I wait patiently for my friend. A few minutes later, I hear a sigh and know she's taken her first sip of tea and is ready to talk.

"I can't believe I'm talking to you. I have so many questions. I'm not sure where to start."

"How about I tell you everything that's been going on since I got here, and then you can ask your questions at the end."

"Yeah, okay, do that."

I spend the next forty minutes detailing everything. My arrival, the changes in circumstances, what happened with my father, the bond with Kali, and finally, Bran. I left nothing out, going so far as to tell her how I felt and the consequences of the partial shifts. When I finish, I release a long, slow breath, my shoulders dropping as some of the tension leaves them.

There's silence on the other end of the phone, and I check to make sure I still have a connection, "Angie, did you hear all of that?"

"Holy... shit. Thea, that's... I mean, what... How can... Fuck me. I don't even know the questions I want to ask."

"It's been quite a ride."

"You can say that again. I know I told you to give them hell, but that's incredible."

"It is, and now you have to help me."

"Help you? It sounds like you're doing well on your own. What could you need my help with?"

"The true mate bond and if I should accept it now?"

"Er, Thea, this is what you've always dreamed of. Why are you hesitating?"

Again, I spill the inner workings of my mind and all the reasons holding me back. Before I can finish, she interrupts me.

"Thea, honey, breathe. I'm hearing a load of noise from you, but no real reason why you're stalling other than fear."

"Fear? I'm not scared of the bond. I just want to make sure I'm making the right decision for us both."

"Nah, sorry, I don't buy it. You're shitting yourself and using that big brain of yours to come up with logical reasons. Let me ask you something. Do you like him? Do you see yourself having a future with him?"

"Well, yes, but—"

"Ah, you said yes, and that's all you need to know. The buts will always be there until you become more confident in yourself. Before that happens, you'll have to go with your first knee-jerk reaction."

"But what if it's—"

"Do I need to come there and beat some sense into you? No more buts. From everything you've said, he sounds like the perfect guy for you. I mean, for shifter's sake, Thea, he's teaching you to become a trainer, something you've always enjoyed and are incredible at. Not only is he sweet and kind, but he's helping you become stronger."

Until I heard it, I never considered that. He's not asking me to stay at home and raise a family. He wants me to become a trainer and excel in it. In fact, he's actively ensuring my success by guiding me through the process.

"I'm taking from that silence you're now catching up with the reality of the situation," Angie laughs. "Stop overthinking everything. For now, just allow your initial reactions to guide you. I promise they won't steer you wrong."

My eyes well with tears, her voice a comfort and homesickness suddenly strikes me, "I miss having you around."

"Sounds like you've found a fitting replacement," she says, amusement in her voice. "Maybe I should come there so you don't forget about me."

"That will never happen, but if you ever want to, just say the word. I'm kind of a big deal here," I laugh, though I don't believe my own words.

"So, have I missed anything at home?"

"Same as usual. Hearing what's going on with you, your father's behaviour makes a lot more sense now."

"Really, why?"

"He was like a lion with a sore ass when he got back. I'd imagine it had some to do with losing an alpha challenge to the daughter he's called a defect her whole life. He stormed around the place barking demands for the first few days, and then yesterday out of nowhere, took that horrible chair he loves so much and threw it out of the house! Came back out a few minutes later and started to destroy the thing with a hammer. I think the pack is worrying he's becoming unhinged."

I burst into a fit of giggles, remembering what I did to his beloved chair. When I tell Angie, she loses it, too, commenting on my evil genius.

"So everything else been okay? You and Jake still good?"

"Yeah, we've been good. He hasn't asked me yet, but he has been talking about mating and our future."

"That's great. I'm happy for you, Angie."

"It is, yes," she responds, but her voice takes on a more sombre note.

"What is it? What's wrong?"

"It's nothing, I'm just being silly."

"Angie, talk to me. You're always there for me. Let me do the same for you."

"I'm just wondering if mating is the right thing for me now. We've had Mrs Wick and Nora disappear in the last two days. Gone without a trace. The pack wonders if they left their mates and went to live somewhere else. Maybe having a chosen mate isn't all it's cracked up to be."

"They just disappeared. No word to anyone?"

"Mrs Wick had a diary that was found. She wrote about not being settled and wanting something more. We were left wondering if Nora went with her in search of something that would make her happy."

I remember cooking the feast for the Wicks because they were expecting, even if she was unhappy, would she leave her mate when they were expecting their first child? The recent disappearances in the human world come to mind, but Applecross is so far away from normal civilisation that I find it hard to believe she would have been taken.

"It seems odd," I admit. "But their actions shouldn't sway you from your happiness. Before that happened, did you still want to mate with Jake?"

"I did, yes."

"Well then, nothing's changed. You and Jake are great together. We're just as bad as each other, afraid of the unknown and what awaits us in the future."

We talk for the next hour, and the only reason I end the call is when someone knocks on my door. The bond pounds maddeningly in my chest, answering the unspoken question of who it is. When I tell Angie I have to go, she ends the call with one last piece of advice.

"Go find your happiness, Thea."

CHAPTER NINETEEN

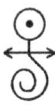

Despite not having had a moment to fully process them, Angie's words linger in my thoughts throughout the morning—Find my happiness. Following the call, Bran and I shared a brief tension-fueled coffee before joining the rest of the group in the canteen. The entire morning unfolded with a sense of normalcy, aside from the time Bran and I shared, which was overshadowed by the persistent urge to mate with him and my partial shifts. Once we joined the others, the distraction provided a different focus, though it was hard for me to completely stop him from invading my thoughts.

We enjoyed breakfast together, exchanging jokes and laughter with the others, and as we headed to work, it dawned on me—this, right here, is my happiness. Bran is my happiness. Kali, the rest of the group, my job, all of it, is my happiness.

Entering The Pit, a small smile tugs at my lips. I am happy and content. Every aspect of this place and the people within it contributes to my happiness, and there's no valid reason to continue postponing what I truly desire.

In response to my thoughts, my animal purrs loudly. I get some questioning looks from the guys, but Bran simply smiles in my direction, not at all caring that his mate is making unnecessary noises. He is utterly perfect, and now that my head and heart appear to be on the same page, I want nothing more than to abandon my job and take what's mine.

Unfortunately, work must come first, so I will stow my desires, be responsible and then take what I want later, provided Bran is on board.

Having made the decision, the morning inches by unbearably slowly, with each passing minute intensifying the pull of the bond. I've partially shifted and remain that way, thanks to observing Bran as he imparts new combat moves to the recruits. Both Bran and Anubis have integrated with their respective groups today to review new combinations and simulate larger-scale scenarios. Witnessing their collaboration is captivating, even if my ability to concentrate is somewhat challenged.

"Thea, care to run through some combat drills with Elias and me?" Bran unexpectedly asks, pulling me out of my wayward thoughts.

Gods, why can't we be alone. "Erm, sure. What did you have in mind?"

"I'm going to fight Elias, and I want you to jump in and defend him whenever the opportunity presents itself. Elias, I want you to keep a close eye on Thea and how she interacts with us. Watch how she intercepts the moves and turns them against me."

Bran is talking me up for a big game, considering he hasn't even seen me fight. Did Castiel tell him exactly how I fight, or does he just have that much confidence in me? Whatever the reason, my animal purrs, happy with this development and Bran's confidence in us.

This is hand-to-hand combat, so there are no gloves, bowing, or timed rounds. It's all out fighting and an opportunity to display as much technique as possible. I watch them go at each other for a few minutes, giving them both time to build up some momentum, but when Elias doesn't move to block a right hook, I step in, hooking my arm around Brans and pulling him back.

I don't give him a second to regain his balance, using his momentum to push him forward so I can swing behind him and put him in a chokehold.

"Don't hold back, will you, babe," he jokes, laughter rumbling through his chest.

I don't mean to be quite so rough, but my nerves are on edge, waiting for the moment I can tell him I'm ready. I relax my grip slightly but don't let him go, enjoying the feeling of his body this close to mine.

"Do you see how she used my momentum against me?" Bran asks Elias. "Now tell me how you would get out of this situation."

Their conversation becomes white noise. All my senses are hyper-focused on Bran, the feel of him, his scent, the pounding of his pulse. I don't know if they've finished talking, but I abruptly let go of Bran and spin him towards me.

"Everything okay, babe?"

If I hear him call me babe one more time, I will combust. The pet name does something to me, and my arousal spikes intensely. Bran growls low in his throat, his grey eyes suddenly flashing orange as he struggles to control his emotions.

"Guys gather round," Anubis suddenly shouts. "Bran and Thea are going to take us through the combinations so you can see how the professionals do it."

My eyes widen in horror at Anubis's suggestion. It's not that I don't want to spar with Bran. I'm just worried I won't be able to control my urges or my animal. Speaking of which, she enjoys this idea very much, that loud purring starting up again as Bran circles around me, the predator in him coming out to play.

"You okay to do this?" He checks.

"Yep, I can do it," I reply, my words clipped.

My animal's emotions surge with exhilaration, and without thinking, I go for it, consequences be damned.

I start with some quick jabs and crosses, all of which he blocks effortlessly. Introducing the combinations the recruits have been working on, I end up clipping him on his hip with one of my kicks. He smirks, looking more turned on than he probably should for the situation we're in. He doesn't hold back either, and I love that he's sparing with me like an equal as I block and move to avoid each hit. He lands one shot to my shoulder, admittedly not very hard.

We continue like this for a few minutes, my tension climbing higher with every glancing blow. Aiming to avoid one of his body shots, his hand brushes against my breast, and I lose my concentration. He takes the opening I present and flips me over his shoulder to pin me to the ground. Though he's technically beat me, I've never been more turned on. With him on top, grinning down at me, I spot the tension around his eyes as they flash between man and beast. Lifting my head off the mat, I slam my lips against his.

I can sense he's shocked when he doesn't immediately respond, but it takes him less than a second to catch up, groaning low when I wrap my arms around his neck and deepen the kiss. I've never been so brazen, but I couldn't stop even if I wanted to. When he subtly grinds his erection between my legs, I whimper.

"Alright, avert your eyes. I think we've all seen enough. Recruits take your starting positions. Bran, Thea, compose yourselves."

Anubis's words penetrate my brain, and I pull away from Bran, feeling slightly embarrassed about how we've behaved in front of the recruits. When I look at Bran, his smile is wicked.

"I need... I want..." Damn it, why can't I tell him that I'm ready.

"Your place or mine?" he asks, apparently understanding my garbled words.

"Mine. Now," I demand, my voice sultry and unrecognisable as the desperation of the bond takes over.

Bran pulls me to my feet before turning to Anubis. "Bro, we're going to need the afternoon off," he tells him, the excitement barely contained within his voice.

"No problem. You guys go do your thing, and congratulations," Anubis smiles proudly. I'm stunned by the emotion displayed in his eyes.

He is genuinely happy for us, and his acceptance of me into his family pulls at a different emotion I, unfortunately, can't examine too closely due to the raging arousal that refuses to be ignored.

We leave The Pit and make it as far as the courtyard before Bran's patience wanes, and without warning, I'm swiftly up in his arms as he charges towards my apartment. He doesn't even wait for the elevator, instead charging up the three flights of stairs like a man on a mission. My animal delights in every second of this display of dominance and once again purrs loudly.

"I love it when you make that sound for me, babe. Now let's see what other noises I can wring out of you."

The ache between my thighs pulses at his words. One touch is all it's going to take for me to unravel. When he reaches my apartment door, I wiggle in his hold, needing to be put down so I can make a proper connection with him. He allows me to slide down his body, and the second my feet touch the floor, my lips meet his in a desperate clash.

This kiss does not start off sweet like last night. This one is fuelled by an all-consuming need. He kisses me thoroughly to the point my legs feel weak, and I break the contact to take in some much-needed air.

"Door, babe," he murmurs against my neck as he turns me round to face the door.

After a few fumbled attempts, I get the door open, and the second I turn to face him, his lips are waiting to pick up where they left off. I jump into his arms, and his hands cradle my ass, squeezing tightly. The kiss grows more aggressive, and my hands slip up his shoulders as he kicks the door shut. Walking us straight to my bedroom, I clutch him closer, the bond taking over rational thought as I grind against the large erection waiting for me.

All too soon, I'm ripped away from him as he tosses me to the bed. His eyes, more orange than grey now, burn with a primal hunger, his pupils enlarging as they drift from my eyes down my body. My heart beats faster when he pulls his shirt over his head. My gaze hungrily rakes over the defined contours of his chest down to the waistband of his trousers. He shoves down his jeans and boxers with no preamble, standing before me naked and proud.

I devour every delicious inch of exposed flesh. His whole body is a work of art. Chiselled six-pack with a light smattering of brown hair that leads down to his happy trail, and that sexy V most toned men seem to have leads to the most impressive cock I've ever seen.

"Condom or not?" he asks as I lay there staring at his very large, very hard cock.

Is that even going to fit? I've never been filled before, and based on his size, I'm wondering if it's something we need to work up to.

"Babe?"

"Sorry, what?" I ask, finally tearing my gaze away from the most gigantic cock. "Oh, err, not," I reply to his question. With the broken connection to my animal, I'm yet to have a heat cycle, so I don't need to worry about the fear of reproducing.

His answering smile causes my nipples to tighten, and he moves with a quick grace to remove my clothes, his hands steady and sure as he lovingly reveals my body. When I'm laid before him in nothing but a shy smile, my hesitance rears its ugly head, but only because of his size.

"Um, Bran," I whisper, mortified I've not mentioned this before. "I haven't, um... haven't had sex before," I say, looking down at him with my head cocked to the side.

"Dear gods, you're going to unman me before we've even started. I figured, based on your past, that might be the case, but hearing it out loud does crazy things to me, babe."

"I'm glad, but... will it fit?"

"We're made for each other, babe, but don't worry, I'll make sure you're ready for me."

He surrounds me with his presence, his weight pressing down on me in the most wonderful way. Our lips meet again, and it's almost like he's trying to consume all of me with a kiss. I can't think straight, can't express what I need from him.

I break the kiss, trying to form some words, yet there is no need. He moves down my body, kissing and stroking my flesh as he goes. I come alive under his touch, arching my back to get closer to him. When he reaches the apex of my thighs and strokes his tongue against my clit, a scream bursts out of me. Before I can get air into my lungs, his mouth latches onto me, and I damn near choke, the indescribable feeling making even breathing hard.

It doesn't take long for my first orgasm to crash through me. There's no build-up, no warning, just the most powerful feeling I've ever experienced. My scream is silent as my back goes rigid, waves upon waves of pleasure flooding me. When I finally gain some composure and begin to breathe again, I open my eyes to see a very happy Bran smiling down at me.

"You look beautiful when you come," he whispers over my lips. A lazy smile spreads across my face as I kiss him, tasting myself on his lips. I suddenly notice my whiskers are out, and when I feel something move beneath my ass, I pull away from our kiss, leaning my forehead against Bran's shoulder as I groan for a different reason.

Of all the times for a partial shift, I was hoping to make it through this experience without my animal's extremities getting in the way.

"Hey, hey," Bran coxes, "Please don't hide from me. I love it when you shift, babe. It's nothing for you to be embarrassed by."

"But my tail..."

"Can I see it? This whole animal look is really doing it for my bear."

I choke out a laugh at the excitement in his eyes and lift my hips a little, revealing the tail I've been trying to hide since it became known I could do this. I study it at the same time Bran does, surprised by the black stripes at the end.

"That doesn't look like a lion's tail," he comments before reaching out to gently caress it.

As with all my animal's body parts, it's as if they have a direct line to my core, and I moan loudly when he does it a second time.

"Oh, babe, we could have some fun with this."

My animal, the bond, and I don't care about fun. All we need is our mate to put out the fire he's started inside us. A little rougher than intended, I bring his mouth to mine, biting his lip as the purr starts up in my chest. The tugging from the bond, which has been getting significantly stronger, lets me know it's no longer satisfied as it becomes unrelenting.

Bran must feel it, too, as his next move is to line himself up with me and smoothly ease his way in. He's gentle, but nothing can stop the pain as he tears past the last barrier between us. He holds steady for a minute, his tongue duelling with mine and making me forget all about the pain.

He moves slowly at first, changing the tempo of his kiss as his cock creates an inferno that has my next orgasm slowly building. I can see the strain in his eyes and in the corded muscles around his neck. He's holding himself back, lovingly making sure I enjoy every stroke. I adore his tenderness, but I need more. I need to see him lose control, the same way I do every time I'm near him. Breaking away from his lips, I trail my tongue softly along the column of his neck before biting him tenderly.

His restraint snaps in an instant, his speed increasing as he lifts my leg and provides a new angle of mind-blowing pleasure. It doesn't take long for the rapture to wreak havoc on my body. When his teeth bite down on my nipple, I lose my mind, grabbing him by the side of his head and clamping my teeth down between his neck and shoulder.

I don't even stop to think about what I'm doing, but when I break the skin, and his blood explodes across my tongue, I detonate into a thousand pieces. The orgasm and his blood mingle together to create a mix so potent that I'm forced to retract my teeth so I can scream.

Bran growls loudly, pounding into me until I feel his teeth break the skin on the column of my neck. The orgasm that was ebbing away abruptly surges through me, and I'm lifted off my back as Bran crushes me to him, a pleasurable fire spreading throughout my body.

When he releases my neck, my eyes meet his and at the height of our combined climax, that's when the bond suddenly snaps inside my chest.

I gasp at the radiant white light wrapping around us, attempting to process the effects of the bond as my orgasm gradually recedes. An extreme rush of emotions fills my heart, and tears well in my eyes as I acknowledge Bran's presence. I not only feel him physically but also his pleasure, his joy and his love for me. It's as if I've rediscovered a lost fragment of myself.

He breathes deeply before gently kissing my lips. "I love you," he whispers tenderly, causing a tear to roll down my face.

He loves me. I can feel it in our bond, and it's the most intoxicating sensation. I am worthy of someone's love.

"I love you too," I respond fiercely, knowing he will feel my words and hear them.

His features light up with happiness as he softly wipes away the fallen tear, "Dreams do come true," he murmurs before kissing me adoringly.

Well, it's about bloody time.

CHAPTER TWENTY

A startled laugh escapes me, "I know, but it was worth the wait." I grin, running my fingers through his messed-up hair.

"Huh?" he says, his brow furrowed as he looks down at me.

Oh gods, don't confuse the poor lad. He's just had sex. His brain cells won't be working properly yet.

What... Who said that?

"Can... Can you hear my thoughts?" I ask Bran, wondering if this is part of the bond that Kali somehow forgot to mention.

He cocks his head to the side, adjusting our position so that we're laying side by side. Bracing himself on his elbow, he studies me. "No, I don't think so. I'm only getting feelings from you at the moment. Why?"

Maybe I'm just imagining things. Great sex could mess with a person's head.

Honey, it may have been great sex, but that doesn't change the fact I'm here.

What the hell! Okay, I am absolutely not imagining this. Is that? Could it be?

Come on, sweetheart, catch up.

"Why do you suddenly feel like you're panicking? We moved a bit fast, but—"

"Bran, just shut up a minute," I quickly cut him off.

Wow, real nice. You get laid once, and you're telling him to shut up.

Oh my God, is that... is that my animal? Thinking that makes me feel ridiculous, but what else could it be.

And she gets it. Well done, honey. Nice to finally speak to you.

I jump up off the bed, pacing as shock travels through me. Bran is frowning at me but isn't saying anything. Is that because I told him to shut up?

Probably.

Oh, this is so surreal. I can't believe I'm hearing her. The bond with Bran has obviously broken down some of the restrictions as it did for Kali. I stop my pacing when something occurs to me. Can I shift?

I seriously hope so because I'm sick of being stuck in here.

"Babe, I can feel several things coming from you, care to fill me in?" Bran finally breaks his silence to ask me.

"Umm, yeah. I can hear my animal," I explain, astonishment lacing my voice.

Bran jumps from the bed, his massive cock swinging between his legs, and suddenly, it's all I can focus on. Even semi-erect, it's still huge.

Now you, my girl, are one lucky shifter. That is one fine-looking specimen.

I snort as Bran takes my face in his hands, his eyes studying me with concern, "What do you mean you can hear her?"

Not that bright, though, is he?

Ignoring my animal, I answer Bran's question, "She's talking to me, in my head."

"Are you sure it's not your bond with Kali?"

"No, it's not," I confirm with complete confidence. I would know if Kali was speaking to me through the bond. "Why do you ask?"

He still appears concerned, but I don't understand why. Surely, this is a good thing. We've broken down a barrier, one I'm hoping gets me closer to shifting.

"Well, babe, it's just... normally, we don't hear our animals talk to us because they are us."

"Oh."

Don't worry about that. We're special.

We are? How are we special?

It's hard to explain. I just know that we are.

Reassuring, thanks.

"This is still an amazing breakthrough," Bran proclaims, his excitement trickling through our new bond. "A closer connection to your animal is incredible. Are you okay?"

"I think so," I nod. "It's a little weird to have someone else talking in my head."

Try living for twenty-one years in someone else's body.

"I wonder if you can shift now?" Bran's tangible joy for me is adorable, and I briefly forget all about my animal as I stand on my tiptoes to meet his lips. The pulsing and torture from the bond may be gone, but I'm very much aware of my newly mated status and the fact my mate stands in front of me completely naked.

As much as I would enjoy a second round, you can't put me back in the box now I'm out.

Feeling Bran's cock growing steadily against me and his arousal through the bond, it's with great reluctance I pull back to break our kiss. "Can you give me just one minute," I tell him, backing away to the bathroom and shutting the door before he has time to answer.

I stand in front of the mirror, taking in my wild hair and rosy complexion. Leaning closer, I study my eyes intently, taking in the golden hue I've never seen before.

Okay... animal, do you have a name?

No. You've always called me animal, which is a bit rude, by the way.

Well considering I don't know what you are, and I believed we were broken, I was afraid to give you a real name, thought it might make things harder.

I know, and I understand.

Wait! Can you tell me what we are?

Nope.

Of course, that would be too easy.

And our path has never been easy.

Don't I know it. I can't believe I'm talking to you. It's truly amazing to finally connect with you this way. Only... I've literally just bonded with my true mate—

Our.

What?

Our true mate, he's mine too.

Yes, sorry, our true mate. I was hoping to spend some more time getting to explore the bond—

You mean having sex. You want to have more sex.

Ahh, yes, I do. I'm sorry. I know this is all new to us both, but if you could just bear with me and maybe stop talking while I get to know our mate, as soon as we're done, we can go outside and see if I can shift. Deal?

Charming, putting your mate before me, but fine. I'm only agreeing because that man is sex on legs, and I enjoy the show. You get two more rounds before I start singing.

I'm not even going to think about the enjoy the show comment.

Thank you. I appreciate it.

Quickly splashing my face with some cold water, I take one last look at my golden eyes and head back out to the bedroom. Bran is still completely naked and lying on my bed with his hands behind his head. When he sees me, his smile spreads further as his eyes rake over my naked body.

I stroll over to the side of the bed and, with confidence I didn't know I possessed, climb straight onto his lap. His eyes widen briefly before a lazy smirk pulls at his lips, "Are we going to see if you can shift?"

"Not yet. I've made a deal with my animal," I tell him, running my hands up his chest. "I haven't had my fill of you."

"Hell yes," he says, palming my breasts and deliciously torturing my nipples. Bran takes the lead like an expert puppet master, working me into a frenzy before lining himself up to enter me again. We spend the next few hours wrapped up in each other, and he brings a whole new meaning to the word ecstasy. As promised, my animal stays quiet, but before I can test our shifting theory, I fall asleep snuggled safely in my mate's arms.

***

Hey. Hey, Althea. Come on, wakey, wakey. You need to get up now.

What? Who's talking so loudly?

It's me, you know, your animal. The one you were supposed to take outside.

I startle upright in bed as a flood of previous revelations rushes back to me, and I realise I can hear her! Memories of the incredible things Bran did to my body throughout the afternoon and night come rushing back. We haven't left my bed since yesterday afternoon, and as I turn to gaze at his peacefully sleeping form, an irresistible urge compels me to reach out and brush aside the strands of hair that have fallen onto his face.

Hey, get your hands off him and let's go see if we can shift!

Okay, give me a minute to wake up.

Silently making my way to the bathroom, I attend to my needs, dressing and brushing my teeth. My animal stays quiet, but I sense her impatience beneath the surface.

Because I've been patient for twenty-one years, now it's my turn.

Sorry. You're right. Thank you for waiting. I know that can't have been easy.

Hmm, it wasn't all bad. Our mate is a virile creature, and he certainly knows how to get—

Okay, that's enough. Something about you watching makes it feel a little creepy.

Her laughter in the back of my mind is strange, but I find myself smiling all the same. Communicating with her after all these years means so much to me. I will take all the creepy comments she has for us to continue with this progress.

Good to know.

When I return from the bathroom, Bran is slowly waking up, "Good morning, my gorgeous mate. Where are you off to so early?"

My heart flutters at hearing him call me his mate. "My animals had enough of waiting, so we're going outside to see if I can shift."

He stretches before throwing the covers back and getting out of bed. When presented with all his naked glory, I find myself torn again.

Oh no, you don't, it's my turn now.

"Give me a second to get dressed, and I'll be right there with you," he says, walking over to me and taking my face in his hands for a toe-curling kiss.

He heads for the bathroom, and I leisurely walk into the kitchen to prepare drinks for both of us, a broad smile gracing my face at the joy of having him in my home.

You want to be careful smiling like that all the time. Your face might get stuck that way.

I don't mind if it does. I've never been this happy before.

I know. It's not easy watching someone you love go through everything you have.

There's a twinge of sorrow in my heart for the things she's witnessed. She has experienced it all alongside me, and she, too, has never been able to distance herself from those experiences.

I would do it all again, Althea. At least sometimes, I could give you peace when you needed it. Fair warning, if we can shift and I ever see your father again, I'm biting him on his ass.

I would pay good money to see that.

When Bran comes out to the kitchen, he accepts the drink I've prepared, initiating a kiss before swiftly consuming almost the entire cup. Without delay, we make our way outside and venture towards the forest. Throughout the walk, Bran maintains a firm grip on my hand, and the contentment and happiness radiating from him leaves me a tad emotional.

I have a true mate, a wonderful one too. All those fantasies as a young girl have paid off tenfold. I never imagined it would feel like this, but Bran's right. Dreams do come true.

Oh dear gods, you're not going to be one of them disgustingly in love people, are you? You need to remember that you're still a strong alpha.

What! Alpha? What do you mean? Is that how I was able to stand up to my father? Except for the occasional feelings I experience from you, I don't feel like we're an alpha.

I can assure you, we are definitely an alpha.

"I think this should be far enough. You ready to give it a shot?" Bran asks before I can speak to her more about that comment. We've paused a few feet within the forest's perimeter, the trees extending for miles and the scent triggering a surge of happiness in my animal.

Oh yes, yes, this is the perfect place. Let me out of here. I've been dying to run through these trees.

Okay, but try not to get your hopes up, just in case.

"How should I do this?" I ask Bran nervously.

Placing his hands on my shoulders, he turns me towards him, "When you partially shift, you said you feel the tingles. That's the point where you let go and embrace the transformation. Imagine your animal coming forward as you retreat to the background." He kisses my lips softly after imparting his wisdom and takes a few steps back.

Okay, I can do that.

Are you ready?

Twenty-one years ready, let's shift.

Taking off my clothes, I smile, ignoring the sensations coming from Bran through our bond. I shut my eyes, concentrating on my animal, exerting all my energy to coax her forward. We struggle with each other, both of us a little too eager. After a few deep breaths, I attempt again, but there's no response, no tingles to signify a shift is even close. When I open my eyes, I gaze directly at Bran, a sense of disappointment washing over me.

"It's okay, babe. It's your first time, and it might only happen as you two grow closer." He moves forward to embrace me, and I soak in his reassurance.

You're not trying hard enough. You only partially shift when you're emotional. Get Bran to fuck you and see if that works.

Laughter erupts from me at her suggestion. Could that work?

"What? What did she say?" Bran asks, releasing me from his arms.

"She thinks I need to be experiencing some form of emotion for it to happen. She suggested we have sex," I giggle, thinking how ridiculous this all is.

His loud laughter makes me jump and his amusement through the bond is infectious, "Oh, babe, I think me and your animal are going to get on tremendously."

Oh yes, we are.

"So, care to help me out?" I flash him a cheeky grin.

His wicked smirk does things to me on its own, but when he reaches for me and claims my lips, I melt into him. The kiss becomes heated as Bran plays with my nipples, touching and squeezing before they trace lower. When he gently glides over my clit, I moan into his mouth. He pushes two fingers inside me, finding that spot that makes me see stars. I'm panting as he works me harder, and the beginning of an orgasm builds. I contrate hard not to lose myself to Bran and the sensations he creates within me.

The tingles come on suddenly, only this time all over me. I reluctantly but quickly yank his hand away as I give in to the sensation.

In my peripheral vision, I notice Bran taking a step back, but that's the final image I register as my body starts snapping and reshaping. The pain is indescribable and is certainly enough to make me forget about my almost orgasm. I seem to endure it forever, my entire body ablaze as bones and muscles undergo the intense transformation process.

When I regain my senses, I'm breathing heavily, the remnants of pain still lingering in echoes.

Holy shit, we did it.

Raising my head, I take a moment to reorient myself as I find I'm closer to the ground than usual. I discover I'm now on four legs, and my perspective reveals tan fur adorned with black spots. My vision has sharpened, and my sense of smell is heightened. Catching a whiff of something pleasant, I lower my nose to the ground and follow the scent. As I locate the source, I gaze up at Bran, observing me with a broad smile.

"My mate is a magnificent, beautiful cheetah."

CHAPTER TWENTY-ONE

I'M A CHEETAH. How is that even possible? My father is a lion, and my mother was a leopard. How the hell did they produce a cheetah?

It can happen. I know your father has lion in his blood for generations, but perhaps there is some connection to cheetahs on your mother's side.

Since I won't be talking to my father anytime soon, and no one else knew my mother, it's unlikely I'll ever find out.

Cheetahs are incredible animals.

Of course. I'm not disappointed if that's what you're thinking, more shocked. I was expecting a lion, and now I've had time to process, I'm thrilled that's not the case.

As my cheetah circles around Bran, exploring the surroundings and nuzzling his leg, I assess my own state. I am still myself, retaining distinct thoughts and feelings, yet I sense her emotions more profoundly. Her joy and excitement filter through me as if they were my own, but with concentration, I can distinguish the difference. I share her sense of smell, and my eyesight and hearing mirror hers. I am a cheetah, but she holds the reins of control.

Damn right I do, it's my time now.

I playfully roll my eyes at her enthusiasm, but the joy of witnessing her freedom fills me with delight. Achieving the transformation and allowing my animal to be herself is a major accomplishment. In such a short time since arriving here, we've managed what I initially believed to be impossible. So many questions still linger, and I'm not naïve enough to think our damage is entirely eradicated, but our progress is undeniable.

Bran suddenly crouches down to our level, his hands tenderly rubbing soothing circles behind our ears before he leans his forehead against ours. My cheetah responds with a deep sense of respect and love, and I can't help but wonder if Bran can feel it.

To my confirmation, the same emotions are transmitted through our bond, and I sense my cheetah and Bran forging a connection that only true mates could share. As I immerse myself in their emotions and my own feelings for them, I detect a subtle undercurrent of longing from Bran. When my cheetah withdraws our head from him and tilts it to the side, I know she's picked up on it, too.

"You are the most beautiful cheetah I have ever seen," he says with reverence before stretching to his full height. "My bear and I would love to connect with you. Would you mind if I shift?"

My cheetah meows our response, only the sound is not what I would expect. Admittedly, I don't know much about cheetahs, but the sound is not like a house cat. It's more of a bird's chirp, and I can't stop the giggle that escapes.

Hey! I can growl, too, if the need arises.

I'm sure you can. I was simply surprised to hear that sound come from a ferocious cheetah.

I'll show you ferocious if you carry on.

I'm sorry, I'm sorry. It was adorable.

I feel her annoyance through the bond and smirk to myself before my mind is consumed by my mate. Bran has started removing his clothes to allow for the shift, and my cheetah and I enjoy the show. When we begin to circle him and purr, I worry about her getting too close when he's in this delicate situation.

Don't scratch him up. I like his human form.

You don't have to worry. Surprisingly enough, I do, too.

Is that normal? Shouldn't you be grossed out by humans?

No, it doesn't work that way with a bonded one. You love whatever form they have.

That's good to know. Please be nice to his bear. I haven't met him yet.

I can't promise anything, I'm afraid.

Watching Bran shift into his bear is like observing the master in how to do it right, the change between human to animal is seamless and over in less than ten seconds. It's almost laughable the height difference between our two animals and I wonder if fate or destiny got a good laugh out of pairing us together.

It doesn't seem to bother either animal that they're not the same. My cheetah circles Bran's massive black bear, rubbing herself against him as she goes. With very little grace, Bran's bear falls to his ass, his huge paws resting behind our head. He carefully guides us closer, placing his forehead against ours.

As with Bran before, I feel respect, happiness and love coming from his bear and realise I am witnessing the bond between our animals. To think we might never have got to experience this if the bond didn't work, if the restrictions didn't waver as they did with Kali. Observing this moment between them brings tears to my eyes, and through the bonds with our animals and as mates, there are a few moments of complete quiet and peace.

My cheetah pulls away first, eager to be free and have fun, something that Bran seems to pick up on when they start to play together. Bran's bear stays on the ground, trying to reach for her as she quickly evades his paws and jumps around him. They play like this for a few minutes before my cheetah licks Bran's bear and then turns towards the forest.

I need to run.

There is a deep desperation in her voice, and after a quick look back to Bran's bear, he chuffs, understanding what's about to happen. She turns back to the forest and takes off.

I'm not stupid. I realise cheetahs are fast, but when you experience 0 to 60 in three seconds, it takes a moment or two for your brain to catch up. It's as if we've been shot from a gun as we hurtle across the forest floor. I close my eyes, the dizzying sensation only lasting a few seconds until I adjust enough to open them again.

How can you even see where the trees are when you're going so fast!

Instinct, Honey. Now focus, use my eyes and sense my movements. Fall into the speed, and it will soon feel like you're the one in control.

Following her instructions and clearing my mind, I immerse myself in the run. The pounding of our paws, the wind as it whips by us and the keen eyesight that allows us to see details I would have never picked up on.

The wind is different when there are obstacles in the way. I'd love to go faster, but in such a tightly packed area, it would be difficult, and as this is my first time in twenty-one years, we better not push too hard.

I think this is fast enough, thank you. Definitely fast enough.

Her joy is contagious as we loop back around the forest. Our sense of smell is stronger than ever, and I easily identify the moment we pass by the canteen, the scent of food easy to detect even from this distance. She starts to slow somewhat, still travelling at ridiculous speeds, but the landscape in front doesn't move so fast as she begins sniffing at the ground.

What are you looking for?

Food.

Okay, we can go to the canteen and get some, but we'll need to shift back.

I don't want that rubbish. I want real food. This forest has no large prey, so I must settle for a rabbit.

What! You can't eat a rabbit. They're so cute!

Oh, shifter spirit, help us. I need to eat in this form to keep my energy up, so you will have to get used to it. By now, we should have already had many hunting sessions together.

She's right. We should have been through this already. I won't stop her from making up for lost time when none of this is her fault.

I am sorry. I didn't mean to make you feel bad. What has happened between us is not your fault either. But I do need to hunt.

It's fine. I'm okay with it. I'll be a bystander for this bit. It's not like I'm the one that will be killing Thumper.

She chuffs in amusement at the reassurances I tell myself but stops suddenly when she catches the scent she wants. A rich, meaty aroma makes my own mouth water, and I try hard not to let it draw me in. Crouching low, she slinks across the forest floor, stomach dragging on the ground. When she stops again, I see the rabbit she has in her sights.

I do not condone rabbit hunting, but the thrill of excitement that runs through her is hard to ignore. I hold my breath with morbid anticipation, waiting to see what she'll do next.

She watches the rabbit for a long time, tracking its movements and gradually stalking closer. One second, we're completely still, and in the next, she pounces. I say pounces, but it feels more like flying. She lands with her mouth already around the rabbit's neck and she gives it a rough shake to kill it.

I feel bad until the smell hits me. It's similar to chicken, and when my mouth starts to water, I realise I haven't eaten since yesterday myself. She doesn't worry about delicately pulling parts of the rabbit off, immediately tearing into it and chowing down. Honestly, I'm so confused. On the one hand, it's disgusting, and on the other, it tastes delicious.

When she finishes her meal, she goes hunting for more, presumably making up for lost time. Through our journey into the forest, we soon come across a stream, and she takes a minute to have a drink and clean herself up a little.

Got to look good for our mate.

I don't think our mate would care what we look like.

Well, I care. I am still a female.

We need to get back now. I have work soon. Cheetah... we need to give you a name. I can't keep calling you animal or cheetah all the time. What do you want it to be?

Cheetah is fine.

It's too impersonal, what about Spot?

Are you seriously trying to give me a dog's name?

Okay, what about Shea? Has a nice ring to it, Thea and Shea?

Perhaps I've been spending too much time with Kali. I've heard all about the adventures of Kali and Tali, and clearly, the idea is rubbing off on me.

As long as it's not Spot, anything is fine.

Her tone makes it seem as if she doesn't care, but when you're bonded the way we are, there's no mistaking the trace of happiness coming from her when I mentioned Shea.

You know I can feel your emotions, right?

Shut up.

I chuckle at my big, ferocious Shea and feel her delight as we return to Bran. We find him where we left him, still in his bear form, sleeping against a rock. I laugh at the absurdity of his giant bear taking a nap in the forest first thing in the morning. Must have been worn out from last night.

You sound very pleased with yourself about that.

Maybe a little.

I figured the extra rabbit she was carrying with her was for later, but when Shea goes bounding over to Bran, she drops it in his lap.

Aww, you got it for him. That's so sweet.

Shut up.

Bran's bear starlets awake when the rabbit falls into his lap, growling low before looking at Shea's gift. If I'm not mistaken, it looks as though he's smiling. He devours the rabbit even quicker than Shea did, and when he's done, both animals sit next to each other, cleaning their paws.

It's a sweet and comfortable moment between us all, one I'll keep with me forever. Something about being in our animal forms and being together settles another piece inside of me as I imagine this is what it feels like to be a real member of a pack. In a way, I'm glad I never shifted in my old pack. Being here with my true mate and having his support throughout the process has made the experience unforgettable.

After our late night and, shall we say, physical activities, I could easily fall asleep nuzzled against Bran's bear. Sadly, we need to get ready for work. Bran must have the same thought as he carefully shuffles away from us before shifting back into a stunningly gorgeous man.

Okay, Shea, let's do our thing.

I wait and wait, but nothing happens.

What's going on?

Don't ask me. You only shift when you're feeling heightened emotions. I don't know how to give you back control.

Well, I can't ask Bran to do what he did before. That's just gross.

"Babe, you okay in there?"

Shea lets out a chirp meow to communicate that no, we are not.

"I'm going to assume you're having some issues transitioning back. You need to relax and push forward in your mind, imagine returning to your human form, picture your legs, arms and so on."

I do as he says and picture myself returning, but nothing happens.

Are you stopping this?

Me? No. I'm tired and could do with a nap. If you take over, then I can have one.

I try several more times, but there's no sensation for me to grab onto, no tingles or connection I can make to return to my human form. Am I going to be stuck this way all the time because of these goddamn restrictions playing havoc on us?

I don't think so. It's more likely because we've never done it before, so it may take longer. Either that, or you can only do it when aroused.

Shea yawns as she lays down, padding our paws and getting comfortable.

Hey! Not helping, Shea. We need to turn back.

Well, when you figure it out, let me know.

"Maybe we could head over to The Pit and ask Anubis for help. He'll be alpha soon and might be able to force the shift," Bran suggests reluctantly.

What do you think, Shea?

I doubt that will work. I'm more alpha than him.

How do you know?

Just trust me on this.

We need to try something. Could you please get up and at least try.

Fine. But when this doesn't work, I'm taking a nap.

Following Bran through the village toward the training centre, numerous pairs of eyes cast glances in our direction. Instead of shying away or donning my usual facade, Shea confidently strides amongst them as if she owns the place. Rather than being unsettled by the stares, she revels in the attention, and her confidence sends a surge of energy along our bond.

When we arrive at The Pit all the guys are present, and thankfully, the recruits are yet to arrive. Anubis sees us first, a smile pulling at his mouth until he catches sight of me and his brows furrow. As the rest of the guys turn towards us, surprise, shock and a little amusement from Castiel register on their faces.

"Urr, Bran, care to explain why you have a cheetah rubbing against your legs?" Anubis asks wearily, taking a slow step towards Bran.

See, I'm a total badass. Even this soon-to-be alpha fears me.

I don't think he fears you, Shea. He is likely confused and concerned for his brother.

As Bran explains to the guys what happened, Shea sits smugly at his side, our tail swinging lazily from side to side. I can sense through the bond that she enjoys Bran recounting the details of how she came to be. When Bran goes one further by describing how incredible we are, I can practically taste her satisfaction. My mate has no idea how perfect he is, both for me and my cheetah. The group offer their congratulation to Shea and me for finally being able to shift, and when Bran asks Anubis to help me transform back, he gladly accepts and gets down to eye level with us.

"Hey, Sis," he addresses us with a grin. Shea cocks our head to the side as my heart fills with happiness at hearing him call us that.

We have family, Shea! A mate, a brother and a sister-in-law.

I enjoy your happiness, Althea, but I think we are about to disappoint our new brother. He is not strong enough to force the shift.

How can you possibly know that?

Alpha's can sense these things. You are too emotional to feel it now, but tapping into our alpha energy is something you must learn.

"Let's give this a go, shall we," Anubis continues. "When you feel my power, you might find it strange. If you don't resist, it shouldn't hurt too much. Are you ready?"

Shea acknowledges by getting to our feet.

When you feel the command, explore our bond and see if you can sense our alpha power.

"Shift," he demands. The alpha command rolls over us, stronger than when my father used to command me. However, before it can take hold, a heat rises within me, within Shea, and the command disappears, lost to the wind.

Told you.

You sound way too smug right now.

"Shift," Anubis says again, with more power slamming into us. Nothing, not even a slight pull.

Just how powerful are we, Shea?

She doesn't answer as Anubis continues to stare back at us. After another minute, he turns to Bran, "It must be the restrictions stopping my commands from getting through."

Yeah, that's not it, alpha.

What aren't you telling me, and what the hell are we supposed to do now?

CHAPTER TWENTY-TWO

"No offence, Anubis, but you're not actually an alpha yet. It may take more power to force the shift.

The others snicker at Bran's comment, and I see the moment he regrets his choice of words. "I just mean, maybe because of Thea's restrictions, it needs to be an official alpha."

Anubis laughs and pats him on the back, "Don't worry, I know what you meant. Despite the fact I've never had a problem with it before, maybe you're right. Perhaps you need to ask Father."

At the mention of their father, my ears prick up. I don't want my first encounter with my future father-in-law and alpha to be when I need his help. What kind of impression would that give. I was hoping to appear composed and well... stronger.

We are strong.

You say that, but right now, we look like a pup who can't control their shift.

Fair point.

"—I'm sure Thea doesn't want to be stuck this way." I only catch the end of Bran's conversation, but he's not wrong.

Hey, I've been stuck in you from birth. You've only been like me for two hours.

Not the point, Shea, I still have a life to live. I want you to be free, but I still need to be me. Don't forget this is my first taste of freedom in twenty-one years, too.

Touché.

The sound of scuffling feet captures my attention, Shea's exceptional sense of hearing allowing me to determine the recruits are approaching. If I'm meant to lead these people, showing them we cannot shift is not the impression I want to give.

Shea, we should go before they get here. Get Bran's attention. We can hide out in the staff room for now.

Hide? Alphas do not hide.

We're not exactly behaving like an alpha, Shea. Do you want them to see that we can't shift back?

How embarrassing.

Shea nudges Bran's leg, and when he looks down, she tries to convey that we need to leave, flicking her head to the side. Judging by the confused expression on his face, I don't think he gets it.

Ha! He's a male. Of course, he doesn't get it.

With a huff, she trots toward the staff room door and scrapes at it, signalling our intentions. I see when he comprehends and rushes over to open the door for us. Once within the confines of the staff room, Shea leaps onto the couch, pawing at it before settling onto the plush surface.

Might as well rest and give you time to think of a way out of this.

Oh, of course, you leave this to me.

Bran stares at me momentarily, then concludes that I will obviously be here while he has a job to do.

He bends down in front of us and scratches behind our ears. It feels fantastic, and when the purring starts, I'm not sure if it comes from Shea or me. "We'll figure this out, I promise," he says softly.

Shea surprises us both when she leans forward and licks his face.

Did you just kiss him?

No, I licked him, and now he's mine.

Her tone is so serious I can't tell if she's being sarcastic or not.

I'm not.

He smiles blindingly before kissing the top of our head and standing. "Don't worry, babe, I won't be too long. I appreciate the situation is not ideal, and we'll have to work through it, but you should know, I am extremely proud of you."

And he is. I can feel it from our bond. His love, pride and slight amusement all come through to me, and if it wasn't for my current predicament, I would explain how much it means to me. Instead, I push my love and gratitude towards him, hoping I convey, without words, how grateful I am for him.

When he leaves and the door closes, I'm annoyed not to be going with him. I've only been shadowing him for two days, and the last time I saw the recruits, I was trying to hump my mate. I don't want them to think I'm a slacker or that I can't control myself, yet at this moment, those things are true.

The job will still be there tomorrow. Enjoy the rest.

It will take some time to adjust to you hearing all my thoughts.

I've heard them since you were born. I simply haven't been able to respond before.

Will you tell me why you think you're more alpha than Anubis?

It's hard to explain. It's instinct, something I am sure of. If you were hoping to join their pack, I'm afraid I wouldn't be settled.

What? Why? You were fine with being part of my father's pack.

Oh no, I wasn't. I just couldn't do anything about it. This is different, now I'm free I can only be in a pack where the alpha is more powerful than I, or we form our own pack.

You make it sound so simple. Who would want to be in our pack when there's already an established pack here?

It's not something we need to worry about for now. We can cross that bridge when we come to it.

But what about the madness that can set in without a pack.

As an alpha, we would not be affected by that.

I'm on the verge of questioning her meaning when I catch Anubis speaking. Despite the considerable distance between us, the clarity with which I hear him is a bizarre sensation. He's informing the recruits I won't be joining them today. It's so frustrating not to be out there with them.

I eavesdrop as they commence their activities and soon pick up on some chatter among the recruits. One voice is instantly recognisable—Jared. Although I've only been observing them for a couple of days, Jared stands out due to his undeniable arrogance. He seems to believe he doesn't need to follow instructions like the others, often paying little attention when Bran gives guidance. I hear him speaking with another recruit in hushed tones, but I catch most of what he's saying.

"She can't even be bothered to show up. Who thought having a woman as a trainer would be a good idea. She's probably on her period," Jared sniggers.

I may not be off to the best start with this job, but it's not like I'm responsible for my own group yet. My not being there is not affecting anyone directly. And what does being a woman have to do with anything! My anger rises at his sexist comments, and Shea lets out a low growl.

Should I rip his head off and deliver it to his parents?

Not yet.

I continue to listen, and it only takes a few more minutes before Jared opens his mouth again, "The guys all seem to think she's some badass trainer, but she looks weak to me. One punch, and she'd be on her ass. She would look good on her ass, that's for sure," he cackles to whoever he's talking too.

I'm used to judgment from others and being called names, but something about this kid speaking about me this way causes my heart rate to increase and my blood to boil. Perhaps it's because I'm mated now, or maybe my emotions are quicker to rise. Whatever the reason, his comments do have an effect on me.

As anger surges forward, I don't even have a chance to get up from the couch as my muscles and bones start to snap and reshape. It takes considerable effort not to scream out in pain, and when the transformation is complete, I'm a panting, naked mess.

"Shifter gods, that hurts," I mutter, pulling myself up on the couch.

So, arousal to get me out and anger to get me back in. Good to know.

I bark out a laugh at Shea's simple way of summarising the situation. I suppose if I stick to those guidelines for the time being, it might work. Now, if only I was dressed and could teach Jared what it means to be a decent human being.

I meander through the staff room, attempting to locate something to cover myself. If anyone other than Bran walks in, they're in for an unexpected sight. I come across a spare set of the recruits' uniforms in the equipment room. After a brief sniff test, I decide to put them on. In situations like these, beggars can't be choosers, but I draw the line at wearing something that reeks of someone else's sweat.

After helping myself to some refreshments, I ponder my options. I could join the others, stopping any further snide comments Jared might have, or I could stay here until lunch and make a discreet exit. The idea of sneaking out doesn't sit well with me, and Anubis has already informed them I won't be present today. I don't want to contradict his words. Besides, I am feeling a bit drained. Who knew shifting took so much out of you.

I did.

I roll my eyes at her response. She sounds drowsy, which isn't helping my own tired state. Pacing around the tables, I reflect on everything that has unfolded in the last twenty-four hours. I have a new bond with my true mate, a connection I've not had much time to savour. Then there's Shea—hearing her voice and experiencing my first shift has been nothing short of extraordinary. I never realised how much I was missing out on. Sure, it always hurt that I couldn't reach her, but I didn't truly grasp what I was missing. Now, the thought of someone taking her away is unbearable. I can't fathom life without her.

I am a true shifter, or at least, to some extent. It appears I still can't shift at will, and that limitation must be tied to the restrictions. The bond with Bran has undoubtedly helped, but a barrier still prevents the complete connection to my shifter side. I suppose it's logical, considering Kali also struggles with mastering her powers completely.

We need to figure out who the hell would do this to us and why? I wonder if I should go help Oberon today. I could—

For the love of the Gods, will you be quiet! Seriously, I'm trying to sleep. Sit down and rest. You can't do anything until the recruits go on lunch anyway, and you've already said you're feeling tired.

I pause my pacing, biting my lips to stop the laughter that wants to burst out over her attitude. Cranky cheetah. Moving to the couch, I sit, figuring it can't hurt to rest my eyes for a few minutes.

***

The press of gentle lips against my neck is what wakes me, and I moan, angling my head to give Bran better access.

"Did you sleep well, babe?" He says between kisses.

"Hmmm," is my only response as his lips slide softly across my skin. When he chuckles lightly against me, it sends goosebumps across my upper body.

He trails his hand through my hair and tugs slightly at the roots, the action causing me to grab hold of him and kiss him with wild abandon. He groans into the kiss, kneeling between my legs on the couch as I pull myself closer to him.

"Ahem." Someone announces from the open staff room door. "Mind if we come in, or are you planning on using the communal couch to devour each other." I know the deep, rumbling voice belongs to Balbur, and when I pull my lips away from Bran's and look over, amusement shines in his eyes.

"Sorry, not sorry," I tell him with a grin. He huffs good-naturedly and walks into the room, followed shortly by the rest of the guys. I'm surprised to see Oberon in attendance and without his laptop! I figured they went everywhere together. They all offer me their congratulations on being mated and my ability to shift, and when Bran takes a seat beside me, his chest puffs up in pride, the same emotion coming from our bond.

"So, Thea, any idea on what it was that helped you shift back?" Anubis asks with interest.

"Oh, um... It was my emotions that seemed to trigger it." I don't elaborate any further because I don't want Bran to know that hearing Jared did it.

Keeping secrets from our mate?

No, not entirely. I just want the chance to deal with him myself. If Bran finds out, I won't have the opportunity to.

I like it. We will see that he pays for his disrespect.

"The same with Kali, too," Oberon speaks up, pulling me away from my conversation with Shea. "I wonder why your emotions seem to be the catalyst."

"Wish I knew, Oberon. I really do. Are you any closer to figuring anything out?"

"Unsure at this stage. I would like you and Kali to review some texts I've found and see if they trigger anything."

"Sure, just let me know when."

Turning back to Bran, who is watching me and playing with a piece of my hair, I smile up at him, "So what's on the agenda this afternoon? Can I pick the training back up now I've sorted myself out?"

"Erm, babe, it's the evening. We're finished for the day."

"What? It felt like I only slept for an hour. How can the whole day be gone?"

"You looked so peaceful when we came in at lunch. I didn't want to disturb you. The first few shifts can drain your energy, and I thought you could use the rest."

"It's fine. I guess that also explains why it feels like I have a hole in my stomach."

"Yep, you'll burn off a lot more calories in shifter form, especially considering how fast you are. The rabbit you caught will only sustain her for a short time. She'll get substance from the food you eat, but you'll have to hunt with her again soon."

I agree. If you don't eat soon, I may... force a shift... and go hunting.

Shea still sounds drowsy and distorted. Her lack of energy is also worrying.

Do you feel this way because you need to eat?

Maybe?

"Bran, if I've slept nearly all day, why does Shea seem so lacklustre?" I ask, noticing the bond between Shea and me feels no different.

Bran gazes at me with confusion before realisation dawns on him, "You named her Shea?" He looks at me with an expression that suggests he finds it adorable, which is puzzling. What's wrong with naming her Shea?

Anubis interjects, providing his own thoughts on the matter. "Our animals are an extension of us. We don't typically give them separate names," he explains.

"Oh. I figured it was better than calling her animal. Calling her Thea just doesn't seem right."

"You call her whatever you want, babe," Bran says, glaring at Anubis. "And to answer your question, she will be exhausted. It's the first time she's been able to run, and it will have taken a lot out of her. More sleep and some food, she will perk right up."

What he said.

"Do you remember the first time you took your wolf for a run?" Bran asks, grinning over at Anubis.

"How did I know you would mention that," Anubis grumbles. "I can confirm it is perfectly normal, Thea. After my wolf and I first ran together, it took him nearly two days to recover. I thought something was wrong with him, and you could say I got a little upset."

"He burst into my parents' bedroom in tears," Bran finishes, causing the rest of us to laugh.

"Thank you for sharing that with me, Anubis. I do feel a little better now."

He nods and smiles at me softly. Standing, he heads over to the couch and clips Bran on the back of the head, setting off another round of laughter.

"Come on, babe, let's go fill your stomach till you can't move," Bran proposes, taking my hand and pulling me from the couch.

"Now, that is a plan I can get on board with."

CHAPTER TWENTY-THREE

My cheeks have barely hit the seat at our usual table in the canteen when Kali's excitement travels through our bond, and she comes barrelling over to me with a broad grin.

"You badass, a freaking cheetah! I'm so happy for you."

Her happiness travels through our bond, and when I stand to accept her hug, I notice my arms are covered in fur. "That's new."

"Still partially shifting then," she asks, inspecting the soft beige fur.

"I've not long since changed back, but... I have no idea what's brought this on."

I wasn't feeling anything particularly strong except Kali's happiness for me. Could that have triggered the shift?

"It will sort itself out. So, tell me everything!"

Kali and I take a seat, and we're completely engrossed in our conversation as I recount my morning with Shea. Kali asks me lots of questions, continuously commenting that she can't wait to meet her. A few minutes into the conversation, my partial shift disappears, and

I choose to ignore the randomness of it all. Bran fulfils his intention, returning to the table with three plates loaded up for me.

"Erm, Bran, I'm hungry, but I'm not sure all this is necessary."

"Trust me, babe, the first time can leave you ravenous," he grins wickedly when he sits beside me.

My cheeks flush. Based on the feelings coming from Bran, he is not referring to my first shift. As the memories of our previous night flood my mind, suddenly, I'm back to a partially shifted state. Ears, fingers, teeth and tail, it seems we're going for the full works.

Are you still sleeping, Shea?

When there's no response, I can only assume these shifts are an overreaction to any slight elevation of my emotions. Could this be me leaking in the same way Kali does? I try to ignore the change, but eating with large canines is a challenge I'm unlikely to get around.

"Would you like me to cut your food up for you," Kali whispers with a snicker.

"Very funnyth," I groan, forgetting I can't talk with these damn teeth.

Frustration and annoyance are predominant, leading to Bran placing his hand on my thigh. I think he's trying to help, but now that I can add horny to the list, this partial shift will not be going anywhere.

"Woah, that's strong. Slow down there, Bran." Kali comments, placing her hand over her chest.

Frowning, I cock my head to the side, "Whath doth you meanth?"

"The spike in your emotions, mainly your arousal. I'm trying not to feel it, but that nearly punched me in the fucking chest. It was so strong."

"Erm, Feisty," Anubis says cautiously, gesturing to the hand on her chest. Each of her fingers has turned into flames. The outline of her hand is still visible, the flames lightly tracing the shape rather than engulfing her hand completely.

"Oh shit," she groans, holding her hand out in front of her. "Though it is kind of pretty."

The rest of the guys, who have been quiet up till now, take an interest in what is happening with myself and Kali. They all ask lots of questions and theorise what new triggers we may have and how my bond with Bran could have an impact on my bond with Kali.

For the love of the gods, would you please eat something!
Shea, good you're back. Are you feeling okay?
Fine, just weak. Please eat something.
That's easier said than done with our canines sticking out.

"Holy shit, Bran! Will you please feed Thea something? The woman is bloody starving."

Bran looks between Kali and me before raising his eyebrows at me, "I was giving you a chance to see if you could work it out, but I have to agree with Kali here, babe. You're starting to feel weak. Can I help you?"

I nod my head, too embarrassed and hungry to care. Between my bonds with Bran and Kali and my connection to Shea, I'm struggling to juggle all the emotions enough to think about reversing the shift. Bran reverently feeds me as the others continue to talk, enjoying the moment more than I would have expected. One whole plate of pasta later, my energy starts to increase, and when I sigh happily, I return to my normal human self.

Kali seeing the change, says exactly what I'm thinking, "This is going to get worse before it gets better, isn't it?"

"You mean us leaking all over the place? Yes, I think it is."

I smile gratefully at Bran, taking the fork from his hand and continue to eat my own food. Now I'm no longer shifted or hungry, Kali's hand has returned to normal, too, and the chatter between our group continues.

"You guys need a new nickname," Castiel says after a few minutes, "I'm thinking the Leaky Ladies."

I'm going to eat him.

Kali and I shoot Castiel a glare, and the poor guy actually winces under our gazes, shovelling a forkful of food into his mouth as he mumbles an apology.

"Dude, you totally crapped your pants," Balbur laughs gleefully. "Just remember you still have to train Kali, and now she has Thea in her corner, you're done for."

Balbur takes great delight as Castiel continues to wither under our attention. After a few more seconds, we burst into laughter, triggering another round of leaking powers.

"For fuck's sake," Kali moans as flowers burst over the table. "This is your fault," she chuckles lightly, pointing at Castiel.

My arms and ears have shifted again, and though the whole situation is amusing, we need to find a way to handle this better.

I think you should let me out and see if the blond hunk still wants to give you a new nickname.

At this point, I might not get much of a choice. Any ideas on how to handle the partial shifts?

No clue, but I like it. Makes it seem as if I have more control.

How?

Your arms are not fully shifted, but I feel the fork as if it were my hand. I believe this is a manifestation of our power struggling against the restrictions, much like our sister.

Sister?

Yes. Why do you sound confused?

You think of Kali as our sister?

Of course, why wouldn't I?

I... I don't know. She does feel like family, but when you said sister, it resonated strongly with me. I guess she is our sister.

"Everything okay, babe? Is Shea talking again?" Bran asks, noticing I've been quiet.

"She is and feeling much stronger."

He leans in a little closer, his scent surrounding me in the best way, "That's great. Can I get you more to eat, or would you like to go to yours for dessert?" He mumbles quietly.

"Dude, seriously. I'm sat right here?" Kali groans.

"What, I was quiet," he defends himself, amused.

"It's not your words that are the issue, or maybe it is, but the feelings they provoke. If you ever want us to stop leaking, you need to stop making us aroused in public."

"Gods, where's my female with leaking problems," Castiel mutters, disgruntled.

"Angel boy, that's just gross," Kali snorts.

"Not from where I'm sitting," Anubis grins, grabbing Kali from her chair and placing her in his lap.

I'd like to say the rest of the evening goes without incident but that would be a lie. The frequency of my shifts is tightly tied to any spike in emotions—happiness, anger, arousal. Any slight elevation seems to trigger it now. Kali is no different, except her leaking causes more of an issue for those around her.

Not once do any of the guys make an issue out of it, get annoyed or make us feel different. Anubis and Bran are understandable; they're our mates, but Balbur, Castiel and Oberon take it all in their stride. They enjoy teasing us but never take it too far and are sympathetic to our situation.

The whole evening is wonderful. Even Shea gets involved, though not directly, and my happiness is complete. Everything I have ever wanted around one table. It's more than I ever could have dreamed of and more than I probably deserve, but I plan to hold onto it for as long as possible.

With the copious amounts of food I've eaten, we're the first to leave when Bran points out how tired I am. I've been leaning on him more and more throughout the evening, and now, full of food, my body is heavy with exhaustion. On the walk back to my apartment, I realise I have no idea where Bran lives.

"Second floor in Oak," he chuckles when I ask him. "Would you like to go to mine instead?"

"Actually, yes, I think I would."

"No problem, babe. Would you be annoyed if I carried you? Your exhaustion feels heavy."

Don't you do it.

Under any other circumstances, I might agree with you, but not tonight.

"I would love that, thank you."

When Bran picks me up, I wrap my arms around him, burying my face against his neck and breathing him in deeply. He holds me tightly to him, and I've never felt more protected and cherished. As he walks me down the stairs and through the courtyard, I relax more into his hold.

"I know everything is overwhelming for you," he begins talking quietly. "I can feel when your bonds become overloaded or when your emotions spike, and I want you to know I'm here for you. I'm incredibly proud of all you have achieved today, babe, but I want you to promise me that you'll share the load with me if it ever gets too much. I realise you've done things alone your whole life, been responsible for yourself all this time and now you have Shea and the bond with Kali, you have plenty of support.

He pauses to open the doors to Oak before speaking again, "I guess what I'm trying to say is I want our bond to be your safe place. When things become too much, if there's too many emotions or noise to deal with, I want to reach for us and know that all you will ever find is support and quiet if that's what you need."

The last twenty-four hours have been overwhelming, in a good way, but still a lot to take on. Throughout it all, Bran has been at my side, and to hear him speak now, to offer me this sanctuary in all the madness, brings tears to my eyes.

"I love you. More than those three words can express," I tell him, lifting my head to gaze into his slate-grey eyes. "You have given me so much, more than I could have hoped for, not just the bond or my ability to be with Shea. It's your confidence in me. How you want me to succeed and be happy, not for you, but for myself. You are a one of kind my mate, and my safe place will always be with you."

He kisses me tenderly, somehow still managing to walk towards his apartment. "I love you too, mate," he breathes before opening the door and carrying me into his space.

Flicking on the lights, his home is a replica of mine, with a touch of masculinity in the black décor. His scent is everywhere, and I find myself immediately comfortable when he places my feet on the ground.

"I realise you need to sleep, but can I worship you before you do?" he asks from behind me, placing his hands on my shoulders and kissing the side of my neck.

"I can't think of anything I want more," I reply in a breathy tone.

Skimming his hand down my arm, he takes my hand and leads me to his bedroom. The same theme is continued here, the black sheets, picture frames and furniture contrasting with the white walls. I don't have the opportunity to take much else of the details in as he turns me towards him and gently runs the back of his hand down my cheek.

His hand continues to my neck, over the swell of my breasts and down to the hem of my shirt. Teasingly slow, he peels my shift off me, his fingers tantalisingly glancing across my skin. My breathing speeds up as he gradually removes every item of clothing until I'm standing before him naked. I don't feel shy or self-conscious under his perusal. If anything, I feel powerful, having my mate look at me with such desire.

When he takes a step back, I nearly reach for him until I notice him lift his shirt. He removes his clothes in a much more hurried fashion than mine, and the result causes me to bite my lip. His toned and golden physique is a feast for my eyes, and as we both take our time visually exploring each other, I'm needy and desperate when he finally reaches for me.

Laying me on his bed with extreme care, he caresses my body, every move, stroke and kiss delivered in a sensual way that drives me crazy. I try to force the issue by reaching for his erection, but when Bran said he wanted to worship me, he meant exactly that.

There isn't an inch of me that hasn't received some attention, and by the time he slides his fingers through my folds, I'm a writing mess. He alternates between kissing my lips and my breasts, his fingers skilfully building an orgasm I can't wait to tear through me. When he inserts two fingers into my core and gently bites on my nipple, a thousand stars burst behind my closed lids. I clench around him, riding his fingers until the orgasm ebbs away, and I'm gasping for breath.

"Stunning," he murmurs, kissing my lips once before gently biting my bottom lip.

Every touch is hypersensitive, and when his cock slowly enters me, I moan loudly. He sets a slow but punishing pace, grinding and rotating his hips, making sure to truly worship every inch of me. His eyes never leave mine, watching my face for every reaction as his hands tightly grip my hair. The intensity of his gaze and his movements prove to be my undoing. When the second orgasm takes me over the edge, I pull him along with me, clenching hard around him as he roars his satisfaction.

We lie there panting for a few minutes, Bran's head resting against my chest as I lazily stroke my fingers through his hair. Our bond is consumed with so much bliss and satisfaction that the feeling causes my eyes to droop, and a smile pulls at my lips. I become vaguely aware of Bran moving from me, cleaning me up and placing me in his bed. When the bed dips beside me, and I'm enclosed in Bran's arms, I finally give into the pull of sleep.

"Rest, my beautiful mate, and have sweet dreams."

CHAPTER TWENTY-FOUR

MY EYES BLINK RAPIDLY, *finding the six wooden posts that represent the dream Kali and I have been having.*

Shea?

There is no response from her, so presumably, this is my subconscious and not something we share. This time, I'm in the middle of the structure, right next to the altar, no running towards it, and I wonder if that's because Shea and I are now fully connected.

The whole place still gives a weird vibe, and after the day I've had, I'm reluctant to touch anything that will trigger the images. Turning towards the altar, my eyes trace over the six symbols. They appear more vivid in the dream than the picture Oberon showed us, the groves deeper and sharper. As I stare at them, the symbol I'm drawn to shimmers gold.

My fingers trace the pattern without stopping to think about what I'm doing. A startled breath leaves me as an image of myself comes to mind, slowly panning out until I leave the dream place behind and become part of the scene. I'm in a clearing, surrounded by trees and a small cottage. Everything is quiet until suddenly, the outer wall of the cottage explodes, and Shea is being thrown through the air towards the trees. My eyes follow her movements, panic and fear pulsing through me as she hits the tree hard and falls to the ground.

Running as fast I can, I find her crumpled on the ground, her eyes closed, her chest moving too slowly.

"Shea? Shea, come on, wake up." I beg, reaching for her, only to have my hand vanish before I can touch her.

Another noise draws my attention as a blurred figure comes hurtling in my direction. I don't get a clear view of what it is, but when I rise to my feet and look over towards the cottage, I spot Kali, badly beaten and being held up by two other figures that I can't make out.

What is going on? Why can't I see everything?

The first blurred figure reappears and stalks towards the cottage where Kali stands injured. I turn back to Shea, screaming at her to wake up, that her sister needs her. A scream of pain slices through the area, and my panic multiplies. I realise this is just a dream, but it feels real, and I can't let anything happen to Kali.

"Shea, please. You're an alpha, for shifter's sake. Wake the hell up!"

When she suddenly shakes her head, I back up a little, checking her over as she does the same thing.

"Shea, Kali is in trouble. She needs your help."

Shea looks in my direction, but her gaze travels straight through me. She can't see me; it's just a dream, but we're connected, so maybe she can still hear me.

"Go and save your sister, now!"

Shea pounces to her feet and watches from the edge of the clearing, stopping next to another blurred figure before pouncing into action. She's too late. Kali is picked up by some force I can't see and thrown against a wall, her head cracking loudly before she slumps to the floor.

I scream, calling out her name before a voice booms around the clearing.

"Is this what Earth considers their saviours? You are a disgrace to all of our kind."

Everything becomes fuzzy as I hear my name being called. The image of the cottage and Kali wobble, and before I'm pulled away, I hear it on the wind.

"Six will connect."

"Babe! Thea, come on now, wake up. Show me those beautiful eyes," Bran's voice registers as the last of the dream fades away.

"Kali," I groan, opening my eyes to the early morning light. "I need Kali."

I hear a heavy pounding so fierce I feel it resonate in my chest before realising it's my bond with Kali. Throwing the covers aside, I jump out of bed, shocked to see my legs have shifted and my toes have turned into claws.

"Hand on a second, babe. I'll get the door, you put some clothes on. My shirts are in the draw over there," he tells me pointing to the dresser.

Only because I can feel Kali near, I agree and watch him leave to answer the door. Looking down at my legs, I groan—this is not attractive no matter how you look at it—my legs look like they've never been shaved a day in my life. I don't have time to worry about it now, and without paying attention, I pull out some of Bran's clothes to cover myself, the image of Kali beaten and broken staying in my mind.

She is okay. You can feel her remember. Just breathe.

Taking Shea's advice, I take a couple of deep breaths, the action calming me until I hear Kali's voice.

"Where is she? Is she okay? What's happened?"

Running from the bedroom, I crash straight into her, my arms squeezing her tight as relief washes over me. She's here and she's okay. It was a dream, just a dream.

"Are you okay?" she asks softly, returning my hug as fiercely. "I felt your panic, your fear. I couldn't find you in your apartment, but I got here as soon as I could."

"I'm okay," I mumble, still reluctant to let go.

"Thea, talk to me," she coaxes, pulling back from me. "What happened?"

"Here, babe," Bran interjects with a cup of coffee. "Why don't you sit and tell us what happened?"

I nod gratefully, taking the cup from him and moving over to the couch. Before I can sit down, Bran pulls me into his lap, squeezing tightly in reassurance as Kali and Anubis, who I've just noticed, take a seat.

"It's silly," I mumble, feeling foolish now I need to explain it.

These dreams are not foolish. They mean something, and we need to figure out what.

Any ideas on how we do that?

No, but you need to share this latest one. It could be something that helps in the future.

"It was a dream, but it felt so real," I start, still seeing everything but the blurred figures so clearly.

"Judging from your reaction when I came in, I'm guessing it doesn't end well for me," Kali laughs, though it lacks any real humour,

"You were still alive, I think."

Anubis growls low at my response, and Kali grabs his hand to soothe him.

As I tell them all the details of the dream, Bran plays with the ends of my hair and by the time I'm finished, I've relaxed into him and finished my coffee. There is silence amongst us for a minute before Kali speaks.

"It always sucks for me in your dreams," she snorts.

"Not funny, Feisty," Anubis utters, annoyed and agitated.

"I'm sorry you're right, but nothing has changed. We still don't know what any of it means, and as it stands now, we're all okay. As horrible as these dreams are, the only thing we can do is capture every detail and see if a picture starts to form that can help us."

"You're right. I'll speak to Oberon after work and give him all the details. I'm not sure it'll help, but keeping a record of all our dreams seems to be the only thing we can do."

Kali stands from her chair, pulling Anubis with her. "We'll leave you guys alone to get ready for work," she pauses, coming over to squeeze my hand. "Thank you for your concern. I can see this has left you shaken, and as bad as it might seem, I love you for it. Nothing will happen to me with you guys around."

I stand to give her a hug and then watch as Bran sees them out. He comes over to me and pulls me in his arms, as always, making me feel safe and secure.

"You want to get ready for work or take the day off and stay in bed all day?"

"As appealing as the second option is, I missed work yesterday and will not be missing another today. I'd like to start training my own group at some point."

"Consider it done," he replies, kissing the end of my nose and walking back into the bedroom.

I stand still for a second, replaying our conversation, when his response dawns on me. "Erm, what do you mean, consider it done?" I ask, following him into the room.

He has that wicked grin on his face I love so much, though I sense this may not turn out in my favour.

"Exactly what I said. Get dressed. You have a group to train."

"Today? You're giving me a group today?"

"Sure, why not. I know watching is useful, but I can also see you're desperate to get stuck in. You know the new combinations. Start on those and then go with what feels right. You'll be amazing."

"Your confidence in me is astounding."

"You are astounding," he smirks back.

We spend the next thirty minutes getting ready for work, the shower calming me enough for my legs to return to normal even though my mind stays wholly occupied. Bran has a coffee waiting for me once I'm ready, and we spend a few minutes talking. He gives me some pointers about the training programme, how best to get things started, and to ultimately trust my instincts. He has total faith in me, and it's heartwarming.

"Will you live with me?" I suddenly ask him.

"Whoa, babe, that's rushing things a little, don't you think?" he jokes, his eyes alight with excitement.

"Well, I mean, it might be. I guess I could get used to staying in a big empty bed all by myself," I pout playfully.

"Holy shifters," he groans, adjusting himself not so discreetly. "And she turns it around so beautifully. I could deny you nothing when you look at me like that."

"I'll remember that," I giggle, kissing him lightly before heading towards the door to start our day.

We stroll out of the apartment hand in hand, heading to the canteen for breakfast and to meet with the others.

"And where would my mate like to live together? Your place or mine?" Bran asks as we walk through the courtyard.

"I'd like to be close to Kali. Would that be okay?"

"Absolutely, I don't have any emotional attachments to my place. I'm happy wherever you are," he says, putting his arm around my shoulder.

"And that is why you are the best mate."

"Babe, please. You'll make me blush," he laughs, the sound doing funny things to me.

Are you two quite done? This mushy stuff is sickening.

You know you love him as much as I do.

That may be true, but I will show that by killing something for him as a gift.

My giggle blossoms into a full belly laugh at the image of Shea presenting Bran with a dead animal to show her love.

I don't see why that's funny. I am sure he would appreciate it.

"What's so funny?" Bran asks.

"Shea was saying the mushy stuff was sickening, and when I told her she loved you too, she agreed but said she would show you that with something dead."

"Aww, babe, that's very sweet. Shea, I would love any gift from you."

Ha!

"Wait? That wouldn't gross you out?"

"Not at all. My bear is positively giddy with the thought."

Let me out. Shift, so I may go and acquire a gift for our mate.

Now who's the mushy one, hmm?

Still you.

My conversation with Shea and Bran helps dispel some of the uneasiness from this morning. Breakfast with our group also does that, and both Kali and I manage to make it through a meal, only leaking on two occasions.

Now it's time to work, and heading towards The Pit, my stomach fills with nerves. With all the emotions pumping around me, I'm guessing it won't be long before I shift again.

CHAPTER TWENTY-FIVE

THE RECRUITS STAND AROUND awaiting their instructions, and I stand tall beside Bran, waiting for Anubis to assign me a group. As much as I wanted this job, standing here now, I'm wondering if I've made the right decision. If it was only about the skill, I'd be fine. It's the leading side of things. I've watched all the guys with their groups, and they all present a strong, superior front for these young people to look up to. How can I measure up?

Why do you doubt yourself so much?

Are you kidding? Look at how I let my father treat me. You might be an alpha, Shea, but I am not.

And do you think you're weak?

Well, yes. I became the doormat to our last pack for years.

Hmm, interesting.

What's interesting?

What you perceive as weak. I watched you from the day you were born, saw you deal with your mother's death, the rejection of your father and alpha and how the pack treated you. I never once thought of you as weak.

You didn't?

No. You took everything and never broke. You did all that was asked of you and never gave up. That, my dear, is strength, not weakness.

But I never stood up for myself.

And how would you have done that? You couldn't shift, couldn't connect with me, and you had no one. Strength is not just about standing up for yourself. Strength is withstanding hardships and not giving up. You are stronger than you know, Althea, and now is the time to start believing in yourself. And this time, you have plenty of support.

I... Thank you, Shea.

Anytime. Now show these pups we are an alpha and we never give up.

"Okay, babe?" Bran asks me quietly as the recruits are divided into groups.

"Yes, I think I am," I tell him with a small grin.

"You got this. If you need me, I'll be right here."

Nodding, I step forward when Anubis calls my name and points to the group I'll be teaching today. From our conversation at breakfast, I already know what Anubis wants me to cover with them. All I need to do now is be confident and teach.

We move over to the side of the centre to make room between us and the other groups. As they expectantly line up in front of me, I adopt some of Shea's overconfidence and channel it through me, using it to sound authoritative.

"Alright recruits, as Anubis said, I am new to the team but have plenty of experience, and I expect you all to work hard. If you struggle with anything, speak up; otherwise, I'll assume you all understand your instructions. Any questions?"

If I could have an out-of-body experience and watch myself, I'm almost certain my jaw would be on the floor. Never in my life have I sounded so sure and in control.

"Yeah, I have a question." If anyone was going to ask one, I knew it would be Jared. I had quickly noticed he was a part of my group, and I'm happy about it. Maybe I can curb some of his attitude.

Or you still have the option of letting me eat him.

"Go ahead," I tell him, ignoring Shea's comment.

"What makes you qualified to train us?" he asks with an arrogant smirk. I'm surprised with the guys around he would question me this way, but he does have an air of entitlement about him.

Just a little nibble, I'll only take a leg.

I cough to cover up my laugh, then answer his question. "I come from a long line of alphas and have been training my whole life to become the alpha of my father's pack." I leave out the part about not being able to do that.

He considers my words for a minute before he nods for me to continue.

"Alright, you all know the warm-up routine. After that, we'll move straight onto the course and cover combat training this afternoon. Let's get started."

Since arriving here, I've become lazy, and the gym I created for myself back at my old house seems like a distant memory. I'm itching to feel the burn in my muscles and decide whatever I put the recruits through, I should go through it, too.

It was a stupid idea!

I pride myself on being fit and active, but after an hour of exercise, I'm trying hard not to show my exhaustion. It seemed like a good way to show them that whatever they're being asked to do, as a trainer, I can also do it myself. It did occur to me halfway through none of the guys do this, and now I know why.

The course itself is set up every other day by the trainers before the recruits arrive. Balbur and Castiel were the ones to configure the set-up today, and it was gruelling. The high-intensity sprint I found easy enough, but by the time I had worked through the agility ladders, tire flips, balance beam, rope climb and pull-up bar, my muscles were burning with an intensity I hadn't felt since I first started training.

On a positive note, my actions seemed to command the respect of most of my group, a few of them commenting on my ability and speed, all except Jared, of course. I'm disgruntled to say that he handled the morning well, displaying enough effort for me to be satisfied with his performance.

When we're finished with the exercise portion of the morning, I allow the recruits a breather for lunch so I can go die in the staff room privately.

I don't know why you thought that would be a good idea. You need to keep up your energy to train them.

Yes, I realise that. I just wanted to see what level I was at. I must work harder to get in shape, to keep up with them.

Fine. But you better eat a lot of food now, or you'll crash this afternoon, and I'll force you to shift so we can hunt.

Always with the hunting. We will go again soon, I promise.

Slumping down on the couch in the staff room with five power bars and a bottle of water, I've just bitten into my first one when Bran walks in. He smiles in my direction, though I feel some concern from the bond when he takes in my defeated posture.

"Don't say it. I've already had a lecture from Shea."

"Wouldn't dream of it, babe. You did fantastic out there, but you know there's a reason we don't train with them, right?"

"So, you can carry on for the rest of the day without dying," I mumble around a mouthful of food.

"Yeah," he chuckles. "And because we usually stay behind after to work on our own fitness."

"And you couldn't tell me this before today? I thought it would do me some good since I hadn't worked out since I got here. If I'd have known we were staying back, I needn't have bothered."

"Sorry, babe. Things have been a bit hectic lately, so our usual routine has fallen off track a little."

The rest of the guys enter the staff room, and I groan when Balbur walks in with several trays in his arms, the smell of warm food making me perk up a little.

"Bran thought you might need something more substantial than power bars," Balbur says, placing all the food on the table for the rest of us to dig into. When I spot a tray of pasta and slices of bread, I jump up off the couch, giving Bran a quick hug and muttering my thanks to Balbur before devouring the food.

"Guess food is the way to a woman's heart, too," Castiel chuckles, sitting beside me. A growl rumbles low in my throat when he reaches for some of the bread. "Though apparently, they don't share."

"Sorry," I mumble around my food. "Shea is hungry."

While I find this gluttonous attitude glorious, could you please not blame it on me.

"I'm impressed, Thea," Anubis says when he sits at the table. "Executing the exercises with the team is a great way to understand the process they go through and identify any weaknesses. It's not something we do anymore, though perhaps it would be a good idea to start, especially with so many coming through the programme."

"What!" Castiel moans. "We did enough of it when we were recruits. The perks of working my way to a trainer were so I wouldn't have to do all that shit now."

"What about if you just did it once with each new group," I suggest. "You still get your perks, and the recruits see how well their trainers handle the routines."

"They've got a point, man," Balbur agrees. "We don't want you getting sloppy in your old age. After all, Thea kicked your ass on the first go, and Kali is getting closer."

"Gods, I'm never going to live that down," Castiel sighs dramatically.

After that, the banter starts between them, and I happily get involved, feeling like one of the guys as we finish our lunch. I especially love how Bran never steps in for me, even though I sometimes sense how hard it is for him. He simply sits back and allows me to give as good as I get. When it comes to the others teasing me, he quickly backs me up, providing extra details about them that I wouldn't have known. So far, I'd say the dynamic we have between mates and colleagues is working well.

After lunch, some of my energy returns, and I feel much better, ready to get back at it, but not before Bran kisses the living daylights out of me.

"Give them hell," he says, leading me back out to The Pit.

For the next three hours, I go through every combination with each of the ten people in my group. Some pick it up better than others, and I get a good idea of their strengths and weaknesses. Unfortunately, Jared has taken it upon himself to try and coach some of the weaker ones, and normally, I'd encourage this behaviour, but he's doing it all wrong.

Walking around the group, I watch him work with a young brunette, waiting and observing to see what his instructions are. The roundhouse kick she is trying to perform is all wrong, and she's going to hurt herself if I don't step in.

Then step in. Go over there and tell him to back off. Show her how it's done before he hurts the pup.

Tapping Jared on his shoulder, he turns to me, "Don't worry, I've got you covered," he says with a patronising smile.

Why that degenerate little—

"I paired you together as you seem to have some experience with the combinations. However, you're teaching her all wrong." I turn to the girl, "Are you okay? You'll end up with a bad ankle if you carry out the kick like that."

"Excuse me," Jared snarls. "I've been performing this kick long enough to execute it properly. You should go back to the weaker ones. I'll handle this," he states dismissively.

"What's your name?" I ask, even though I know it; we just haven't been formally introduced.

"Jared."

"Okay, Jared, why don't you show me how it's done."

He eyes me suspiciously but then shrugs his shoulders and performs a roundhouse kick. When he lands, his footing is all wrong, so

I gently tap his ankle and he falls to the floor. He growls as he stands back up aggressively, crowding my personal space.

"What the hell are you doing!" he yells at me.

I smirk at him, about to tell him I'm making a point. Before I get the chance, Bran's menacing growl can be heard across The Pit. I quickly send him some reassurances that I'm okay, trying to convey that I don't need his help.

Our mate is about to rip his head off. Let's just sit and watch. Maybe he will gift it to us.

Why are you so bloodthirsty?

Because this child deserves it.

"As I was saying, Jared," I say scornfully. "If you don't land your feet correctly with this move, you leave yourself open and will get hurt. One small tap is all it took."

"You did that on purpose," he accuses, his face tinged red, either with embarrassment or anger.

"Yes, I did. To teach you a lesson." Regrettably, my own anger spikes and I'm surprised I've gotten this far without shifting. My nails transform into claws, and I feel my ears shift, the sound of Jared's heartbeat growing louder. The young girl who was training with Jared stands in the same spot, gaping with wide eyes. I turn to Jared, maintaining a calm composure even in my shifted state, "Are you ready to learn the correct way now?"

He looks at me with disgust before his eyes dart over to Bran. Whatever he sees in my mate has him turning back and nodding at me. Keeping his distance, he eyes my hands warily as I demonstrate the correct way to perform the kick. Once the girl, whose name is Jess, has perfected it, I move on to Jared.

"I've got this," he seethes in a snobbish tone. "I have been performing this kick long enough that I don't need a wom—"

"I would think very carefully before finishing that sentence," I warn, already knowing where he's going and not favouring my reaction if he does.

He performs the kick twice with the correct manoeuvres, looking back at me with that smug look on his face.

He disrespects us on purpose and sees us as weak.

Then we'll prove him wrong.

Shouting over one of the recruits, Dax, I pair him with Jared and tell them to finish the combinations together. Dax is stronger than Jared with the techniques and has proven himself skilled in combat. Jared knows this, and because of the pairing, I'm signalling him out as the weaker of the two.

He doesn't say anything, but his eyes flash with anger as he tries to stare me in the eye. I could get into an alpha challenge with him now and make him suffer a little. Instead, I choose to walk away and train with Jess one-on-one as she masters the manoeuvres.

See, you are stronger than me. I would have eaten both legs and an arm.

The rest of the day goes by without incident, and by the late afternoon, my group is executing the routine perfectly. I had so many doubts about this job, but I've loved every second. None of my recruits showed any aversion to my shifted state, which lasted for at least half an hour. By the end of the day, I feel confident and proud of myself.

It's not often I think about him, but I would love to see what my father would make of this. What he would think of who I'm turning out to be. His defective daughter is a trainer of the prestigious SNHQ programme.

I told you if I see that man again, I'm biting him, and I may not stop there.

I know, I don't want to see him. Well, maybe I do, but only to show him how wrong he was.

You don't need to prove yourself to anyone. You were perfect before, and you are perfect now.

Aww, Shea, you say the sweetest things. My mushy cheetah.

Shush.

CHAPTER TWENTY-SIX

LATER THAT EVENING WE dine in the canteen with our usual group, which also includes Oberon and his laptop. As Bran prepares my food, I spend a few minutes detailing the dream for him as he takes notes and asks a few questions. He doesn't pick out anything of importance but thanks me for providing him with extra details. He's still no closer to understanding how everything ties together, and his frustration is evident, the unknowns causing him concern.

When Bran and Anubis return, we enjoy our meal, and I'm telling Kali about my group and all we did today, when Damiean enters the canteen. I've not seen him much over the last few days, but the difference in his appearance is like night and day. His clothes are rumpled, and the strain around his eyes is telling. He doesn't come with good news.

"I am glad to have found you all. May I join you?" Damiean asks hurriedly.

There's a chorus of agreement, and as he takes a seat opposite me, his expression transforms into a smile. "Congratulations to both of you. It appears that true mates are discovering each other at a much higher rate lately."

It's said with genuine happiness, so I start to relax a bit more against Bran. "Thank you. I haven't seen you properly, I feel I should—"

"No need for words, Althea. Your joy radiates so visibly, I am pleased you've found that here, and we can share that happiness with you. I only wish my presence here wasn't about to disturb some of that happiness," he says, looking between Bran and me.

A feeling of dread settles in my stomach for a split second as I imagine getting sent back to my father's pack. Then I quickly realise that could never happen—I beat him in an alpha challenge. I have a mate, and I can shift. There is no way I would ever go back there.

"What's going on, Damiean?" Anubis asks, going straight into leader mode.

"I have held off as long as I possibly can, but I'm afraid I'm going to need your assistance now," he declares, looking at each of the guys. "The human situation is deteriorating rapidly, and I need you to step in. I've been in ongoing discussions with the government, attempting to mitigate any supernatural involvement. However, they are no longer entertaining the possibility that this isn't directly linked to the supernatural, particularly to us here at SNHQ."

"They can't be serious?" Castiel yells. "We've been sending out so many teams to monitor the streets, how they can't possibly think we're involved."

"They're growing desperate, and frankly, so am I. We are without leads, clueless about who's involved, the method of how these disappearances are occurring or the nature of their agenda."

"What do you need from us?" Anubis demands, getting directly to the point.

"You're needed for a mission," Damiean states ominously.

A thunderclap vibrates loudly throughout the canteen as Kali's emotions spiral through our bond. I didn't sense any reason to be worried. Now I'm not so sure.

"Where?" Kali asks, the hint of fear in her voice unmistakable.

Damiean sighs heavily, "London."

More thunder and a flash of lightning, and suddenly, I'm reacting. Hand, ears, teeth and tail all come out simultaneously, reacting to Kali's distress.

Anubis leans over to whisper something to her, and whatever he says has the desired effect. The thunder quiets to a low rumble as Damiean continues.

"The government is relentless, demanding information from the supernatural community about the unfolding events. Despite deploying tracking teams and witches casting protection spells, nothing seems effective. Additionally, we're receiving increased reports of teams of supernaturals disappearing. I need my most proficient team to investigate and gather whatever information you can."

"How many people are missing now?" Oberon asks, his fingers tapping away on his laptop.

"According to the intel I've received from the government, we're looking at a grim situation—no less than a thousand humans, perhaps even more," Damiean declares.

"How many supernaturals?" Bran asks, his arm squeezing me a little tighter.

"Forty-three at the last count."

"Fuck," Anubis hisses angrily.

"What the hell is going on?" Kali mutters, shaking her head. "I feel like I've asked this question too many times. I just don't understand."

"And unfortunately, we're no nearer to obtaining any answers," Damiean responds. "That's precisely why I need your team in London, Anubis. I appreciate leaving your mates won't be easy, but I assure you, they'll be safe in your absence."

"When do we leave?" Balbur asks, already pushing his unfinished meal aside.

"I'm afraid time is of the essence. I need you to leave first thing in the morning."

The guys unanimously agree without hesitation, and I'm glad they're offering their help, but I can't shake the creeping fear within me. It doesn't help that my feelings are mirrored through my bond with Kali. I've only recently mated with Bran, and the thought of him entering a place where people are disappearing doesn't sit well with me.

Calm yourself, Thea, our mate is not weak. He is a warrior, and he will return to us.

I do love your confidence, Shea. You keep feeding me that, and I'll keep calm.

Deal.

As Damiean delves into the specifics of the mission and outlines the expectations, I absorb every detail, etching it into my memory so I have a clear understanding of what lies ahead for them.

"Considering the team will be away, we'll require assistance with the recruits," Damiean mentions, turning his gaze toward Kali.

"You want me to help?" Kali asks surprised, the thunder abruptly cutting off completely. If only I could get my shifts to work that way.

"If you're willing. I'm aware that your skills have advanced significantly, and having your support would be beneficial for Althea."

Say yes, say yes, I think strongly, pushing it through the bond. I may have enjoyed myself today, but I'm not ready to take on the whole group alone.

"Okay, yeah. I can do that," she responds, looking at me with a slight smile.

We will make a formidable team with our sister.

"Oh, thisth is goingth to be funth" I say in response to Shea's comment but forgetting about my teeth.

It seems everyone understands me enough as there's a collective groan at mine and Kali's growing excitement and mutters about the poor recruits. I can already see the wheels turning in Kali's head about what we can put them through tomorrow.

There's more talk between us about the government's demands and where the area of focus needs to be. The guys don't seem fazed about what they could be potentially walking into, and the confidence coming from Bran helps settle me enough that I'm able to shift back into my full human state.

When Damiean stands up to leave, Bran also stands, "If I'm leaving tomorrow, then I need alone time with my mate," he states, smiling down at me.

I don't hesitate to stand, taking his hand as he practically pulls me from the canteen. I giggle, saying goodbye to the others, also noting Kali is now in a similar position and being dragged from the room.

They catch up with us outside the canteen, and we all head back towards Oak. You can sense we're all lost in our own thoughts, so I ask the question niggling in my mind, "How dangerous is this mission?"

Bran sighs, no doubt feeling some of my tension, "Honestly, until we get there, we have no way of knowing. Humans have been going missing for weeks now and leaving no trace at all."

"So what do they expect *you* to find?"

"Not to sound arrogant," Anubis chimes in. "Our team is in high demand due to our exceptional skill set. Oberon's tracking abilities are renowned, Castiel is highly sought after for his formidable spellcasting, and Bran, Balbur, and I are seasoned operatives specialising in rescue, recovery, and protection. We pride ourselves on a flawless mission record, attributed to our keen observational skills that allow us to see details often overlooked by others."

"Do you think you guys will find something others have missed then?" Kali asks, her apprehension running through our bond.

"If anyone can, we can," Bran says solemnly. "All this time, I've been hoping and praying the teams on the ground would come back with something. The fact there isn't one lead is worrying. Either someone is not doing their job properly, or we're dealing with something we've never seen before."

"That's what worries me," I respond honestly.

"Babe, you have nothing to worry about, I promise. It's more of a recon mission. We just need to gain knowledge at this point," he says, pulling me closer and opening the doors to Oak. "Do you think I would go if there was any chance I wasn't coming back to you?"

"I would sure hope not."

"Never would I leave the woman I love if I didn't have to."

"Have no fear, Thea. I will bring him back to you in one piece," Anubis states as we enter the elevator.

"Oh, and who makes sure nothing happens to you?" Kali scolds, crossing her arms over her chest.

"I do," Bran says. "There is absolutely no way I would risk your wrath if something were to happen to him. I happen to like my balls."

"Damn straight, and you'd do well to remember that," she nods, sidling up closer to Anubis.

We say goodnight to Kali and Anubis when we make it to our apartments, but when I head inside, I still can't shake the anxiety pooling in the pit of my stomach. It all sounds straightforward enough, so why do I get the feeling this is more dangerous than they are letting on.

"I know, babe," Bran says, pulling me into his arms. "I feel it too, but I don't think it's just the mission. We're newly mated, and being pulled away from each other is bound to have some emotional consequences."

"You think that's all this is?"

"I do. You just love me so much, you need me here," he smirks trying to lighten the mood.

"Oh, absolutely," I grin. "Until you return, I won't function. Getting dressed, eating, and even talking will be more difficult without you here. How will I ever survive?"

"It's insufferable, I know. Before you turn into a naked, starving, mute, I must have you." His lips pull at the corner as he suppresses a smile.

My hands trace their way around his neck as I pull him closer, my lips gently probing his until he deepens the kiss. When he lifts me into his arms, my legs automatically go around him.

He doesn't move me into the bedroom like I expect, instead pushing me up against a wall and taking everything he needs from me in one kiss. Using his hips to brace me against the wall, he reaches around and removes my top in one swift motion. When my breasts are free, he removes his lips from mine to trail them down my collarbone, kissing along the swell of my breasts before he sucks my nipple through my bra.

The action creates a wave of desire through my centre, and I grind down against the erection I can feel through his trousers. He allows the motions for a minute before his hands reach around me to remove my bra. When he cups both of my breasts in his hands and alternates between kissing and sucking, I pull his head back roughly by his hair and devour his mouth.

He groans against me, and my feet suddenly fall to the floor, making me shout out in surprise. A wicked grin takes over his face, then he drops to his knees and removes the lower half of my clothes. Staring down at him, my legs tremble, heat rising to my cheeks when he buries his head between my legs.

Lifting one of my legs over his shoulder, he wastes no time consuming me, raking his tongue from my entrance to my clit until he sucks me into his mouth. The orgasm builds so quickly that I can only hold on and scream his name to the heavens. He pleasures me with wild abandon, and getting caught up in the sensations, I ride his face until the orgasm crashes through me. Bran continues to draw out every drop, and when he's satisfied, small wet kisses pepper me as he works his way back up my body.

"You are so beautiful when you come," he murmurs, his hand gently caressing my cheek.

Not having any response to that, I simply smile as Bran removes his own clothing. Now naked, he steps forward, his hands on my hips as he lifts me once more.

"Hop on, and don't let go," he smirks, lining his cock up with my entrance.

"Never," I breathe, moaning when his first few inches stretch me.

He fills me all the way to the hilt, and in this position, he has a direct line to my G-spot. Raising my hands above my head, he holds both against the wall with one of his hands, the other supporting my ass as he sets a slow but torturous pace. I'm unable to move, completely at his mercy as he pins me against the wall and uses his body to show me how much he loves me.

Watching me intently, he absorbs every sign of pleasure as he grinds his length against me. His rhythm is agonising; every stroke makes my legs quiver, and the pace is slow enough that the orgasm sits just out of reach.

"Please, babe, more," I beg, using his name for me.

His eyes light up with excitement, and he releases my hands from above my hand to grab me more securely.

"Anything you need, babe."

And then he really starts to move.

With a brutal rhythm, my back slams against the wall as he pounds into me from beneath. My hands grip his shoulders tightly, my nails digging into his flesh as that delicious build-up takes over until it slams into me. My body tenses, ecstasy sweeping through me as I clench around him and arch my back from the wall.

He moans with me as the orgasm lasts and lasts, my legs shaking so much I have to lock my ankles together. He slows just enough for me to catch my breath and regain some of my senses but soon picks up that merciless pace again. I love it. Revel in it.

His groans and grunts suggest he's close now, too, and when his hand reaches between us to stroke my clit, I scream out from the sensation overload. A few more strokes of his cock and a pinch to my clit, and I ignite, sailing over that euphoric edge once more and taking him with me.

Roaring out his release, he slows, gentle strokes drawing out our combined orgasm until he sags against me, his head leaning against my chest as his breaths come in heavy pants. He holds me steady, never faltering or losing his grip, and when he peels me off the wall and walks me into the bedroom, I'm astonished at my mate's strength.

That was epic.

Shea! Way to ruin a moment.

Sorry had to be said. I admire our mates' skills and virility.

I can't argue with you there.

"Babe, care to tell me why I feel humour coming from you? I wasn't trying to be funny," Bran murmurs against my ear as he lies down beside me.

"It wasn't funny. That was epic, and apparently, Shea thinks so, too. She said she admires your skills."

I feel his smile against my cheek, "Ah well, I appreciate the compliment, but I think my stunning mate may be more skilful than I."

Turning over, I kiss every inch of him I can reach. Starting with his chest and slowly moving up until I finally claim his lips.

"I love you," I whisper softly.

"I love you too, my beautiful mate."

CHAPTER TWENTY-SEVEN

THE NEXT DAY WE'RE up early to see the guys off, and after some rather pathetic goodbyes from Kali and I, we make our way to the canteen to strategise how we'll manage the recruits. Being at our table without the rest of our group is an odd sensation. Their collective presence has been instrumental in my life here so far, and without their banter and comradery, it leaves a significant hole.

Will you get a grip and stop being mopey. We are a badass woman who does not need her mate by her side all day, every day.

I'm aware. I know you miss him too.

Yes, but in the meantime, we have pups to train.

Her tone sounds way too sinister for what should be a straightforward training session.

Once we're seated with our breakfast, Kali emerges from her dejected demeanour. "So, how are we dealing with these recruits?" She's likely trying to distract herself from our mates being away and the sense of loss.

The bond is still there, I can feel Bran, but I'm very aware of a distance between us, as if he's been misplaced.

"I was thinking we deal with them as one large group," I reply, glad for the distraction. "Keep it simple with exercise and have a combination of hand-to-hand and weaponry. It's probably best with our track record if we avoid anything magic-related."

"Okay, sounds good. I have no clue what I'm doing, so I'll follow your lead."

"In all honesty, it's only my second day going it alone. I don't know how some of the recruits will take to us leading today.

"Oh shit. Have you already had trouble with some of them?" Kali asks, an aggressive edge to her question.

I haven't told anyone about Jared and this blatant attitude towards me. Somehow, telling Kali seems like both a good and bad idea.

"The reason I could shift back when I turned into Shea was because of one of the recruits, Jared."

"Judging from the look on your face, I'm guessing he's a twat."

"You could say that. He basically implied women are not good enough for training them, something about me being on my period and looking good on my ass. Then yesterday, when he was performing a manoeuvre wrong, he got instantly defensive, and when I shifted, he looked disgusted."

"What an asshole!" She yells, an evil smile pulling at the corner of her mouth. "You know what, this is going to be fun."

We will make this Jared pay for his disrespect.

We can't hurt him, though, in case that's where your thoughts were going.

Do you have to ruin everything?

I chuckle at her sulking tone. I think my cheetah has some anger issues.

"What does Shea think?" Kali asks randomly.

"How did you know I was talking to Shea?"

"You sometimes get this faraway look in your eyes. I figured you're either talking to Shea or planning world domination."

"No, that's more Shea's deal. She's a little bloodthirsty, so I'm trying to talk her out of physically hurting anyone."

Kali bursts into a fit of laughter, resulting in an explosion of flowers landing on our table. Their sudden appearance makes me startle, and a shift naturally takes over.

"Oh my... you look fricking adorable," Kali exclaims, looking just below my eyes.

I can feel something has changed with my face, and I expect to find whiskers when I reach my hand up. I do not expect to find my nose shifted along with my whiskers.

"Not now," I groan, touching my face before noticing the dozens of smells surrounding me. The aroma of the flowers is magnified by ten, and the scent tickles at my shifted nose.

"This isn't going to make training any easier." I moan, pointing at my face. "Why did you have to laugh?"

"I'm sorry," she snorts. "Don't worry, it gives you a mysterious edge. If anyone has a problem with it, they can deal with Shea."

See, our sister understands us completely.

"Please don't encourage her."

"I find it hilarious that she's bloodthirsty when you're not. She's like the other half of your personality, the one you don't show."

I never thought of it that way. Is that why we're able to speak to each other the way we do, because my personality is fractured, and she has the other half of it. It might explain our unusual situation.

Would it bother you if that was the case?

No. Not at all. I enjoy being able to talk to you. Although I have to say, if that is the case, I'm a little scared of that part of me.

Shea's amusement trickles through me, but she refrains from commenting.

We finish the rest of our breakfast quickly, both eager and a little apprehensive to get to the training centre before the recruits so we can set up.

On the way to The Pit, I give Kali a brief overview of the normal daily schedule, and we devise a plan to incorporate some of their routines into the day. As we finish setting up, my shift thankfully reverses, and by the time the recruits make their entrance, we're ready for them. Jared's disdain is plain when he realises the guys are absent. His sneer doesn't go unnoticed either, instantly triggering a defensive reaction from Shea and Kali.

If I strike him with our claws, that should take him out for the rest of the day.

No. We want to torture him a little, remember.

"Doesn't take a genius to work out who Jared is," Kali scoffs, glaring at him.

Jared strategically stations himself alongside four other recruits, who, if my memory serves me right, typically align with Anubis's group. Their collective demeanour exudes a clear indication they have no intention of making things easy for us.

"Let's get started and see if we can wipe that cocky look off his face," Kali whispers as she cracks her knuckles.

Gathering the recruit's attention, they quickly line up in their usual formation, though Jared and his group are slower to move and stick to the back. I introduce Kali as a fellow trainer and let them know we're in charge today.

"I'm sure you've probably noticed we're down a few trainers today, so Kali has graciously offered to step in. I expect you all to treat her with the same respect you do the other trainers."

There are a few mumbles from the back of the group, but nothing I can solidly hear.

He thinks this is ridiculous.

Internally sighing, I pull on some of Shea's strength, steeling my spine and addressing the group.

"Today, we'll be training as a unified group. The schedule stays mostly unchanged, and you're all aware of the expectations. The fact that there are only two of us doesn't diminish my expectations for the same level of commitment. Anyone found not pulling their weight will face appropriate consequences."

I look over to Jared and his little group to see him raising his eyebrows at me like he's not the one muttering under his breath as I'm talking.

"Everyone spread out. I want you all in rows with plenty of space between you to go through your warm-up."

"You're so commanding," Kali praises before moving over to the far left to watch over the recruits.

The recruits begin and, after completing the warm-up, transition into a standard exercise routine to test their strength and endurance.

It catches my attention that Jared and his group appear less invested than the rest, giving little to no effort. As I approach, I see that Kali has already noticed and is conversing with Jared.

"Is there a problem?" It takes all my self-control not to snarl at him, especially given the rage I'm getting from Shea.

"Nope, just saying to blondie here how pretty her eyes are," he comments, a smile on his face but his tone insulting.

Kali's smiling, too, but I guarantee it's not for the same reason Jared is. How can he possibly not know that Anubis is her mate, or is he too stupid to care? If my senses are correct, he will learn the hard way that you don't mess with the soon-to-be alpha's mate.

I will rip him apart if he degrades our sister one more time.

"Jared, her name is Kali," I state, asserting a little dominance into my voice. "And you will address her such. If you are performing as you should be, there will be no time for small talk with anyone."

"It's alright, Thea," he replies, his tone condescending when he uses my name. "Why don't you and blondie, sorry Kali, go chill in the staff room and the guys and I can take care of the schedule for you." He laughs as if he's made some hilarious joke, and I'm disappointed to see the other three recruits joining in.

You must let me kill him or at least maim him. I can avoid all vital organs.

Trying to keep Shea under control, I don't get time to respond before Kali steps right up to Jared. She looks sweet and innocent, but the bond clues me in that she's plotting something.

"I think you might need to take a break, Jared. Looks like you've had a little accident," she says, discreetly waving her hand in his direction before his trousers become saturated with water.

"What the... What did you do to me!" he yells, stepping away from us.

Kali and I don't bother to hide our smiles, and I hear some other recruits sniggering, "Well, Jared, since you've already had a bathroom break, why don't you start some laps around the centre."

I can tell he's on the verge of arguing, so before he can utter a word, I draw on Shea's power. "You will complete one hundred laps. Given your blatant disrespect, that is more than fair."

If looks could kill, I would be dead three times over. I watch him struggle against my command, surprised to witness his reaction and realise I must have pulled too much from Shea, issuing the instruction as an alpha command. Jared is unable to resist, my request not only heard but felt by him as he stomps away to start his laps. Turning to the others in his group, I add, "And since you pack of hyenas find Jared so amusing, why don't you go join him."

They groan but say nothing to contradict my order and set off running.

"Wow, four pissed-off males in less than an hour. We're doing great," Kali cheers quietly as we turn to the rest of the group.

"Nice work," I grin, nodding towards Jared and his soaked trousers.

"To be fair, I was going for a small wet patch, not his whole bottom half."

She did an excellent job and should be proud of herself. I would have done much worse.

"Shea's impressed," I tell her as we round up the rest of the group for combat training.

The remainder of the morning swiftly passes, and after lunch, we progress onto weapons training. I must admit, this is not my forte, having only practised with wooden versions. As Kali has been training with the guys for longer, she has more experience in this area and so steps forward to take on lead trainer. This also affords me a good opportunity to monitor the group more closely.

Throughout the program, the recruits will receive training in handling various types of weapons, but today, the focus is on the Bo Staff—one of Kali's favourites.

When Kali calls for volunteers, and Jared is the first to step forward, I'm tempted to interfere. However, sensing Kali's enthusiasm, I choose to let it unfold. Kali begins by demonstrating some basic moves the recruits must follow.

Instead of waiting for Kali's signal, it becomes apparent Jared is quite proficient with a Bo Staff and has taken it upon himself to showcase his skills. He starts by following the instructions but that doesn't last, taking it one step further and showing off. Kali impressively matches him move for move, and it evolves into an all-out battle between them. I step forward to intervene when Shea stops me.

If you won't let me have any fun with him, at least allow our sister to annihilate him.

But this training, and he's taking it too far.

Is she bothered by it?

No, she feels... excited.

Then let her have some fun.

I continue to watch, captivated, as Kali skilfully counters every move Jared throws her way. She executes a particularly impressive move involving a flurry of spins, but midway through, I notice wisps of smoke. When Kali completes the move, her Bo Staff is engulfed in flames.

With a shocked cry, Jared jumps back, eyes wide with fear and mouth twisted with anger. Kali's eyes quickly find mine, and I feel her panic through the bond. As I move forward, Jared recovers, "Are you fucking stupid? You could have killed me!"

Immediately, I stand in front of Kali, the heat from her Bo Staff surprisingly comforting and not at all burning like I thought it might.

"Just wait until Anubis and Damiean hear about this. I knew I was right, fucking defect's not fit to teach the next generation of a supernatural army!" he shouts, pointing at Kali.

I'm not sure how he knows about our situation or why he chooses to use that word, but what unfolds next is beyond my control. When I hear his words, I hear my father. The combined anger from myself, Shea and Kali is too intense to ignore, and the shift forces its way through me.

Before my body can fully complete the shift, I'm already pouncing through the air as Shea. Upon landing, I immediately sink my teeth into Jared's thigh, his shrieks of surprise and pain echoing around The Pit. Shea doesn't bite down as hard as she could, but it's enough to draw blood and tear through some tendons.

No one speaks to our sister that way.

Giving his leg a rough shake, Jared screams louder, falling to the floor.

I realise he deserves it, but I like this job, and I don't want the other recruits thinking we're unhinged. Can you please let go now?

Shea reluctantly releases her grip on his leg before getting right up to his face, unleashing the most menacing growl I've heard from her yet. Kali steps into our peripheral, the heat from her Bo Staff still flaming. I can smell the fear wafting from Jared in waves and can only imagine what we must look like. My snarling cheetah and Kali with her flaming stick.

We are fierce, and he will remember that now.

I agree, but how do we shift back?

We'll worry about that later, for now, we hold our dominance.

Kali places her hand against our back, smiling over at Jared. "Maybe you should go see the healers. We women need to show these recruits what it means to be a real supernatural."

He scrambles backwards, all traces of humour or disrespect gone. There's only fear now. Even his following hyaenas are no longer laughing. In fact, they look a little pale.

"You," Kali points to one of the recruits, "Make sure he gets to the healers, then come straight back."

She surveys the rest of the group, "You've seen how it's done. Choose a partner and practise."

Our sister is strong. She would make a good beta for our pack.

We don't have a pack, Shea.

We will someday.

Watching for a few minutes, Kali makes sure everyone executes her instructions before nodding towards the staff room. When we step inside, I worry she might set the place on fire with her staff, but it seems to be contained to the weapon. Once the door is shut, she turns to me, "Well, I think that went well, don't you?" she snorts. "It's nice to finally meet you, Shea."

Shea meows at her and then nudges her hand in greeting before circling her legs. We follow Kali to the couch and jump up to sit beside her. It's fascinating that this close to her flame and I still don't feel its burn.

"So, what now? I'm not sure I can put this out, and you can't teach for the rest of the day by growling or whatever that noise was you just made."

Kali starts to chuckle before it blossoms into peals of laughter. She becomes louder, snorting in between as her giggles take control and tears run down her cheeks. "What... the... hell... is that... noise, Shea," she wheezes between bouts of laughter.

Her amusement through the bond becomes infectious, and soon, I'm caught up in the jovial atmosphere with Shea. When Shea expresses her delight, emitting what I assume is laughter, it further increases Kali's reaction, and she crumples to the floor, bent over and holding her stomach.

"Oh... please... stop. You're... killing... me," she wheezes. Witnessing her in such a state after a somewhat stressful morning is a relief, and as my own amusement grows, I feel a tingling sensation coursing through my body. Amidst the joy, the unmistakable sound of my bones reshaping penetrates the air.

The impact is far more sudden than I anticipated, and returning to my human form, I find myself landing unceremoniously on my ass, completely naked.

"What the... Ow."

Kali's laughter momentarily cuts off, her eyes widening with surprise before erupting into another bout of hysterical laughter. Despite my shock and abrupt return, I can't resist joining in.

When she's finally able to get herself under control, the flames have died out on the Bo Staff, and she pulls off her hoody and throws it over to me. I quickly put it on, grateful to have something cover my nakedness and enjoying the surprisingly comfortable material. She might never get this back.

With mirth still shining in her eyes, I lean next to her on the floor. "I don't think that went too bad for our first day."

This sets us off laughing again, and that is how Damiean finds us.

CHAPTER TWENTY-EIGHT

AFTER DAMIEAN'S INITIAL SHOCK subsides, we gather ourselves enough to provide an explanation for my half-dressed state and the lingering scent of smoke. He had caught wind of the incident with Jared and stopped by to check everything was okay. It turns out Jared is a familiar figure to him, and his troublesome behaviour has been a concern since the moment he arrived.

It seems Jared's father is a powerful alpha to a pack in Devon. As a result, Jared has grown up with a sense of entitlement. I still offer my apologies to Damiean for Shea's bite. As a trainer it's not responsible to let my emotions get the better of me.

Had he not spoken to our sister that way, I probably could have held off.

Really?

No, not really. But you can tell this leader that if you like.

Thankfully, Damiean doesn't appear too troubled by the incident and assures me this is all part of the learning process regarding my shifting abilities. I'm fairly certain as Kali recounts the events, I see a smirk trying to break out across his face.

The more I get to know Damiean, the more he surprises me. As the leader of SNHQ and an elder, I would've expected a more formal demeanour, but he's strangely down-to-earth. He comes across as one of the guys, rather than a high-ranking elder, defying my expectations of someone in such a prominent position.

By the time we've finished giving Damiean a run down, it becomes clear, considering my half-dressed state, that it's time to call it a day on our first day of being in charge. Damiean offers to speak with the recruits and once he advises they can finish early, a few cheers can be heard before they leave The Pit.

Finding some spare trousers in the storeroom, Kali and I stay behind to pack the equipment away, talking with Damiean who has remained behind to help us.

"Has there been any contact from the guys yet?" I ask, trying to keep the question light and casual. I can still feel Bran through our bond, though it's somewhat muted, so I'm not getting a precise range of emotions as I usually would.

"Not yet, but that's a common practice. When they initially arrive, they go dark, severing contact with everyone and focusing solely on the essentials. That's what makes them my top team. Their commitment to covering all bases is well-known."

"Do you think there will be anything to find if no one else has found anything?" Kali asks, voicing my next question.

"We're overlooking something crucial, some vital piece of information about how these disappearances are happening. What's intriguing is that the supernaturals who've vanished were perfectly fine. They made their usual checkpoint calls, and then they simply disappeared. No calls for help, no distress signals for backup. They would have signalled for assistance if they had encountered anyone attempting to apprehend them."

From the lines on Damiean's face and the frustration in his voice, you can sense how much the whole situation is weighing on him. I suppose that's the role of a leader, but this is different. How do you control something you can't see.

"So that would suggest powerful magic is involved then?" I query, dusting off my hands as I put the last of the mats away.

"Yes. Very powerful indeed, which again causes further issues. I have been around for a long time and could count on one hand the number of beings powerful enough to do something like this. All of them are accounted for with alibis, suggesting it's either something we've never encountered before or we are being deceived."

Neither of those options sounds good, and a sudden spike of worry pulses through me at the thought of Bran in the middle of it all.

Fret not, Althea, he is fine.

If Shea says he's fine, I believe her. Her instincts are better than mine, and she can feel him through the bond just as I can.

With the last of the equipment packed away we leave The Pit and head home. The shift to Shea has exhausted me, and my appetite has increased immensely. With Kali going through the same and our latest mishap, we've agreed to eat at her house tonight. I also think sitting at our table without the guys will make us long for them more.

Before Damiean leaves us to return to his office, he asks for our assistance. "If you don't have any plans for tomorrow, I would be grateful for some help going through all the prophecies. Oberon left quite a list, and they could be relevant to what is happening with you both."

"Absolutely," Kali replies. "I feel bad leaving it all to Oberon anyway, but any time I ask if he needs help, he says he's got it."

"The man has a thirst for knowledge like I have never known," Damiean agrees. "Excellent. Come by my office in the morning, and I will set you up with the reading materials."

"We will be there," I reply, saying goodbye and continuing to our apartment block.

I'm lost in thoughts of Bran for a few minutes as we walk through the courtyard. Damiean's words were reassuring, and the bond is helping me not to lose my mind completely, but the unknown is the worst. All the what-ifs tumble through my mind before Shea brings them to a crashing halt.

This is not how we are spending our evening. I understand you are worried, but Bran is not the only strong one. He has a strong mate, and we must prove that now. We are a mate he can be proud of. Remember that.

"That was strange," Kali comments suddenly. "One second, you were freaking out, and the next, calm and in control. Can you teach me how to do that?"

"I wish I could. That's all Shea. Whenever I'm spiralling, she gets me back on track."

"That sounds nice. I could use a Shea."

"How about a Thea instead?" I smirk. "Shea has me covered for my freakouts, so I'll cover you with yours."

"Deal! Be warned, it could be a full-time job."

"I can handle it," I say, reaching the floor for our apartments. "I'm going to have a quick shower. You better not be lying about all the food you have because I will eat you if you are."

Kali giggles, and some of her tension lifts. "I think you're hot, Thea, but I don't swing that way."

"Ha, ha. Go shower, and I'll be over in ten. I mean it, lots of food!"

"Yeah, yeah."

Leaving her to enter my apartment, which feels cold without Bran's presence, I quickly strip off my borrowed clothes and rush through a shower. To avoid thinking more depressing thoughts and worrying myself, I sing random songs mashed together the entire time to keep my mind occupied.

Will you please hurry up. If I have to listen to any more of your so-called signing, I may shift just to shut you up.

You know you threaten that a lot, but could you actually do it? I mean, without a spike in my emotions.

Shut up.

I'll take that as a no, then.

I knock on Kali's door before opening it, letting myself in case she's still in the shower. The smell of food slams me in the face as soon as I step over the threshold. Meat, bread, and fruit combine in a wonderful assault on my nose, and I groan loudly.

"Good enough for you?" Kali asks, coming out of her bedroom.

"Where did you get all this food?" I reply, noting the numerous pies on the counter and more in the oven.

She waltzes over to the kitchen, nodding her head towards one of the stools for me to sit. "Anubis's mother. She brings us food nearly every day. I think she's trying to make up for her husband being such an asshole."

"What's the story there?" I ask with interest. Kali briefly mentioned there was a problem with her in-laws, and as my mate's father could potentially be my alpha, I'd like to know more about him.

As Kali completes the task of warming the food, she shares the entire story of her encounter with Bran and Anubis's parents, and it sounds distressing. Aria sounds loving and kind, and I'm relieved she had the wisdom to support Kali. As someone labelled a defect throughout her life, I find it unsettling that the alpha has an issue with Kali simply because she's not a shifter. It doesn't bode well for me and my current situation.

It's unlikely he'll be alpha enough for us anyway, so it's not an issue.

What about Bran, Shea? Would you want to be in a separate pack from him?

That won't be a problem. He will leave his pack to join ours.

But we don't have a pack, and that's awfully presumptuous of you.

Enjoy your evening. We can worry about those details another time.

"Come on, whatever you and Shea are disagreeing about, you can do it on the couch and stuff your face."

"Sorry," I mumble, helping grab some of the food and move over to the couch. "How could you tell we were disagreeing about something?"

"It's just something I've noticed. When we're close, I get a much better read on your emotions. I think I'm beginning to distinguish the difference between you and Shea."

Carving into a meat and potato pie, Kali serves half of it onto my plate, and I don't even flinch at the generous portion. When she hands me a glass of wine afterwards, I silently express gratitude for having someone like Kali in my life.

"Here's to terrorising recruits," I say, clinking my glass against hers.

I think you'll find it was me that did the terrorising, thank you.

"Yes, and here's to you my fearless cheetah," I smirk, raising my glass in a toast to Shea.

Kali chuckles as she turns to face me, "Girl, what in the unholy bird noises was that sound Shea made? I never realised cheetahs could even sound like that."

Laughter sparkles in her eyes, and I giggle, recalling our earlier fits of hysterics.

"I didn't either. Apparently, she can growl, but her bird chirp is her way of speaking."

It is NOT a bird chirp. I'll have you know that many prey fall foul with our meow.

Kali uses her wine glass to cover the grin spreading across her face, "Shea's not happy?" she asks, her voice laced with humour.

She may be our sister, but I will nip her if she does not stop laughing at me.

"Okay, fine. Kali, she says even though you're our sister, she will nip you next time if you keep laughing at her." Relaying what Shea said would sound more convincing if I wasn't so amused by the whole conversation.

Kali's laughter slower dies off, "Shea thinks of me as sister?"

"Yes. That's the reason she bit Jared. She is very protective of you, and when we felt your hurt, it was enough to force a shift."

I see and experience a whole range of emotions from her before the sensation of raindrops falls on my head. "God, you must think

I'm so pathetic," Kali says, wiping a tear away. "I swear I'm normally a lot more level-headed, and I've never been bothered whether people like me or not. I blame all these bloody bonds for making me more emotional."

Taking a large gulp of her wine, she looks up and groans in frustration at the small rain cloud gathered above our heads.

"I don't think you're pathetic at all," I tell her, squeezing her hand reassuringly. "I think we can both agree our emotions are on a much shorter fuse these days. I admire you a lot, Kali. You're strong, straightforward, honest and caring. I've always wanted siblings, and I'm honoured to have you as a sister."

"I feel that too," she says, taking a deep, controlled breath. "I'd been alone for too long, and then I got here, made all these new friends, and found my true mate and a sister. It's unbelievable to where I was two months ago, and it makes me wonder."

"Wonder what?"

"Is it all too good to be true? What's the price going to be for this kind of happiness? The issues we still have, the dreams and the other girls, I worry it will all be ripped away or implode in my face."

I contemplate her words and come to the realisation that she's right. Since arriving here, I've gained everything I ever desired—a home, a mate, a job, friends, and family. Is fate truly this generous, or will there be a price to pay for it all?

"Honestly, Kali, I have no idea what's still to come. I guess all we can do is enjoy the happiness until we have more to go on. Whatever unfolds for us, we'll get through it together.

With that sentiment in the forefront of my mind, the rest of the evening is perfect. We indulge in a feast, consuming far too much food, and share laughter over several bottles of wine. I offer Kali a more detailed glimpse into my previous life, the wine bringing out all sorts of depressing aspects. When I mention Angie, Kali insists she must meet her, and I promise her it's something I'll organise at the next available opportunity.

As the night progresses, we decide to have a sleepover, realising neither of us has experienced one before. In her living room, we fashion a makeshift bed and settle down to watch a movie, polishing off the remaining wine. Before long, my eyes start to flutter, and I drift off to sleep.

***

I become aware I'm no longer in Kali's living room but rather in the middle of the same field that has appeared in my dreams too many times. Knowing it will be one of those dreams fills me with dread, especially after the last one.

Observing the structure in the distance, I hesitate to approach. This place, this seemingly tranquil and innocent setting, fills me with anxiety every time I find myself here. I'm unsure what to expect—whether I'll uncover new nightmares or face an attack. Yet, as I stand amid the grass, surrounded by silence and a stillness that should resemble paradise, I find no joy in being here.

A part of me is tempted to test how long I can avoid the structure and witness the dream's progression. Will I remain standing here until I wake up, or will something compel me to approach? Unfortunately, I don't have to wait long to discover the answer.

"Six to save all."

It begins as a faint whisper, gradually escalating in volume as it persists. The same four words echo in an unending loop, causing a growing headache. As if I've been standing in the same spot for days, the urge to escape intensifies. I know what I need to do to break free from this unnerving cycle.

The moment I take a step forward, the structure materialises right in front of me, and the incessant words abruptly cease.

Choosing one post at random, I angrily press my hand against it, wanting this over with. The images unfold, and I see myself and Kali wearing some strange uniform but looking happy. The following image shocks me—it's clear. The next woman in the sequence has sleek black hair and the most unusual eyes, one blue and one purple. She is undeniably stunning, but I have no idea who she is. I'm confident I would remember someone with such distinctive features.

As I concentrate on the face and commit the details to memory, the name Seraphina is whispered close to me, and I almost jerk back from the post. It takes all my resolve to not move away as I wait for the next images to appear.

The subsequent three images feature other women, but none are as distinct as the first three. Then, the darker ones follow—a scene resembling some kind of battle. It's unclear whether this is in the past, present, or future. The imagery is filled with blood and carnage, and as they accelerate, a sense of nausea overtakes me. As I go to pull away from this distressing display, a solitary figure emerges, standing alone and observing the battle. I can't discern any features except that they are exceptionally tall.

A peculiar creature materialises beside the figure, and unless this is some kind of illusion, the creature has two heads. Two dog-like heads, if you can even call them that. Each head boasts a long snout and striking red eyes framed by impossibly tall, pointed ears. The creature's heads pivot to gaze directly at me, and when their colossal jaws part to reveal two rows of razor-sharp teeth, my heart beats erratically.

In an instant, the beast transitions from staring at me with its massive jaws open to being right in front of me. It's no longer an image. It's real.

I'm not ashamed to admit that I scream so loudly that I might have pierced my eardrums.

My screams still echoing in my ears, I gradually come to, only to realise it's not just my screams filling Kali's apartment—it's hers too. Our screams taper off as we lock eyes, simultaneously yelling, "Two-headed beast?"

We remain silent for a few minutes, the only sound being our ragged breaths in the quiet apartment. Suddenly, Kali's iPad emits a noise, causing us to shriek and leap up from our makeshift bed. Kali rushes over to answer it, and I hear the panicked voice of Anubis.

"Feisty, what's wrong? What's happening?"

"We're fine, we're fine," she sighs. "Just... a bad dream."

"We? Is Thea there?" Bran's voice comes over the speaker.

"Yes, I'm here. I'm okay," I tell him, relieved at hearing his voice.

"What happened?" Bran and Anubis ask at the same time.

"We had a sleepover, fell asleep, had the same dream, and both woke up screaming like a couple of banshees," Kali summarises.

"It doesn't sound bad when she says it like that, but it was terrifying," I clarify.

After reassuring our men that everything is genuinely okay and expressing how much we miss them, they inform us of their plan to return tomorrow. They don't share any specifics about their experiences, and since they haven't been away for long, I assume they haven't come across anything noteworthy yet.

However, after hearing Bran's voice and experiencing that nightmare, I eagerly anticipate the moment I get to see him again.

Have no fear. No two-headed beast can strike fear in me.

Oh, Shea, to have your confidence all the time would be amazing.

When the guys hang up, Kali immediately goes into the kitchen and puts the kettle on, "I need a fucking tea," she mutters. "We need tea, lots and lots of tea," she shouts back to me.

Following her to the kitchen, I take a seat on the stool, "Do you have any coffee?"

"Uhhh, I knew this was too good to be true. Where are all my tea drinkers at?"

I snicker at her as she sets about making the drinks. The dream lingers, and I can't get the image of that damn beast out of my head.

"So, you want to tell me about me about yours?" I ask Kali as she hands me over a poorly made coffee.

Her shoulders tense for a second before she takes a sip of her tea. I feel and see her visibly relax the more she drinks.

"Same as usual, weird structure, the images of women and then the blood and stuff. The beast was new though," she looks at me, "It was right in my face, Thea. One minute, I was looking at it through the images, then next, it was right there."

Getting up from the stool, I approach her, putting my arm around her shoulder and giving her a little squeeze.

"It was the same for me. Scared the absolute shit out of me," I shudder thinking about it.

Kali huffs a laugh, "That's the first time I've heard you swear, so it must have been bad."

Taking our drinks back over to the couch, something else from the dream suddenly dawns on me, "Did you see the woman, the third one?"

"Yes," she exclaims. "Seraphina."

"You heard the name too, then. Let's go to Damiean and see if he can help us figure this out."

CHAPTER TWENTY-NINE

Despite the additional details from the dream, as I leave Kali's place, I find myself no closer to figuring out what it all signifies. My mind is a cyclone of images, from the lone figure to the beast and the woman with the unusual eyes. It's the first time Kali and I have shared the same dream simultaneously, and I don't believe that was a coincidence. Whoever is orchestrating the chaos behind all this intended for us to experience that shared dream, but to what end?

Now we've had a glimpse of what one of the other women looks like and a single name—the challenge is clear. How does this information aid us in finding her? There could be thousands of Seraphinas, and we're left clueless about where to start the search. Even if we do manage to locate her, what next? We lack any real substantial information, except that we had a dream involving her, accompanied by a sense of foreboding.

Will she laugh in our faces? Tell us to go away? Has she been having the same dreams? The questions pile up at a rapid rate, and I see no way of getting any answers.

You are giving me a headache. Solve each problem one at a time, and maybe take some Valium.

Thanks, Shea, fantastic insight. The chaos in my mind will not be resolved by Valium. The least you could do is offer some words of comfort.

There, there.

Wow, you're in a great mood today! Did you see the beast?

Not in the dream, no. Since you continue to think of its appearance, I have an idea of what we are dealing with. I am not worried.

If we ever come face to face with something like that, I'll be relying on you to deal with it.

And I will.

Shea's certainty helps as I finish getting ready. It's not merely the words, snarky as they may be, but the genuine emotions she conveys—she is not afraid. It doesn't completely eradicate my fear, but it does help alleviate some of the anxiety caused by this situation.

When Kali knocks on my door, I head out to meet her, my thoughts slightly more settled now I've had some time to process the dream. It's still early this morning, and no one is around when we enter the courtyard.

"One good thing to come out of that horrendous fucking dream was at least we got to speak to the guys. They sounded okay, right?" Kali asks, wringing her hands through her hoodie.

"Yes, they sounded fine. More worried about us, I think. It's incredible when you think about it. Even with our distance, the moment we were truly scared, they could feel it."

"Would be nice if I could feel Anubis properly right now."

The bond tells me my sister is not doing all that well. There's anxiety coursing through her, but I don't mention it until we're in the canteen and seated at our table with breakfast.

"I hate picking out my own food," she mutters glumly.

"Kali, talk to me," I say softly. "I'm your Shea, remember, and I can feel you're anxious."

"It's... ahh... it's everything. Anubis being away, not feeling him enough through the bond. The dreams, the next woman, our powers. And... I have a bad feeling, Thea. Something is coming for us, or we're mixed up in all the blood and death. The rug is about to be pulled out from under us, and I have no idea why."

I can only squeeze her hand to comfort her because she's right. We're stuck in the middle of something we know nothing about, and the more clues we get, the worse the bigger picture seems.

"As your friend and sister, I would love to tell you not to worry, to promise everything will turn out fine, but I'm not going to lie to you. I agree we're entangled in something bigger, and until we know what it is, we can only rely on each other, our mates and our friends. Whatever it is, we won't be alone, and as unpredictable as our powers are, we are far from powerless. We have both grown up with uncertainty and loneliness, yet we are not those same people anymore, and I take comfort in that. We are stronger, and most importantly, we are together. Let that fact help guide you through this next bit, alright?"

Her body deflates as my words wash over her, some of the anxiety leaking out of the bond as she slowly builds herself back up again.

"Damn, that was good," she sighs happily. "You should be a spokesperson or something because shit, did that have the desired effect. Thank you."

"You're welcome," I chuckle. "Just remember this moment for when I have a wobble because, believe me, it will happen."

"So, how do we figure out our next steps?" Kali asks, starting on her breakfast and seeming a little more relaxed.

"We start with research," I state, the beginnings of a plan starting to form. "We need to go through everything that Damiean and Oberon have managed to find. To them, it may be useless information, but for us, it might spark some kind of recognition, some clue we need to follow."

"You think they've missed something?"

"Not necessarily. They've been searching based on the information we've given them and our current condition, but what if it's not enough?"

"How else would you go about it?" she questions, her brows drawn in confusion.

"I'm not sure, but something tells me if there are clues out there, it will be us that find them. Think about it: we're experiencing the dreams, seeing the faces of the women, the lone figure and the beast. Perhaps the dreams are guiding us more than we think."

"I don't want to research that beast or the lone figure. Bloody thing gave me the creeps," she shudders, recalling the image.

Tell her not to worry about that. Neither of those things will get near her.

That may not offer much reassurance, Shea, when we don't even know what they are.

Regardless, she should feel safe.

"What? What is she saying?" Kali prompts impatiently.

"She told me to tell you that you're safe, that neither of those things will get near you while she's around."

"Aww, she's so sweet. Thank you, Shea, I appreciate that."

Shea's satisfaction thrums through me, and I have to smile at my overprotective cheetah. She truly loves Kali as much as I do. As we finish the rest of our breakfast, we dissect the dream, trying to pick out any details that may lead us to another clue. Other than the dream place with the posts, when the images of blood and death occur, there's nothing much in the way of a location, though granted, it would be hard to focus on, given what we're seeing.

Before we can leave to head to Damiean's office, the familiar figure tracks us down, smiling as he takes a seat beside me.

"Good morning, ladies. How are we today?"

I don't get a chance to formulate an answer before Damiean starts to chuckle. I cock my head to the side, wondering over his reaction.

"You do have such a wonderful way with words, Kali," he comments, eyes shining with amusement.

"You would know when you're always in my head," she scolds lightly. "Am I not getting any better at all?"

"You are. Though you were practically screaming those thoughts at me. Sounds like a rough night."

Ah, now it makes sense. Kali will have automatically answered truthfully in her head on how our morning is going. Based on last night, I can only imagine what her answer must have been.

"We need every bit of research you have," I tell him, getting straight to the point. "Something is triggering these dreams and the images we're seeing. There must be a record of the dream place, the symbols and posts somewhere."

"Nothing to my knowledge, but then you both challenge what I know constantly, so perhaps you're right."

"You seem a little put out by that, Damiean," Kali sasses.

"Not at all. I do love a good challenge," he grins mischievously. "If you're finished, we can head over to my office now."

We stand to leave the canteen, and it dawns on me that Damiean didn't come in here for breakfast. It's still early, so how was he sure we would be here?

"I received a call from two frantic males," he tells me, answering my unspoken question.

"You did?" I ask, surprised. I would have thought after our brief conversation, they would have been straight back to the mission, returning to dark mode.

"It's amusing that you're surprised. Did you think one phone call would assuage their fears? They are your mates."

"Did they ask you to come and find us?"

"More like demanded it."

The thought of Bran being so concerned he demanded Damiean find us is worrying. They need to be focused on the mission, not fretting about us having a dream. What if we compromised them and gave away their purpose there. I would never forgive myself if something happened to him because I had a bad dream.

"Althea, if I may, it's a little more complex than a bad dream. You have both experienced physical manifestations while in this dream place. It's only rational, Bran would worry. Trust me, they are very experienced and will have ensured it was safe to call before doing so."

"I... Yes, I suppose you're right."

He nods slightly as we enter the elevator and head towards his office. As we ride the elevator, I can't help replaying the last time I was in this building, going towards Damiean's office. I was with him and my father, and my whole world was about to change because of an arranged mating. I can almost see my hunched form, waiting for my life to be handed over to someone else and dreading what came next.

If only I could go back and reassure my past self that everything would be fine, that my life would change for the better. I likely wouldn't have believed it, but it could have saved me some stress.

The setting is the same as last time when we enter the office. The sizeable imposing desk, the bookcase taking up a whole wall, the chairs, and the windows bring back memories, and I see my father the way I did that day. He stood by the window, radiating tension and alpha power, looking down his nose at everyone. Seeing his image in my mind, I ask myself what I was so scared of.

Yes, he was my alpha, but he wasn't necessarily powerful. He didn't have the same air of authority that Damiean does, the same imposing command that Bran and Anubis possess. And yet, after all the years of rejection, name-calling and demands, I was terrified of him. Coming here has opened my eyes to what a real alpha should be, and I promise myself that if I ever become an alpha, I will never behave the way my father has.

Like I would let you.

I know. Still, the reminder of what we've come from is always good—the pitfalls to avoid. You're also new to the shifter world; you've got a lot to catch up on.

It's different for me. I am an alpha who has had to watch a pack follow an imbecile, all the while knowing he was not fit to lead. I understand the pitfalls and will be a good alpha.

Always so confident.

"Let's start by you telling me the specifics of the dream?" Damiean says, sitting behind his desk and pulling a laptop in front of him. "Oberon has been compiling a report, then analysing and cataloguing any similarities or identifying factors."

Kali begins to describe the particulars of the dream, and I add my input when required. Listening to Kali recount the details confirms our dreams were identical, not a single difference. It strikes me as strange. Until this point, they have been similar, but this seems purposeful, as if having the same dream is trying to drive home a message.

The question is, what message?

"Any ideas?" Kali asks Damiean when she's told him everything.

He continues to work on the computer for a few more minutes before leaning back in his chair with a sigh.

"Based on my knowledge, the dreams, and the bonds, I'm reasonably certain that this indicates some kind of prophecy. The challenge lies in the fact that supernaturals have a penchant for prophecies. As a result, there are literally hundreds to sift through," he pauses, allowing that information to settle in.

Prophecy? It's a word that has been thrown around a few times, and I can see why he would deduce that. What makes us special enough to be part of a prophecy?

"And if there are hundreds of them, how do we determine if our situation lends itself to one?" Based on Damiean's expression, I think I can guess the answer.

"Oberon began compiling a list of prophecies he deemed potentially relevant to the ongoing events in the world. He has narrowed it to one hundred and ninety-seven prophecies requiring more in-depth examination."

"I'm sorry," I stammer. "Did you say one hundred and ninety-seven?"

"I'm afraid so."

"Fucking fantastic. You sure you want to be more hands on with the research?" Kali asks me with a raised brow.

"And just how many doomsday events are supposed to happen over the years?" If Oberon has it narrowed down, how many more did he exclude?

"Not all of them are necessarily tied to doomsday events," Damiean explains. "Some may pertain to specific races, individual families, or even planetary realignment. As I mentioned, the range is extensive. I suggest we start by delving into Oberon's list and focusing on elements related to the number six, dreams, bonds, women, restrictions—"

"Yep, we get it," Kali interrupts.

"Any clue on how we find a Seraphina?" I ask, circling back to what might be the easier task.

"I'll look into that aspect as you are examining the prophecies. Our extensive database contains information on the whereabouts of thousands of supernaturals. With a bit of luck, she might be in the database. However, given the lack of additional information, it could potentially yield a lengthy list."

Fantastic, another long list to go through.

It may not be the greatest plan ever set out, but we need to start somewhere, and this is our current direction. If luck is on our side, we'll find something. If not, we should be able to rule out many possibilities.

Kali and I make ourselves comfortable in Damiean's office as he allocates the first thirty books to start trawling through. He also provides a large pot of tea and coffee, gods bless him.

We divide the books between us and spend the next few hours meticulously examining each prophecy. The supernatural world is filled with some truly bizarre content, and considering I've always been aware of my identity, I can't fathom what must be going through Kali's head as she reads through some of this material.

"I've heard everything now," Kali says, closing the book she was reading.

"What?"

"There's a freaking prophecy about the uprising of gargoyles. I thought they were just weird-looking statues stuck on buildings. Now I know there's going to be an uprising. I'll never look at them the same again."

I snigger at the horrified expression on her face. If only all the prophecies were that simple.

I've read through an entire book about Fae prophecies, and some of them are so complex I can't even begin to understand the intricacies of their race.

It takes an additional two hours before I come across anything vaguely resembling our situation, and even then, I'm unsure about its relevance. The prophecy discusses the alignment of six planets in our solar system and the advancement of the human race. The only reason I've singled it out is because it mentions the number six.

I place it in the maybe pile and move to the next book. As the hours pass, I sense my determination from this morning draining away. This task is monumental, akin to searching for a needle in a haystack. It's no wonder Oberon and Damiean haven't unearthed anything yet.

We've worked through lunch, only snacking, and as the sun begins to set, both Shea and my body yearn for some nourishment.

Yes, you must eat now. You cannot concentrate any longer when your focus is on food. You need steak, lots of steak.

"Kali," I call, pulling her away from the research. "Let's leave it for today and go get some food."

She slams the book closed that she was reading, "Hell yes. I need three plates full and two desserts."

As we're about to leave, Damiean comes back into his office. He's been stuck in here with us for most of the day but has been gone for the last hour. I can't imagine he's eaten yet. "We're calling it a day and getting some food. Care to join us?"

"Yes, I will. I can inform you of what I've been able to find," he replies, following as we leave his office.

Thank goodness for the canteen, otherwise, we wouldn't eat as well as we do. The three of us proceed to fill up several places, and once we're seated with our food, Damiean shares his findings.

"I've narrowed down the search for Seraphina to three individuals. Assuming she's around your age significantly reduced the search criteria. One of them is located overseas, and the other two are based here in England. Though we have no indication that all the women from your dreams would be in England, it seems like a reasonable place to start."

"That's great! So, where are they? Do we just rock up to each one and say, 'Hey, you've been in our dreams, come with us?'" Kali says with a touch of sarcasm.

Damiean smiles, taking a moment to finish his mouthful of food before responding, "I believe a more tactful approach might be necessary, Kali, but essentially, yes. Considering you both had the dreams before arriving here, it's plausible the others are also experiencing them. That should make it easier to persuade whichever woman it turns out to be. Additionally, the bond the two of you share might play a crucial role. If you're all connected, perhaps you'll sense a bond with Seraphina and be able to confirm if she's the right person."

That hadn't occurred to me before. I sensed something was unfolding even before Kali entered the room, and the bond fell into place the moment our eyes met. If a similar connection occurs with Seraphina, it would be a definitive confirmation that she's the correct one.

"Then let's plan a trip."

CHAPTER THIRTY

FINISHED WITH OUR MEAL, we strategise on the best way to handle the situation—who to visit first and what to say. I can't gauge how the scenario might unfold. Two unfamiliar women arrive at your doorstep to explain they've been having dreams about you, and you need to leave with these strangers to unravel a mystery we hardly grasp ourselves.

If it were me, I'm not sure I would believe it.

We also know nothing about this person, what her life has been like up to this point. Is she aware she's a supernatural, or will she be new to it all like Kali? If her situation is the same as Kali's, then trying to explain the circumstances will be even more difficult.

We bring up the prophecies Kali, and I considered as potential possibilities with Damiean, getting his insights on whether they could align with our current experiences. He dismisses most of them, only a select few carrying a sense of familiarity he wants to explore further.

By the time we're ready to head home, we've discussed so many different theories I'm starting to feel depressed.

You are? Try sitting here and listening to it all without being able to input. If I hear apocalyptic one more time, I may rip my ears off.

Excessive. What is your take on it? You've never actually mentioned anything about it since our connection became whole.

We are a part of something big. Unfortunately, I don't know what that is. I can sense we are different, not like other shifters.

In what way?

Well, for starters, we can communicate with each other. I also know—with certainty—we are an alpha that needs our own pack. Not just any pack, we need strong members, powerful. And I...

What? Why are you hesitating?

I didn't want to mention it because I can't be sure if it's a by-product of the restrictions we still have or if it's something else.

Oh god, what aren't you telling me?

"Thea? Is everything okay?" Kali interrupts with concern.

"Not sure," I reply. "I'm just talking with Shea about something. I'll explain in a minute."

Go on, Shea, tell me.

We are different. I can sense we are more powerful than most, but I do not believe all the power comes directly from me.

Where else would it be coming from?

That's why I never said anything, because I can't be sure.

Do you think the restrictions are keeping all this power at bay?

Yes. Even in shifted form, I can feel it, but I can't access it.

What does that mean for us?

You're not going to like my answer.

Tell me anyway.

I don't know what that means for us because I can't identify where it's coming from.

Are you telling me this is another question we don't have an answer for?

Essentially, yes. As I've said, all I can tell you is that we are different.

I don't want to be different.

I'm afraid you don't have a choice in the matter, dear. It is my belief that we are destined for great things.

Based on the dreams and the images I'm seeing, I'm not sure I'd agree with you.

Sadly, only time will tell.

I sigh deeply, wondering what else this life has in store for me. I'm not exactly sure what to do with the information Shea has shared and if any of it is relevant to what is happening now.

"Thea?" Kali questions again. "I don't like what I'm feeling from you. What's going on?"

"Did you hear any of that?" I ask, turning to Damiean.

"No, I can only hear your responses, not what Shea is saying."

"Shea thinks we're different," I explain to them both.

"Erm, not to be rude, but yeah, obviously," Kali snorts. "That information is not new, so why are you freaking out?"

"Different, as in we're not like other shifters. Shea can feel something powerful within us but believes it's being blocked by the restrictions."

"Oh. Oh well, that is new," Kali remarks.

"And this power, is it a part of you both or separate?" Damiean probes.

"She can't be sure. In shifted form, Shea can feel it but can't access it. Until the restrictions are gone, we'll have to wait and see."

"Is it something you can feel?"

"No. I don't think so. I feel my connection to Shea, though it's not as strong as it should be. My bonds to Bran and Kali are strong, but I don't know what else to search for."

Damiean nods in understanding, "At this point, I don't see this being a cause for concern. We're aware Kali has the potential to be the strongest of her kind. Perhaps the same is true for you also. It would certainly make sense in terms of a prophecy. Usually, only the strongest are chosen."

"So we wait and see," I repeat sombrely, fed up with the same answer for everything.

"I'm afraid so. I understand this must be incredibly frustrating, but I firmly believe you wouldn't have been placed in this situation if you weren't capable of handling it. In your brief time here, both of you have made significant strides and should take pride in your accomplishments. I believe we have not seen the best from you yet."

"You sound like Shea," I huff.

"Then a very wise cheetah she must be," Damiean chuckles.

He has no idea.

With nothing further to discuss, we call it a day, say goodbye to Damiean and make our way to Kali's apartment. After last night's dream, we both agree to spend the night together, neither wanting to be alone.

When we enter her apartment, the first thing Kali does is pull out a bottle of wine. "No more doomsday talk, no more asking questions we can't get the answers to. Tonight, we drink and bond."

"That sounds like a perfect idea!"

Grabbing two glasses, we head over to the couch, and I pour us both a generous measure as Kali does something on her iPad. A couple of seconds later, music flows through the speakers dotted about the living room.

"Can you believe this shit?" she laughs lightly. "At my old place, I had a couch, coffee table and crappy TV. Now here I sit, surrounded by lovely furnishings and the latest technology, drinking wine that doesn't taste like vinegar while sitting with a friend who is fully aware of my secret powers."

"It is something. Tell me about your old place, where you lived. What was it like?"

Over the next hour, I get an animated rundown of Kali's life before SNHQ. I admire her resilience in facing her challenges solo, and I can't help but laugh when she describes some of the 'mishaps' she's experienced over the years. I sense some of these incidents scared her, as having little control over the outcome can be terrifying. However, the story she shares with me now seems to be one of the happier moments in her journey with her powers.

"There I was standing in line, arms full of chocolate and two tubs of ice cream, when this woman starts getting all bitchy with me," she huffs, taking a gulp of her wine.

"Admittedly, I didn't do myself any favours by mumbling under my breath about what she was wearing. I mean, who goes to the shop in their dressing gown and slippers? Anyway, she hears me and starts bitching at me to mind my own damn business and blah, blah, blah.

"Now, if it hadn't been that time of the month, it probably would've panned out differently, but as it was, I was already feeling a little ragey. So I stand there, taking the abuse this woman is giving and not noticing that my hands are getting hotter and melting my bloody ice cream. As the line starts moving along, the woman steps forward and slips into the ice cream. Her legs spread eagle as she goes down, and the whole store gets a front-row seat to what's under her dressing gown!"

"You're joking," I cackle, my sides hurting from laughing as I place my wine on the coffee table to avoid dripping on the couch.

"Honestly, I'm not sure what was worse," Kali snorts, trying hard to finish the story through fits of giggles. "The fact that her pubes were in the shape of an arrow pointing down... or the tattoo she had on her inner thigh of Popeye."

I lose it, bursting into hysterics along with Kali. It takes minutes for us to calm down enough that I can wheeze out my question. "What... what happened after?"

"Well, after she exposed her bare ass trying to get up, she left that store so fast, she left one of her slippers behind."

The end of her story promotes another round of hysterics, but as we're in the throes of laughter, something strange happens. As if our bond has become overloaded with emotions, a pulse of energy is released from Kali, causing the TV and the coffee table to explode. As if that wasn't strange enough, my own emotional overload happens, and I abruptly shift into Shea.

Gods! I wasn't ready for that. What the hell is going on.

I... I... don't. One minute, we're enjoying ourselves, and the next...

Shea turns our head to Kali, who is as still as a statue, staring gobsmacked at the TV.

Shea, make sure Kali's alright, please. I think she's in shock.

Shea jumps back up onto the couch and nudges Kali's arm with her head. The motion prompts Kali to turn. "Shea," she gasps, grabbing onto the fur around our neck.

"I... I didn't... I didn't mean to do that. I don't even know how I did it."

If I had to guess, we were a little too happy, causing our powers to leak out of us. I can feel Kali freaking out, but not being able to talk to her, all I can do is send her reassurances down the bond.

Shea pushes Kali back on the couch and lays herself halfway across her lap, purring gently.

She will be okay. She just needs to calm down and regulate her breathing.

We sit like this for some time, Shea purring as I send comfort down the bond.

"This is what I did at the coffee shop," Kali confesses quietly. "I got so angry that I blew up the front of the store. I'm a danger to everyone."

Shea growls low, disliking where Kali's thoughts have gone. I need to speak to her, to restore her confidence and tell her she's not a danger. Nobody was hurt, and though my reactions may not cause such a destructive effect, I understand, and I'm with her.

It's so unfair. Someone like Kali, the most loving and kindest person you will ever meet, should not have to deal with this. We should have never been tampered with, but the fact that someone thought it was okay to do this to Kali, makes me livid.

Calm yourself, she is okay.

No! She is not okay. She is hurting, and none of this is her fault!

Shea jumps off Kali's lap and starts to pace around the room.

You're right. It's not fair, she deserves better. So do we, but this is our situation.

At least we've always known what we are. Kali has done this all alone, and when she should be enjoying herself and her powers, she's terrified of them!

Althea.

Stop it. I know what you're going to say, and it's wrong. I want—

"Shea, what's going on? I can feel your anger."

You need to calm down before you upset Kali any further.

I... I can't. My blood feels like it's burning, and I want to burn the people that did this to us.

You need to run. Too much is built up in you, and you need to expel it somehow.

But Kali...

"It's okay, Thea, go. I'll be right here when you get back. Go, I promise I'm okay." Kali walks over to the door to let us out, and without waiting for me to agree, Shea takes off.

I have no idea what's going on, how I went from happiness to shock to anger and why the latter is taking over me so completely. I feel the red-hot rage burning through me and grit my teeth against the scream that's lodged in my throat.

Okay, Althea, just like last time, immerse yourself into the run. Think of nothing else but running.

When Shea's paws pound against the grass and the forest looms ahead, I focus on seeing what she sees, hearing what she hears. By the time she's made it into the forest and sets off at an alarming speed, I'm fully immersed, and the rage simmers.

I can't tell how long we stay out here, only that we circle the village perimeter seventy times before Shea starts to slow.

Better?

I think so, yes. How did you know that's what I needed?

It was more of an educated guess. You were overloaded with too many emotions, and anger tends to be the one most people can get lost in. You just needed to focus on something else.

Can we go back to Kali now?

Sure.

Even though we are far from our apartment block, it takes less than three minutes to reach Kali's door. Shea raises our paw, using our claws to scratch against the door. When Kali opens the door, her face reveals she's been crying. Shea enters the apartment, winding around Kali's legs and offering her comfort in the only way she can.

The glass has all been cleaned away, and Kali has made a bed in the living room again. Gently grabbing Kali's sleeve with our teeth, Shea guides her over to the makeshift bed. She deflates on the spot, turning on her side and making herself small.

Shea places our head against Kali's legs and gently begins to purr. "I'm not sure why, but I find it comforting when you do that."

It's because we are alpha and have the ability to comfort our pack when they are in need.

I thought Kali was our sister, not pack?

She is both, and this confirms it. Only pack can feel comfort from this.

Well, if it's helping her, please don't stop.

I won't. You rest, too. Don't worry, I will look after you both.

I don't feel like resting, but after thirty minutes of listening to Kali's deep breathing and Shea's purr, I fall into a thankfully, dreamless sleep.

CHAPTER THIRTY-ONE

At some point throughout the night, I'd shifted from Shea back to myself, waking up still laid on Kali's legs. When I move away and straighten out, she wakes, murmuring Anubis's name.

"Hey," I croak, voice still thick with sleep. "How are you feeling?"

"Like shit. You?"

"Hungry. Like I haven't eaten for weeks."

"Now you mention it, I'm starving," she agrees, sitting in the makeshift bed. When her eyes land on the broken TV, she sighs deeply. "Blown up TV from bloody laughing. Could our lives get any more weird?"

"Yes, I believe they can," I huff. "You know it's not your fault, right?"

"I know. I had time to think about it when you were freaking out and went for a run. It was more of a shock. I haven't used that power since the day I blew up the coffee shop. Doing it again brought back all the fear I felt then."

"But you're—"

"I am stronger now, I realise that. Still didn't stop me from freaking out. What about you? What was with all the anger and confusion? It was as if you had a split personality. You kept flitting from one to the other so quickly, you were giving me whiplash."

I don't understand it myself. The thought of Kali being upset sent me spiralling. "It was like an overload. When I sensed your fear, it triggered something in me that kept building and building. All I could focus on were the people that did this to us. I wanted to find them, to hurt them the way they have done to us. Once I'd been for the run with Shea, it settled. Either that or I was too exhausted."

"Jesus, you on a murderous rampage and me blowing shit up for fun. What a pair we make."

"No one would mess with us."

"I guess there is that," Kali chuckles.

We get up, and I tidy away the bed as Kali makes us drinks. It's still early morning, but neither of us is getting any more sleep, and with the guys hopefully returning today, I'm too eager to just sit around. We discuss last night a little more, both coming to the same conclusion that wine and laughter are not a good combination for us.

"When we eve—" My words are cut off by the pounding in my chest, the feeling of excitement overwhelming me from my mate bond.

"The guys are back!" Kali squeals, jumping up and scrambling for her shoes.

I follow hastily, my own joy and relief filtering down the bond. Until now, I didn't realise how muted the bond felt with our distance. Now he's close I can feel him so much clearer. We exit Kali's apartment in a rush of limbs and crazy hair, neither of us taking the time to check our appearance before leaving.

It's only when we step into the elevator and catch our reflections in the mirror that we groan in unison. Both still dressed in our sleep clothes, our shoes not even tied properly, we're quite the sight.

"Here," Kali says, handing me a hair tie. "You need this more than I do," she laughs, looking at the wild mane I'm currently sporting.

I would've liked to look a little more put together when we were reunited, but my excitement outweighs my worries about appearance. When the elevator doors open, we eagerly exit, bursting through the doors of Oak and into the courtyard.

It takes us less than two seconds to locate them at the other side of the courtyard, walking our way and both wearing the same big smiles. Kali takes off running, and I go to follow, utterly thrilled to see my mate in the flesh again. Only the excitement becomes too much. From the corner of my eye, I notice flowers following in Kali's wake. Dozens of white lilies litter the ground the closer she gets to Anubis.

Please, Shea, not now.

I'm sorry, I can't stop it.

The emotions from Bran and I are too much, and it can only result in one thing. My bones start snapping mid-run as the shift takes over me. I fully transform into Shea, only to land in Bran's arms as my cheetah self.

This is not the reunion I wanted.

Don't blame me. Although I am liking the outcome.

Shea licks Bran's face, and in that moment, I want the ground to swallow me.

"Hello, my beautiful mate," he practically purrs at Shea. "Did you miss me?"

Shea nips at him playfully, and he chuckles, the sound moving through me, sending a pleasurable shiver down my spine.

I hate my life right now.

No, you don't. You're just jealous.

Of course, I'm jealous! I missed him and wanted to express that.

And you still can. You seem to think that when you're in this form, you are no longer you, but this is still you, and you can still express yourself, just in a different way. Now stop being spoilt, and let me enjoy our mate.

You don't have to sound so smug about it.

"I can feel your disappointment, babe, but don't worry, we're still together," Bran murmurs, leaning his forehead against Shea's.

The connection between us soothes my worries. To feel him this close, to have his scent surrounding me, is precisely what I need. I pour my love, relief and happiness through the bond, and I feel those same feelings coming from Bran. He's home.

The sound of Kali's voice interrupts our moment, "Oh, Thea," she says, her tone sad but slightly amused. "It sucks to be you right now."

Don't I know it.

Bran places us on the ground, but his hand never leaves us, his fingers stroking through the fur behind our ears and neck. I've never been petted before, and it feels incredible. I want to curl up in his lap so he can do it all day.

"The others have gone straight to Damiean's office, and we need to head over there now to debrief. Are you joining us?" Anubis says to

Kali before looking down at me with a smirk. "Nice to see you again, Shea."

Shea nods our head in acknowledgement before following the group towards SNHQ. We stay practically glued to Bran's side the whole way there, and none of the curious looks bother Shea, striding confidently next to her mate.

"Was everything okay here? No more dreams?" Anubis asks Kali when we enter the elevator.

"Dreams? No. Okay? No. I owe you a new TV and a coffee table," Kali offers sheepishly.

"Why? What happened? Are you okay, who—"

"Anubis breathe. I'm fine, we're fine. We decided to have a drink last night after a depressing day of doomsday prophecies. I was telling Thea a story, a fricking hilarious one."

"The one with the woman at the supermarket?" Anubis guesses.

"Yes, that one. Anyway, we were laughing and the next thing my powers reacted, and I blew up the TV and coffee table. I'm sorry."

"Feisty, you have no reason to be sorry. I'm just glad you're okay."

"Was Thea okay?" Bran asks Kali as he looks at Shea.

"Erm, not exactly. She immediately shifted into Shea and had trouble calming her emotions. She needed to run it off and only woke up as Thea this morning."

Bran reaches for us again, both hands cradling Shea's face as he looks deep into her golden eyes as if he's trying to reach me inside her. "I'm sorry I wasn't here, babe. I'm glad you're okay."

Our mate is very caring. I am enjoying this feeling.

You sound a little surprised, Shea. Does the big bad alpha feel all mushy for her mate?

Yes, I believe I do. He is gentle with us but still allows us to be dominant when we need it. He is the perfect match for us.

I couldn't agree more.

Everyone is already waiting for us by the time we reach Damiean's office and when he quickly realises there isn't enough room for us all, we relocate to one of the conference rooms. Bran immediately pulls out one of the chairs for us to jump into, and with him seated beside us, he returns to his petting. For the first few minutes I find it hard to follow the conversation, the rhythmic movement of Bran's hand soothing me enough that I want to sleep.

"Was your mission successful? Did you find any new information?" I hear Damiean ask and force myself to focus on the conversation.

Anubis sighs before answering, "Not sure I'd call it successful. It was much worse than we've been led to believe."

"How much worse are we talking?" Damiean questions, looking between them all.

"From what we saw, the whole south side of the country is going through mass panic. Riots, looting, protests, the government controls what's being broadcast to the rest of the country and shows only a small amount of what's happening there. It's bad, Damiean."

"Do we have estimates of how many are actually missing?" Damiean asks, taking out his notepad and writing the information down.

"Closer to two and a half thousand now. Whoever is doing this is branching out. Cases have been reported from all over the country. The highest count is mainly in the south, but more reports are also being received from the North now."

"Has anywhere else in the world reported any mass missing people?" Kali asks what I'm thinking.

"No, from what we know, this is all isolated to England only," Anubis responds grimly.

"The government are restricting the information released to avoid a countrywide riot, but I'm not sure how much longer they're going to be able to keep that up," Balbur explains.

"What about magical signatures?" Damiean asks.

"Well, this is where it gets interesting," Oberon starts. "It's undeniably supernatural related, only it's something we've never come across before."

Castiel paces the room as he adds his conclusion to the mix, "We were lucky enough to find a trace in Oxford, where the most recent missing case had been reported. It was slightly stale when we got there, but the energy was unreal. Something extremely powerful is behind these missing people, Damiean, and we need to be prepared for it. The intent behind the magic was teeming with darkness."

"What does that mean?" Kali questions, her bond pulsing with worry.

"Every spell, potion, power or magical ability leaves a trace, an energy trail to follow. Whenever a supernatural uses their power, there is always intent behind it. If you shift with the intent to kill people, the energy will be dark, and if you shift with the intent to enjoy being one with your animal, the energy or intent will be light. Some spells and potions can have both depending on what they were created for and how they are used."

Castiel's explanation is news to me, and there are so many questions I want to ask. As if sensing my frustration, Bran scratches behind my ear, comforting me in the only way he can.

"So, this power used to take the people is all dark?" Kali clarifies.

"Not just dark, Blondie, black hole, ancient dark. I excel in reading energy signatures and have experienced nearly every type there is, until now. I've never felt or seen anything like it. I was almost compelled by it," Castiel shudders, slumping into one of the seats.

"What do you mean?" Damiean snaps out, instantly concerned by Castiel's words.

"As I was reading the signature, something was pulling at me," Castiel says but then shakes his head. "No, that's not quite right, something was trying to influence me, whispering in my head, and I could feel my free will being sucked from me, almost like it was trying to suck my soul out and leave me an empty vessel."

Silence descends over the table as we picture what Castiel is describing. As someone who's had their free will taken from them, I understand how that might feel, just maybe not quite as forceful.

"How did you break the compulsion?" Damiean asks Castiel.

"To be honest, I'm not sure. One minute, I'm reading the signature, and then next, the guys are all screaming at me and slapping my face. If it was that powerful against a supernatural, I can only imagine what it would be like against a human. They wouldn't stand a chance."

"So, what now? And if someone says more research, I might actually lose it," Kali says, looking around at everyone.

"The government obviously wants us more involved. They want sizable teams of supernaturals stationed at every major city, ensuring we're on hand if or when it happens again. After hearing your report, I must agree. Whatever is causing this, for certain, is supernatural, making this our responsibility," Damiean states gravely.

I tense under his words, as two days without Bran here was bad enough. I can't imagine him being gone longer than that.

"You need to call in reinforcements," Bran says, speaking up for the first time. "I can't go back down there yet. My bear did not take too kindly to being separated from our mate after only just finding her."

The relief is instant, and I'm happy we're on the same page. It was exactly what I needed to hear.

"Absolutely, I shall start making some calls. This is not something the other headquarters can ignore now. They will send reinforcements," Damiean assures.

Bran relaxes his touch slightly as they continue to talk about where the teams will be needed and how they will manage the government going forward. From the sounds of things, this has now become a supernatural problem, and the government will follow our lead. I'm sure they're going to love that.

I lean further into Bran, enjoying his warmth as my mind turns over everything I've heard. The words from my dream keep popping into my mind, 'six to save all' and 'six to determine the fate'. Do all the missing people and this ancient energy have something to do with our dreams, our restrictions? Seems coincidental for it all to be happening at the same time. Are we meant to stop whatever is doing this? Or are these two completely different issues?

You are giving me a headache again.

Get used to it. It seems this is only going to get bigger. What do you think?

I have been learning with you, but I'm afraid I have no theories other than the instinct to find the other women is strong.

Why?

Because if we are bonded to these other women, they could be members of our pack.

This again. Why is it so important that we have a pack, that we don't join the one here? Also, I'd like to point out that Kali is not a shifter, and these other women might not be either.

They do not need to be shifters to be in our pack. I need to meet the current alpha here to determine if this feeling driving me is correct. Once I meet the alpha, I'll be certain.

Okay, I'll ask Bran to set something up with his father. If you are wrong, then we must join this pack.

Agreed.

"All okay, babe?" Bran murmurs softly as everyone else continues to talk.

Looking at Bran through Shea's eyes, he's even more striking than I remember. The grey flecks in his eyes are different shades, making it seem as if a storm is brewing.

I can't tell him what's going on in my head, so I simply show him I'm okay through the bond.

As Kali talks about the books we went through yesterday, I hear a fly close by, the low buzzing distracting me from the conversation. When it hovers past my head, Shea reaches out with our paw to bat it away. Unfortunately, now our attention is on the fly, and even though the situation is serious, and I'd like to know all the information, I'm overcome by instinct to get this damn fly.

Our head whips from side to side as the fly torments us. I can feel Kali and Bran's amusement through the bonds, but neither of them stops to question my unusual behaviour.

Shea, can we not just leave it alone and concentrate on what's going on?

Sure, you do that.

I try, I really do, but the fly persists, and no matter how hard I focus on the words, the fly continues to capture my attention. When it suddenly passes by our head, Shea snaps our teeth, capturing the flying creature and swallowing it whole. Castiel is looking at us with a mixture of amusement and disgust. I don't care, though—I'm just happy we got the fly and can concentrate again.

Did you find anything in your research yesterday about people going missing or large numbers being needed for a sacrifice? Damiean questions Kali.

"No, nothing," Kali answers. "Do you think these two events are related?"

"I'm afraid I say this a lot lately, which is unlike me, but I'm unsure. The timing is remarkable, though."

"You've been going through the books?" Oberon asks with surprise and excitement.

"Yep, couldn't leave all the fun to you. After the last dream Thea and I shared, we wanted answers. Didn't realise there would be so much to go through."

"Can you tell us about the dream?" Oberon asks, his trusty laptop open in front of him.

Kali keeps it short, detailing the specifics of the dream and the fear we both woke up with. I can see from their expressions it's hard for Bran and Anubis to hear and they're disappointed they weren't here for us.

"We have narrowed down the location of two women named Seraphina. The sense of urgency to find her hasn't left since we had that dream, meaning we need to find her soon. It might help us unravel more details and put the pieces of this puzzle together," Kali asserts.

"And where might she be?" Balbur asks.

Damiean flips through his notes. "Well, if the database is correct, there are two living in England, one in Grimsby and the other near Cumbria."

"We need to find her within the next few days. Thea and I need to go on a road trip.

Bran tenses beside me, and I feel it through the bond. He does not like that idea. When Anubis speaks next, he confirms the same thing. "You cannot go alone."

If I could talk, there is much I would like to say to Anubis and his slightly demanding tone. I understand their need to protect us, but whatever these dreams mean, and whatever these restrictions are, is something we need to figure out. They have enough unfolding here, and this is not a dangerous thing for us to do. Thankfully, Kali agrees and says what I'm thinking, almost word for word.

"I never said we would," Kali responds, cocking her eyebrow at him and his demand. "But we also don't want to go in mob-handed. We have no information about her, and she doesn't know us. If we all turn up at the wrong person's house and she sees us all, it will raise more questions. If we find the right one and she's been having the dreams, she might recognise us, or we're hoping she might feel a bond like we did. Either way, it will be easier for either woman to just deal with me and Thea when we first meet her."

"I will take them," Damiean says, stepping in before any further protests can be made.

"But can you guarantee their safety when they leave here?" Anubis pushes.

Why does he think we can't defend ourselves? Does he believe that we only need mates to protect us, that we're incapable of doing something alone?

Althea, I'm sure that's not—

No Shea. This is ridiculous. We do not need his permission to do this. We are an alpha, and we will—

"Thea?"

"Babe?"

Kali and Bran call out in concern, but my anger takes over, forcing Shea and I to growl in Anubis's direction. He maintains a calm demeanour, which, for some reason, angers me more. Before the emotion can take over, my bones snap and pop, signalling the shift about to happen.

When I fully transform into myself again, I hear Bran barking at the others to avert their eyes, my now naked appearance doing nothing to help calm my mate. Bran's shirt is swiftly placed over my head, and when I look up at him, his eyes shine with happiness.

"Hello again, Beautiful."

"Mate," I breathe, overjoyed to be in his arms again.

His lips gently brush across mine, and it's not nearly enough after two days apart.

"Are you okay now? I thought you were going to attack my brother and have him for breakfast?"

I smile sheepishly, recognising I may have overreacted to Anubis and his protective stance on the situation.

"I'm sorry, Anubis," I say as Bran positions me on his lap to cover my behind. "I'm not sure what came over me. I seem to be quick to anger at the moment."

"You do not need to apologise, Thea. This is normal for a shifter, especially an alpha," Anubis responds kindly.

"It is?"

"Oh yes. It's almost like going through adolescence again. Only anger seems to be the defining emotion. Your instincts will kick in when you feel threatened or questioned, or your pack is in danger. It usually results in quite a bit of anger."

"He not joking," Bran says from behind me. "He was a complete asshole to live with when he was going through it."

"How long does it usually last?"

"Depends on the alpha. Some can overcome it quickly, others, a few months, a year maximum."

"And how long did it take you?"

"Eight months," the guys proclaim in unison.

"Aww, Wolf Man, you were a pain in the ass for eight months?"

Anubis smirks, proud of himself and not in the least bit bothered Kali's statement seems true. Still, I feel better knowing there's a reason for my sudden rage. I've never been an angry person, and I'm usually level-headed. Once again something else I will need to adjust to, but I will learn to control it.

"Are we all in agreeance that Damiean will go with the girls, or do we need an alpha show down before that's decided," Castiel questions cheekily.

"I have no objections," Anubis quickly declares, resulting in the others all declaring the same.

Laughing at their behaviour, Damiean agrees, and I'm thankful these people in my life know how to make me feel at ease. I all but challenged their leader, and rather than making an issue out of it or making me feel awkward, they joke about it like it's an everyday occurrence.

A few more details get discussed, but now I'm sat on Bran's lap in only his shirt, I couldn't tell you what they were.

CHAPTER THIRTY-TWO

There's not much left to discuss that can't be revisited later, and with our mates back home, my primary focus is on spending time together. The others in the group quickly grasp this, so once the debrief is completed, the four of us are told to leave.

In Castiel's words, the tension is too much, and he's sick of looking at our happy faces.

I haven't eaten anything last night, and with my most recent shift, as we leave SNHQ, my stomach reminds me of that fact. In my half-dressed state, Bran drops me off at my apartment and quickly leaves to retrieve food for us. While he's gone, our bond practically sings with joy and anticipation, which gives me an idea.

Moving some of the furniture around, I create a larger space to lay a blanket down. Next, I gather every cushion in my apartment and arrange them comfortably on the blanket. Finally, routing through the kitchen cabinets, I find a few candles and scatter them throughout the room.

It's not quite as romantic as what Bran did for our first date, but I'm hopeful he'll appreciate the sentiment.

I take a quick shower, and by the time I get out, Bran is back with the food. I don't bother putting any clothes on, instead entering the living room in just a towel. He stands staring at the makeshift picnic until I enter the room. When he sees me, his eyes trail over my body hungrily.

"On our first date, I wanted nothing more than to lay you down on that blanket and make love to you," he tells me, his tone husky as he places the food on the counter. "The next day, when I arrived to see you in only a towel, I wanted to ravage you, to claim you forever."

He steps towards me, his fingers slowly trailing down my face until he tilts my chin up towards him, "I'm going to play out both of those fantasies today," he growls, his lips claiming mine as if I was his salvation.

My arms wrap around his neck as I savour his taste, the feel of his soft lips against mine, and his tight hold around my waist. Being together and connecting in the most intimate ways after two days without each other is an overload to my senses. As if on cue, parts of my body start to shift, yet I'm too engrossed in Bran to care.

When he pulls away for air, his chest heaving with heavy breaths, his eyes swimming with the orange of his bear, I have never felt more turned on.

"Take me, Bran," I whisper. "Take me hard, soft, slow or fast. I don't care how, just... take me."

"There is nothing that would bring me greater pleasure, babe. And I intend to take you in all of those ways."

The towel is ripped from my body before he leads me over to the blanket. He steps away from me as I stand before him, completely naked, delighting in the look of hunger and desire reflected back at me. His eyes trail over every exposed inch of my flesh, his pupils growing larger and his nostrils flaring as my own desire burns through me.

He seems to decide what he wants to do with me first, gently taking my hand and lowering me to the ground so he can situate me against the cushions.

"Open your legs for me."

Following his order, I open my legs and display myself to him, becoming more aroused when a low groan rumbles through his chest.

"A perfect Goddess, ready to be devoured."

Whipping off his shirt, he kneels on the ground in front of me. Taking his time, his lips start from one ankle, moving his way up my leg until he's kissed every inch. By the time he gets to the apex of my thighs, I'm writhing and desperate for his touch. He continues to tease me by giving my other leg the same treatment, but when he reaches my hip, he kisses slowly along my pubic bone before unexpectedly burying his head between my legs.

I scream out at the contact, his tongue playing my clit so perfectly that the orgasm barrels through me with no warning. He continues his sweet torture, not letting up for a second after my first orgasm ebbs away, and a second quickly follows.

As his tongue continues to lavish me, he circles my entrance with his finger before inserting two and finding that spot that makes my eyes cross over. He's relentless in his pursuit to bring me to orgasm, and when I reach the crescendo of my third, a loud growl rips from my throat.

A victorious smile pulls at his lips, and when he slows his actions but doesn't completely stop, I beg him to. "Please, Bran, no more. I can't...I need..."

"Okay, babe, but I'm not done with you yet. I want at least two more of those sexy growls from you."

Falling flat against the cushions, no longer able to hold myself up, my legs shake as Bran pulls me closer. Garbled words leave my lips when his tongue traces a pattern across my stomach towards my breasts. My skin is over-sensitised, every stroke creating goosebumps to flare across my body. When his tongue circles my nipple, I moan before gripping tightly onto his hair.

"Now, Bran," I demand, pulling on his hair harshly so his eyes meet mine. "I need to feel you, now!"

"Your wish is my command," he grins before kissing me harshly.

Without further preamble, his cock stretches me slowly, inch by inch, until his hips meet mine. In my sex-addled state, I wasn't aware he was naked, and the sudden intrusion forces my head back, and a pleasure-filled scream echoes around the apartment.

He teases me with slow thrusts, hitting every nerve end as he grinds in and out of me. The pleasure builds, and my body shakes with the need to come, for him to move faster and shatter every inch of me.

"Harder... Harder, Bran, please. Make me come."

A deep growl resonates from him, one I feel in my chest as he pulls out and then slams himself inside me. He sets a relentless pace, spearing me against his shaft as I quiver around him. His grunts and groans turn me on more, and all too soon, my orgasm crashes through me, battering me with its intensity. I scream, growl and moan my way through the longest orgasm I've ever had. Bran never lets up, his masterful pace drawing my pleasure out longer than I thought possible.

"You are glorious when you come," Bran murmurs before biting down on my nipple. "Now show me that sexy ass."

Still inside of me, Bran moves me, positioning the cushions underneath my stomach and chest to ensure I'm comfortable. He slows his rhythm slightly to allow me to adjust to the new position. Leaning close, his breath flutters over me as he kisses from my shoulder up to my ear.

"Hold on, baby," he says in a low husky tone.

Hold on is all I can do when he slams into me over and over, his hands gripping my hips tightly. With another orgasm building, I whimper and shudder, not sure my body can take anymore.

"You have one more for me. I know you do."

When Bran reaches around to pinch my nipple, I arch my back, unexpectedly desperate and needy again. He pulls me backwards until I'm kneeling with him, and he has access to both breasts. Somehow his pace never changes, and when his hand softly grazes down my stomach towards my clit, I explode. Coming so hard, I clench around him until he can barely move, the action causing him to roar loudly and, after a few more strokes, spill his release inside of me.

I shudder on his still-twitching cock as he gently lays us down and pulls me towards him, my back to his front. My eyes close of their own accord, and my body feels heavy with satisfaction. Bran gently trails his fingers up and down my arm, and the moment is so perfect I never want it to end.

"Gods, I love you," I murmur breathlessly.

"And I love you, my beautiful mate. Forever and always."

We lie quietly for a few minutes, basking in the glory of our lovemaking before my stomach interrupts the beautiful moment.

"Babe, I have to ask, did you eat at all in the time I was away?" he chuckles softly, his hands moving my hair to see my face.

"I did, but nothing yet today. Between the shift and your expert skills of wringing every inch of pleasure out of me, I'm tapped out."

"Then let me remedy that quickly before you decide to take a bite out of me," he says, kissing my cheek.

"Hmm, don't tempt me," I utter lazily.

When he pulls out of me, I groan at the loss but have no energy left to move. My body is completely sated, and if it wasn't for the naked view of my mate, I wouldn't even open my eyes. Watching Bran, he gets up from the floor, heading into the bedroom before returning with a towel to gently clean me up.

I smile softly at my mate as he takes care of me, arranging the cushions so I'm more comfortable and placing a blanket over me so I don't get cold. When he's satisfied with my position, he moves over to the counter to retrieve the food he brought earlier. Gathering everything he needs, he joins me on the floor, sharing the blanket with me as he serves up a generous amount of pasta, bread, and a large glass of juice.

Seriously, after that workout, all you're eating is pasta! You need meat, woman.

I've had plenty of meat, thank you.

I laugh internally at my joke, and I can practically see Shea rolling her eyes.

Bran turns on the TV, and after fiddling with the remote, soft music fills the apartment. I sigh happily, stuffing my face with pasta, and when I look over at Bran, he has a satisfied smile on his face.

"What?" I ask in a very unladylike manner with a mouth full of pasta.

"I was thinking about you the whole time I was away," he starts, taking a bite of his food. "It was this exact scenario. Spending time with you like this after ravishing you. Seeing you eat naked with mussed-up hair. For me, it doesn't get more perfect than this."

"Me either. I am one very lucky lady," I smile, still shoving food into my mouth. "So, how was it? I heard the debrief, but I imagine it wasn't as straightforward as that."

"The worst part was my bear," he admits, setting his food aside. "He was not happy about being separated from you. I kept to myself the first day and watched, convincing myself I needed to be there and not come home. When I felt your fear the next morning, I shifted and destroyed some of the house we were stationed at. I almost came home. Only after talking to you could I calm down enough and remember the mission."

"I'm sorry. I didn't mean to make you worry like that."

"No, you have nothing to apologise for. I knew it would be more difficult for us with our bond being so new. Anubis struggled too, which helped," he laughs. "What about you? How was your day training the recruits? I'm sorry you didn't get more time to do things on your own, but I'm not sure I could have stayed away any longer."

"It's a good job your back." I start to tell him everything that happened the day Kali and I were in charge. His expression is murderous when I tell him about Jared, not just what went on that day but the other times I've heard his derogatory comments. The anger coming from the bond burns through my veins as if it were my own, and I quickly finish the rest of the story, telling him in detail how Shea bit Jared.

Thankfully, it seems to calm some of his rage, though he assures me he will speak with Jared and his father about his behaviour. I describe everything else that happened and the state Damiean found us in, which he finds hilarious.

When we move on to the subject of Kali's and my shared dream, he asks for the specifics, and we discuss the best way to approach the other woman from our dream. He offers some good advice and shares his concerns about us going to meet her, but ultimately, he supports our decision.

"There was something I discovered while you were away," I tell him as he plays with the ends of my hair.

"Oh? You were busy while I was gone," he smirks playfully.

"Yeah, it's something Shea mentioned, and it's been on my mind a little."

He straightens up from his slouched position so he can see me better. "What's been on your mind, babe?"

"According to Shea, and this is all based on her feelings, I haven't felt anything, so I'm not sure—"

"You're rambling, beautiful."

"Right, sorry. Well, Shea is sensing something inside us—a great power she can't tap into but is certain is there."

"Okay, and you think the restrictions stop you from accessing it?"

"Possibly. I can't feel anything other than my bonds and Shea."

"Then why do you seem worried?"

"Because there's still so much I don't understand about myself. These bouts of anger are worrying and though I'm happy to learn it's an alpha thing, that poses a different problem."

"Let's come onto the alpha thing after," Bran says softly. "What worries you most about this extra power, that you can't access it or that you might not be able to control it?"

"The latter. I don't need any extra power, but if it's there and we somehow get the restrictions lifted, what will the consequences be? I already can't shift on command. Will I become more unstable with more power?"

"Firstly, I'll have a badass mate," Bran huffs with amusement. "Secondly, you could never become unstable. You're already so conscious about your abilities, and you're careful. I don't see the extra power taking over you if that's what you're worried about. I think, no, wait, I know, you will handle it as you have everything else that life has thrown at you. With grace and tenacity. You don't give yourself enough credit, my beautiful mate."

"And you give me too much. You're biased," I scoff.

"Perhaps," he smirks. "I do know you won't be on your own. Whatever power you have, whatever worries are going through your mind, if it's too much, I'll be there to take on the burden with you."

"Thank you." Trailing my hand across the column of his neck, I pull him close and press my lips to his. I pour my affection and appreciation into the kiss, desperately hoping the physical act will communicate his importance to me. As he deepens the kiss, his tongue dominating mine, I unload some of my worries to him.

It feels wrong at first, but when I sense his acceptance, his happiness at being able to help me this way, I continue to pour it all out. By the time he pulls away from our kiss, I feel lighter. There is only one thing left to discuss.

"I know," he murmurs, kissing the end of my nose. "You're an alpha, and I don't think you can join the pack here."

"Does that upset you?" I ask, searching his mesmerising grey eyes for the answer.

"Not as much as I thought it would," he replies, honesty brimming in his gaze. "Wherever you are, that is where I'll be. Could I ask something of you?"

"Of course, anything."

"Before I tell my father I'm leaving his pack, which, by the way, might not go down well, would you meet him and my mother?"

"Yes, I can do that. I would never expect you to give up your pack life for me, Bran. We could make it work."

"We might, but I don't think my bear and Shea will be quite as understanding."

He's not wrong. We need our mate by our side.

"Okay, so you might be right there."

"My only concern at the moment is that you don't have control enough to start your own pack, and with that comes some worry."

"The madness?" I question, wondering if he's considered it too.

"Exactly. I've witnessed first-hand the effects that being without a pack can have on a shifter. I wouldn't wish it upon my worst enemy."

"So, what do you suggest?"

"Meet with my father. Let Shea meet him. The restrictions are new territory for us all, and while Shea is restricted, she might find she can join the pack temporarily. I know your experiences with your father have scarred Shea as much as they have you, but contrary to recent opinions, he is a good man. A temporary spot in the pack could also ensure the madness stays at bay."

"Do you think it would still be a problem with us being mated?"

"Honestly, I have no clue. Can't hurt to try, though, right?"

What do you think, Shea? Will you meet the alpha and consider a temporary spot in the pack?

I will. I beg you not to get your hopes up, though. I cannot join the pack if I feel more dominant than the current alpha. It will cause untold heartache in the end.

Fair enough. Let's meet with him and go from there.

Very well.

"Shea's in agreement. We'll meet with your father and see how it goes."

"Perfect," he smiles brightly before kissing my lips softly. He doesn't take control of the kiss, instead trailing his lips across my cheeks and down my neck. My breathing picks up as he works his way to my collarbone, soft, wet kisses trailing down my chest to my nipples.

"Enough talk. My mate needs to be ravished," he growls low, nipping at my other breast.

He spends the rest of the day doing exactly that.

CHAPTER THIRTY-THREE

THE ALARM BLARES THE next morning, signalling our time alone has come to an end. Bran groans, his hand reaching over me blindingly to stop the awful sound. I beat him to it and stop the squealing, rubbing at my eyes as the late night catches up with me and makes my eyes feel gritty.

We took full advantage of our time together, now faced with a full day's work, it was not the wisest decision. Bran pulls me close, his face nuzzling into my neck as he shows no signs of moving from the bed.

"Bran, it's Monday. Time for work," I tell him softly, my fingers pulling through his hair.

"Hmmm, loving you is my new job," he responds, his voice rough and husky as sleep still clings to him.

"I'm not sure I can provide the same benefits," I giggle.

"Babe, being with you is all the benefits I need." He kisses my neck, and I groan, desperate to take this further but also wanting to be responsible.

Bran takes the decision out of my hands when he continues to kiss his way down my body.

"Bran, we should get ready," I murmur half-heartedly.

"We will," he says, his lips vibrating against my nipple. "But not until I've had breakfast."

He moves so fast, his mouth suddenly gone from my nipple, now caresses my clit thoroughly. He wastes no time eating me out—his actions are frenzied, as if I'm the greatest meal he's ever tasted. My voice cracks as the orgasm rushes through me, and my mouth hangs open on a silent scream.

Still in the full throes of my climax, Bran enters me with a grunt, and my orgasm continues until my legs are shaking and my breathing is harsh. The pleasure seems to touch me everywhere, and when I feel Bran's lust through the bond, it magnifies my own.

He's lost to his own arousal, my desire and ardour turning him on further and pushing him to satisfy me more. He pulls my hips off the bed, holding me steady in his hands as he thrusts into me with slow and hard strokes. The combination drives me wild, and I whimper as the next orgasm builds.

"Eyes on me, babe. I want to see you when you come," he demands in a low, gruff tenor.

I'm helpless to deny his request, my eyes glued to his passion-filled gaze. The intensity, love and desire reflected back at me is my undoing, and my core trembles around him. My climax triggers his own, and I force myself to stay focused on him, not succumb to the pleasure so I can watch him unravel.

"Gods, babe," he growls, his body tensing and his strokes becoming jerky as we both ride out our orgasm together. I have never witnessed a more erotic sight than my mate losing himself in me.

He grins salaciously at me, leaning forward and capturing my lips in a soft kiss. "Best morning ever," he breathes against me before kissing me hard enough to make my toes curl.

It takes us a few more minutes until either of us moves, but when I notice the time, I jump out of bed and quickly rush to the shower. He laughs at my attempts to sneak in before him, and I find myself grinning all the way through my shower.

Having Bran home and being together like a normal couple is perfect. I can be myself around him, and I've never felt so settled or at ease. It gets me thinking about our conversation last night and if the madness could truly affect me when I've never been happier. I understand it's a needless risk to take when there's a pack I can join here, but if that doesn't work out, something tells me I won't need to worry.

I'm not worried.

Are you ever? You're always confident that everything will work out.

Not necessarily that it will work out, but more that we are meant for great things.

You've said that before. How are you always so sure? And please don't say instinct. It means nothing to me.

Fine, but that is part of it. The other part is the evidence. We already know we are powerful, more than we should be considering our heritage, and then there are the restrictions. Someone did this to us for a reason, and the logical explanation is to stop us from becoming who we are meant to be. Why would they do that if we weren't made for something great?

Or it could be the opposite, and we end up destroying everything.

No, I don't believe that for a second. You are far too kind-natured for evil.

I hate to say it, but only time will tell.

Contemplating Shea's observation as Bran takes a shower, I continue preparing for the day. Numerous coincidences are piling up, and until the bigger picture comes into focus, all we can do is gather the pieces. I'm starting to believe Kali and I are integral pieces of this puzzle, alongside the other women, and until we all come together, we might not see everything we need to find answers.

After making coffee for both me and Bran, unintentionally, I end up pacing around the living room—the habit returning as I consider various possibilities. I'm not even aware of it until Bran stops me, placing his hands on my shoulders.

"Your analytical brain is turned up full this morning, huh? Perhaps I didn't wear you out enough."

"Oh, you most certainly did. Any more, and I wouldn't make it into work today."

"Well, in that case," he grins mischievously.

"Ah ah, no, you don't. After Friday, I need to turn up and be professional. Get through a day without biting someone."

That means you too, Shea.

I make no such promises.

Rolling my eyes, I quickly drink my coffee and pull Bran out of the apartment before he can talk me into staying in bed with him all day. Out in the courtyard, we bump into Balbur and Castiel, who are on their way to the canteen.

"And there was me thinking we wouldn't see Red today. Based on how Bran's bear behaved, I figured he would have you tied to the bed for at least a week." Castiel teases, his blue eyes shining with mirth.

"As if Shea would ever allow that. We need to be free to keep you lot in line," I sass.

"Never a more truthful word spoken," Balbur snorts.

"I don't need anybody to keep me in line," Castiel protests. "I behave in a gentlemanly manner at all times."

"I don't count flirting with my mate gentlemanly," Bran argues.

"Hey, I didn't know she was yours then, so you can hardly blame me."

"No, I guess I can't," Bran answers begrudgingly, pulling me under his arm in a show of ownership.

As an alpha, I'd expect Shea to be annoyed by the gesture. After all, alphas are usually the strong, independent types. Instead, she preens under his attention.

I am still a female and can appreciate when our mate claims us so publicly. He understands we are his, just as much as he is ours. Now grab his ass and make it known.

In my head, I'm laughing at Shea's request, but externally, I take her advice and slip my arm around Bran's waist, squeezing his ass and smiling up at him. My action creates a burst of joy and arousal from our mate, and I second-guess my decision to listen to Shea when his eyes fill with heat.

"If this is how these two behave after two days apart, I can only imagine what Blondie and Anubis will be like," Castiel grumbles.

"Has anyone seen them yet this morning?" Balbur asks.

I try not to actively sense anything through my bond with Kali when she is alone with Anubis, so I haven't been paying much attention. However, when I check in now, she appears happy but anxious. Communicating through the bond is challenging unless you're experiencing a specific emotion, so asking a question is not easy. Despite this, I give it a shot, trying to communicate my concern over her feelings.

If I'm correct, what she sends back is that she's okay and will see me soon. I'm unsure how I know that based on emotion alone, but that's the sense I'm getting.

"They're on their way," I mention to the others.

"Can you talk to each other through the bond?" Balbur questions with surprise.

"No. But I can feel her emotions enough to clue me into what she's doing and if she needs anything."

"I'd be useless with that type of bond," Castiel comments. "I barely know what I'm doing half the time, let alone what someone else is doing and how they feel about it."

"You'd be surprised," Bran replies. "You don't have to actually discern what the bond is telling you because you can feel it yourself, almost as if they were your own emotions, but you can easily recognise they're not."

"You're not making it sound any less complicated, dude," Castiel snickers.

When we make it to the canteen, I sit at our usual table as Bran gets my breakfast for me. I would never admit out loud but when Kali said she missed Anubis providing her food, I secretly agreed. There is something intimate about him knowing my tastes so well, and it always tastes better when he prepares it.

When a sudden burst of relief washes through my bond with Kali, I turn to see her enter the room, Anubis draped around her. She appears happy and content, yet the feelings inside don't match the exterior. When she reaches the table, I pull out a chair for her, and as Anubis arranges breakfast for her, she turns to me.

"Any dreams last night?" She asks in an almost panicked state.

"No, why? What happened?"

"I saw that girl, Seraphina, or at least I think it was her. I saw her dying."

"Oh Kali, I'm sorry. That can't have been easy to see." I wrap my arm around her shoulder and hug her close. "How did it... was it in the images?"

"No. That's the strange thing. I wasn't in the dream place or near the posts. I was standing on the side of a road near a wooded area. At first, I thought it was a regular dream, but then I noticed a girl with black hair running by me. I didn't see her eyes so I can't be sure if it was this Seraphina, but that was my first thought when I saw her."

Kali gazes off across the room, her eyes glazed as if she's reliving the dream. I tune into her emotions so I can gauge how she's feeling.

"She was running, like one of those crazy people that enjoy it. I watched her briefly before I heard the noise from an engine. It was a blacked-out car, so I couldn't see anyone inside, but it was barrelling down the road, going way too fast. I screamed to the girl, but she didn't hear me. It hit her so hard she went flying, at least three feet."

Kali's anguish pours through the bond, and I squeeze her tighter. "I tried to get to her, but I couldn't move. The driver of the car stopped to check, and then I woke up. I can't be sure, but I have the strongest feeling that she's dead. Whoever was in that car was aiming for her, Thea. It was deliberate; the driver intended to kill her."

She releases a shuddering breath and snaps out of her distant gaze. "I don't have visions, Thea—all I've ever had are dreams. I can't be sure if I made it all up, if it's already happened, or if it's going to happen."

"And you say you're first thought was this Seraphina girl?"

"Yes. But even when I got close to her, I couldn't tell if it was her or not. What do you think it means?"

"Nothing from our dreams has turned into a reality yet. Maybe this was a warning, a caution of what could happen if we don't find her. There was nothing you could do, and whoever is sending us these dreams is responsible for what happens to her, not us. We just don't have enough information to go on."

"So, should we do anything about it?"

"Let's talk to Damiean first, see when he's available to take us to meet these two Seraphinas."

"Okay. Yeah, you're right. It should be soon, though, Thea. I've got a bad feeling about it all."

"We'll go to his office today after you're done with your training, yeah?"

Kali agrees as Bran, Anubis, and the others arrive at the table, arms laden with plates of food.

"Woah, ladies, who died?" Castiel asks, looking at us both.

Anubis grumbles and rolls his eyes before hitting Castiel on the back of the head.

"What was that for?"

"Have some tact, man."

"Tact about what?"

"It's fine, Anubis, he didn't know," Kali says, defending Castiel's question.

"Oh shit," Castiel says, whipping his head around to Kali. "Have I put my foot in it, Blondie?"

"Just a little."

Even without knowing who this woman is, there's a sombre mood at breakfast when thinking about someone being murdered. Kali explains the details of her dream to the guys and there's a subtle shift in their attitude about us going to find Seraphina. Initially, they believed the plan was too risky, and we didn't have enough information about what was going on. Now, a woman's life could potentially hang in the balance, and they're all more understanding than the day before.

Castiel offers some suggestions regarding a spell that could protect the women. Still, with only a name and possible location, it's not enough information for him to create an accurate spell. Ultimately, they all agree that finding these women needs to be a priority.

Unfortunately, it's not something we can get to immediately, as work is also a top priority. After the recent visit to London and everything the guys witnessed, we need more recruits than ever, trained up and ready to go. In the debrief yesterday, Damiean mentioned getting more resources from other SNHQ branches, which means we'll need to set up even more training soon. Every team sent out must be adequately equipped.

It's not an ideal time to leave, but if Kali's gut feeling says something bad is about to happen to this woman, it must be taken seriously. It also begs the question why I didn't dream last night. I didn't sleep much, but the little that I had was restful. Why are we no longer getting the same messages?

As usual, the question will have to remain a mystery as it's time to go to work.

CHAPTER THIRTY-FOUR

Arriving at work after last Friday, I hold my head high as I enter The Pit, glad to see most of the recruits ready and waiting. I'm told by Anubis that Jared will not be in attendance today. Since learning about his blatant disrespect towards Kali and me, he is not someone the guys want as part of the team. It would have been nice to see his reaction when he was told.

The laughing hyenas that joined in with him that day have been assigned to me this morning, and when Bran finds out, he tries to protest.

"Bran, it's fine, honestly. After biting Jared, they were more afraid of me. I can handle them, I promise."

"I don't doubt that for a second, babe. I just don't want them anywhere near you."

"I know, but we all have to work with people we don't like sometimes."

"I hope you're not referring to me when you say that, Red," Castiel jokes as he walks over to his group.

"Go on," I say, pushing Bran away. "I'll be fine."

"If I hear one disrespectful word, I will not be responsible for my bear's actions."

"Fair enough," I smile, going over to my group.

"Good morning, recruits," I yell to be heard over the noise of the others. "Friday was a prime example of our emotions coming into play when you're in a simulation. I'd like to focus on that more today. Start with your warm-up drills and be back here in thirty minutes."

Dismissing the recruits, I observe them as they depart, standing proud with my hands behind my back. For the first ten minutes, my time is spent with a surprisingly uncoordinated vampire, constantly correcting their position to prevent self-injury during a warm-up routine.

Afterwards, I monitor the group, keeping a watchful eye on them and noting who is putting in their best effort and who is lacking. I'm pleased to see the young men who aligned with Jared are taking things more seriously today. Unfortunately, I can't determine if that's because the guys are scattered throughout The Pit or if they're beginning to respect me.

When they've completed their warm-up, I pair them up, instructing them to engage in hand-to-hand combat. I dedicate equal time to each pair, offering corrections when needed and introducing different stimuli to catch them off guard. Hearing the debrief from the guys and what is happening in London, I can't help but look at the recruits and wonder if they are ready for what's unfolding out there.

It changes my approach to how I would typically train them, provoking them in unorthodox ways to ensure they are prepared for various emotional situations.

A witch in my group, a little on the short side, struggles the most with my teaching methods. I've commented on his size and made a point of pairing him with one of the tallest in my group, hoping he would adjust his fighting style to accommodate the height difference.

Observing him, I can see from his expression my comments are not appreciated. When his shots start to go wide and energy dips, I take him off to one side.

"Do my comments about your size bother you?"

"What do you think?" he snarls, clearly not impressed.

"I think they do, and that is precisely the point of this lesson. What's your name again?"

"Connor."

"Well, Connor, my whole life, I was told I was useless and a defect, and do you know what I did? I fought harder than ever to prove that was not the case."

"Not much I can do about my size, is there?"

"Oh no? And why do you think that is?"

"I'm a foot shorter than everyone here. I'll never be able to get any taller or be as strong as them. I only joined this stupid programme to shut my parents up."

It's a shame about his attitude towards the programme, but apparently, it's seen a lot. Parents like to boast about their kids, and it's seen as a high honour when they are accepted into the programme.

"Look, I don't know your story or the reasons that pushed you to be here. What I do know is that you're quick. You don't have to be the strongest or the tallest to be the best. You need to use your height to your advantage and take away its power over you."

I can see from his expression he doesn't believe me, that my words are not getting through to him.

Don't give up. Show the pup how.

"Come with me," I tell him, walking him over to Balbur. Connor suddenly looks nervous, and I smirk slightly when Balbur raises his brow questioningly at me.

"Connor, you know who this is, yes?"

He nods his head rapidly but doesn't respond in any other way. Their height difference is almost laughable, but I need my giant friend to prove a point.

"Balbur, this is Connor. Would you mind sparring with him for a few minutes?"

"Sure, show us what you got, kid," Balbur says, nodding towards some spare mats.

Connor nervously moves into position, adjusting his stance to start the combinations.

"Balbur, if you would please, spar with him as you would any of the others."

Connor's eyes go wide at my statement, but he stays where he is, and when Balbur gets into position, Connor begins his routine. There is no energy or enthusiasm coming from him, and when Balbur easily bats away his shots, Connor's frustration mounts.

"Okay, stop," I tell him, moving closer so I can talk quietly to Connor. "What do you think Balbur's biggest strength is?"

"His height, obviously. And he's strong."

"And his weakness?"

Connor looks over my shoulder to where Balbur is standing. "He doesn't have one."

"That is where you are wrong," I say, bringing his attention back to me. "Everyone has a weakness. Do you see the distance between his feet and his hands? All that area is unprotected for someone of Balbur's size. You have good technique, so push harder and use whatever you have to gain an advantage. Now spar with Balbur again and aim for the areas he's too big to protect."

He heads back towards Balbur again, taking up his stance, his shoulders straighter and his eyes more determined. He struggles at first to gain access to the areas where he could do the most damage, but after a few adjustments and words of encouragement, his confidence starts to grow.

I'm pleased Balbur doesn't let him off lightly, he doesn't pull his punches or kicks, and he doesn't allow him an easy session. With every hit Connor connects to Balbur, his smile becomes bigger and soon a crowd has gathered to watch them spar.

Connor pulls off a particularly hard move, and when he races quickly between Balbur's legs, the big guy trips and falls backwards onto the mat. I don't know if Balbur did it intentionally, but Connor doesn't seem to think so. He raises his hands and cheers victoriously, the other recruits cheering with him.

"Alright, everyone, back to your positions," I call, getting my group under control. I turn to Balbur before going over to them, mouthing a thank you. He nods in acknowledgement and picks himself off the floor.

"Well done, Connor," I smile when I return to my group. "And for the rest of you, let this be a lesson. No matter how tall, short, fast or strong someone is, there is always an area of weakness to exploit. If you become emotional or distracted on a mission, you'll miss it. Stay focused and look for the weak spots. Let's break for lunch, and when you get back, we'll begin with weapons training."

The recruits disperse to cool off and get a drink, Connor the only one to hang back. "I get it now, thank you. I won't let my height bother me anymore."

"You will, and that's okay. We all have our insecurities. You just need to remember when you're on a mission, you leave it behind. Your height is an advantage out there. Use it."

"I will, thank you, ma'am."

I nod, acknowledging his gratitude, before heading to the staff room to take a break.

Very well done, Althea. It was a pleasure to watch you grow that way. So confident and sure of yourself.

I have you to thank for that. My weakness is doubting myself. My strength is you.

Well, I could take all the credit, but I noticed how you thrived when you could feel our mates' pride.

Yes, I guess there is that too.

Your mother would be very proud of you.

Shea!... I...

Her comment strikes me straight through the heart, and my eyes unexpectedly well with tears at hearing the words I always wished my father would say.

Thank you, Shea. That means the world to me.

I only speak the truth. Now, pull it together, our mate approaches.

The door to the staff room opens and Bran comes striding in, not stopping until he's in front of me and his lips are sealed to mine.

"That was the sexiest thing I've ever seen. Will you train me, please?"

"Oh, give over," I laugh, kissing him once more.

"I'm serious. I didn't know whether to be impressed or turned on. It was all very confusing."

"I just did what any of you guys would have done."

"Err, not really. Don't get me wrong, we point out weaknesses and strengths, but the way you showed him, explained it to him and encouraged the lad was more than any of us would have thought to do."

I grin shyly at his comment, "Thank you. I do feel like I'm becoming more confident in myself and my role here."

"And it shows. I'm proud of you."

I pull him close, demanding a kiss so I can show my gratitude. He allows me to control the kiss, groaning against me as the heat builds between us. When he grabs my hips and pushes me against the wall, my control is over. Bran encourages me to grow at every opportunity, but when we are intimate, he dominates me in the best of ways.

"Ahem, this is the communal staff room," Castiel's voice breaks through our moment. "None of that, thank you, especially because some of us are not getting any."

I feel the blush work its way from my neck to my face at the position Castiel has caught us in. It's not very professional on my part, and I quickly wriggle out of Bran's hold.

"I'm sorry, you're right. It's not professional to behave like that. It won't happen again."

"Like hell it won't," Bran growls, pulling my back against his chest.

"Relax, Red, I'm only playing," Castiel says, that cocky smirk of his coming out to play. "First time I've seen that one on you. It's cute," he comments, looking at my face.

My hand touches my face, confirming I've partially shifted my nose. When I feel higher, my ears have also shifted.

"What you do to me," I mutter, turning to Bran to see a smug smile on his face.

"Me?" he queries innocently. "I believe I turn you on too much, babe. What can I say—it's a gift."

"Or a curse, depending on your perspective," Castiel chortles.

Ignoring them both, I head to the vending machine, looking for something for lunch, since I don't have time to go to the canteen now. Before I can make any selection, Bran twirls me around and plants another kiss on my lips.

"Lunch will be here any second. No mate of mine will be eating vending machine crap if I can help it."

As if on cue, the others enter the room, a large box full of burgers and fries. With my shifted nose, I can smell every ingredient in the box and moan at the overwhelming scents as my stomach rumbles.

As we sit and eat, the others comment on my interaction with Connor, and I receive some glowing praise from Anubis for how I handled the situation. Balbur tells the others how well Connor exploited his weak zone but admits he fell easier than he usually would. He could see the kid needed a confidence boost, so he allowed him the victory.

By the end of lunch, my face has thankfully shifted back to normal, prompting Castiel to comment, "Food is definitely the cure for you and Blondie. Whenever your powers are leaking, if you eat, it seems to resolve it."

"Note to self: always have food on hand," Bran chuckles to himself.

"Works wonders for me. I've started carrying chocolate wherever I go now," Anubis adds.

I splutter in surprise, "You have not!"

"Yep. Whenever Feisty is hungry, her powers leak more, and she loves chocolate. It's a win-win all round."

"Do you like chocolate, babe?" Bran grins as we tidy up and get ready for the afternoon.

"Can't say I've tried a lot of it. In fact, I've only had it twice in my life.

"Gods, don't tell Feisty that. She'll have you on a chocolate diet for the next few weeks," Anubis laughs, leaving the staff room with the others.

"Babe, before you go, I've been thinking. Would you be okay with going to my parents for dinner tonight? I figured if you were going to find Seraphina tomorrow, there might not be another opportunity for a while?"

"Erm sure... that sounds great."

Bran snorts, his eyes beaming with mirth. "You're not a very good liar."

"Well, I can't be when you can feel everything?" I point out.

"True. Don't worry, they're excited to meet you. My mother assured me that my father will be on his best behaviour."

"Okay. Then let's do dinner."

He kisses me briefly before we head back out and over to our groups. The rest of the afternoon passes by quickly and I'm convinced that's because of the nerves and dread about the upcoming meal. Hopefully, it can't go any worse than it did for Kali.

CHAPTER THIRTY-FIVE

IT'S LATE BY THE time we finish with the recruits, and Kali has done her afternoon training, so instead of going home to shower and change, Bran and I head straight over to his parents. I question him several times if this is the right thing to do, considering we're both sweaty and dirty from working. He assures me several times that it is.

Kali wishes us luck as we leave, the thought of me meeting Bren leaving a sour taste in her mouth. I can sense through the bond she's worried for me, and after her experience with the alpha, I'm a little concerned, too.

My perception of alphas isn't great, thanks to the damage my father did. After hearing the details of how Bren behaved with Kali, I can't say I'm looking forward to this meeting.

Let me state for the record now, I will not tolerate any disrespect from him. He may be our mate's father and alpha, but I will not sit by if his attitude is anything less than welcoming.

I understand, Shea, but you need to also remember we are a guest in his house and technically his daughter-in-law.

That plays no relevance to pack hierarchy, and he will know that.

Okay fine. Let's not cause a scene, though, right? If you are agitated or annoyed by him, tell me, and we will leave.

"Shea is not looking forward to this, is she?" Bran asks as we make our way to the family pods.

"She's very protective over Kali, and knowing how your father has treated her has left Shea underwhelmed. She has promised to be good, though."

I did not say that.

I know, but this is Bran's family, and I can feel his tension. I want to avoid putting him in the middle.

"I can understand that. I wasn't impressed with him myself. It's strange, all this time, I never knew my father until that night. We're shifters, so we mainly stick to the pack, but I'd never noticed him have a problem with any other species of supernatural. I guess Anubis's mating with Kali brought out his true side."

"At least we won't have that same problem," I say, trying to lift Bran's spirits when his worry filters down through the bond. "We're both shifters, and your mother sounds lovely. I'm looking forward to meeting her."

"She is," he smiles. "And her cooking is incredible. You're in for a feast tonight."

I continue to ask him questions about his mother and his favourite meal of hers, hoping to distract him enough that he doesn't worry about tonight. It must be hard for Bran because he loves Kali like a sister, and his father's treatment of her creates tension in an otherwise happy family. Anubis seems to have minimal interaction with him now and no longer turns up for the family dinner once a week, which, in turn, upsets his mother.

Yet for some reason, even knowing all this, Bren has done nothing to try and apologise to Kali. They haven't seen each other since that night, and it surprises me as an alpha and a mate, he wouldn't do something to try and mend the gap in his family.

Approaching the quaint cottages, my mind goes back to the pack life we had in Cumbria. The layout was very similar, except the dwellings were not nearly as fancy as these ones. The smell of lavender permeates the air, and the fairy lights dotted around the cottages provide a tranquil scene. I'd imagine growing up here would be a perfect place for young pups. Plenty of open space, rich earth for growing and a forest right on your doorstep. It's no wonder so many families still live in this village.

We pass three of the cottages before Bran takes a slight left, and when I see where we are heading, I notice the front door is already open, and a woman stands waiting at its entrance. The closer we get, the more nervous I become. The woman in the door is Bran's mother, and after all the wonderful things I've heard, I want her to like me.

She is just as beautiful as Kali described, and her welcoming smile puts me at ease immediately. Dressed in a stunning dark purple dress that pairs perfectly with her olive skin tone, her soft grey eyes regard me warmly. Completely ignoring Bran, she moves to me and envelopes me in a loving embrace. Kali was not exaggerating when she said she emits a maternal quality that makes you want her to be your mother. From a single hug, I already sense how much I'm going to love her.

"Another beautiful woman to welcome into the family. We have been truly blessed," she says, holding me at arm's length to look me over.

"It's very nice to meet you, Mrs Thorne."

I like her. Her animal gives off nurturing vibes and is not threatened by us.

"Oh, please call me Aria. Your family now, no need for formalities. Come, come inside. I've made pies." She takes my hand, leading me inside, when I hear Bran chuckling behind me.

"Hello, mother, nice to see you too!"

She turns to him with a playful smile, "I see you every week, my dear son. Don't be so needy." She winks at me as she leads me through her lovely home.

"Needy! How... What... How..."

"Do try to finish your sentences, Bran. No one can understand you otherwise," Aria says mockingly as she leads me into the kitchen.

My burst of laughter won't be contained at Bran's look of utter confusion. I know his mother is messing with him, but clearly, he doesn't.

"Babe, I was hoping to introduce you to my mother. She's a sweet, loving lady who is evidently not around today."

Aria laughs lightly as she waltzes around the kitchen, producing three glasses that she places on the kitchen island.

"And how is my wonderful son today?" she asks in a more serious tone, placing a kiss on his cheek.

"Better now my mother has returned," he smirks, his eyes shining with humour.

Aria steps away to retrieve a bottle of wine that she hands over to Bran as she tends to the oven. The smell of meat and pie crust invades my nose, causing even Shea to make a noise of approval. The scent fills the air, and as Bran fixes us a glass of wine, I turn towards his mother to see her taking several freshly baked pies out of the oven.

"Mother, did you really need six pies just for the four of us?"

"Bran, you can eat one whole pie yourself, so don't act shocked. I don't want you eating any furniture tonight."

"Oh, Mother," he groans disapprovingly, shaking his head in despair.

I watch the back and forth between them, fascinated by the loving but hilarious relationship they seem to share.

"I'm sorry. Did you say you don't want him to eat the furniture?" I ask, speaking up for the first time.

"Please, Mother, no," Bran whispers not at all quietly.

"I'm afraid it is a mother's prerogative," she helplessly shrugs her shoulders. "And yes, dear, I did say that. When he was younger, Bran had the awful habit of always munching on the dining room furniture."

My giggles quickly blossom into full-blown belly laughs at both the hilarity of the tale and Bran's look of horror as Aria continues her story.

"At first, I didn't notice the teeth marks on the table legs, but when he started working on the tabletop, it suddenly all clicked into place. The little bits of wood I would find on the floor, how quiet he was before meals. Whenever he got hungry and impatient, he would start on the furniture."

"How old was he?" I ask between fits of laughter.

"I believe it started just after his third birthday and continued until he was five. We were concerned, but it didn't seem to be causing any issues other than my need for new furniture."

Bran sits with his head in his hands, the bond telling me he is embarrassed and amused. I control my giggles and send him loving feelings through the bond. When he looks up at me with his eyes filled with mirth, I smile warmly.

"I didn't realise bears had a thing for eating wood?" I question with an arched brow.

He narrows his eyes at me playfully, "It was my teeth. Whenever I was hungry, they would ache. Chewing on the wood lessened that until I was fed."

"For a while, we did consider he might have been part beaver," Aria adds.

"Yes, thank you, Mother. Can we move on to something else now?"

"That, my dear son, is payback."

"Payback? For what, I haven't done anything," Bran protests.

"Do you remember when we first met Kali? How you told her many embarrassing stories about Anubis as a child. Well, Anubis asked me, since he couldn't be here, if I could return the favour," Aria smiles mischievously, and I see where Bran gets the look from.

"Why that little shit."

"Bran! Language."

"Sorry, Mother. I will get him for this, though," Bran promises.

My smile is wide as Aria laughs and continues to tell me stories about Bran and Anubis when they were younger. She has the same enthusiasm as Bran when she tells a story, one that makes you feel as if you're a part of it. Her easy-going nature makes it seem as if I've been reunited with an old friend, and she continually keeps me involved in the conversation.

We converse for a few minutes before Aria begins to ask questions about me. Bran already said he had told her a little about my circumstances, so I don't go into too much detail and keep my story light. Aria is in the middle of telling me about her old pack before she came to SNHQ when Shea bristles.

He will never be our alpha!

Okay, okay, calm down. What is it?

His animal is threatened by us, and his intentions are unclear.

Does it have to be this way for the first meeting? I can't just meet my mate's parents before shifter politics comes into it.

Do not avoid eye contact with him. You must be steady in your gaze.

As Bran's father comes into view, I try to keep calm and remember I am here as his daughter-in-law first, not an alpha, so I should remain polite. When he steps into the room, his eyes meet mine and there is most definitely a challenge there. Shea's dominance flows through me, and so I do as instructed and maintain eye contact with him.

Bran and Aria are quiet as we continue our stare-off, and the tension in the room rises, a bead of sweat breaking out on Bren's head. For now, I feel nothing other than annoyance. There is no pull of alpha power, just like there wasn't with my father.

How strange that for most of my life, I've been treated worse than dirt. Now, in the face of all these alphas, I'm more alpha than them both.

I have been trying to tell you this.

Yes, but hearing it and experiencing it are two entirely different things.

I feel Bran reach for my hand and squeeze it. I can't get a good read on his feelings now, too busy concentrating on his father. Bren now has more sweat running down his face, and it looks like he's been for a major workout. There's a slight ache in my body, but that could be down to work and other activities.

He is trying to assert his dominance over you. I say try because he is failing miserably. Even Anubis has more power than him.

From my peripheral, I notice Aria looking at her husband with concern, and she eventually reaches over to take his hand. The touch from his wife is all he needs to break our contact. I release a quiet breath, satisfied with my strength. If it wasn't for the fact it was Bran's father whom I was challenging, I might have enjoyed it.

The kind of power that comes from asserting your dominance over another shifter is heady, not in a controlling way, but more of a confidence boost. Validation that I am more than capable of taking care of myself. Well, with Shea's help.

"I guess it was too much to ask that one of my son's mates would be a nice, quiet, submissive girl who would settle into our pack with no issues."

"Excuse me?" Aria snaps angrily at him.

He seems to realise he said that out loud and quickly backtracks, "What I mean is they will both have their hands full. After dealing with you all these years, I can see they will need lots of advice," he gives her a cheeky smile, and I suddenly see the similarities between father and son.

Anubis looks more like his father than Bran, but the resemblance is unmistakable when Bren smiles. I decide to introduce myself first, considering he's not bothered to do that yet. I stand up and reach out my hand, "It's nice to meet you, Mr Throne. My name is Althea."

My voice is strong and steady, my handshake firm and I feel pride coming from both Shea and Bran, which relaxes me somewhat. I did the right thing, and hopefully, from one alpha to another, we're still able to get along.

"Please call me Bren. It's nice to meet you, Althea. That is quite the animal you have there."

Shea preens, and I almost roll my eyes.

"Thank you. We are still getting to know one another, but our bond strengthens daily."

"Ah yes, Bran told me you have a similar story to Anubis's mate."

It doesn't escape my attention that he doesn't bother to use Kali's name. With that one sentence, no matter how nice he is to me, he will never be anything more than a polite acquaintance.

Aria appears to relax now the introductions are over and ushers us into the dining room. Once seated, she serves up several helpings of pie, and I beam when I notice there is more on my plate than Brans. He notices this, too, but rather than commenting, he rolls his eyes and smirks at his mother.

We settle into a comfortable conversation, and when Bren asks for details about my life and previous pack, I tell them more of my story and how Shea came to be. I honestly expected more judgment from Bren, yet if anything, he seems impressed. He's not rude to me and acts openly interested in what I have to say.

Sadly, this doesn't endear him to me and only serves to annoy me. I can only assume it's because I am a shifter or an alpha that he is treating me better than Kali. Either way, it doesn't sit right with me. Several times, I deliberately drop Kali into the conversation, commenting on how wonderful and supportive she is.

Aria doesn't miss the opportunity to join in, reflecting on her own experiences with Kali. It's interesting to watch Bren when this happens. He doesn't openly display any disdain as we talk about Kali, nor does he get involved. I'm left to wonder if he realises his mistake and is just too stubborn to fix it.

"I assume that with your recent connection to your animal, you will no longer be joining the pack?" Bren asks, derailing the conversation away from Kali.

"I'm afraid not, no."

"Does this mean you will be creating your own pack? I'm sure you're aware of the hierarchy per territory, yes?"

"I am aware, thank you. My intention will eventually be to create my own pack. However, that is not something I will be rushing into. I also understand there can only be one pack at SNHQ, and I do not intend to challenge you for that."

"I'm glad to hear it," Bren smiles tightly.

Bran doesn't seem to appreciate his father's response, and a jolt of anger spikes through our bond. Strangely, his response doesn't bother me. It seems to me he is protecting his pack and their way of life—I can respect him for that.

A few hours pass, and all six pies have been demolished. I have to agree with Kali, Aria's cooking is better than the canteen, and that's saying something. When we stand to leave and say our goodbyes, Aria hugs me tightly, requesting a girl's night with me and Kali.

"I think that's an excellent idea. We'll set something up soon, I promise."

She smiles brightly and steps back, allowing Bren to reach out his hand towards me. "It was a pleasure to meet you, Althea," he says, shaking my hand.

"And you," I respond politely.

Bran is wrong. You're actually very good at lying.
Ssshh.

Bran and I stroll through the village hand in hand on the way back to my apartment. We've left his parents all of thirty seconds before his questions come flying at me. "That went well, right? I felt my father annoyed you a few times, but you stayed till the end, so it went well, right?"

"Yes, Bran," I laugh. "It went well. Your parents are lovely, and I can't wait to spend more time with your mother."

It has been a rather interesting visit, and though I look forward to seeing Aria again soon, I can't say the same for Bren.

CHAPTER THIRTY-SIX

BRAN AND I RETIRED early after meeting with his parents, exhaustion catching up to me after a day at work and the late night the day before. When I wake up the next morning, I'm surprised to find myself alone in bed.

"Good morning sleeping beauty," Bran says from the doorway, fully dressed and leaning against the door frame with a coffee in his hand.

"Morning, what time is it?" I yawn, rubbing the sleep from my eyes.

"It's seven-thirty. You were out cold, so I figured you could use the extra sleep."

"Oh, thanks. Is there more of that delicious-smelling life fuel?" I query when the scent of coffee fills the room.

"There is, and if you get your sexy ass out of bed, I'll have one waiting for you."

"Deal."

He walks over to me and places his cup on the bedside table. Sitting on the bed, he reaches for me, his lips meeting mine, and I fully come awake in the best way possible. He doesn't take it any further than a kiss, but when he pulls away, his eyes regard me with love, though frustration comes from our bond.

"What's the matter?" I ask, wondering over his emotions.

"Oberon called this morning. He's found something he would like you and Kali to look over before you leave."

"And that makes you frustrated because?"

"Because I would love nothing more than to have more time in bed with you, but I get the sense you would want to see this information."

"Ah, I see. Well, my insatiable mate, I won't be gone long today. When I return later, you can have your way with me." I kiss his lips, nose, and cheeks, peppering him with soft kisses until he laughs.

"Babe, if you continue down this path, we will never leave. Up you get, and I'll make you a coffee."

"As you wish," I giggle, getting out of bed and heading towards the bathroom.

I'm washed, dressed, and ready in less than ten minutes, choosing blue jeans and a plain black jumper. Except for my uniform, I still haven't had the opportunity to get any new clothes. It should be a priority soon, considering most of my clothes are no longer fit for purpose. There just always seem to be other, more important things going on.

I opt to wear my work boots because they're the only decent footwear I have, and I love them. Tying my hair up, I glance in the mirror and, for the first time, notice my fresh appearance. I've put weight on, have more colour on my face, and I look happy.

Incredible how far one person can come with the proper support.

Leaving the bedroom, I approach the kitchen where Bran is preparing my coffee. I wind my arms around his waist from behind him, soaking in his presence and filling my nose with his scent.

"You sure you don't want me to come with you today?" He asks, talking about our trip to find the next woman.

"I'm sure. I think it might be a little intimidating for us all to turn up. Besides, I'll be back before dinner."

He turns in my arms, holding me close and kissing the top of my head. "I know. Seems as if we're being pulled apart a bit too often for my liking."

"Then the sooner we get to the bottom of this, the better. I have a feeling it will get worse before it gets better."

"Yeah, that's my worry too," he replies, handing me the cup of coffee.

I don't say anything because I don't want to give him any false optimism. Kali's feeling that something bad is coming is one I share, and to think that once we find this Seraphina, our lives will be better is just naïve. Who knows what information there is still to uncover? Based on the images from our dreams, there is still a lot more, and none of it looks good.

Bran and I make our way to the canteen to meet up with the others. The rest are already seated at our usual table when we get there. Damiean and Oberon are also in attendance. I say good morning to everyone, and I'm pleased when I see Kali looking happier than yesterday. She confirms she hasn't had any more dreams but is eager to get going on our mission to find Seraphina.

Bran asks Oberon to wait with the latest news until he's retrieved some breakfast for me, so I take the opportunity to catch up with Oberon, realising I've not spoken to him properly since he returned.

"How are you, Oberon? I feel like we only talk lately when you have information."

"I apologise, Thea. The mystery surrounding you and Kali certainly keeps me enthralled in my tasks."

"Oh, don't apologise. I just hope you remember to rest in between all your research. We only had one day of it, and it was exhausting."

"Fear not, Thea," he chuckles softly. "When you enjoy something, it's not all that tiring. I get the sense that the unknowns surrounding you both will keep me occupied for some time."

"As long as you're enjoying it, I guess I'm happy for you. I did say to Kali we should get more involved after seeing the number of prophecies you marked as potential."

"That would be great. It's always better to have you there in case of questions."

"Then consider it done. Evenings, weekends, whenever you need us there."

"Thank you. I'd imagine we'll have more to investigate with the introduction of the next female."

When Bran returns with my breakfast, Kali moves closer towards me, both sitting directly opposite Oberon and awaiting his latest find. He pulls out what looks like a journal and turns his laptop so we can see the screen.

When he opens the pages of the journal and pushes it towards us, a chill runs down my spine. For the first time outside of my dreams, I'm looking at the structure I've seen so many times.

Six posts with an altar in the middle.

"Er, Thea, you're seeing what I'm seeing, right?" Kali asks her words barely above a whisper.

I not only see the place that haunts our dreams, but the words carefully etched into the wood cause me to pause. I've never noticed any engravings before, but I've heard some of the words. I trace my fingers over the pages, half expecting the images to start assaulting my mind. I'm thankful when they don't, though the evidence in front of me still leaves me filled with apprehension.

"Six lost souls, six powers unknown, six will connect, six to determine the fate, six will make the sacrifice, six to save all," I say aloud and immediately find Kali's eyes when I finish.

You could hear a pin drop. That feeling of dread I've been trying to ignore comes back in full force and punches me in the gut. Bran's hand squeezes my knee in comfort, and I look up to find Oberon studying Kali and me.

"Where did you find this?" Kali whispers as if afraid to disturb the silence. "This is what we see in the dreams. This place and some of these words are whispered or shouted at us."

"I had a feeling based on your descriptions that would be the case," Oberon says. "I'm afraid I can't say where I found it. I stumbled across this journal when I was looking through some of Damiean's books in his office."

"Damiean, did you know you had this?" I ask, surprised it's not been shown to us before.

"No. And until yesterday, this was not a part of my collection," he states adamantly.

"What? How can that be if Oberon found it."

"Kali, I have searched those shelves a thousand times, and I have never seen this before," Oberon confirms.

"So someone put it there," I comment, trying to connect the dots.

"That's what we believe, yes," Damiean declares. "However, I have seen this before, many years ago."

"You're going to need to elaborate, Damiean. Do you recognise this place? Have you been before?" Bran asks.

"It has been on our radar previously. It was the strangest thing. One day, there was nothing there, and the next, these posts appeared," Damiean responds, a faraway look in his eyes as if he's remembering something.

"Earth to, Damiean, what are you talking about," Castiel asks him.

"I'm slightly embarrassed to admit I didn't think of this location when you mentioned your dreams," he says, looking at me and Kali. "As I'm sure you are aware, Stonehenge has been a mystery for thousands of years and has always been a place of interest for supernaturals and humans alike—it has an energy that calls to us. Around twenty-five years ago, this structure appeared not far from it," he says, pointing towards the picture in the journal.

"We receive lots of reports about these types of things, so it wasn't taken too seriously at the time. At first, it was just six wooden posts, and we left it to the humans to investigate. After a few years, a witch friend of mine was in the area and came across it. He said he felt an intense energy coming from the centre and wanted to investigate. This is the journal of his findings.

"Did your friend say what type of strong energy he felt?" Anubis asks Damiean.

"No, only it was something he had never felt before. He is an elder witch and a wise man. If he did not know, I'm not sure who would."

"Great, more freaking weird energy, just what we need," Kali says, throwing her hands up in exasperation.

"What else does the journal say?"

"Not a great deal, I'm afraid," Oberon replies. "It details its proximity to Stonehenge, the surrounding forest and earth. The writer talks a little about the words, theorising a prophecy. Besides that, not much else."

"No mention of the symbols you found on that piece of paper?"

"No, nothing," he confirms.

I reach for the book, flicking through to see the notes scrawled across the pages. There are many drawings of the surrounding areas, but only one of the hexagon structure and altar. The writer certainly believes the words play an important part in something, his notes referring to several other prophecies where six have been mentioned.

"So, these wooden posts popped up twenty-five years ago. Were there any other investigations done?" Balbur asks Damiean.

"Yes, I attended the site myself, but nothing was there. No energy was present, and when we probed further, it all led to a dead end. Unfortunately, the hexagon symbol appears countless times throughout the centuries, and it's used heavily for spells and rituals. We chalked it up to a ritualist altar, and with other urgent matters to attend, the information was stored and forgotten."

"I've seen hexagons used a lot in spells," Castiel adds. "The number six can also represent both good and evil."

"Exactly," Damiean agrees. "Which is why our research led us nowhere. There are several ways the hexagon symbol may be interpreted. Many believe it represents nature and balance. It ties everything together and links everything back. It has also been known to be used in dark magic rituals to call forth evil spirits and create evil spells. The number of points on a hexagon is also significant to the number six, which can represent a balance between the earthly and spiritual realms."

"Great, so there could literally be thousands of texts, stories or whatever relating to the hexagon and the number six?" Kali sighs in frustration.

"I'm afraid so."

"We need to go here," I tell Damiean with certainty.

"We do," Kali says, "But only after we find Seraphina. I reckon the more of those women we find from the dream, the more clues we'll get."

"I don't like these words, Feisty," Anubis interrupts, pointing to the words carved in the wood.

"Six lost souls, six powers unknown, six to connect. Those words certainly sound like your situation at the moment. Especially considering your unique bond," Oberon mentions.

"It's not those words that bother me, O, it's what comes after. Six to determine the fate, six to make the sacrifice, and six to save all. That sounds like a doomsday prophecy, with my mate right in the centre of it."

"We can't be sure of anything at this point," Damiean cuts in. "All we can say for certain is there appears to be a link between this place and what you see in your dreams."

Anubis tries to interrupt again, but Damiean stops him, holding his hand up in acknowledgement. "I appreciate, Anubis, that there are other similarities, the restricted powers for a start, but we can't know anything for sure. This could be one of many prophecies that refer to six and hexagons."

There is every chance Damiean is correct, but still, something nags in my gut. We need to go there and see if it reveals any answers. All the signs point to it, and there are too many coincidences for this not to be an important part of our situation.

It would benefit me greatly to see this place in person. I am not a part of the dream and, therefore, only catch glimpses of it in your mind.

What do you think about the words?

Based on what you've said and seen, I don't think it's a stretch they are about you. As I've said, we are destined for something big, something life-altering. If the one with the laptop thinks this is a prophecy, I'm inclined to agree with him.

The one with the laptop? His name is Oberon.

It is not in an animal's nature to remember people by their names. We use scents or distinctive qualities. As this one is never without the laptop device, he will be laptop man.

I try very hard not to laugh out loud at Shea calling Oberon laptop man, and when Kali frowns at me, I shake my head discreetly, expressing that I will tell her later.

When Oberon taps the map on the screen of his laptop, I suppress the smile, trying to pull at my lips. "This is where the site is and where you'll need to go. I've printed out a copy to keep with the journal and will add it to the list of potentials, but based on this new information, I think this should be the first place we investigate."

"Once we have found Seraphina, I will take you there," Damiean states.

"Until then, I will continue my research," Oberon adds.

"Is there anything you need from us?" Castiel questions, eyeing the journal curiously. "I know we're not as good as O with the research, but there might be other ways we can help."

"Could you please talk to your mother about the grimoires, see if there is any reference to this type of thing. I know she has a penchant for reading anything she can get her hands on," Damiean smiles fondly.

"Sure. I'll be seeing her this afternoon."

"As for the rest of you, the human situation is not improving. We have another group of recruits arriving tomorrow afternoon from Europe. I would like you to assess their abilities and determine how soon we can get them on assignment. I'm told they are well trained, but I would still like the assessment to be made by your team before sending them out there."

"We're on it, Boss," Balbur rumbles.

"Then there is nothing further we can do. Ladies, if you are ready, let's head to the first location."

CHAPTER THIRTY-SEVEN

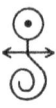

As Damiean finishes chatting to the guys, I turn to Bran, who has been surprisingly quiet throughout the most recent discovery. Our bond suggests he's a little agitated, which I would expect.

"Everything okay?" I ask, grabbing his hand and pulling his attention away from the journal.

"Sure," he smiles, though it fails to reach his eyes.

"Let's go outside," I tell him, pulling on his hand so he stands.

I inform Kali and Damiean that I will wait outside for them, pulling Bran along as we exit the canteen. We stroll together for a minute until we find a quiet spot.

Our mate is not happy. You need to fix it.

Yes, I'm aware, Shea, that's why I've brought him outside, so I can find out what's going on.

I don't like it. You need to fix it immediately.

"What's going on in that head of yours?" I ask, ignoring Shea and focusing on Bran.

"It's..." he sighs heavily, his arms wrapping around me and pulling me close. "It's everything. It kind of seems like we're battling a war from all sides. I'm concerned about things going on out there and how it impacts not just humans but us too. I'm worried about you and who did all of this to you. I'm anxious the more you find, the more danger you'll be in. I want to protect you from it all, but I have a feeling there will be times I will be helpless, and it's not sitting right with me."

My poor mate. In his efforts to be my shoulder to lean on, I forgot all about the strain that may cause him. His ability to stay positive and not let anything bother him is incredible, but seeing those words and that picture has affected him more than I could have realised.

"Bran," I say softly, pulling away to see his face. "I won't lie and say everything will be fine, but we're strong. You, me, Kali and the guys. We have a great support system, and none of us have to deal with this alone. I'll admit part of me is scared to find out what this all means. I must find out, though. I need to know who did this to us and why. If that means uncovering something dangerous, then so be it. Just understand that whatever information we find out, if it's something you can't be a part of, I'll always consider your feelings before making decisions. We are a team now, and I'll do everything I can to prove to you what a great team-mate you have."

This time, his smile reaches his eyes, and his fingers softly stroke down my face before winding around my neck. "Just be safe, babe. That's all I ask."

My lips mould to his before he can utter another word, and I pour every ounce of love into our kiss. Through our bond, I show him everything. My fear, anger, and worry over the situation. I let it all go for him to feel, and when he understands, I show him what is most important to me. My hope, desires and my love. All my emotions for him flow out of me in a rush. To have a mate who truly understands and supports you is a dream I never thought possible. He bolsters me in a way no one else could, not just by looking after me but by encouraging me through everything, never asking me to be something I'm not.

Our kiss gradually comes to an end and when we pull apart, his eyes shine with the orange of his bear. So much unspoken emotion swims within their depths, but I feel every ounce of it coursing through the bond.

"Beautiful," Bran says, looking deep into my eyes. "Make sure you bring your delectable ass back in one piece," he smirks, lightening the mood.

The sudden burst of emotion that comes from Shea catches me off guard, and before I know it, I've shifted. Shea pounces on Bran the second the shift is complete, licking his face and nuzzling his neck. Bran laughs heartily, and my heart warms at the tender moment between them.

She was worried when she could feel his uneasiness, but forcing the shift like that, I didn't realise just how much it affected her. She appears happier now, held closely by Bran as he breathes in her scent.

"My bear thanks you," he murmurs softly. "And he will miss you too."

"Althea?" Damiean's voice abruptly penetrates our moment. "I'm sorry... hello again, Shea."

Shea jumps out of Bran's arms and stalks up to Damien, nudging him with our head as gratitude pours from her. I'm confused about why she would react this way and even more surprised when Bran vocalises the reason for me.

"Shea is saying thank you," Bran tells Damiean. "Without your easy acceptance of Thea and her restrictions, Shea would not be here."

Damiean looks taken aback for a second before he bends down and scratches behind our ear. "You are most welcome, Shea. I am happy you found your way to your family."

And just like that, another burst of emotion, except this time it's from me. I did find my way to family, and it is the most perfect family I could have ever asked for. Being reminded of that overwhelms me, and as I look around our group, I've never been more thankful or happy.

The change in emotions causes yet another shift, and when I'm back in my human form, I pant heavily, the two sudden shifts causing havoc on my body. Thankfully, Bran seemed to pre-empt what was about to happen and is already there, waiting to cover me so I don't expose myself to everyone.

"And they call me leaky," Kali huffs happily.

"Here, let me help with that," Castiel says, waving his hand in my direction and muttering a few words quietly.

A tingling sensation slithers across my skin, the feel of material brushing across me. When I look down, I see I am dressed head to toe. Soft suede boots cover my feet, blue denim jeans encase my legs, and a beautiful dark purple cashmere sweater covers my top half. My clothes have never been so lovely.

"Thank you, Castiel, I love them," I beam, turning from side to side.

"Dude, not sure how I feel about you dressing my mate," Bran grumbles. "You're lucky she is stunningly beautiful."

Saying goodbye to the rest of the guys, Bran delivers one more toe-curling kiss before I leave. "Be careful, babe. I love you."

"I will. I love you, too. Stay out of trouble."

Even though I don't expect any danger on this little mission, I do feel some apprehension about leaving my mate behind. It's crazy. If all goes well, we'll be back before dinner, so why does leaving him feel so hard.

Because the bond is still new.

So are you saying, over time it will get easier?

No.

Helpful, thanks.

"So, I've been thinking," Kali says as we walk through the courtyard with Damiean. "When I first met you, I recognised you from the dream. If we've seen these images of the other women, then it's likely they have, too, but what if they haven't? Do we tell them everything and hope they believe us, or do we let them be to continue their lives?"

It's a difficult question to answer. I think I'd want to know if it were me, but I didn't have the greatest life and would have done anything to escape it. What if this other person is happy? They could be married, have kids or anything. Given what little information we have to share, do we upset all that?

"Would you want you know?" I ask instead.

"Hell yeah, but I was miserable in my old life, so I'm not sure my opinion counts."

"For now, perhaps just a meeting is all that's required to determine our next move," Damiean comments. "If all six of you are connected in the way that you and Kali are, I suspect they may already have some idea of what's happening."

We continue to follow Damiean through the courtyard and out of the village towards Candor Forest. It occurs to me I have no idea how we are travelling to these locations. Presumably there are vehicles somewhere, not that I've ever seen any.

"How are we getting there?" Kali asks, vocalising my thoughts.

"Magic." is Damiean's only answer, and as we step through the tree line, he turns to us. "I'm going to need you to hold onto one another, and I will need to touch one of you."

"Kinky," Kali snorts.

Damiean chuckles but doesn't comment any further. I hold out my hand, and Kali places hers in mine as Damiean holds onto her shoulder. My curiosity is piqued, remembering the portal-like entrance I came through when I first arrived here—I'm expecting something similar.

One second, we're in the forest surrounding our home, and the next, I feel as if my body has been stretched to its limits and then put back together again. I wouldn't say it was painful, but it's certainly an experience I won't forget. By the time the sensation stops, we're standing on a quiet street with small, detached houses on either side of us.

I can't explain why, but I feel like I need to catch my breath. Bending over with my hands on my knees, I take deep lungfuls of air. I spot Kali doing the same next to me.

"Perhaps... a bit of warning... next time you do some... magic mojo on us," Kali says between breaths.

"What... was that?" I pant.

"My apologies, I thought this way would be more fun," Damiean answers with a sly grin.

"Seriously, what was that?" I ask again.

"Teleportation. Don't worry, you'll get used to it," he says with far too much humour.

"What the hell are you, Damiean," Kali queries now she's got her composure back.

"A tale for another time. Come, this is her house," he responds, pointing towards a small but cosy dwelling at the end of the street.

I shake off the last remnants of the teleport and set off with Kali and Damiean towards the house. The street is clean and quiet and appears part of a larger estate. All the houses have neatly attended gardens, and most are two stories. The house we arrive at is enclosed by large bushes that circle the garden, with only the driveway visible until we pass through. Flowers are everywhere on the other side, along with little garden gnomes scattered around. It's clear that whoever lives here spends much time out in the garden.

"So we just knock on the door and ask for Seraphina? See if a bond kicks in?" Kali asks quietly as we approach the door.

"Perhaps not. They were in the database, so they are supernatural. We can say we are from SNHQ and are currently searching for a Seraphina to help with a situation we have. Keep the details vague," Damiean advises.

"Okay, then let's do this," I declare, strolling towards the door and knocking.

After a few minutes of silence, the door opens slowly, and an older woman greets us. She has a kind smile and warm eyes as she takes in the three of us on her doorstep, yet I'm not getting any supernatural vibes from her.

Shea, are you getting anything?

No, nothing. She is either human or is masking herself.

"Good morning, ma'am. We are sorry to bother you. My name is Damiean, and this is Kali and Althea. We were wondering if Seraphina was available to speak with us?"

The woman's demeanour changes in an instant. Her eyes shine with tears, and she suddenly becomes unsteady on her feet, falling into the door frame. Damiean quickly reaches out to her, carefully grasping her arms to ensure she doesn't fall.

"Are you okay?" I ask, concerned at her abrupt change.

She composes herself before looking the three of us over again. Shaking out of Damiean's hold, she stands up straighter and opens the door wider, "Why don't you come in and tell me what you need Seraphina for."

Before we can answer, she shuffles down the hall and into a kitchen, the three of us share a look before Kali shrugs and steps into the house. Damiean and I follow down the same hall and enter the small, bright orange kitchen.

I'm all for having colour in rooms, but the orange is so bright I feel like I should be wearing sunglasses.

The woman ushers us to a small table, indicating that we sit down as she busies herself, putting the kettle on. 'So why do you need to speak to my granddaughter? Three people arrive early on my doorstep; it must be quite important."

"We are from an organisation that helps people, and we have reason to believe that Seraphina may be of help to us," Damiean answers carefully.

Once again, the woman turns her eyes on us. She seems to study Kali and me a little longer than what is considered polite.

"So you're supernaturals then?" She comments, setting up four teacups.

"Are you?" Kali blurts and then winces.

"No, dear. Well, maybe?" The woman answers cryptically.

"What do you mean?" I ask, looking for some understanding of this slightly confusing woman we have come across.

"Three strangers turn up on my doorstep, and yet I knew immediately you didn't mean any harm. You all have a good energy about you. So maybe I'm a touch supernatural," she replies with a slight smirk, placing a tray of drinks on the table.

I don't have the heart to tell her I don't like tea, so I politely take the cup she offers. I notice Kali has a big smile and roll my eyes at her love of tea. Kali proceeds to drink the whole cup, and I'll never know how she does that without scalding her mouth.

"Is it possible to speak with Seraphina, please?" I ask, ignoring the drink in favour of moving things along.

At my question, the woman's face drops again, and I have a sinking feeling something is wrong. She places her cup down before answering, "You cannot speak to Seraphina."

"May I ask why?" I probe gently, concerned for this woman and her change in behaviour.

"Because she died two days ago."

Kali gasps at the woman's words and my eyes close in despair. It wasn't just a dream Kali had—it was some sort of vision. How that's possible is irrelevant. My heart breaks for the clearly distraught women before us.

"I am tremendously sorry for your loss," Damiean says, placing his hand on hers to offer some comfort. "Could you tell us how it happened?"

"She... she was killed," the woman stutters with watery eyes. "The police showed up at my door two days ago saying she's been in some sort of an accident. They found her body by the side of the road."

"I am so sorry," I comment sadly, reaching for Kali under the table when I feel her hurt and anger through the bond.

"She was such a lovely girl," the woman cries softly. "She came to live with me two years ago when her parents decided to travel. She was never bothered about going to see the world, just happy to be in her little family bubble. She would help me around the house and was always smiling."

"I'm sorry, Mrs..."

"Please call me Gina," she pats Damiean's hands, then moves to pick up her cup.

"Gina. You said the police called it an accident, but you believe she was killed?" Damiean queries, quickly glancing at Kali with concern.

"The police are wrong. It was no accident," she says, her voice full of conviction.

"How do you know?" I pry, believing her but needing to understand more about the circumstances.

"Because my Seraphina was a vampire. A vampire cannot die without being beheaded or having their heart taken out."

Oh crap. She was murdered.

We talked with Gina for another hour, listening to her theories on why Seraphina may have been targeted. Her father is a vampire, but her mother is human and there doesn't appear to be any link to us or any other supernaturals. Maybe a case of the wrong place at the wrong time?

Kali is quiet throughout the conversation, her emotions all over the place as guilt eats at her. I can only hold her hand in mine and send reassurances through the bond until we leave.

By the time we leave Gina's, my heart feels heavy. Of all the things I expected when we got here, this was not it.

CHAPTER THIRTY-EIGHT

AFTER OFFERING OUR CONDOLENCES once more and leaving Gina's, we walk down the street and away from the house before I turn to Kali.

"Please, Kali, you have to listen to me. There is nothing anyone could have done about this. By the timing of her death and your dream, it had already happened."

"Then why show me! Why give me the details if it had already happened. Was I meant to save her and failed? Was it a clue to something else? I fucking hate all these unknowns," she yells, her bond displaying her hurt.

Damiean leads us towards the end of the street and across the road to a small park. Finding a bench, he sits Kali down and sits beside her.

"The most frustrating thing about my job is the aspects I can't control," he says, causing Kali to look over at him in question. "For me, it's the worst experience. I like to be in control to ensure everyone's safety, and if I cannot do that, it drives me insane and makes me feel like a failure. I don't need to hear your thoughts to know what you're telling yourself and what you are questioning."

"How do I stop it, the doubt and the guilt?"

"You don't. You channel it into something else. You make peace with things being out of your control, and you focus on the things that you can. I am telling you both now that whatever this journey you are on, it will not be easy. There will be moments when everything is out of your control, and how you focus when that happens will make the difference. Use what you're feeling to move on to the next task—to keep going. I promise it will get easier."

"And if it doesn't?" I question, using Damiean's advice to quell my own fears.

"It will. Nothing bad lasts forever. Look at how your lives have turned out now compared to what they were. That is all the evidence you need to have faith that things will work out. This death is not your responsibility or your burden to bear. You were shown what happened for a reason, and I believe the reason will reveal itself when the time is right. Until then—"

"We keep moving forward," Kali finishes for him.

"Exactly," Damiean smiles. "You move forward until you find your happiness. You are both incredibly brave and strong. Remember that for the difficult times ahead."

"Thanks, Damiean. It's good to have a wise-ass... I mean, a wise man around," Kali smirks. "But what do we do now?"

"I think we should still investigate the other location if you feel up to it. I appreciate it looks bleak given the dream, but I think it's still worth exploring." I offer, looking to them both for confirmation.

"Yes, we complete our search, to be sure," Damiean agrees.

Kali stands from the bench with a sigh, "I'm not sure what good it will do, but you're right. We're here now, so we might as well."

"Let's move further into the park so I can teleport us," Damiean says, leading the way.

"Oh joy, another trip of having my guts turning inside out," Kali mutters, and I can't help but laugh at her attitude towards Damiean's particular brand of travel.

"Something strikes me as odd," Damiean comments as we wander a little further towards some trees.

"What's that?"

"The incident was not reported to us. Usually, if the police encounter a deceased supernatural, it is reported so we can investigate."

"Do you think it's been kept from you intentionally?" I query.

"I'm unsure, but I will be looking into the matter as soon as we get back," he replies adamantly, turning to us and holding out his hand.

"Let's hope the next Seraphina is still okay," Kali comments as she takes his hand and then mine.

We're teleported again, and though I don't like the feeling, it's certainly better than the first time. Coming out the other side, I still feel like my insides don't belong to me and have to catch my breath again. I'm not sure what to make of it, though the convenience is outstanding.

We appear to be in someone's back garden right next to a swing set and sandpit. I belatedly notice one of my feet has ended up in a paddling pool and jump out of it, shaking the water off my foot. This is a family's back garden, and my heart drops at the implication this could mean for us. If there was any possibility this Seraphina was the one from our dreams, her having a young family could complicate the situation even further.

"Umm, Damiean. Why the hell are we here?" Kali asks, looking around in surprise.

"I transported us to the last known address in the database," he replies, also looking around and likely coming to the same conclusion as me.

"Maybe we should get out of the garden before the family comes out wondering why three strangers are standing in their back garden," I suggest.

Damiean reaches for us again, and we teleport to the end of the street, where a few trees hide our appearance. I quickly glance around, my head spinning from the sudden teleportation as I check to make sure no one has spotted us.

"That's still not getting any easier," Kali grumbles, stepping from behind the tree.

"Perhaps we should try walking to the door this time," Damiean says, trying hard to hide his amusement.

"The super-powerful, almighty Damiean landed us in a paddling pool," Kali snorts, her voice higher as she tries to control her laughter.

"Yes, well, it's not always an exact science," he grins.

We walk back up the street to the house we landed at, and walking straight up to the door, I knock. The sound of tiny feet running, laughing and shouting indicates someone is home, and it takes a few minutes for someone to come to the door.

A young woman with brown hair and tired blue eyes stands in the doorway holding a baby, "Can I help you?"

"Um, yes. Sorry to bother you, but we're looking for a woman named Seraphina. Does she live here?"

"Who? There's no one here by that name," the woman says as she looks past me to Kali and then Damiean. Her eyes widen when she sees Damiean, and she straightens up a little, messing with her hair.

"I'm sorry, we must have the wrong address," I say and start to turn away.

"Sorry, did you say Seraphina?" she calls out, and I turn back to face her.

"Yes, is she here?"

"No. But I think the girl who used to live here was called Sera. Crazy girl with different coloured eyes."

I'm not sure about the crazy part but you would undoubtedly remember someone with her eyes, "Do you know where she lives now?"

"Not sure. Think she moved to the woods or something. She was always causing trouble here and had to move somewhere more isolated, or so the other neighbours tell me. I only met her once."

"Did she happen to leave a forwarding address?" Damiean asks, stepping towards the doorway. The woman's breathing changes and her smile gets a touch wider. She is clearly attracted to Damiean and happy to provide him with the information.

"Hang on one minute, and I'll check," she says, shutting the door.

"I think you have an admirer, Damiean," I tease as we wait.

"Please, I'm probably old enough to be her great, great, great grandfather," he comments dryly.

"Eww," Kali laughs.

We wait a few minutes before the woman returns, passing Damiean a piece of paper and smiling, "I'm afraid this is all I have."

Damiean doesn't bother looking at the paper as he puts it in his pocket, "You have been most helpful, thank you," he tells her before walking away. I witness the woman checking out his ass as I thank her and follow Damiean and Kali.

"And where are we going now?" I query as I catch up.

"Asher's Farm, somewhere near the Lake District," he announces.

"Great," I sigh. "That should narrow it down. The Lake District is huge."

We walk to the trees at the end of the street, and Damiean teleports us again. It doesn't seem as bad this time. A little more natural than before and something I'm getting used to.

You might be, but I'm not. Feels like I'm being shaken like a rug.

I'm sorry, Shea. I thought as a shifter, you would have a stronger constitution.

Very funny.

Looking around our new location, I'm not surprised when I feel Kali's hopelessness matching my own. We appear to be in the middle of nowhere on a long main road with trees on either side.

"Are we going to walk until we find her?" Kali moans.

"I'm afraid we don't have any other option. I can't teleport us everywhere in case we miss the location. Let's walk for an hour and see if we find anything. If not, I'll teleport us to a different area." Damiean suggests.

It's not much of a plan, but without knowing where Asher Farm is, there's little we can do. So far, our search for Seraphina is not yielding the results I hoped for. From the young woman's description of this Sera, she could be the person we are looking for. Her description of Seraphina's eyes is the only positive we've received today.

We walk south down the road for over an hour before Damiean teleports us to another location, the surrounding area looking the same.

"Please tell me you didn't teleport us to where we started?" Kali grimaces as she looks up and down the road.

"It may not be an exact science, but I can assure you, we are in a different location."

We set off north this time, and after fifteen minutes, my chest starts to feel strange. It starts as a flutter, but the more I walk, the stronger it becomes.

"Do you feel that?" I ask, stopping and getting Kali's attention.

"Oh, thank God. I thought I was having a heart attack from all the walking."

"You feel her?" Damiean checks.

"I'm not sure. I feel something in my chest, but it's not very strong."

If you could shift, I'd likely be able to sense her.

That's not helpful, Shea, when we have no control, and I don't want to scare her by meeting her as a cheetah for the first time.

Fine, but it will take longer this way.

We continue walking for another ten minutes, the feeling becoming stronger with every step north we take. It seems to be pulling us off the path we're on and into the trees. I look over at Kali, and when she nods, we both step into the trees simultaneously, Damiean right behind us.

"Okay, it's definitely getting stronger now," Kali confirms.

We wind through trees, jumping over fallen logs. All the while, the tugging sensation becomes more substantial and more insistent. After a few more yards, the landscape changes. All around us are holes in the ground, as if landmines have been detonated throughout the woods.

They're scattered everywhere, and there doesn't seem to be any pattern to their location.

"Should we be walking through here?" Kali questions, stepping around a large hole in the ground.

"It does seem as if the area has been used for some form of training or maybe weapons exercise," I comment, noting how the ground appears to have been patched up in places.

We keep walking, avoiding the holes and logs set up like bunkers. This area has either been a battle site at some point or is used for military training. I can't think of any other explanation for the randomness of destruction here.

What's also strange is it appears the area has been patched up at some point. Some holes have been recovered, and many smaller trees are randomly dotted throughout as if they have recently grown.

Passing through another line of trees, the area gets brighter, and there are fewer trees the further we walk. There are many more bunkers in this area, and as I pass a particularly wide one, a large house comes into view.

"I think this is the place. The tugging is pulling me in that direction," I tell Kali and Damiean, pointing towards the farmhouse.

Before we take our next step, an almighty boom rattles the trees and my bones. I exchange a startled look with Kali and Damiean, and we quicken our pace, running towards the house.

As we make it to the steps of the house, another loud boom rattles the land, knocking us off our feet. "Where the fuck is that coming from?" Kali shouts, jumping back to her feet.

"I believe from over there," Damiean says, pointing to the other side of the house where there are more trees. Instead of knocking on the door, we set off running to the other side as another boom rocks the ground.

"I hope there's a reasonable explanation for all of this, and we're not about to be thrown into our first battle," Kali declares as we keep running.

When we make it to the tree line, there's dust everywhere. There are no more explosions, and as my ears stop ringing, I'm convinced I can hear singing. When the dust begins to settle, I spot a flash of yellow but lose it before I can confirm what it is. The three of us approach cautiously, and as the dust settles, I can make out more details.

There, in the middle of the trees, is a woman with straight black hair in a bright yellow onesie, dancing around like she hasn't heard the explosions rocking through the Lake District.

She has her back to us as she throws little potion bottles into the air and mumbles some words. The bottle explodes, and the trees rattle again. As pieces of trees and leaves fall from the sky, she starts dancing around, singing it's raining men, only changing men to leaves.

I'm not sure my brain is truly processing what I'm seeing, but when she turns full circle, still singing her heart out, her eyes finally find us.

"Oh, hey, sisters!"

To be continued...

AFTERWORD

What did you think to Althea?

She's been on a ride, and it's not over yet!

Thea, Bran and Shea's journey has been told but you will see more of them throughout the rest of the series.

Each book will be centred around a different couple, with the main story continuing throughout.

As an avid reader, I understand how frustrating it is to wait for a series to be complete. Rest assured, I am aiming for a quick release of the others, so you won't have to wait too long to find out how the story progresses.

To keep up with the latest releases, please follow me on Facebook or Instagram - ZK Cole Author.

Also, if you enjoyed this book, please leave a review.

Book 3 - Seraphina coming soon.

ACKNOWLEDGEMENTS

Thank you for reading the second book in the Destiny's Glitches series. I hope you enjoyed Althea's and Bran's story, and it left you craving more.

My first acknowledgement will always be to the people who gave this book a chance. You, the incredible reader. Of all the books out there, it makes me immensely happy that you chose mine. There is still much more to uncover, and I hope you'll continue with me on this journey.

To my amazing editor, Sarah, you've been a constant support throughout this process, and most of this series would not be possible without you. Thank you for continually checking over everything and spending far too many hours helping make this book the best version it can be.

As always, you knock it out of the park with the cover design, too! Every time I see these beautiful books, I'm reminded of all the effort you have put into this series and how each cover gets better and better. Your attention to detail is outstanding, and I thank you for all the hours you patiently put in to get every aspect just right. From the bottom of my heart, thank you.

To Laura, you have been instrumental in championing these books. The work you have done in getting the word out and promoting means I have enough hours to continue writing, ensuring the series is released quickly. I would not have half of the reads I do if it wasn't for you. Thank you for all your hard work and support.

To my beta readers, you guys are awesome. Your feedback spurs me on and helps keep the creative juices flowing. You guys rock, and I couldn't do this without you.

Finally, to my husband, you once again stand beside me throughout this whole journey, offering words of encouragement and making me cups of tea. I love you!

ABOUT THE AUTHOR

Z.K. Cole is a UK paranormal romance author and working mum — an IT Analyst by day and author by night. On the weekend, you will either find her spending time with her two amazing children and very patient husband or setting the world to rights with her mum and sisters.

She is also a reading fanatic who loves nothing more than discovering new authors who write great fiction while drinking copious amounts of tea.

If you want to find out more about upcoming books, please visit her Facebook page or contact directly via email – zkcoleauthor@gmail.com.

facebook.com/profile.php?id=61554307850448

instagram.com/zkcoleauthor1/

Printed in Great Britain
by Amazon